PUG
SHERIDAN

* * *

PUG SHERIDAN

A Novel

Sandra Cline

Autumn Leaves Publishing
ALBUQUERQUE, NEW MEXICO

First printing 2004

ISBN 0-9754554-4-3
LCCN 2004105905

Cover art by Mimi Von Litolff, an award-winning artist
whose work can be found in collections throughout the United States.
Access her website at: www.mimiv.com

1   3   5   7   9   10   8   6   4   2

For Maude,
who taught me how to live.

For Ron,
who showed me how to love.

AUTHOR'S NOTE

Every tale has a hero who takes a journey of one sort or another. There is usually a villian to stir things up, create conflict, and shine a mirror upon the face of truth. If it's a good story, the bad guy doesn't always know that he's really an evildoer. A strong narrative is purposefully crafted to awaken, entertain, challenge, and even shock the reader. Words become seeds of meaning, floating beyond the everyday world to crystalline realms, germinating answers to profound questions.

Within a limited, artistic context, the word *"nigger"* has been used in the story that *Pug Sheridan* has to tell. In my opinion, no other word elicits more feelings of disgust or revulsion than that racial epithet. In this case, the vile expression is not designed to offend. Rather, its necessary use serves historical accuracy and is meant to be that *needed mirror upon the face of truth.* Put simply, Pug's story *is* the way it *was*—the good, the bad, and the ugly.

Finally, to any young readers who might be holding this book in their hands, a special message: To caretake the future, it is important to know what has gone before, not just the polished facts, but an understanding of the *human* toll that resulted from individual and cultural choices. Versions of Pug's tale could be (and are) played out any number of ways across the world. In actuality, it is only the time and place that change, or as Pug would say, the characters remain as "interchangeable actors wearing the same wretched masks."

It is this writer's great hope that *Pug Sheridan* will serve as a lighted signpost, reflecting the path toward a brighter, more peaceful tomorrow by marking some of yesterday's detours.

S.C.
June, 2004

They that love beyond the world cannot be separated from it.
Death cannot kill what never dies.
Nor can spirits ever be divided,
that love and live in the same divine principle,
the root and record of their friendship.
If absence be not death, neither is theirs.
Death is but crossing the world, as friends do the seas;
They live in one another still.

—William Penn, *More Fruits of Solitude*

PREFACE

It's better to be hated for who you are than to be loved for who you're not, so the old saying goes. I hope that old proverb is true because I have blood on my hands.

I'm a marked woman. The man I shot had friends whose hearts and minds remain as closed as his once was. It has become my habit to listen for footsteps behind me in the dark.

This is the story of how it happened, as true as I can tell it. To understand the end result, you must know the beginning well. As I stir the smoldering ashes of the past, I can feel the searing heat on my face.

ONE

I was born to be a teller of stories. Mama says I've been a chronicler of local events since I was "four going on forty." I'm twenty years old, this summer of 1918, but I've already had some of my poems and short stories published in fancy Yankee magazines.

I write about what I know, the heart and soul of rural Alabama. I cherish the slow, clean fires of hickory coals, the whirring wings of yellowhammers, and the people of Village Springs, those who cling to the bosom of the earth for their survival. Some that *haven't* survived now lie buried beneath overgrown honeysuckle vines and fig trees. Their untold tale is part of mine.

My given name is Sadie Lou Sheridan, but I'll answer only to my nickname, Pug. The diminutive suits me fine, though I'm not sure who first called me that, or why. Daddy says it was in answer to my short, turned-up nose. Mamau Maude, Daddy's mama, says my name fits my pugnacious personality.

I can be hotheaded at times—there's no denying it. Such temperament is part of the total picture, one that includes Irish red hair, pale blue eyes, and long skinny limbs. My milky skin turns red if I even think about sunlit days. Every square inch of me is as freckled as a guinea egg.

There are those who can testify to the deceptiveness of my lean frame. I've more than once held my own in a fair fight. Lad or lass, I've whipped both. It's said by some that my unladylike behavior embarrasses the Sheridan name. "That Pug Sheridan," I hear them whisper, "she's as wild as Burwell's Buck!" I just smile; such talk furthers my aims, convincing local evil-minded, two-legged beasts to leave me, and mine, alone.

Strong women remain the tradition—no, make that the *necessity*—in my family. Charmed and charming as they might be, Sheridan men tend to be flighty like bullbats and as lazy as Uncle Deal. When I was a girl, there were three living in our house: Tyne Herbert Sheridan (my daddy, known to everybody as T.H.), Finas Sheridan (Daddy's brother), and Azberry (my younger and sole sibling).

Sheridan males have always shared a peculiar characteristic, a propensity toward superstition adhered to with religious fervor. No self-respecting Sheridan gent would consider so much as a visit to the outhouse without first checking "the signs."

Anything and everything could be a sign. The weather, dreams, curious animal behavior, the twelve signs of the Zodiac, nothing escaped the scrutiny of the aforementioned philosophers. Wives' tales became wives' truths with their interpretations.

Daily, with infuriating reason and calm, the men I lived with expounded on biblical passages, quoted in support of their metaphysical cause. ("Let them be for *signs,* and for seasons, and for days, and for years," Genesis 1:14.) It's astounding that the Sheridan clan has come as far and lasted as long as it has. However, the truth is—for reasons I've yet to fathom—their daffy predictions often came to pass, and even I have learned to pay attention.

We are, by any Southern standard, well-off. Some might call us rich, but that would be stretching the facts. The perception that we are wealthy has made us a powerful local force. An influence to be reckoned with, if not respected.

Our continued upstanding position was assured a few years before I was born. It was then that one of the Sheridan brothers' cockeyed business schemes actually made good. After seeing a mysterious liquid oozing from the ground, they drilled around our family property for oil. One of their wells was unusually deep; the hole in the earth plunged 985 feet.

The ole boys soon hit a reservoir of gushing terrestrial secretion all right, but it wasn't oil. The narrow crater sprang to life, first with a trickle and then a loud burbling sound, like some enormous underground monster with indigestion. The reddish-white liquid that began to percolate at an ever faster rate smelled like rotten eggs. The Sheridan patriarchs discovered a genuine artesian well, a fountain of free-flowing sulfur. They had the water analyzed and determined it to be high in minerals, the kind of water long believed to be a recipe for good health.

For a time, the brothers became men of limitless ambition. They scooped out mountains of dirt and created themselves a mineral-rich lake five acres in size, reaching sixty feet down at its deepest gorge. Three narrow streams flowed from the well's mouth to form Sheridan Lake. To this day, the hallowed waters continue to rise from the depths of the earth, backed by underground pressure.

Our home grew into a country resort, Sheridan's Artesian Mineral Springs. Many sought joy and a myriad of cures there. The steep, sloping road to our place contributed to its nickname, The Hill. Scores of people, white and colored, traveled to The Hill from all over Alabama on weekends.

Segregation occurred by common consensus. The colored families migrated to the east side of the lake; white relations purposefully meandered to the west. Children from the East and West contingencies were forbidden contact. It was a long-lived division that my family neither encouraged nor approved of.

We Sheridans have always been stubbornly at odds with most folks living in Village Springs. "Judge people by their deeds" was the family motto we lived by, a dictum that separated us from other white, God-fearing families. This attitude was regarded as an eccentricity, a result of our diluted (pronounced "deluded" by the gossips) blue-blooded genealogy.

The truth was much simpler. Essie, my black nanny, taught us about what mattered. She'd also been a loving nursemaid to my father and uncle. Over the decades, Essie had become as much a part of our family as any of us. As she became a precious part of our lives, we learned to correct our own past mistakes.

I wish everyone could've seen things the way I did, not just in black and white. But sadly, while most colored families politely welcomed me to their lakeside district, I could tell that my close proximity made them uncomfortable. They'd come to The Hill to forget their troubles, not to create new ones with the nosy, uppity white folks across the way. I learned to avoid the tension my innocent offers of open friendship caused by staying on the western lakeside slope.

As for our numerous visitors to The Hill, my watchful family left the established tide of peace to its own rhythm and course. To do otherwise would've hastened the drifting, rising tide of discontent. Thankfully, adversity was only a subtle undercurrent during those early community holidays at our tranquil resort.

Everyone who came happily paid a small fee, which allowed them to picnic, swim, or fish for two-foot-long bass. Some came just to sit in the naturally warm water in amphibious communion, believing their silent prayers invoked the water's magic to cure their physical ills.

At times, The Hill did indeed seem enchanted. A sacred grove of ancient cedars stood sentinel over the rust-colored waters. Huge oaks and pines also bordered our land; they offered strong limbs for rope swings and circus games.

Being the highest point in Alabama, The Hill was usually pleasant and cool, even in summer. Our patrons sat on the banks of Sheridan's Resort and studied the shadows of the big trees. The eerie flickering of sunlight in the surrounding woodlands was truly wondrous.

Other customers roamed the nearby area to gather sweet moss and ferns. Many kisses were stolen as young folks strolled and courtships blossomed. The would-be lovers were encouraged by the excited cries of wild turkeys and the fragrant aroma of the passion flowers that sprang up everywhere. Cares and woes melted away with the passing of the day and its rainbow of colors, the hazy, ever-changing hues.

Inevitably, the attention of all would return to the sparkling lake, the magnificence of it. On one side, its beach was made of sawdust. Across the way, the water's sandy edge boasted great, vine-clad rocks. The water rose from deep within the body of the earth where there was no division of spirit. It offered exquisite silence.

Significant numbers of dry-landers also pondered the mystical properties of another liquid, the sort found in wide-mouthed mason jars. Home-brewed wines and whiskeys were surreptitiously passed from one gent to the next.

The ladies didn't approve of this activity, especially when it occurred so close to countless frolicking children. However, they also understood that their menfolk wouldn't stay hitched to the matrimonial post for very long if they tied the reins too tight.

In compromise, everybody pretended that all comers found redemption in the lemonade we sold and served from five-gallon tubs. It usually wasn't long before each player, be he pious or potted, grinned like a dead pig in sunshine.

Their resort complete, Uncle Finas and T.H. contributed doodledum-squat when it came to running things. Successful management of The Hill depended upon their female kin. But, as the old saying goes, "There's no use goin' back on raisin', and denyin' heritage."

I, for one, haven't denied my heritage, though I have resisted looking back on the latter-day past. Much of the truth that rests there is painful and ugly, but it must be told. Dark times have fallen on Alabama, and the darkness has a name: it calls itself the Knights of the Ku-Klux.

Many are responsible for what has followed; someday, the true criminals will be known. I now realize that recent, tragic events were inevitable, even predestined. They resulted from decades of ignorance and hate. It's as though every person I've ever known was born to play a role in the drama; by being themselves, in the act of living, the stage was set.

*　*　*

Two significant events occurred during my childhood. The first, my earliest memory, heralded Egypt. I was two years old when she came to live with us at Sheridan House; hearing the story retold throughout my life has crystalized it in my mind.

It was late, long past ten, when the rapid, desperate knocks rattled our back door. Daddy cradled me in his arms as he slowly lifted the metal latch, allowing the heavy, pine door to swing open.

Reverend Watkins stood before us. The sleeves of his shirt were singed, and the rest of him was covered in soot. He was breathing hard, his face red with excitement. The preacher shuffled from foot to foot, but his arms remained stiff as he awkwardly held a tiny, black newborn infant.

The mute child was a bundle of confusion and fright; she lay stone-still in the man's arms. The babe was swaddled in a worn, homespun, woolly blanket. Tiny pieces of ash could be seen in the folds of the cloth that warmed her.

"She was abandoned," the preacher said, his words ragged puffs of air. "I found her lyin' in the dirt underneath the church steps." Reverend Watkins was overcome by a coughing spell before he was able to say, "Somebody put her there, then set my church on fire. Their intention was to murder us both."

A shocked, agitated silence followed. Finally, my father found his wits and said, "Come inside and sit down, Samuel. We'll get to the bottom of this thing." Daddy paused, cocked his head, then added, "I don't hear the fire bell."

Brother Watkins' voice broke when he replied, "That's because there's nothin' left to save."

Mama walked up behind us and whispered, "Lord have mercy. Give her to me." As the reverend gingerly passed the baby to my mother, she turned to my father and said, "Go find Essie."

Egypt's eyes met mine; an innate recognition of one another, special to young children, gave rise to an instant trust and strong bond between us. Egypt relaxed, rendering her first audible sound, a tiny squeak.

Essie arrived. Like someone reacting to the arrival of a long-anticipated package, she lovingly took the babe from my mother's arms. Her subsequent, unexpected words hung in the air like stardust. "I had a dream you was comin'," she cooed to the child. "I've been waitin' a long time. They told me to call you Egypt. Praise the angels, here you are. Granny Essie will take care of you from now on."

Essie's last name, Lovall, adequately described her inner nature. God never created a more gentle spirit. Already in her late sixties, she had tended many white children, but she'd never had a child of her own. That is, until the night God sent Egypt to her.

We watched with fascination as Essie prepared a bottle of formula, carefully testing its temperature on the soft side of her dark wrist. The baby was hungry. Watching Egypt suckle on the bottle's rigid nipple with determined relish, Essie guessed that she'd never been fed. Neither had the babe been bathed; when the blanket was pulled back, birthing blood, dried and caked, covered her tiny body.

Essie laughed when Egypt's diminutive lips formed a suction hold rivaling a baby bull's. As Essie fed the newfound orphan, Brother

Watkins passionately related the horrifying, yet miraculous, details of that evening's events.

Though Brother Watkins was white, his Pentecostal church was one of the rare places where black and white folks worshiped together. Nobody could remember how long this had been true for the Holy Church of the Brethren, but it'd occurred naturally during his thirty years as pastor, a fact that remained a thorn in the side of local, self-proclaimed Christian "purists."

On this night, the minister had lingered at his pulpit, long after a lively snake handling service, to prepare his sermon for the following Sunday. At first, he thought he heard a cat scurrying on his roof. Then, he heard a slight bumping noise near the church entrance.

Believing he had an unexpected visitor, the preacher waited. When nobody entered, he walked to the door and found it blocked from the outside. Try as he might, Brother Watkins couldn't force open his only exit.

Sounds of breaking glass from one side of the little church, and then the other, startled him. Burning torches ignited the wooden pews around him with terrifying precision. They'd been thrown through the small ventilation windows that bordered the ceiling.

Praying aloud, the minister tried to smother the growing flames with the altar cloth, to no avail. Thinking quickly, he retrieved an ax from the forward closet, on hand for the sanctuary's wood-burning stove. He hacked his way through the pine door as the smoke threatened to overcome him.

The preacher claimed that as he left the burning sanctuary, the Holy Ghost came upon him, took his hand, and showed him where to find the deserted, sleeping child.

Neighbors who had seen the flames rushed to help, but too late. The smell of burning kerosene was unmistakable. The chapel went up like a match stick, aided by the fuel that doused the outer walls and roof. Holding Egypt tight, the minister prayed as the House of Worship burned to the ground.

Then, he climbed upon his horse and headed for our place. In deciding where to go, Brother Watkins realized two things. As a U.S. Marshall, my father was the highest ranking local lawman. And, even though Egypt was colored, the preacher knew our family would take her in.

Later that night, after Brother Watkins' departure, my father told my mother that he had a gut feeling the reverend had left out some important part of the whole truth.

As the years passed, nasty things were whispered about how our family included Essie and Egypt. Some folks gossiped about who Egypt's parents might have been, and how she looked only "half-colored."

Prejudice was like a dusty, ill wind that regularly blew across our valley. Under cover of the "Devil's paintbrush," with its pretty orange dandelions, it carried the aged barb of the thorny briarroot that pierced and stung everyone it touched.

The sum of it is, despite our critics, Egypt and I were raised together. She was a nervous tot, needing constant companionship. For a full year after she was found, Egypt wouldn't sleep until she was placed beside me in my crib. Nightly, she'd grip my forefinger with quiet desperation, added insurance that she would never be left alone in the dark again.

I often felt hateful stares bore into me from behind whenever I was in town with Egypt. As a young child, she was extremely shy, a regular stutterer. She never, ever spoke in public. The morning following my tenth birthday, I stood before the candy counter at Marsh's Grocery, watching with amusement as Egypt tried to decide which sugary treat to buy with the three pennies Daddy had given her.

Fanny Holt, my closest white friend, came into the store with her older, depraved brother, Grady. Like Grady, Fanny was as ugly as a mud dauber, but there the likeness stopped. On most days, Fanny's pure, unspoiled spirit was mirrored by her quick wit and unassuming charm; but that day was different, and it became a signpost for the future.

Grady Holt invented juvenile delinquency. His Baptist preacher father had a son as mean as old Satan wanted him to be. But I held Fanny to a higher standard.

"Boo!" Grady snuck up from behind and scared Egypt by goosing her in the ribs.

"Leave her alone," came my exasperated challenge. "I'll make you sorry if you don't." I raised my fist, and Grady hesitated before taking two steps back. I assumed he was remembering the time, three years earlier, when I'd broken his nose for being too forward.

Several adults had gathered to watch this local form of entertainment, my unpredictable behavior regarding senseless insults leveled at Egypt. It surprised me when, with stuttering words meant to mimic Egypt, Fanny decided to show off for everyone. "Try those chocolate covered nuts over there, darkie. The ones that look like nigger toes. Don't all you blackies suck your muddy feet when nobody's lookin'?" Fanny's audience rewarded her with clamorous laughter.

Though tears stained her long, thick lashes, Egypt stood ramrod straight. For the first time, she didn't look to me for comfort or protection. Instead, she turned to face Fanny. Eight-year-old Egypt slowly walked toward her tormentor, head held high like a queen, while I held my breath. With angelic dignity, she gently lifted Fanny's hand; Fanny was too stunned to resist. Then, Egypt pushed her three precious pennies into Fanny's palm. "You're the one that needs sweetenin' today, Miss Fanny," came Egypt's timid murmur. "Try the jawbreakers."

Fanny's gaze met mine. Her expression belied anger, confusion, and shame as she and I held a mad-dog staring contest. Unspoken words and accusations passed between us like static-filled air.

During our formative years, Fanny and I usually played at her house, apart from Egypt. But sometimes, she'd bravely defy her parents, sneaking away with me and Egypt for covert fun in the shadowy woodlands near our homes. With time, uncertainty had turned to familiarity where Fanny and Egypt were concerned. But on the day that found us in Marsh's Grocery, stubborn pride combined with choice words to spell betrayal, the most hateful kind. All for a laugh at Egypt's expense.

An unfamiliar adult voice said, "That nigger's been livin' with white folks so long she's forgotten her place, gotten uppity. Needs to be taken down a notch or two."

That's when I rushed forward to slap Fanny. The room was absolutely quiet after that. Curious bystanders waited for the show's finale. Dumbstruck, Fanny stood still as a statue.

I took Egypt's hand and kicked in Grady's direction when he moved toward us. Egypt and I slowly backed away, step by step, until we reached the door. Fanny softly sobbed while I addressed the room, saying what they all needed to hear. "Unlike *some* people," I declared, "Egypt *does* know her place. She belongs with those that love her. Something you'd all do well to remember."

I narrowed my eyes, looked back at Fanny and added, "A person without real friends is no better than a bug in the dirt."

We hotfooted it back to The Hill, my black sister and I, hand in hand. After that fateful day, she never stuttered again. But the many similar scenes that played out during our life together, though at different places and times, would find interchangeable actors wearing the same wretched masks. By the time we were grown, Egypt and I knew our lines by heart.

When Egypt was nine, Daddy gave Essie and her grandchild their own cottage. It sat on a cleared patch of ground on the west side of our home known as Posie's Peach Orchard. It was a stone's throw from the main house, and I often went there to hear Essie's unusual yarns.

Essie was a natural storyteller and teacher, a weaver of tales; she held Egypt and me spellbound for hours on end. As she sat in her worn, upholstered chair beside the fire, Essie talked of family who came from Africa, a land she called, "the lost place in time." Essie's stories advanced a sacred oral tradition that stretched across oceans and generations. She also had a hidden agenda—to plant seeds of meaning that would germinate and sprout with age.

A favorite spooky tale, passed down by tribal bushmen, revealed why the wind blows. "On the day we die," Essie would dramatically and somberly begin, "the wind comes and blows away our footprints. The dust covers our tracks. The great, dark goddess livin' under the ground knows for sure, then, we're gone. Otherwise, she'd lose count of her creatures, get flustered, and cause mayhem. If the ghost wind does its job, calamity is stopped. It howls and fusses for good reason, 'cause on the day of our passin', its breath blows away any trace that we walked this earth."

When I told Mama about Essie's tales, she smiled and said, "Maybe *we're* the ones livin' in the lost place in time."

It would be many years before the reason for the Pentecostal Church fire was explained; the answer would unearth secrets from the graves of both the innocent *and* the guilty. In the meantime, the dead remained a patient bunch. They'd wait their turn to talk. For most of her life, Egypt wondered if the facts of her parentage would ever be known.

The main question that needed answering was why somebody had tried to burn her alive.

* * *

Egypt was delivered to me, but I found Fawn. We were ten years old when we met—or I should say, when she saved my life.

I had a vague idea of Indians living down in Spunky Hollow; the recent arrival of these curious neighbors had created quite a stir in Village Springs. After listening to the offhand rumors and careless hearsay of several local townspeople, all kinds of foolish notions presented themselves to my uninformed childish mind, especially at night. I took to sleeping with my hat on, to up the chance of holding on to my flattened-down scalp.

One spring day, I'd wandered a fair distance from my home in search of wildflowers. I found myself in a colorful field of blooming foliage. An orchestra of Bluebonnets, Red-topped Sheep Sorrel, Granny Gray Beard, and Wild Iris played for me, luring me farther into the patch. I stood alone, eyes closed, imagining myself inside an enormous bouquet arranged upon a docile giant's table. For a while, time eluded me.

As I reached out to pick a pretty, daisy-shaped cluster, I heard a voice say, "You better not touch that. It's a chigger plant."

I jumped and swung around in one continuous motion. There, three feet from me, was a girl my own age. Somehow, she'd sneaked up from behind without a sound. *Where did she come from?* I was mad as fire for being given such a start.

Fawn stood straight and still; I thought her beautiful, even then. Her skin was tanned a golden brown. Shiny thick strands of black hair caressed her shoulders and back. Her eyes sparkled, the color of hickory nuts. There was an undefinable quality about her manner, like a graceful untamed creature. It was a regal charm that I mistook, at first, for overbearing biggity.

I closely examined the flower in question, then loudly declared that I saw *nothing* that looked like a chigger bug.

"They're so tiny they'll fool your eyes," Fawn said slowly, the way one patiently explains something to a small child. "Those red bitin' bugs'll dig into your flesh and cause it to welt up. When you pinch your skin, you can sometimes see 'em and scratch 'em off. Otherwise, they've got to be scraped out with a knife or have kerosene poured over 'em. You can be itched to death after pickin' those 'gussied up' chigger plants."

I was still bending close to the bloom as I watched her out of the corner of my eye. This young stranger had my undivided attention. I decided not to risk such a cruel and untimely death, so I drew away from the flower in question.

We faced off, sizing each other up. Our puckered lips reflected mutual irritation. Suddenly, our bodies collapsed to the ground, paralyzed by waves of helpless laughter. Every time we looked at each other, the howling, tittering commotion began all over again. Our bellies ached with spasms as tears streamed from our eyes.

Finally, a breeze-blown, gentle quiet settled over our meadow as Fawn and I lay in a clump of mashed-down wildflowers. Staring at the sky seemed the safest. It wouldn't have taken much to start us laughing again, and I was tuckered out.

"I didn't mean to scare you like that," I heard her say. "I thought you would notice me comin'."

"Never mind," I answered. "Mamau Maude would've said I was asleep at the switch."

"It's awful hot," Fawn murmured. Her voice carried a kind of purring quality, soothing and nice.

My reply came slowly, words subdued by fatigue and heat. "T.H. Sheridan is my daddy; he says the hotter the summer, the colder the winter."

Whereupon, Fawn made an uncannily accurate observation. "Sure sounds like your family's got a lot of sayin's."

It was almost enough to get me laughing again, but I controlled the urge. I swallowed hard and asked her if she was new to Village Springs, though I already knew the answer.

"Badgerwoman and I moved to Spunky Holler about a year ago. My daddy had bought the place and was fixin' to come with us before he died of the flux. He's with my mama now. She died when I was a baby." Fawn paused, then added, "We've kept to ourselves, settlin' in and all."

"Badgerwoman?" I asked, nonplused.

"She's my granny, my daddy's mama. Badgerwoman's full-blooded Cherokee like Daddy was. Granny knows things. *Secret* things." Suddenly, Fawn appeared much older than her years. Her overall demeanor changed; this shift was subtle, yet unmistakable. For a moment in time, she loomed as Artemis personified, the way I'd envisioned the Greek heroine in mythic tales I'd read: Artemis, virgin goddess of the wilderness and the sacred hunt.

Like an old habit, my romantic nature distracted me. I hadn't thought to ask this girl's name, yet I wanted to know *everything* about her and her mysterious granny. Here I was, talking to one of the "fierce Injuns" of Spunky Hollow; the adventure was just too delicious.

Excitement swelled inside my head, and I was, once again, lost in another daydream as my nostrils took in the pungent aroma of wild sassafras and wormwood. Suddenly, Fawn's voice, low and whispery, interrupted my reverie. She was begging me not to move, but my unqualified amazement upon seeing her standing shadow, knife in hand, had the opposite effect. I sat straight up, realizing the problem too late.

The air around me hung in heavy stillness. I recognized the brown and orange checks of a copperhead. It'd slithered in our direction as we rested from our childish cackles. Instinctively, I rolled away from the moccasin. The creature's rough skin shimmered majestically in the sun as it struck out, biting hard into my bare leg.

As I continued rolling, a dull thud shook the ground; Fawn's knife had made its mark. I raised my head to see the snake skewered to a mound of daisies. It wasn't quite dead; its tail moved slightly, while the woods around me appeared to blur.

A trickle of blood oozed from the puncture marks just above my ankle while I let loose with every cuss word I'd been able to acquire in my few short years. I then did a most peculiar thing; I ate clumps of dirt, handful after handful. It tasted warm and rich. The coarse, musty aroma soothed me somehow, and kept the panic down.

Fawn tightly locked her arms under mine, dragging me to the nearest shade tree, a weeping willow. I tried to stand but felt dizzy and overbalanced.

"What's your name?"

"Pug." My voice sounded separate from myself.

"I'm Fawn. Fawn Storm. I live in that holler by the creek. I'm gonna run over there and get Badgerwoman. I'm sure she'll know what to do. You hunker down here and lie still." Fawn ran toward the little valley where she and her grandmother lived.

The world around me appeared queer and dreamlike. I found myself lying in a big bed of red ants. It was as though every one of them took a notion to bite me. Before I could react to the pain, I realized they weren't really there.

I remembered my mother; I thought about how mad she'd be that I was lolligagging in the fields with dinner waiting. Then, with a wrenching that reached down into my soul, I vomited all the gritty earth I'd consumed minutes before.

I took a mild oath and spoke it aloud with as much earnestness as I could muster. "Bless God! If I ever get done with this thing, I'll always do right for as long as I live! I'll even go to church. I won't go back on you, Jesus, I swear…" I intended to go on praying for a while; I figured an oath needed to be long on words to take adequate hold. However, my soul sounds soon sank into merciful blackness.

I awoke after sundown, in the pink of evening. I wanted very much to go back to sleep, as I was in a tremendous amount of pain. An old woman lit a kerosene lantern in the small room I found myself in. Even in my stupor, I noticed the character lines etched in the weathered face, illuminated with a red glow. It was an Indian face, with strong features and dark, leathery skin. Silken hair, pulled back into a tight bun, was black with wide bands of gray streaks. Long years had left their mark, a humped back and shoulders. She looked like an aged soul, one who'd carried a heavy load for a considerable time.

My sympathetic benefactor moved slowly and deliberately to my bedside; her wrinkled hand held a small pottery mug. "Drink this, child. Sleep more."

"What is it? Who are you? Am I dead?"

A flicker of a smile crossed the old woman's face. Before she spoke, she studied me with serene, black eyes. "I'm Badgerwoman. You're in my bed. This is rattleroot tea. Works best for rattlesnake bites, but we can't be fussy. You need to sweat out poison. Now drink." The concoction put to my lips was as bitter as bile. I gritted my teeth to get it down. Once I'd swallowed all of it, my body felt warm and loosened.

I'd been placed in a feather bed, soft like the down of a goose's breast, laid atop a corn shuck mattress. It felt like a womb, one that protected me from the darkness both inside and outside myself. As I passed the night in a fitful doze, Badgerwoman stayed by my side, chanting in modulated tones so powerful I knew God was listening. Mamau Maude says, "Kind deeds are a balm to the soul." That night proved the truth of such a simple expression.

A rattle passed over me more than once; herbal tea was administered every hour. I was vaguely aware of pressure being applied to my wound. Cries for my mother were soothed with gentle words and caresses.

Some part of me hovered above the rest. I imagined my body to be a soft dessert and I, the real me, was a mound of whipped cream floating on its surface.

Past the window hovered a purple sky, covered with a blanket of stars. I knew that—if I chose—I could take flight, ascend to the Milky Way, and discover once and for all what lay on the other end of a sparkling night sky. *If this side appears so radiant and beautiful, how glorious Heaven's Gate must be.*

That's when a bizarre buzzing noise rattled my brain, followed by a voice that sounded neither male nor female. A proclamation reverberated loudly around the corners of the room: "No, little one. Put away your wings. The time hasn't come that you may fly like an eagle. You must stay where you are." I tried to reflect on this message, but awareness trailed off into sluggish slumber.

I awoke to familiar voices. It was well past the crack of day. "We were nearly out of our minds with worry," my mother was saying. "I'm so thankful we came upon this girl when we did."

Fawn had gone out at sunrise and found my posse; many in the search party were strangers to me, folks who cared enough to look for a lost child. Within minutes, the modest cabin overflowed with warm bodies. I hadn't had that much attention since the day I'd cold-cocked Grady Holt for trying to look up my dress.

For a few local citizens, Fawn and Badgerwoman became folk heroes. Commonalties were recognized, including their desire to live a quiet, steadfast existence in our little town. Still, most Village Springers stubbornly held to ignorance, seeing all people of color as dirty or beneath themselves. Regularly, I'd see neighbors I had cared about while growing up intentionally cross the street in front of us, simply to avoid the two people who had saved me from certain death.

Small-minded spirits thrive in the dankest of places, the coldest of hearts, that's what Daddy always said. From my perspective, and that of anyone who wasn't lily-white, Village Springs was one of those bleak places. I was ashamed, determined to change things, starting with my own life.

Ignoring community-wide disgust, the Storms were made honorary members of the Sheridan clan. Like Fawn and me, my grandmother and hers became fast confidants during my convalescence; it was as though the four of us had known each other before.

My consummate fatigue, a remnant of the snake's venom, was slowly but surely remedied by Mamau Maude and Badgerwoman. In due course, after weeks of soaking my leg in turpentine, the swelling died down, and the soreness lifted. However, for years after my recovery, whenever springtime revisited, my leg would ache and swell around the puncture scars. I know it doesn't sound reasonable, but it's true.

TWO

Awarm Sunday in late summer found me tolerably mended, standing by my window at daybreak. My room appeared different in the glimmer. Everyday items glowed with mystical hues from the first tinge of dawn. My oak bed looked huge, its four posts casting enormous shadows. A canopy top held draw curtains, partially opened, tempting me to return. The mattress was so high from the floor, I had to use a stool to climb in. There was a trundle bed stored underneath, allowing extra room for an overnight guest, though four children could've hibernated an entire winter on the main bed frame in relative comfort.

My father adored space. That fact was reflected throughout our house; he had designed and supervised every solid inch of its construction. Our ceilings stood extraordinarily high, making all of the rooms in Sheridan House large and airy. T.H. told newcomers to The Hill that he would give them his house if they could find a knot in it, knowing full well it was built with Heart Pine lumber.

I padded across the wooden floor to admire the carved front of my chifforobe. The ornate armoire had arrived from France for my seventh birthday. Its beauty was awe-inspiring; made of polished mahogany, it had a narrow chest of drawers on one side, and a space for hanging clothes on the other. Each end held a separate door that opened out, with a mirror attached to the back.

I pulled out my coveralls, slipped them on, then quickly scooped my chamber pot from beneath the bed. I set it on the ground outside my window and climbed out, headed for the woods to empty the pot while pondering the virtues of piety and persuasion. Stopping on the well-worn footpath at the wooded edge of The Hill's east side, I gazed back at my home; the whitewashed structure gleamed in the sun. A one-story colonial design, the house boasted several wings, marked by chimneys that spread out beyond a central location. Its front emphasized a wide verandah supported by square pillars.

Sheridan House overlooked the L&N railroad, separated from it by a long, grassy slope. The sight was both endearing and enduring, a century of family memories. On that particular day, resort activities had commenced in a full-blown flurry. The dawning sun had barely burned through an overcast sky, but already there was bustling commotion. Hired hands and resort guests awaited breakfast; additional preparation of food was needed for the coming day visitors. Tending the grounds and animals also required careful consideration.

The Hill's Supreme Commander was Cora Sheridan, my mother. She maintained the image of a woman given to uncommon energy and business capacity, even though she moved with a halting gait. Mama was afflicted with milk legs, a painful, chronic skin infection that set in after Azberry was born. She treated her pain with Saymen's Salve; the remedial effects were short-lived, but I never once heard her complain. For her, it was bad manners to lament publicly about anything, much less personal suffering.

My mother was a black-haired, green-eyed Irish beauty with fair skin and delicate features. One of Charleston, South Carolina's genteel creatures, she'd tamed my giant of a daddy with feminine charms that bewildered my young girl's heart. She brought a rustic elegance into our home that soothed the eye and spirit of all who entered. Decorating with finery came naturally to her; she had a flair for combining such diverse particulars as imported velvet and home-grown, hand-polished leather. Etiquette and good form flowed in Mama's veins like a birthright, her connection to a more refined past.

Mama hated the local vernacular and was always correcting Azberry and me. "There's something called proper grammar," she'd sigh, exasperated. "I swear, if my friends up north ever come to visit, they'll think you were raised in a barn the minute you open your mouth."

At Sheridan House, Mama was a rainbow trout swimming upstream against a bunch of boneheaded pikes. Her frustration at our inability to understand the value of cultured decorum would sometimes invite tension. However, with earthy, rough-and-tumble humor, Daddy could always find a way to make her laugh, and she'd relax. It was a paradox I never understood. As different as my parents were, their mutual devotion to one another was obvious, even to total strangers.

Since she'd attended a fancy girls' school while growing up in South Carolina, it was Mama who patiently guided me through our immense and amply stocked library. She emphasized a variety of subjects: music, history, literature, science, and art. She also tried to teach me the basics of feminine skills, focusing on the spinning wheel and the handiworks of crochet and embroidery, to no avail.

To Mama's obvious disappointment, my complete lack of aptitude in the culinary arts was established early. It was downright dangerous for me to have anything to do with an egg pudding or sweet potato pie. Food seemed to explode, without provocation, under my watch. Still, Mama clung unflinchingly to the belief that my true nature, some unforeseen latent gift, would find its way to public notice. My mother was an incurable romantic.

Duty completed, I returned to my room and stretched out atop my bed, absorbed with thoughts of my family, particularly how I might handle my father's lack of religious zeal. I dreaded telling T.H. about my newfound commitment, the promise I had made to God, vowed on the day I met my death adder in the form of a copperhead.

Though I'd gone to Old Bethlehem Methodist with Mamau Maude a few times, Daddy discouraged it. "The only church that needs belonging to is the *Big Church!*" he'd bellow in that baritone voice of his. (My knees shook when Daddy bellowed.) Convinced that preachers prevent folks from thinking for themselves, T.H. held stubborn convictions about belonging to any organized religion, though he professed an abiding belief in God.

Daddy was a complicated man in other ways, too. Though he could be a braggart, T.H. was also beguiling, with flamboyant style and charm. Even those who disagreed with his radical views liked him, in spite of themselves. In his role as a part-time U.S. Marshall, T.H. looked dashing in his fancy clothes. The man had charisma! He stood a good height, wore black suede, wide-brimmed hats, and often holstered a gun high on his hip. He was an expert at putting on the dog, impressing people.

Also, because Village Springs had no real dentist, Daddy had long ago discovered another hidden talent—he was good at pulling teeth. He provided that free service to whoever requested it, and sometimes to those who didn't.

I didn't fear my father, but I knew him to be a formidable opponent. Butterflies danced in my stomach as I considered the challenge; my mind was an overflowing chalice, brimming with contradictory beliefs and opinions. Ivy-covered theological ideals crept and twined inside my know-nothing, budding intellect.

There were three Houses of Worship within close proximity to The Hill: Old Bethlehem Methodist, Mount Hebron Baptist, and the Holiness Church of the Brethren. How was a soul to know which one God really lived in, or at least visited occasionally? Each denomination claimed to hold the key to salvation, exclusively. It was a dogmatic dilemma, but I quickly settled on a course of action: I'd join all three. Proper amounts of time would have to be spent among the trinity of doctrines, to cover my aces.

I foresaw one major problem, however: official baptism at Brother Watkins' Pentecostal Church, now located in the old schoolhouse, would be impossible. That special service included snake handling. I prayed that God would understand the ironic contradiction.

Eventually, I came up with a workable plan for presenting my righteous aspirations to T.H. With renewed resolve, I raced off in search of my grandmother. I found her at the well, drawing water. "May I go to church with you this morning, Mamau?"

"Child, you know you're always welcome to come worship with me." A pause, and then, "What does your daddy say?"

"I'm headed in now to talk to him," I answered. With that piece of news, my granny's forehead wrinkled like a bull's back. Through my young eyes, she appeared to be as tall as her son. I marveled at the muscles in her legs, strong yet feminine. Golden hairpins held her long, silver hair on her handsome head in a coiled braid.

With a few historic exceptions, I'd never heard anything other than words of loving kindness escape my grandmother's lips. I wondered why folks would sometimes say to me, "Are you sure you're Maude Sheridan's grandchild?"

Mamau was my ally, but doubtless would remain a silent one. I knew she wouldn't interfere in the parental decisions of her son, even though I was certain she had strong opinions about religion—and me. When it came to T.H., I was on my own, unless I made sure that Mama was within earshot.

I found my father in the dining hall, dipping into "mountain oysters," otherwise known as fried hog testicles. As with most things T.H. undertook, he watched the cycling orb of the moon until the time was right to harvest such a manly feast. Then, he and his helpers would alter (that is, castrate) the latest litter of newly weaned pigs. Whereupon, they'd have themselves a big mess of tender vittles. Southern folklore imparted the belief that this delicacy, in the truest sense of the word, would enhance virility. Man's best friend is *not* the dog.

I stood in the doorway and judged Daddy's frame of mind on that warm summer morning. He was obviously enjoying the special dish he seemed so partial to. The time was right for what needed saying. Azberry and Uncle Finas were there, along with several guests who'd already meandered down from their lakeside cabins.

Our beamed dining hall, with its gigantic oak table, reminded me of the one King Arthur and his knights must have used. My favorite picture hung on the wall behind my father, a painting that also evoked medieval times. It brilliantly captured an old monk sitting at a table, gray-headed, wrinkles in his face; he looked like he'd been battered by life. On the monk's table lay a bowl of soup, a piece of bread, the Holy Bible, and a pair of glasses, nothing else. He was saying grace, and that was also the title of the picture. Grace. The painted scene suited my virtuous intent and bolstered my determination to walk into the lion's den.

Glancing across the table, I spied Essie's artwork: fried chicken, pork chops, grits, gravy, assorted homemade jams and jellies, scrambled eggs, pots upon pots of steaming coffee, and of course, the private parts of several unfortunate shoats. Mama passed by with a fresh tray of biscuits and said, "So there you are, Sadie Lou Sheridan. It's about time you joined us. A girl your age needs a good breakfast!"

I sat down, stuck my thumb in a biscuit, and poured the hole full of syrup. Mama threw me a disapproving glance, so I added eggs and chops to my menu. My style of eating hasn't changed; I attack my food with ravenous zeal, mouth chocked full. That day was no different, and Mama took notice. The sound of "Sadie Lou!" once again burned my ears.

Azberry snickered at the use of my despised given name, something Mama tended to call upon when irritated, either at me or life in general. While wondering what had riled her that morning, I almost lost my courage to speak to T.H. Defiant, I stuck my tongue out at my five-year-old brother, and my moment of spinelessness passed. I slid into an empty chair, next to Daddy's, and nodded a greeting to everybody present. Then, I set to work. "Good mornin', Daddy."

"Hello Puglet, you look mighty pretty today." It was a good start considering what I was facing.

"Sleep well, Daddy?"

"Dead to the world. And you, Daughter?"

"Actually, I was awake a good part of the night's hours studyin' on something. I was lookin' up in the sky yesterday when I saw a buzzard sail past; he was all by himself. I remember you tellin' me that folks should watch a lone buzzard 'til he flaps his wings." I now had T.H.'s attention. He was a true believer in that folktale, having what you might call a "bird-brained fetish" about such skyward happenings.

"That's right, my girl. If you see a buzzard flyin' by himself, it's important he flaps his wings, at least once, before movin' on. It's a real bad sign if he doesn't. Bad luck even; it can bring dire consequences to the watcher."

I'd grown up as a keen observer of those solitary soarers, searching as they made their way over meadows and mountains. I'd learned they could glide on unflapping wings for hours before becoming foreboding black specks in the distance. This had become an accepted occurrence of nature to my young eyes, but I knew that to T.H., each one carried a message of doom. If he was right, I'd already been damned, many times over, by a bunch of flying turkeys.

"My buzzard didn't flap, Daddy." I glanced sideways to see a dark frown pass over my father's face. I didn't like causing T.H. grief. He'd anguished enough during my recent reptile-induced illness. Still, I saw no other way of becoming a good, churchgoing, promise keeper.

"Like an omen, could that spiteful vulture be tellin' me I should do something I've put off? Could it be…" I spoke the last three words very slowly as I waited for T.H. to catch up with my conniving young mind.

"A warnin'! Yes, for sure that's what it was!" Relief washed over him.

"That's what I thought, Daddy! I'll bet that buzzard was tellin' me to repent, and stand good for what I say."

Then, I dramatically recounted what had happened between me, the Almighty, and the death adder, flatly stating it was time for me to embrace religion. When I was finished, T.H. sat in his chair, as still as death. His manner was so strange; it was like a trance had come over him.

I began to squirm in my seat, thinking he must be madder than I'd ever witnessed before. I took some comfort from the fact that Mama poured herself a cup of coffee and sat down nearby; Mamau Maude came in right behind her. Resort guests who knew T.H. were headed *out* the dining hall, toward greener pastures.

"What church did you say you were thinkin' of attendin'?" he finally asked in a voice I recognized as being too controlled. We were more alike than either one of us knew. Seeing as I was, like the Bible says, "fruit of the father's loins," I'm sure T.H. knew he'd been had.

"All of 'em," I boldly replied, marveling at my own pluckiness. That's when the bellowing started; T.H. thundered like a Brahma bull. I thought the earth had begun to shake, but it was only my skinny bones trembling uncontrollably in my chair, next to the fiery passion of Irish Gaelic.

"Dammit lassie, a mouth might open and shut like a prayer book, but that doesn't mean it is one!" While Daddy continued flinging his Joe Blizzard fit, Mama and Mamau Maude sat quietly in their chairs, waiting until the heat died down to a smoldering ember. Finally, my father said, as if wondering out loud, "I swear, I don't know what's gotten into you girl. I ought to forbid you from takin' in such foolish notions."

T.H. was up against it with the trio of wily women he found himself facing that day. "Pug's old enough to know her own mind about such a sacred thing," Mama said softly.

"There was an age, not long past, when a man was master of his own house," he grumbled.

Then Mamau Maude spoke, her voice sweet and kind. As I listened to her words, my spirit felt cradled, gently rocked by the peaceful tide of hope. "Tyne, this is about acknowledgin' a greater Master. God has put his mark on the child, and He commands her to follow her heart. Your daughter comes to you not for your blessin', but for your acceptance and your love."

From the next room a pendulum clock chimed seven times. Mamau's brief discourse had sounded like poetry, the only time I ever heard her admonish my father. She did it with such sympathetic style, there was nothing for him to do but gradually smile and say, to no one in particular, "If it doesn't rain today, it'll miss a mighty good chance." Daddy's words trembled with emotion as he ran his big, callused fingers through my tousled hair. His touch reassured me. I felt safe, affirmed.

✳ ✳ ✳

After breakfast, there was still plenty of time before church, so I headed down the well-worn trail that led to my thinking place. Strolling along, savoring sweet summer smells, I munched on wild huckleberries and honeysuckle. I stopped and stared at some blooming High Buck, fascinated by the phallic-shaped, hairy flower that hung down low, about six inches. It looked alive—I reached out to touch it and shivered.

I walked the line of stones set across Hog's Creek, then traversed a wide meadow of budding mayapples on the far side. After moving away the brush I'd so often laid across the opening to Horseshoe Cave, I entered the chamber and searched rock ledges by feel until I found the strategically placed matches. I lit several candles before opening the cigar case that contained my smuggled treasure. I reclined comfortably on a pallet, designed with scraps of cloth I'd pilfered from Mama's sewing room, and lit myself a homemade cig made from rabbit tobacco.

Attempts to manufacture my own cigarettes had begun two years earlier. Experience and determination guided me in the perfection of this craft. Trial and error proved corn silks, grapevines, and coffee grounds to be the choicest packing materials. Hours spent watching my elders had aided me in the pursuit of authoritative rolling techniques. I was now a master. As I inhaled long and deep, I thought about the important role Horseshoe Cave now played in my life. Three months earlier, Egypt, Fawn, and I had discovered the place together.

That first time inside its dark domain was a terrifying experience. The cave's mouth was small; a full-sized man couldn't have entered. At the time of our original discovery, I peered into the darkness for a minute or two, then ducked inside, alone. For my prepubescent form, it was one short dive, combined with a level roll, and I was in—underground and blind as a bat.

I thought the opening would provide more sunlight than it actually did. For several moments, I was paralyzed with fear, consumed by the tangible, enveloping blackness. Though the air was cool, I began to sweat. All kinds of pictures took shape in my mind: huge, hibernating bears, spiders the size of my fist, and gigantic snakes with keen-edged fangs.

An inadvertent moan escaped my lips; its echo sounded like someone answering back. A few moments of silence followed, then I heard the whispers. They weren't the murmurs of living beings. The rustling noise sounded more like the sighs of ghosts. I panicked, screamed, then crawled in the direction I'd fallen, clawing stone walls until Fawn and Egypt pulled me out.

Two days later, our courage bolstered, we returned to the cave armed with tallow candles and matches. This time, we entered together and immediately saw there were no animals, large or small, lingering about. This in itself was odd, as though the cave had been waiting for someone, for us, to discover it. I was taken aback when Fawn and Egypt were unable to hear the manifest, eerie whispers. To my ears they were easily perceived, distinct from anything I'd ever heard before. But the sorrowful, haunting racket seemed meant for me alone.

To their credit, my two friends never questioned my sincerity about hearing the creepy sounds. Fawn had a chilling theory. "Badgerwoman says that caves like this were buryin' grounds for the Creek and Choctaw. Their spirits might warn us to keep our distance. Maybe, that's what Pug hears. I don't think we should ever go too far back into the crannies of this place."

Scared speechless, Egypt and I nodded; we had no argument with such astute, disquieting counsel. Nor were we about to pick a fight with spooks, especially phantoms staking a claim. As long as there was the tiniest light, the whispers lessened. Gradually, with the passing of time, they stopped altogether. Or more correctly, I no longer heard them.

We always met in the main chamber, just inside the den's opening. Egypt gave the cave its name because of a perfect earthen horseshoe, a natural formation she discovered over the cave's mouth. The interior was extremely wide; the cave's ceiling was high, like that of an unadorned cathedral.

Our girlish, high-pitched voices loudly resounded around the spacious walls. Strewn along the smooth dirt floor were fragments of lead, shells, and Indian-looking trinkets. Horseshoe Cave offered perfect shelter; some unseen crevice in the rear of the cavern caused the air to blow inward in summer and outward in winter, allowing fresh air to circulate.

During the weeks that followed our discovery, Horseshoe became the perfect hideout. It was an intrigue we kept to ourselves, offering covert amusement and sought-after freedom from adult scrutiny. Whenever there were paying customers on The Hill, Egypt, Fawn, and I knew the cave's existence allowed our multi-hued group to steal away. To frolic together with impunity, away from frowns of disapproval. My parents let us work this out on our own; foolish, impossible rules are best taught that way.

Then, things got complicated. One day, while playing Chinese checkers within the safety of Horseshoe, we heard rustling near the entrance. I peeked out in time to see Fanny trying to hide herself behind a nearby tree. We'd avoided each other since that infamous day, months earlier, when she'd acted like a horse's ass in Marsh's Grocery.

With the speed of a bear cub, I rushed out of the cave and bounded toward my traitorous friend; Egypt and Fawn weren't far behind. Together, we cornered Fanny, then tackled her. "What are you doin' here?" I demanded, feeling madder than a pitbull.

Fanny stared at the ground and confessed, "I followed you. I'm dyin' to know what you're doin'. Why you're always sneakin' off in the same direction."

"You had no right to do that," I hissed. "This is *our* special place. Nobody knows about it but us!"

"Until now," added Egypt, annoyed.

"I wanna play, be friends again," Fanny pleaded. She looked up into Egypt's eyes, then Fawn's, then mine. "With *all* of you."

"Is that so?" I said, making no attempt to hide my sarcasm. I looked at Egypt; she shook her head *no*.

"Fanny is a weeny," came our simple chant, delivered with the sharp, cruel edge of children.

Fanny was so angry that she began to cry, but she tried one more peace offering. "What can I do to show how sorry I am for...you know..." Looking at Egypt, she continued her awkward apology. "What happened in the store, it was stupid. Sometimes, I can't stop my own big mouth. I admit I was a showoff, but I take it all back. I never meant what I said; you know I didn't, don't you Egypt?"

Egypt was clearly moved by Fanny's words and seemed close to forgiveness when I stepped in. "It ain't that easy, and you know it. Are you always gonna act like an idiot whenever your brother's around? Maybe once a Holt, always a Holt, is that how it is?"

The situation boiled over with pent-up feelings. "Who are you to be callin' me names, Pug Sheridan? You think you're Miss Perfect. It's time you came off that mountain you're standin' on."

"You're the one on her high horse, Fanny Holt. Or maybe, you're just full of horse *shit.*" That's when a full-blown cat fight erupted. Fanny attacked with all her might, knocking me to the ground. Entangled, we rolled in the mud, pulling each others' hair out in clumps.

Fawn and Egypt finally managed to drag us apart, but not before we were both bruised and bleeding from deep scratch wounds. I knew how a mad dog must feel; I wanted to bite somebody. Fanny looked rabid too. The pair of us was pushed down into the cool shade of separate trees.

It was Fawn who patiently negotiated a civilized solution, an arm wrestling match. If I won, Fanny would leave and never come back, telling nobody about Horseshoe Cave. We'd let her join our group should she beat me.

"Also, if I win, I get to be the boss!" Fanny yelled her challenge across the narrow space between us.

I nodded, cocksure I'd win.

"By God, let's do it. All or nothin'...*right now,*" Fanny spat.

She and I lay upon our stomachs on a nearby grassy knoll, clasped hands, then dug our elbows into the soft earth. We stared angrily into each others' eyes as Egypt gave the signal to begin. Our bodies jerked in tandem. *God, Fanny's strong,* I thought.

"Dung eater," Fanny growled.

"Buffalo butt," I snarled.

Minutes passed. We both groaned with the effort our demanding contest exacted. I feared it was a stalemate; we seemed equally matched.

But I found the strength for one final shove. That's when I heard it. A stomach-turning pop. Fanny's wrist snapped liked a mop handle and she cried out in agony. Stunned, I let go of Fanny's hand. It involuntarily flopped forward like wet cloth, her forearm bent where it should've been straight. "Please stop. I give up, Pug," my opponent sobbed.

I felt like a criminal. "Lord…Fanny, I'm so sorry. I should've known when to quit." As I put my arms around her, she began to shake.

"Oh sweet Jesus! It hurts; it aches real bad!" Fanny's high-pitched wail was unnerving. I felt helpless, unsure of what to do next.

Like an expert, Fawn calmly examined the break. "I know how to fix your arm, Fanny," came the soothing, assuring words. "I saw Badgerwoman help somebody with a sore arm like yours. It's gonna hurt for a second, but I know it'll work."

Breathing hard, the injured girl studied Fawn for a long time. "All right." Fanny's voice betrayed her fear. "Fix it, if you know how."

"First, we need to walk over there," Fawn answered, pointing to a large, nearby log. She lowered Fanny down, next to the old timber, then told her patient to close her eyes. Without warning, Fawn slammed Fanny's arm against the hard wood. Fanny screamed like there was no tomorrow, but her arm was straight again.

Egypt disassembled my knapsack and produced a wide, sturdy board. Fawn carefully lay the swollen limb on the wooden splint, and I secured it with my sock. Then, we focused on keeping Fanny comfortable until she felt like walking home.

Exhausted, our little band made its way back to the cave, helping Fanny negotiate the opening so she wouldn't injure herself further. Once inside, Fanny rested upon my pallet, whimpering like a sick puppy when I clumsily covered her with an old blanket.

Nobody said anything for a long time. Words seemed inappropriate. Finally, all four of us spoke at once, asking the same question, "Now what?" It broke the tension and paved the way for laughter.

"You broke my damn arm, Pug!" Fanny cried out, her smile coy, not angry. She slapped me on the backside with her good hand.

"I know, you win," I joked.

"What is this? Some kinda warped rule y'all have to play here? All those with broken bones are allowed in?" Fanny's question was part serious, part tease.

In answer, Fawn handed Fanny an Indian-styled rawhide rattle. The image of a bear was drawn with black paint on one side, the outline of a sparrow on the other. "We call it our talkin' stick. You deserve to hold it now," Fawn murmured.

We'd already used the stick many times, as part of a game we'd invented. The girl to whom the stick was passed asked the others a riddle or told a joke or bawdy rhyme. Sometimes, she simply shared a story or bit of gossip. A girl never wanted to pass her turn if she could help it; the goal was to think of a waggish, entertaining ditty to say, each and every time the stick came one's way.

I knew what Fawn was up to: she was trying to take Fanny's mind off the pain. I could see that Fanny also understood this and was grateful. Visibly moved, Fanny asked, "What's no better than a bug in the dirt?"

"A person without real friends," replied Egypt. "But that's nobody here." The moment felt timeless.

Overwhelmed with guilt for what had happened, I remained quiet as I added more wood to the dying flames of our small fire. The four of us listened to the popping and crackling echoes as they bounced around dirt walls.

Fanny, now one of us, returned the talking stick to Fawn. In a low, mischievous tone, Fawn asked, "What is that which is enough for one, sometimes too much for two, and nothin' at all for three?" Silence. "A secret," she whispered before passing the stick to me.

Like a bolt of lightning, it hit me. "Maybe we can prove that riddle wrong," I said, raspy-voiced. "By startin' a secret club. With real initiations and the like. Usin' Horseshoe as our base, nobody will ever know what we're doin' here. Nobody but us." I thought the idea would make up for Fanny's arm, as well as months of bad blood and hurt feelings, but palpable resistance was in the air.

"Who'd want to join?" Egypt asked, nonplused. "Most white girls make fun of us when we're together. The colored ones are more scared than ever of doin' something bad, causin' trouble by makin' the wrong person mad. You and me can't even be on the same side of Sheridan Lake on public days."

"Egypt's right, but so is Pug," Fawn chimed in. "Why can't we have our own kind of fun? The grown-ups around here don't understand. *We do.*"

Fanny nervously protested. "I still want to play with y'all, if you'll let me," she said. "But joinin' a formal club, Daddy'd kill me if he ever found out." She looked at Fawn and Egypt. "Don't misunderstand. I like you and all…It's nothin' personal…It's just that you don't know my father."

I feared that the day was ending up the way it started. "Nobody should be forced to join," I cajoled. "But that shouldn't stop us from havin' our own hideout, with rules that *we* decide on."

"Seven." Fawn sounded excited. "Seven girls in our club would be a lucky count. Badgerwoman uses that number for all her totems."

I gently laid my hand on Fanny's shoulder and coaxed, "Your daddy's a preacher. He's not about to hurt anybody. It's your decision, of course. But you can't let your family run your whole life, Fanny. You're already part of the secret now. Part of Horseshoe. There's no turnin' back. Not for any of us."

Fanny bit her lip as she thought out loud. "I guess I *did* follow y'all here today." She winced as she cradled her broken arm, then smiled. "And I fought to stay and be the boss. I'm good at sneakin' out of the house after dark." Another long pause and then, "I'm in if you'll have me."

Our idea was a novel one—based on friendship, not skin color—born at the height of childhood innocence. We invited three more of my white friends to join, and they accepted, though such an alliance was a big risk. As children, they were in danger of receiving a terrible whipping from their parents.

But unlike most youngsters, Violet and Ruby Seay, along with Newt Yetter, had families that ignored them most of the time. Those particular three girls had few friends and were known as troublemakers, nuisances of the neighborhood; they were used to getting in and out of mischief, a talent I knew would come in handy.

We called ourselves "The Secret Society of the Seven Sisters." Our sense of adventure allowed us to throw caution to the wind, even though the stale breeze of prejudicial threat was gathering strength throughout the South. Still, with our childish naiveté, none of us could've foreseen the emotional chaos our friendship would bring as it rubbed certain people the wrong way, people whose tolerance level was already inflamed.

As a half-baked, rough-and-tumble tomboy, however, I believed good times were there for the taking. On the morning I'd butted heads with T.H., I stashed stolen, leftover corn cakes in Horseshoe Cave, along with a change of clothes. I hurriedly snuffed out my smoke and raced home to get ready for church.

THREE

I whistled as I skipped toward the washroom. Essie called out behind me, "A whistlin' girl and a crowin' hen always come to some bad end!" When I whistled louder, I heard her boisterous laugh echo down the hall.

Daddy built our unique bathing room with Mama in mind. It had a window in the roof where sunlight filtered through in a giant beam of heavenly heat. The other windows were high up, offering the bather a private refuge. The floor and walls were constructed with blood-red bricks. A wood stove rested in the corner. Soft white towels and matching rugs invited touch. Earlier, water had been added to the oval-shaped aluminum tub positioned in the center; morning's light had warmed it.

I washed with diligence, wanting God to find me squeaky clean. I even remembered my neck and ears. The soap was formed with hog's grease combined with homemade lye leached from hickory wood ashes. The lye from our ash hopper was ten times better than the store-bought stuff. Mama had poured lemon juice into the mixture; sometimes she'd add mint leaves or rose petals before the homemade soap was poured into molds. It left a body smelling like fresh morning dew.

After slipping on my dressing gown, I hurried to my room. Fawn had climbed through the window and was sitting on my bed. Her solemn expression relayed the fact that Badgerwoman wouldn't permit her to accompany me to church. "Can you come to Horseshoe early tonight?" Fawn whispered, making sure no one overheard the name of our secret meeting place. She was trying to act cheerful, but a single tear rolled slowly and sadly down her face.

"Sure," I answered, "I'll see ya at the cave as soon as afternoon services are over." Fawn smiled faintly, nodded, then climbed soundlessly out the window.

With relish, I put on my favorite outfit, a cotton dress with tiny lavender and gray checks; a purple taffeta ribbon was attached at the waist. I wore matching shoes, which Essie had polished with a greasy biscuit. Mamau Maude braided my long red hair down my back. Atop my head, I placed a gray velvet hat with a narrow brim. All modesty aside, I looked good enough for burying.

My grandmother appeared distinguished and refined in the dress and matching coat she'd made from scraps of fancy Italian drapery. The ivory brocade complemented the color of her hair. She wore no jewelry. As the first lady of simple elegance, she didn't need to.

Daddy's voice boomed as he shouted orders and joked with hired hands. Mamau Maude and I walked outside to discover that he had harnessed two of our Kentucky thoroughbreds to the surrey we used on special occasions; it had a green top, decorated with fringe that bounced happily during travel.

Lester Goff, a man Daddy tolerated because he was a cripple and couldn't get work elsewhere, hollered, "Come and see the mess those niggers left over yonder, T.H. There are peanut shells everywhere. It'll take 'til Doomsday to clean 'em up. Why can't they act like civilized folks?"

"Now Lester," T.H. replied, his voice stern, "you know I don't care for such talk. Peanut shells are harmless enough. Go help Jack move that lumber. Then see what you can do about cleanin' the stables."

I rolled my eyes at Lester's comment, then climbed in the surrey alongside Mamau Maude while Daddy held the horses. He walked purposefully around the restless animals and handed the buggy whip to his mother. At first, I thought Daddy wasn't going to look at me. But as our horses trotted away, he turned and gave me a wink, his eyes glistening. Relieved, I smiled back.

Hansel and Gretel unified their step, putting on airs of arrogant superiority; Mamau Maude and I laughed at the uppity horses. The rhythmic sounds of their trip-trot gait calmed and lulled us. Mamau didn't like driving the team, but I did. She let me have the whip for most of the way; I felt free, alive, and powerful while guiding them forward. We rounded a bend and saw Old Bethlehem Methodist in the distance; our horses picked up speed as we got closer to our destination.

Built in a grove of trees located atop a rounded, grassy knoll, the church was shaded by richly-boughed oak branches that draped themselves over the roof. On that summer's day, there were bird calls in the air and butterflies flitting about. As the buggy pulled to a stop, I noted who'd arrived and who was wearing a new dress or hat.

Violet and Ruby Seay were playing out front and were surprised to see me. Their mother let them sit in a pew with me and Mamau Maude. The three of us were excited to see each other, and we eagerly whispered among ourselves for as long as possible. When we thought nobody was looking, we crossed our wrists with seven fingers extended outward. It was the Seven Sisters' secret signal of recognition. Our covert cleverness made us giggle hysterically. A fixed stare from Mamau Maude told us to settle down in a hurry.

I squirmed on the hard, homemade pew; it was held together with large, square nails that bore into my rump. My sweaty thighs stuck stubbornly to the pine slab. As I tried my best to sit still, the combined, pungent aroma of wood, cut flowers, mildew, cologne, and sweat distracted me. *God's Perfume,* I thought to myself.

I jumped when Reverend Horton Tidbow's resounding greeting demanded my attention. "Let us rise and sing Sacred Harp number 231, in recognition of God's Promise, liftin' our voices in praise and thanksgivin' to *The Unclouded Day.*"

Mamau knew the words of the hymn by heart; Ruby, Violet and I shared a song book. Even though my singing voice sounded like a mule in labor, I had a hankering to "rise and sing" full-out, ignoring all sideway glances in my direction:

> Oh they tell me of a home far beyond the skies,
> Oh they tell me of a home far away.
> Oh they tell me of a home where no storm clouds rise,
> Oh they tell me of an unclouded day.

After hymns, the sermon began. I remember brief passages spoken by Reverend Tidbow that day. He had some first-rate lines too, worked the crowd real good. "We may talk of presence of mind, but there's a rarer quality we should all strive to have. That is presence of heart." He preached with a no-frills approach, plain and loud.

I don't remember much more because I fell in love during the twenty-five minutes he spoke. Most folks don't believe young girls can feel true love, but they're wrong. Though a sudden thunderstorm rattled our chapel walls, I took no notice. A storm-free paradise had settled within my own, fast-beating heart.

Alton Strawbridge and his brother, Arious, had come into God's House late. The pews were packed with parishioners, so they reluctantly sat in one of the Amen corners. The side benches were so named because of the older folks who regularly sat there, calling out "Amen!" anytime they approved of the preacher's message.

The two brothers attended boarding school up North. They rarely came home, and I hadn't laid eyes on either of them in years. Arious was sixteen, Alton fifteen. Their mother succumbed to childbed fever a few weeks after Alton was born. Judge Thurmond Strawbridge, their father, had recently died a peaceful death in his sleep. The severity of Judge Strawbridge's sentences, and his reputation along the circuit as a "hanging judge," worsened after the death of his wife. Similarly, as a parent, he'd shown little patience with his boys; they were better off being raised by schoolmasters.

Alton and Arious were alone now, without living relatives except for the Judge's sister, Caroline Strawbridge; they had returned home to help their old maid aunt sort things out. Caroline's expression appeared sad even when she smiled. Her nephews also carried themselves with a melancholic bearing. It wasn't grief alone; the family bloodline conveyed a dominant gloomy gene. I, for one, thought it added character and intelligence to Alton's perfect face.

Alton was tall with deep-set, light blue eyes; his skin was darkly tanned like his brother's. Patrician would describe his nose and other features. The color of his lips reminded me of running roses in early bloom. Sleeping feelings were aroused inside me, hinting at the essence of something previously unknown. Some might call it lust. At age ten, I didn't know what to call it, but in one short hour it was decided; I'd save myself for Alton Strawbridge, until Doomsday if I had to. I made a wish on an eyelash and blew it away.

Sometime during my lovelorn daydream, I heard the pastor ask if there was anyone present wanting to join the membership. All churches in Village Springs had a similar diametric rule: you couldn't get baptized unless you joined the church, and if you joined, you were automatically baptized. The next thing I remember is standing in front of the entire congregation, with Preacher Tidbow on one side of me and Mamau Maude on the other.

My grandmother removed my hat. The Reverend reached into a wooden bucket and scooped out an impressive amount of water, holding it easily in the reservoir of his large, curved palms. With practiced deliberation, he let the cool liquid cascade down upon my head. "As this water flows, may it remain a symbol of God's Purity and Mercy. I baptize you, Sadie Lou Sheridan, in the name of the Father, and of the Son, and of the Holy Ghost. Amen."

I waited for the preacher to say, "Go forth my child and sin no more!" But he didn't. Instead, he continued to pray silently while his hand remained firmly planted atop my head. I tried not to wriggle when the baptismal water dripped down the back of my dress and seeped into my undergarments. Pastor Tidbow prayed for a distressingly long time. I figured he thought me a challenging specimen for theological solutions; my soul obviously needed extra attention. When, at last, the preacher reached down and shook my hand, I risked a glance in Alton's direction; his smile met mine and my face turned ten shades of scarlet.

An offering was taken, the doxology sung, and when it was over, everybody gathered out front. Grown women talked among themselves while their men hitched horses. Ruby and Violet whispered in my ear, assuring me they'd be at the club meeting that night, but I barely heard them; my attention was elsewhere. Alton and Reverend Tidbow were having an animated discussion on the church steps, eagerness pouring forth from Alton's side of the conversation. Eavesdropping proved impossible; the churchyard echoed with what sounded like a multitude of chatty voices.

From the corner of my eye, I saw Mamau Maude walk toward Arious and his Aunt Caroline. I studied Arious for a few moments; he was actually the more handsome of the two brothers. Even so, my gaze fixed on Alton.

"Pug Sheridan, what's the matter with you? You haven't listened to a word we've said!" It was Ruby. She grabbed my hand and added, "Come with me. I have something to show you." We ran back into the church, and Ruby took a small package from her mama's hand. "Look what Grandpa sent us all the way from Boston!" There, in a little tin box, were sticks of red and white peppermint candy.

Violet chirped, "There are seven pieces left, enough for each girl to have one at the Seven Sisters' meetin'!" Violet caught herself; her excited voice had been too loud. She quickly brought her hand to her mouth, then carefully looked around, chagrined. No one had heard her. The three of us breathed a sigh of relief.

"You've gotta be more careful!" I admonished. "What if somebody had been standin' nearby?"

"I'm sorry, Pug," came Violet's embarrassed apology. "Sometimes, I just get so wound up! I look forward to our meetin's more than words can say. I promise it won't happen again." Her mother's voice echoed in the distance, calling Violet and her sister by name, ending the tense moment; they raced toward the sound, headed home.

During the return ride to The Hill, I plied my grandmother with questions while a soft rain pelted the surrey. "Mamau, do you know what 'Amen' means?"

"It means 'may it be so,'" she smiled. Mamau went on to say how good she thought the sermon had been and how proud she was of me.

I loved her dearly, like a second mother. Mamau Maude always made time for me, and I felt older in her presence. I then asked if I could go with her to deliver a baby, the next time she was summoned as a midwife.

"I'm sorry child, but you haven't had a baby yet. There's a legend from the old country that cautions against you seein' childbearin' too soon. If a childless female watches another woman in labor, she might have *that* woman's pain, as well as her own, when her first lyin'-in time comes. Best not risk it."

Best not, I thought, still wondering if I'd ever learn the secrets of female mysteries. I pressed for more information. "Where in blazes do all those babies come from? I've noticed that most are born in the middle of the night. Does that mean something I should know?"

My grandmother acted embarrassed, an unusual occurrence, and summarily answered, "Babies can be born anytime. I've delivered as many at noon as I have at midnight. But, nighttime does play an important role; husbands and wives tickle each other in the dark, then the baby starts to grow in the woman's stomach."

"Well that does it!" I loudly declared, incredulous. "Nobody is ever gonna tickle me again!" I waited for my grandmother to spill the real beans, a truth I suspected yet hadn't confirmed. But she stayed silent, and so did I. We were almost home before Mamau Maude mentioned that she'd invited the Strawbridge family to Sunday dinner. I was speechless for a moment or two before I heard myself say, "Amen!"

✳   ✳   ✳

"Alton, did you know that we call our little Pug the 'Poetess of the Hill'?" Bragging doesn't suit most people, but it heightened T.H.'s jubilant spirit as he lavished unwanted fatherly praises in my direction. Our family's private dining room found Daddy at one end of the table, Reverend Tidbow at the other. Uncle Finas, Azberry, and the Strawbridge brothers sat across from Mama, Mamau Maude, Caroline Strawbridge, and me.

"Young one, you look pale. Are you ill? You haven't eaten a thing." It was Mama, and she reached over to feel my forehead.

With exaggerated annoyance, I leaned away before her hand met its mark. "I'm not a baby, Mama!"

"Don't you go sassin' your mother, lass." Daddy's tone, as well as his gaze, was stern and rigid.

It was the longest meal I'd ever known. My parents were making it impossible for me to appear the seasoned and sophisticated *femme fatale*. I wished they could see the newfangled me, the ripened core, flowered and blossomed since breakfast.

Azberry sat hunched in his chair, sopping up gravy, grinning like a possum. If the preacher who'd just baptized me hadn't been there, I might have strangled the little scrunch.

"Would you read us one of your poems after dinner?" Alton was offering me a face-saving diversion in the conversation.

I was able to say, "If you like," before my throat closed up tighter than a tick. I watched with fascination as a ray of sunlight danced in the air above Alton's head, creating a halo effect around his dark brown hair.

Reverend Tidbow's deep voice was like a low rumble. He looked Daddy straight in the eye and said, "Young Alton tells me he's aimin' to be a preacher, gonna study theology when he goes back to school." Countless debates had raged across our table between the Methodist minister and T. H., invigorating them both. For Pastor Tidbow, Daddy was a thrashing flounder, a prize fish. Like Jesus, he saw himself as a devoted fisherman, the angler who'd reel T.H. in. The problem was, where Horton saw genuine bait dangling on his hook, T.H. saw artificial flies.

Mama was determined there would be no "fly-fishing" that day. She meaningfully touched Daddy's arm and promptly changed the subject, asking Arious what he planned to study after returning to Maryland.

"I'm preparin' to be a doctor, Ma'am," he proudly answered.

"So you'll minister to festered hides while Alton sees to their depraved souls!" The words popped out of my mouth before I could call them back. A painful silence filled my ears until Uncle Finas burst out laughing, a kind of howling that immediately infected the entire room. After that, we passed the afternoon in a better, profoundly relaxed mood. Everybody talked and joked more; even the gray cloud over doleful Aunt Caroline lifted for a while.

Azberry dropped his fork, and the Sheridan men, true to form, looked to see from what direction visitors would be arriving; the errant "sign" couldn't be ignored. Uncle Finas mentioned he'd seen a snake coiled in a tree while walking across the pasture. "A clear signal," Daddy agreed, "that for sure means more rain than we've already had."

I faked a sneeze to see if my menfolk would suggest that sneezing at the table meant you'd soon hear of a death, but they took no notice. Mesmerizing everyone, the Strawbridge boys were telling juicy stories about boarding school life. As the blackish-red pokeberry wine flowed, the tales got funnier. The brothers cheerfully told us about their eccentric headmaster, a man who'd had his tombstone carved ahead of time to read: SENSIBLE PEOPLE CHANGE THEIR MINDS, FOOLS NEVER DO. Arious swore to us that the monolith sat, waiting for sentry duty, in a corner of the man's office. "Important for such a thing to be done right," added Alton, mimicking Mr. Riddles.

The brothers elicited more belly laughs by insisting that their headmaster's stated professional intent was to eradicate all "murderers of the English language," either by education or by hanging. This compulsion evidently brought forth proper grammar and diction at the Zabiel Boylston School for Boys, with unprecedented success.

I joined in the laughter, but as the Strawbridge siblings expounded on their educational adventures, I grew uncomfortable. For me, their good-natured humor served as a bittersweet reminder of my own short-comings. It was the first time I felt embarrassed by my lack of formal schooling. I stared down at the table, overwhelmed by a sense of intellectual inferiority. *Alton could never be interested in a girl as flat-headed as me,* came the devastating thought. I pushed away my serving of rhubarb pie, no longer hungry. "Nothin' ever happens in Village Springs. Arious, maybe you'll be made a doctor in time to save me a slow death, Hum-Drum Fever," I stammered, fighting back tears.

Mama sensed my changing mood and sweetly murmured, "Maybe we'd better have that poetry readin' before we discover our 'Poetess of the Hill' buried under Boredom's Mountain."

I nodded and, with a heavy heart, trudged to my room to decide upon a dissertation. I settled on the latest work recorded in my diary, then ambled to the living room. When reading aloud, I always tried to muster the same passion and fascination I'd felt while writing the words. So, with artistic flair, I stood in our sizable salon, before my captive audience, and said, "'Moon Mill' by Pug Sheridan."

Azberry started to applaud, and Mama whispered, "Not yet, son."

I took a deep breath, then read my poem: "A green fountain sparkles while echoes of owls roll around in the air. Above night's enchanted forest, the moon circles and weaves her web of time." Then everyone applauded, and Uncle Finas whistled. The resulting encouragement and compliments lifted my dark humor and prevailing bashfulness. I curtsied, then walked across the room to sit between the Strawbridge brothers.

"What else do girls write in those little books?" Arious teased.

"Shh! Secrets of the heart!" Alton answered.

"Now, you boys leave the child alone. She shows promise for one so young," Aunt Caroline chided.

Alton took my hand in his and said, "Your mama tells me that you're goin' to the Bible service at Mt. Hebron this afternoon. May I escort you there, Miss Sheridan?"

Speechless—a rare occurrence for me—I nodded with a sheepish grin.

* * *

Vigil Holt was a Baptist minister and ventriloquist. When he preached about Hell's horrible particulars, it sounded like wrathful demons from Satan's fiery Underworld were coming through the walls of Mt. Hebron Church. "Someday, unbelievers will be able to open the gates of Hell and see for themselves, but by then, it'll be too late!" Preacher Holt's voice steamrolled over the squirming congregation.

"Imagine for a moment, the possibility of drillin' a hole nine miles deep into the crust of the earth, then hearin' millions of tortured screams, agonized cries comin' from the sufferin' souls condemned to the pit of eternal damnation! Doomed for all time!" From below the floor, we heard a human voice wail in pain; the horrific sound was enough to curdle the blood.

"Salvation must come before that hole is dug! Don't wait until the evil powers of Hell are raised up, let loose to roam. Declare yourselves the sinners that you are. Redeem your souls from that ragin' inferno!" By the time Preacher Holt ended his sermon, all the young children were screaming. Their distress was made worse by the sobs and weeping of their parents, well-meaning folks who dealt with their own fear by loudly begging the heavens for forgiveness. The collection plate was passed among the blithering throng; tear-stained money filled the basket.

Soon after, I found myself standing on the bank of a nearby stream that ran behind the church cemetery. Those of us to be baptized, me for the second time that day, had on robes made of unbleached cotton. Reverend Holt waded into the water, explaining that only those who allowed themselves to be completely submerged would have their sins washed away. He delivered a long harangue about other denominations that did not immerse their members; then the baptizing began.

One by one, we waded to where Vigil Holt stood. I watched those who went before me. Their faces had a queer, strained expression; the younger ones looked bewildered as they rose out of the water. When my turn came, Preacher Holt gripped my shoulders unreasonably tightly, as though he thought I might spook and run. "In the name of Jesus, child, I baptize you." The pronouncement seemed to come from the sky, like the voice of God. As I leaned back, the minister pushed me underwater for several long seconds. I remained strangely unafraid while being baptized—head, ears, and all—in the icy cold water of Billy Branch.

Dripping wet, I scrambled up the slope to find Alton. Instead, *I* was found by Grady Holt. He had fancied me since kindergarten, and was always trying to impress yours truly by saying outrageously shocking things. Since Alton was nowhere in sight, I felt flustered, not knowing what to do next. Grady saw his moment and pounced. Thinking himself clever, he asked, "Do you know that if you cut a nigger baby's fingernails too soon, it'll die before it's six months old?"

Grady sounded determined to addle me, but I just stood there, wringing out the hem of my baptismal shift, trying to maintain my dignity. "I suppose *you've* tried it, Grady Holt!" My teeth chattered as I spoke, more from feeling self-conscious than cold. I guessed that Grady could see through the thin material of the water-soaked garment clinging to my skin. He seemed to be enjoying the view. I modestly wrapped my arms around myself.

"If they haven't been baptized before they die, do you think those little dead babies spend eternity bein' licked by the flames of Hell?" He followed the question with a high-pitched shriek, similar to the ones we'd heard during his father's sermon. His mischievous laughter pursued me as I ran away.

A loud clap of thunder was followed by a sudden cloudburst; the large drops showered me as I made my way back to the church. The rain felt warm and clean on my skin, a refreshing downpour delivered by the Rainmaker Himself, the ultimate Baptism.

Once I'd changed into dry clothes, I found Alton sitting in a back pew, soaking wet. He'd been on a mission, picking flowers in nearby pastures, when the thundershower began. With a hint of coyness, Alton handed me a bouquet of pink honeysuckle and wood violets. "Today has been a big day for you, Miss Sheridan. Two baptisms on a single Sunday sure is something."

"Three if you count the rain," I grinned. Alton looked perplexed. It was the kind of puzzled stare I'd become accustomed to whenever I expressed myself freely. "I figure at least *one* of those baptizin' rites will catch hold," I continued, "but dogged if I know whether it was the Methodists or the Baptists keepin' company with the Lord today. I can't say for sure 'cause I ain't no judge, and there's not enough of me for a jury!"

Alton's belly laugh drew stern stares from old-maids Ledbetter and Washburn, surreptitiously gossiping in the choir platform. "Land sakes Pug, you're a little squirrel turner, aren't you?" His voice was a chortle. "A genuine Wunderkind!"

I lowered my eyes demurely as we walked outside, pleased by the accolade. "You're goin' back to Maryland tomorrow?"

He nodded.

There was a long moment of silence as I gathered my courage. "Will you write me?" My face flushed as I asked the question.

"Do you promise to send me original works by the Poetess of the Hill?" His question sounded serious.

"I promise," I shyly answered. Like an English Lord, Alton gently lifted my cold hand and kissed it. I continued to stare at the spot where his lips had touched my skin while he walked to his horse. I was still in a daze as he waved affectionately, then rode away on his rust-colored mare. "Wunderkind…" I softly whispered.

Fanny Holt walked up behind me. "Hi, Pug. Talkin' to yourself again?"

I dodged the question, and asked her what time she'd be coming to Horseshoe. "I'll sneak out after everybody's asleep," she answered. Taking note of my unconvinced expression, she added, "Don't fret, Queenie, the initiation doesn't start 'til midnight, anyway."

"You know as well as I do that Fawn will perform the egg tree rite at twilight, and we *all* have to be there to cheer her on." My admonishment sounded more bossy than I'd intended.

"Don't give it a second thought, Miss S! Fawn was there for me on my special night; I'll find a way to do the same for her. You can write it in your little red book and stamp it with your royal seal." Fanny gave me one of her impertinent grins, and we both burst out laughing. Impudent, bold, and saucy, she was one of my own kind, and we both knew it. "Hey, why was Alton Strawbridge givin' you flowers?"

"I'll tell you later," I smiled. "I'd better get goin' while the skies are clearin'." I waved to my friend and ran to my little horse, patiently waiting at the hitching post. A few weeks earlier, Daddy had won Blue in a poker game. When I saw him, it was love at first sight. A highland pony, he was a thick, gray saddle animal with a sweet disposition, standing about fourteen hands high. The pony nuzzled me as I patted his mane, and I gave him the expected sugar cube before we headed off.

I guided my horse toward Mt. Hebron's cemetery, to visit the grave of my Granddaddy Sheridan. The story of his death had been oft recounted in our home. "It's important that we *never* forget," cautioned Mamau Maude, always beginning the grim tale with the same words of warning.

Granddaddy had crossed rebel lines to fight with the Yankees during the Civil War. He survived the bloody battles, rising to the rank of lieutenant while still a young man. Shortly after the surrender at Appomattox, he found himself among Army troops that were sent south to stop a massacre.

It all happened in North Carolina during a regional conflict between the federal government and such self-named, night-riding vigilantes as the Yellow Jackets, the Redcaps, and the Klan. The locals called it "Ku-Klux fever," and lots of folks died of the disease. The victims included legislators, sheriffs, and countless black leaders, anyone who supported the new laws. Some were shot, while others were whipped, hanged, or drowned.

Granddaddy wrote to Mamau Maude about such terrible tortures, including the night he found one poor soul who'd had his ears cropped. "These acts are disgraceful to humanity," he declared in his final letter; they were the last words he ever wrote. My grandfather was killed, one hot August night, in a shoot-out with the Klan. The words on his tombstone read, "Peace is Mine."

Whenever I visited his grave, however, I couldn't help feeling that Granddaddy hadn't really found "peace." I sensed something important was left undone when he died, that a torch was passed to the next generation of Sheridans on that fateful day. The thought made me shiver as I sat rigid upon my pony.

To cheer myself while passing through the boneyard, I made up an epitaph for Grady Holt and recited it aloud: "His illness lay not in one part, but over his frame it spread. The fatal disease was in his heart, and water in his head." As we turned south at Billy Branch, Blue snorted his approval of my wicked verse. I giggled and loudly continued, "This stone was raised by Grady's Lord, though not his virtues to record. Since it's well known to all the town that it was *raised* to keep him *down!*"

FOUR

Blue trotted onward through tall, wet grasses. The enchanting music of nearby Katydids, hidden in lush meadows, filled my ears. My young mind's eye conjured fantasy picnics under moonlit skies—images of *amour*. Our cross-country path led to an ancient Indian trail, given the colorful name Bear Meat Cabin Road. The name "Bear Meat" belonged to an old Cherokee chief who'd lived in the area, long before the first white man had ever passed foot. The dusty byway shimmered, polished by rain; my pony chose his footing carefully in the hoof-deep mud.

I scanned the nearby fields, filled with bright yellow flowers that bestowed a golden glow on the environs, like the haze from a fire. I thought about something Badgerwoman once told me; the early Cherokee called themselves "Cha-la-Kee," chosen from the word "Cher-fire," meaning men of divine fire. Perhaps some of those Cha-la-Kee were buried under the incandescent yellow blossoms, the wisdom of a lost age reflected in the surreal light of a hazy afternoon.

"It's beautiful!" I shouted. Out of nowhere, a hawk swooped down and playfully circled overhead before disappearing into the brightness of the sun.

I neared Horseshoe with growing anticipation. An old wives' tale goes, "In the dark all cats are gray." That evening, Seven Sisters would declare that saying true as we completed the final, formal ritual to establish our club. Breaking long-standing southern taboos, we'd blend our assorted hues, becoming *one* in sisterhood.

But first, Fawn had to complete the egg tree rite. On the appointed night, each sister was required to make such a tree, following a strict protocol. A small hole was poked into each end of several eggs and their contents sucked out, one egg for each year of the initiate's age. Egypt, being the youngest, had sucked eight eggs; the others had swallowed nine. Ten was the required number for me, as it would be for Fawn. Vomiting was allowed, but every egg had to be devoured.

The initiate used the "blown" eggs to decorate a small, dead bush, dug up before the ceremony. After cropping its limbs, the girl tied the eggs on to the little tree with bright, shiny threads. Then came the scary part. With her sisters watching from a safe distance, the new recruit set the bush into the ground near the cabin of Rola Moon, the rumored witch of Village Springs.

Rola lived alone and was feared by most people who knew *of* her, though I'd never heard anybody say they really *knew* her. I could count on one hand the number of times I'd actually seen the witch. Remarkably self-sufficient, she came in contact with other people no more than she had to.

In desperation, some folks would go to Rola Moon for help when sickness, or other calamity, struck their family. They said her spells always worked; payment was a chicken, a blanket, whatever they had to give. It was whispered that Rola used her conjuring magic to do other things, like keeping a husband or wife from flirting around or giving a rival bad luck. Her "customers" always kept their business with her to themselves; conspiring with Rola was denounced by all the local preachers. In fact, she was condemned to Hell from some pulpits.

According to the Seay sisters' granny, a woman born and raised in the blue hills of Kentucky, an egg tree limited a witch's powers. If caught in the act, however, Seven Sisters never doubted we'd be boiled alive. The terror of the deed was surpassed only by our impishness. Six of us had succeeded without incident; this night was Fawn's turn.

I tumbled into the hidden grotto to find a fire already burning. Fawn, as usual, was one step ahead of me. We'd settled into a comfortable routine over the summer; I always slept at Fawn's house on Sundays, so Mama would habitually assume that's where I'd be, except she didn't really know. My mother would've thrown a conniption fit if she knew that I often slept in a dank cave on cold ground.

No living adult knew about our meetings in Horseshoe Cave, except Badgerwoman. Weeks earlier, Fawn had shown the hidden chamber to her granny while they were roaming the woods, grubbing for herbs. Badgerwoman never gave away our secret, not even to Mamau Maude. With the passing of time, the old Indian became a mentor to us all through Fawn's stories. During the initial stages of our clandestine assemblies, we came together on an irregular basis. Eventually, a full moon signaled that it was time to meet, a gentle light that guided each girl's path through the woods.

"Badgerwoman packed a good dinner tonight," Fawn announced as she laid out the squirrel that her grandmother had parboiled, then recooked in fresh water with sassafras root. My mouth watered at the sight of walnut bread smeared with pumpkin butter; it was earthy food, well-suited to the coarse surroundings. "Too bad, I can't eat any of this since I'll be havin' eggs for supper," Fawn cracked.

"You ready?" I asked, knowing what lay ahead.

She rolled her eyes and nodded. "Let's talk about something else before the others come. It'll help me calm down. I can't stop thinkin' about the tasty 'girl stew' the witch will make if she catches me."

"Don't worry," I reassured her. "Rola Moon wasn't even home all the other egg tree nights. At least, I'm pretty sure she wasn't. I think she prowls around after dark; she'll never even know you've been there."

Fawn shook her head, insistent. "Not this time. She's waitin'. Somehow the witch knows I'm comin'. I can feel it." She shivered and rubbed her arms in the passing chill.

I searched my mind for something to say, but drew a blank. I was thankful when Fawn spoke again. "You look starry-eyed. Anybody I know?"

"I doubt it, since you could count on five fingers the number of boys you're acquainted with," I said, teasing.

"Around here, boys worth talkin' to are as scarce as hen teeth," she shot back.

"Well shut my mouth, Fawn Storm, you're startin' to sound like me!" It was good to see her brief smile. "Put another log on the fire, and I'll tell you about my day," I cajoled, realizing a way I could divert my friend's anxiety.

Fawn listened intently as I told her about being baptized twice, how different the church services were, dinner at my house, and the Strawbridge brothers. It took more than an hour in the telling, my mouth chugged full, running over with the details of the day's events.

"I'd say this was an important afternoon in your life, Pug. What granny calls a 'starhawk' day." Fawn didn't talk much after that; she didn't need to. We'd become such good friends that we now thought alike; much of our communication was body language, an intuitive link.

Whenever the other girls would ask why Fawn's words could be so few and far between, I'd answer, "It's just her way. Remember, she's part Indian."

By the time I'd finished embellishing that day's adventures, the other five had arrived. What a ragtag bunch we were, with our torn coveralls and colorful, short sleeved shirts. (Except for Newt, who insisted on wearing a dress every day of the year, winter blizzards included.)

Violet's and Ruby's clothes always appeared a size too small, but they were clean. The Seay sisters quickly unfurled the candy they'd brought, delighting in our squeals of appreciation. "We'll eat it later, you know, after all the excitement," they stipulated with knowing looks.

Newt was as fidgety as a cricket, her usual state. Egypt glowed with unmitigated joy, a heightened reflection of her happy-go-lucky self. Fanny's high-spirited presence filled the room. Fawn remained in a hushed daze, absorbed in thought; we assumed it was a Cherokee approach to what was coming, a kind of mental preparation.

The group's overall excitement was palpable. No verbal mention was made about what could go wrong; everyone knew Fawn's dread. She watched with interest as each sister, in turn, silently pulled out a pocketed egg and placed it into the ceremonial basket. Fawn added two, and I contributed the final three eggs to the collection, part of the stash I'd pilfered at breakfast. But it was still too early to begin the rite. Instead, we passed around the talking stick as we waited for darkness.

We kept a tally of achievement after talking stick "events," with scrape marks rasped upon the cave wall. Fanny and I were in fierce competition for the Seven Sisters title of "Miss Mouth of the South."

That night, after drawing for straws, Violet went first. Unprepared, she made up a crack-brained fable as she went along. "While walkin' here tonight," she began, "it looked like the full moon was swallowin' the silvery clouds. Maybe the moon's really alive, a monster that eats vapors to stay afloat and keep its inner glow. But when it looks watery, like last week, it has gobbled too many wisps and is feelin' poorly, soggy even, like when we drink too much cider." Good-natured moans and groans noisily resounded in the chamber. Violet shook the elaborate rattle to signal the end of her time and eagerly passed it to her sister.

Ruby was ready with a riddle. "When was the first talkin' stick created?" Itching to give the answer, she impatiently waited until we'd hushed, then yelled, "When Eve gave Adam a little Cain! Get it, a little cane?"

Egypt, always shy when it came her turn, often had something original to say; she was good at eliciting red-faced giggles, a natural comedian. "Granny showed me how to cure my hiccups by holdin' my breath for a whole minute. If y'all promise to stay quiet and count, I'll prove I can do it."

An electrifying stillness filled the cave as Egypt held her breath for an impressively long time. Just before a minute had passed, Fanny leaned over and wickedly tickled her under the chin, forcing Egypt into a giggle. Fanny leapt up, and the chase was on as Egypt playfully pursued her around the cave. Ultimately, Egypt caught her rascally friend, then tickled her bare feet until Fanny begged for mercy, evening the score.

Fawn passed her turn, giving the floor to Newt, who often came primed with queries that ran along a never-ending thread. Her mind was a surplus of opinions and inclinations about the lives of the lovelorn. "What's the difference between a taken lover and one who's been turned down?" Newt's body was all aquiver. An inadvertent belch erupted as she cried, "One kisses his miss, and the other misses his kiss!"

Fanny took the rattle and declared, "Daddy never lets me play cards; he says they're of the Devil. I think he's wrong; cards are fun. So here's a trick my Granny showed me. If you want to win the game, stick a crooked pin inside your clothes." Fanny theatrically revealed the rusted hat pin attached to her inside pants cuff, and hysterics ensued.

After an hour of informal comedic competition, we'd almost tittered ourselves out. When my final turn came, I could smell victory.

Feeling smug, I asked, "Why does a dog's nose always feel chilly to the touch?" No answer. Whereupon I began to recite: "There sprung a leak in Noah's Ark which made the canine start to bark. Noah took its snout to plug the hold. That's why a dog's snoot is always cold."

"Pug Sheridan, you just made that up! In all my born days, I've never heard a more ridiculous poem!" It was Fanny. With a self-satisfied grin, I returned the talking stick to her, an obvious challenge. "All right, Pug. You win!" Fanny announced good-naturedly. "But don't get too cocky. I'll be ready for you next time, with some stupid rhymes of my own."

That night, we reveled in our perceived wickedness as we sang forbidden Yankee songs, then passed the "peace pipe" that Fawn filled with her own unique recipe, comprised of cinnamon, sage, and lavender petals. It was past ten when the carefree interval ended. Our pent-up, girlish energy was spent, allowing us to focus on the weighty matters at hand.

The egg tree rite began. Seven Sisters transformed themselves into prim and proper young ladies. We were the picture of decorum as we exited the cave. Beneath the light of a silver-gray moon, we formed a cohesive circle around our final initiate.

Fawn's breath appeared fast and uneven as I wordlessly handed her a canteen of water, but the young Cherokee then calmed herself, closing her eyes while inhaling, slow and deep. She waited several minutes before uttering her special chant (each girl's was different), repeating the prayer three times, her voice clear as crystal. "The river will watch over me. The ocean's tide shall carry me. Like a mother, the waters of Spring."

Ruby handed Fawn a thick, straight sewing needle. With expert precision, Fawn took an egg and poked the first hole in the larger end of the oval, gradually widening the opening with a circling motion; she repeated the deft action at the narrower end of the egg. Watching her, I suspected she'd been practicing for days. Fawn put the shell to her lips and rapidly slurped the contents as her sisters applauded, reciting in unison, "Seven Sisters hatched like an egg. Swallow the golden egg."

Fawn stared fixedly into space while exhibiting superior control over her gag reflex. Amazingly, she vomited only twice while sucking all ten eggs, a Seven Sisters record. She also proved to be the nimblest when it came to tying her eggs onto the tree branches. The rest of us had hurried to end the rite, but not Fawn. She insisted on drawing a charcoal picture on each and every egg, creatures mostly: birds, fish, spiders, and others.

When the egg tree was ready, the seven of us walked to Rola Moon's cabin in tense silence, traveling in a scraggled line hand-in-hand, our only protection against otherworldly, threatening sounds coming from the blanketed woods. Wild boar were on the hunt, running in packs, their grunts and snorts too close for comfort. Panther screams, far off in the hills, sounded like a terrified woman.

Occasionally, we'd hear the screech of an owl, an eerie sound in a darkened forest, warning off any enemy endangering its young. "Owls will gouge out your eyes for gettin' too close to their nest," Fanny volunteered with perfect timing. Terrified, Egypt squeezed my hand so hard it grew numb.

"This is scary enough, Fanny, without your two cents' worth," I whispered.

"Some folks just don't know how to have a damn good time," came Fanny's retort. She defiantly pressed on, "By astral light, by moonbeams bright, I make the wish I want tonight…"

I couldn't resist the dare, so taking her cue I responded, "The hag is old, bent like her cane; we'll soon take all the power she's gained."

Newt spoke for the other five girls. "You're scarin' the dickens out of us! You may think it's funny, but this isn't the time for a cursin' contest. You two don't know when to quit. Besides, did you ever stop to think that your hexes might backfire?"

Chagrined, Fanny and I kept close-mouthed for the rest of the trip. When we reached our destination, all was quiet and dark, both inside and outside the witch's house.

Six of us sought safety within a large sunflower patch while Fawn cautiously approached the house. She turned and whispered, "I don't like it when the crickets are this still at night. It means something's wrong."

Fawn's worst fears were quickly realized. As she prepared to set her roots into the ground, Rola Moon bounded onto the porch. The sorceress squatted, hooting like an owl, "Whoo, Whoo?" It was a perfect imitation of the real thing; the owl cries in the forest had been Rola all along, stalking us as we approached her property. The witch stood and faced the sunflowers that shielded us from view; we held our breath, feeling naked and exposed.

At first, the witch acted like she couldn't see Fawn, frantically digging in the earth six feet from the porch step. "Who goes there? Is it the rites of ancient ripenin'?" Rola shouted. "Answer me now! Do you lie with silence?" She sounded furious.

Fawn quickly shoved her egg tree into the hole she'd dug, then filled it in with dirt. With catlike agility, the witch was off the porch, facing Fawn, nose to nose. Fawn tried to flee, but Rola grabbed her by the shoulders.

"Oh my God," whispered Ruby. "She's gonna eat her alive if we don't do something."

"Ruby's right," said Egypt. "If we tackle her all together, we can knock the harpy down, grab Fawn, then run like Hell."

"I'll stab the old shrew with my hat pin," chimed Fanny, loud enough to draw Rola Moon's attention.

When the witch turned to look in our direction, the woman's expression startled me. An inkling of understanding crept into my mind. "Wait," I said, addressing my friends. "Nobody move. Stay where you are 'til I say."

"This ain't no time to act like the boss," argued Fanny. "Are you just gonna stand here while Fawn has her tender giblets cooked at a slow simmer?"

"Shh!" I flashed Fanny a look that could kill, and she hushed. What I'd noticed was incongruous; the witch appeared sad, confused, on the verge of tears. "*Who's scarin' whom?*" I wondered.

Still grasping her by the shoulders, Rola Moon studied Fawn's face for the longest time, like she wanted to ask a question but didn't know how. She looked our way again and hollered, "Mirror, clear mind. Let it be renewed this time!"

"She's crazy I tell you," Fanny insisted. "Has been for years, accordin' to Daddy."

Rola looked back at Fawn and said, "Be gone red-lettered signs. Looking glass of doubt! A puzzle. Whoo, Whoo?" Rola inexplicably loosened her grip, allowing Fawn to escape. Our Indian friend unleashed a raw, grizzled howl, the victory cry of the Cherokee, as she raced across the witch's yard. Seven Sisters waited until she reached us.

"Whatever happens, don't look back!" came Fawn's excited words. Together, we scampered back to Horseshoe, empowered by the force of female friendship. We drank strong coffee until midnight, recounting Fawn's daring escapade again and again.

The final initiation had been completed. Now, we came together for our most important moment, the consecration of our club, which would unite us in a bonding ritual and pledge. Fanny dramatically produced a gleaming razor blade, and our nervous breathing conjoined as one breath, a seven-part harmony.

Hesitantly, Egypt reached into her pocket and unfolded one of my father's old handkerchiefs, holding it securely by the sides so that it sagged in the middle. Fanny sheared off a piece of her thick, brown hair and placed it in the center of the cloth; then she held the ritual fabric so that Egypt could cut a sizable length from one of her own pigtails. I was next. One by one, we added large chucks of our long locks to the growing pile.

The razor came 'round again and, expectantly, Fanny held the handkerchief near me. I loudly sighed, then pricked my right forefinger, letting the bloody, dark droplets fall on the silky border of the snowy cloth. I focused on remembering the Seven Sisters' secret oath as I recited it aloud: "In the name of the seven daughters of Atlas: Maia, Electra, Calaeno, Taygeta, Merope, Alcyone, and Sterope, who under the moon of long nights were metamorphosed into stars, I give you my solemn pledge." The oath was my own creation. I'd read and re-read the story of Atlas, and his daughters, from a book on Greek mythology; it captivated the Seven Sisters' romantic spirits.

Fawn didn't flinch as she coolly sliced her own soft flesh, allowing the blood to spurt forth and join mine. There were sharp gasps, and stifled moans, as the keen bite of the razor traveled farther around the circle. Violet was last; her voice squeaked as she announced, "I know I'll faint if I do this standin' up. Y'all mind if I sit down to draw my blood?" As if unified by a group spell, everyone nodded a silent assent. We were seven, synchronized in our goal, when Violet added her blood to ours, the handkerchief now dyed red, the color of ripened pomegranate.

I lifted the small basket that contained seven slips of paper, bearing the names of Atlas's daughters. As the basket was passed, each girl spun outside the circle in rounds of seven, then drew a name, permanently capturing her secret sobriquet, known only to the other six. Egypt drew Taygeta; Violet became Maia. Fawn pulled Calaeno; Ruby became Merope. The luck of the draw made Fanny Alcyone and Newt Sterope; I was Electra.

We wrapped the papers bearing our secret names in the damp cloth that contained our blood-splattered hair. As I tossed the sacrosanct material into the fire, we held hands and repeated the pledge as a group. *At that moment, the Seven Sisters' covenant was sealed.*

We celebrated with the Seay sisters' gift of peppermint sticks. The fancy candy was sugary rich, offering a needed energy boost. For several minutes, words were supplanted with cheeky giggles.

Finally, Fanny spoke for us, her thoughts bursting forth like rapidly fired bullets. "Tonight has been the happiest night in my life. I can't wait to see what happens next! If we stick together, we're unstoppable. You're the best buddies I'll ever know." As Fanny made eye contact around the circle, she added, "Each and every one of you can count on me in a fight, even to death. I keep my promises."

With reluctant good-byes, and a lot of foot-dragging, we ended the evening. Our circle broken, Seven Sisters left the cave to creep back into their respective houses—that is, except for Fawn and me.

Before we scrambled into our bed rolls, Fawn ran outside to vomit one last time; she was clearly tuckered out when she returned. "You look tired enough to be makin' three tracks in the sand," I joked.

Fawn smiled. "Badgerwoman ends her prayers with the same words every evenin'... 'Blessed be this night for dawn is sure to follow.' Now I know what she means."

By the time I lit a long-burning candle, my friend was sound asleep. "Blessed be this night," I whispered before closing my eyes to welcome the dark.

FIVE

Seven Sisters' first few years together were a time of slaphappy simplicity. Within Horseshoe's protective womb, there were birthday celebrations, tea parties, and endless games. As individual parts of a whole, we took equal portions of everything life offered—handmade toys, books, even chicken pox.

Shielded by ghostly shadows, childhood confidences were entrusted that are still guarded today. Orally shared stories, both real and imagined, cemented our commonality. Egypt was fond of small trickster fables, especially those involving a larger person or animal being outwitted. The *Uncle Remus Tales* ranked among her favorites.

Fawn often spoke of Cherokee nature spirits; when called upon, she assured us, they could bestow the believer with uncommon strength. At those times, it was possible to outrun deer, win a barehanded fight with a wildcat, or survive falls from great heights.

As for the rest of us, our own Bible described the defeat of giants and even the vanquishing of the Devil by God's faithful. If you had "right" on your side, all things were possible. The unique blend of stories filled our youthful hearts with the self-righteous conceit of ingenuous dunderheads. The thought-provoking yarns combined with our innate, fiery personalities to create an unstable mixture, a catalyst for activism. This set the stage for my later deed, the one that ultimately led to the death of an enemy.

The *first* time I took the law into my own hands, however, I'd barely turned thirteen. Seven Sisters formed a self-styled vigilante group after Fanny heard a rumor that the Connolly family had a blind son with mental problems. "They say he's called Moody," Fanny somberly explained as we sat around our fire one memorable, frigid evening. "His folks have locked the poor thing in a room under their house. They keep him down there like a dog."

Following Fanny's cue, I said, "He's probably never known what warm sunlight feels like. I say we rescue him!"

So, one moonless November night, we Seven Sisters dressed in dark colors and smudged our faces with black flag bark. Like outlaws on a mission to pull a jailbreak, we set out to free Moody. We weren't certain he really existed, but we saw ourselves as heroines for justice, his liberators from inhumane treatment. At the same time, the freakish *idea* of Moody scared us, heightening the adventure.

We arrived at the Connolly place in the dead of night. Right away, we found a boarded-up space that might've served as a window in warmer months. Employing the wide-tip screwdriver that Fanny was clever enough to bring, we tore away the thick plywood. A small opening was revealed, about the size of a washboard. I lit a tiny candle and held it aloft in an attempt to peer inside, but the meager light did little to illuminate the darkened recesses of the makeshift chamber. "Is anybody down there?" My voice was hushed but friendly. "We're here to save you," I continued, feeling brave and important. "Answer me, if you're there. Before somebody hears us!"

A screech, rivaling that of a banshee, loudly erupted. We'd managed to terrify the poor soul locked inside the basement prison. I snuffed the candle as all seven of us ran to the shelter of nearby shrubs. Staying out of sight, we watched as Tom Connolly stepped onto his porch, intently looking and listening for signs of mischief. He walked to the side window, carefully examining the torn plywood and one lone screwdriver. Tom called out, his voice more sad than angry, "Whoever did this, come forward. Let me see your face."

The others stayed behind while Fanny and I held hands and walked toward our accuser. Tom Connolly was about forty years of age, though he looked much older as he stood before us in his long johns. He sighed deeply, then wearily said, "Come on inside. I'll show you what you came to see. You should've just knocked on the front door. Would've saved a lot of upset." Fanny and I obediently followed Mr. Connolly into his house; neither of us remembered meeting Tom before, but he knew our names.

The Connolly home was small, plainly decorated with homemade furniture. A hole had been knocked in the back wall; a short stairway led under the house. The door to the makeshift, underground niche was open, and a dim light shone from below. Fanny and I were still holding hands as we made our way down the stairs behind Tom.

The glow from a single oil lamp illuminated the pitiful scene. A grown man, dressed in faded dungarees, whimpered like a baby as he buried his head in his mother's lap. "I heard the thunder, Mama. Can you smell the smoke?" Moody's repeated words were occasionally punctuated with a bloodcurdling shriek. Jan Connolly reassured her son with soft, motherly caresses.

In unison, Fanny and I blurted out, "We're sorry."

"We didn't mean to scare him," I added, embarrassed.

Then came Fanny's blunt question, "Why do y'all have him caged up, anyway? What's he done to deserve it?"

A pain-filled glance passed between Tom and his wife. "Moody gets real mad sometimes. Unlike most folks, he doesn't need a reason." Tom's voice was low and resigned. "When our son goes out of control, he breaks things, includin' my nose. Jan's nursed so many black eyes, we've lost count." Tom sunk down onto the stairs, and put his head in his hands. "One Easter, a few years back, Moody lost his temper like never before. He killed his little sister, Janie, with a blow to her windpipe. We couldn't stop him; he's too fast and strong when he's like that." It was a shock to see a grown man sob.

After a long silence, Mrs. Connolly said, "Most of the time, he's like you see him now. A frightened child who needs his mama. We can keep Moody here, or send him to a crazy hospital, where nobody would love him the way we do. Since Janie died, Moody doesn't want to come up from the basement. This is his world now. He's happy here. Except, when it's stormin'. He gets real upset, then. We don't know why. When you tore away the wood, and he heard your strange voices, he thought it was thunder. Moody can't help the way he is."

I didn't know what to say in response to their misery. Lacking words, I reached into my pocket and pulled out a handful of candy. "Please give this to Moody when he calms down," I said. "Tell him it came from the thunder."

Eight months after our encounter with the Connollys, there came a rumbling, late summer storm. Moody's house was struck by lightning, then burned to the ground. The troubled family moved to Texas, forced by fate to live with relatives. Seven Sisters avoided the Connolly place after that. The entire incident became another secret we kept to ourselves.

✳ ✳ ✳

One damp and chilly night when I was fourteen, I lay in bed, rankled by the sound coming from the next room. It was Azberry, humming in his sleep. Every time he got his breath, he'd make a little droning noise. I listened to that purring, human motor every night, hoping he would grow out of such an annoying habit. With such a racket distracting me, I wondered if I'd ever get to sleep. Soon, there came a sound I didn't recognize. I felt a sinking feeling when I realized the scratching noise was coming from my window.

It was overcast and pitch-black outside. I peeked around my canopy, but couldn't see what sort of night crawler had come calling. I lit the candle on my nightstand and cautiously crossed the room. At the window, the flame illuminated the elfish face of my friend Newt. She motioned for me to come outside.

I pulled a sweater over my nightgown and put some boots on. Once on the damp ground, I measured my way by the light of Newt's small carbide lamp. We walked away from the house, far enough that our voices couldn't be heard.

Newt plopped down on a log, and I sat beside her. She was near the same age as me, but much smaller in size. In the murky darkness, she looked like a pixie, one of Azberry's flower fairies on a midnight frolic, itching to tell me her news. "I done it!" Newt was breathless with excitement.

"Done what?"

"You know, you've got to guess!"

"Dogged if I do!" Sometimes Newt could be aggravating. It was the dead of night. I was tired. I was cold.

"Emmer Faulk and me, we run off and got hitched today!" The words blurted from her mouth.

Now, I was also speechless.

Newt was a "briar patch" child, born out of wedlock. Her mother had deserted her when she was three; her father was the local miller. From the time I could walk, I accompanied my family whenever they made their regular visits to Clifford Yetter's Millworks. As the grinding, rotating millstones pulverized our grain, Newt and I would happily chase each other around the nearby pond; it was a high-energy exuberance that left us both used up, ready for naps.

Early on, Newt best expressed herself by staying in motion; she was slow-witted and hard-headed, a challenge to raise. To his credit, Clifford Yetter had taken in his abandoned child. But, even though he provided adequate food, shelter, and clothing, he remained emotionally detached from his offspring.

I knew about Newt's infatuation with Emmer Faulk. I didn't think it unusual, considering her melodramatic nature. She had known multiple crushes through the years, was forever madly in love with somebody. Most of us ignored her crazy talk, accepting it as part of her humor. Now, at thirteen, Newt had gone and *married* the dirt-poor, thirty-one-year-old widower and father of five.

"Daddy will want to kill Emmer when he finds out. You've got to help us, Pug!"

"Me? What can *I* do?" My words sounded numb. Subsequent thoughts ran along a very different line. *You empty-headed fool! You're ruining your life, shackled and chained. I should drag your silly self into the house, and let T.H. take you home, while there's still hope of an annulment. What can a man possibly give you, under the covers or otherwise, that makes you act like such a moron?* My internal rampage was interrupted by the memory of a promise, the Seven Sisters' oath.

"We're hidin' out on Nine Mile Creek behind Crooked Shoals, Grandpa's old place. Emmer's there now. Bring us some food tomorrow, if you can get it without nobody noticin'. We need somebody to check on Emmer's younguns, too. Things should quiet down in a couple of days, then he can take me home. He's gonna lift me over the threshold, like a grown-up bride!" Newt didn't seem to notice the cold. After I climbed back into my room, I shivered enough for both of us.

✳ ✳ ✳

The next morning, I woke up late, an unusual occurrence. The blood on my sheets made it official; I'd entered womanhood, or it had entered me; I'm not sure which. Mama helped me with my personal hygiene and tidied the bed. To settle my aching belly, Mamau Maude brought me some tea made from mountain mint plant. A soft wind kissed my face as I sat on our porch, sipping the warm liquid.

The breeze was suddenly cut short. I looked up to see Newt's daddy approaching our house on foot. His burly frame came storming through our yard. I knew, as sure as a dog will bark at the moon, the man had murder in his heart. "Did you know that girl of mine has gone and jumped the broom with clabber-toothed Emmer Faulk?" Clifford growled at me.

I stared down into my mug; it seemed like a mighty good time to learn to read tea leaves.

"Is she here?" he thundered.

I shook my head, *no*, which was the truth. Thankfully, Clifford didn't ask me if I knew where Newt was. I was feeling green around the gills, unsure about how well I'd carry off a lie.

Dumbstruck, I watched while Newt's daddy ranted like a rabid mule; I remained mesmerized by the slobber that trickled down his chin as he yowled. "Emmer Faulk is a no-good, low-life, son of a bitch! He'll always be suckin' a hind teat. In fact, he's as useless as teats on a bull! In two shakes of a sheep's tail, I'll hoist his carcass up so high, he'll catch a glimpse of Heaven before he falls back to the depths of Hell!"

I wasn't sure how long T.H. had been standing behind me, but was grateful to hear his voice. "Now Clifford, there's no need to go off half-cocked. Come on in. We'll throw back some bellywash and think this thing through." Daddy's tone was soft and soothing, like he was talking to an agitated animal on the verge of attack. Clifford followed him into the house; his respect for my daddy had a calming effect. They sat in our living room, talking while T.H. poured Jim Beam bourbon into crystal glasses. Those two were "saucered and blowed" by the time I gathered my burlap sack filled with contraband, climbed on Blue's back, and headed for Nine Mile Creek.

As I rode, I peeled the stem off some sugarcane and made myself a homemade sucker, enjoying the earthy sweetness while considering the two suckers awaiting my arrival. I was seriously depressed. And angry. Furious with Newt for becoming a self-made slave, mad at Emmer Faulk for needing one.

Some things can't be fixed. For the first time I understood the saying, "Live and learn, or die and forget it all."

A beautiful waterfall graced my destination, spilling over wide, sandstone ledges. The water fell into a circular pool, with a tall bank to the west that was a profusion of pale pink mountain laurel. It was here I found the honeymooners. I delivered the nuptial supplies without saying much. They weren't interested in having company, and I wasn't interested in being any.

My next stop was Emmer's cabin, about two miles away. It was an untidy, four-room house, with trash scattered about the yard. The steps leading up to the porch were broken. The walls were made of unsealed planks; there were also cracks in the floor. I could see chickens walking under the house, along with some pigs and an old hound dog. I saw no windowpanes, just shutters. There were flies everywhere.

Inside, Emmer's five kids were huddled around the fireplace. The oldest child, an eight-year-old girl, was stirring something in the wrought iron Dutch oven that hung over the tiny flame. The younger ones were eating out of a bucket lid, slurping mush that resembled the sludge Uncle Finas had used to slop the hogs that morning.

The two-year-old tottled over to a corner and sat down to suck on the dry leg bone of a chicken. The little tike had the squirts, and as she walked, soft globs of excrement plopped onto the floor.

The two youngest children were naked as jaybirds; the others wore rags. Each pair of britches was ripped; every foot was bare. Ulcerated sores infected various parts of reed-thin arms and legs.

An uneasy feeling burrowed down and settled in the pit of my stomach. My entire body was a bundle of nerves, drawn up tight. A biting autumn wind passed through the patchwork mess of a cabin, creating a bone-chilling draft. I quickly realized that I was looking at a family dying on the vine—Newt's family.

Five pairs of wide eyes ogled me as I talked up a blue streak, thinking aloud. "Emmer Faulk, the next time I see your worthless self, I'm gonna clean your plow! You're a sorry, good for nothin', top water minnow! You were born tired and raised lazy! You don't deserve to have our little Newt. You don't deserve *anything!*" Screeching like a bobcat, I'd flown completely off the handle.

The pitiful wailing of young voices, responding to my outburst, brought me to my senses. It hadn't been the best way to introduce myself to that pathetic group of suffering waifs. I soothed their crying as best I could, but all five remained skittish and easily frightened.

"What's your name?" I asked the eldest.

"Darlene," she coughed.

I touched Darlene's forehead; her skin felt like a hot poker. I examined the other children and discovered they also had high fevers. While leaning over to smell the gruel bubbling in the pot, I grimaced, then groaned with disgust. It was rancid.

"Darlene?" The sour taste of bile rested on my tongue.

"Yes," came the soft reply.

"Don't eat any more of this. It's gone blinky."

"Yes, Ma'am, Miss Sheridan." Darlene made a determined effort to smile. It broke my heart.

Those children were really sick. I had to do something. Fast. I ran outside and jumped on Blue.

"Please don't go!" Darlene called from the porch.

"Don't leave us, Miss Pug!" *All* of the tiny curtain climbers were begging me to stay.

"I'm runnin' for help. Then I'll ride right back."

"You promise? Cross your heart?"

"Yep. I'll be here before *you* can say, *abracadabra!*" I assured them while patting the tops of moppet heads, gathered all around the pony. Finally, I signaled for Blue to move on, letting him know we needed to hightail it. "Ride like the wind, Ole Blue," I cried. "We've got a bona fide crisis on our hands!" My little horse galloped as fast as he could to Fawn's place, two miles due north.

Nobody seemed to be home when we arrived in Spunky Hollow. I cupped my hands together and "blew a fist," the Seven Sisters' emergency signal. A minute passed, then Fawn was there; Badgerwoman appeared a few moments later.

"We were in the garden. What's the matter? You look upset!" Fawn was out of breath. She'd raced from the other side of the vegetable patch in a full-out run.

I described where I'd been, and what I'd just seen. Then, I began to cry, another rare occurrence for me, but I'd felt out of sorts all day. Badgerwoman began giving orders like a Confederate general. "I go back with Pug. Fawn, ride to Maude. Tell her about sick babies. Bring soap, food, blankets."

Fawn left, and Badgerwoman hurriedly threw needed items into a flour sack. She moved with lightning speed, an amazing sight to one who considered her the resident aging sage. She grabbed her mysterious medicine bundle, then signaled that she was ready.

Fawn had taken their only horse, a Tennessee Walker. (The mare was a gift from T.H., his thank-you gesture for saving my life.) I helped Badgerwoman onto Blue, then led the way to the Faulk place. When we arrived, Badgerwoman wasted no time; I watched her bowed-back form carefully inspect one child, and the next, down the line. "These children starve, much work to do here. Pug, draw a bucket of water."

With her first command issued, Badgerwoman nonchalantly walked to one of the chickens pecking in the yard. She held its neck in her hand, then swung the bird's body around in a cranking motion, until the head separated from the rest of it. Wrung its neck faster than I could blink.

Sometime later, Mama and Mamau Maude arrived. Their first reaction to the disaster known as the Faulk place came as a joint exclamation. "Lord have mercy on our souls!" Then, there were *three* determined women giving orders, quicker than Fawn and I could fetch and tote.

Badgerwoman and Mamau Maude soaked and scrubbed the puny children. "Why, you're just knee-high to a duck," my grandmother would say as she lifted each filthy cherub into the washtub filled with warm water.

There were lice in the young ones' hair, so Badgerwoman made a potion from a plant called Devil's Shoestring. The noxious mixture killed those crabby creepers deader than a doornail.

Mama, Fawn, and I boiled clothes and linens in a large cast iron kettle, outside, over an open fire. I could hear soft curses, spoken under Mama's breath, as she added lye to the steaming cauldron. "You're the one I'd like to boil, Emmer Faulk—alive and screamin'—you horse's behind." The continuous wave of murmurs coming from my mother was accentuated with thick, throaty noises. Her anger was downright frightening; Fawn and I were determined not to cross her.

With each batch of laundry, my mother made certain that the bug-killing lye was strong enough; she had her own, unique method for measuring the potency. After dipping the headless chicken's wing feathers into the acrid liquid, she checked to see if the feathers parted from the stem; if they did, it was ready. We scrubbed the clothes on a corrugated washboard, wrung everything by hand, then hung them on a clothesline until they were dry, stiff enough to stand by themselves.

After chicken soup was spoon-fed into every young, eager mouth, Badgerwoman made blackberry tea to treat the diarrhea. She gave each child one tablespoon of the cooled liquid with each attack. The old Indian also burned dried, white sage inside their rooms. "Sacred leaves burn away foul smellin' evil spirits," she insisted.

At the same time, Mamau Maude bound sliced onions to the bottoms of tiny feet. The layered, pungent pulp absorbed the heat as she lovingly sponged the children's fevered bodies, letting the soothing water cascade down their backs.

Later, while I nursed the blisters that'd erupted on my hands, I noticed my grandmother and her Cherokee friend huddled together, conspiring in a nearby corner. Badgerwoman whispered something funny, and Mamau Maude giggled. "That'll set him straight," I heard my grandmother say.

What are they up to? I wondered.

After breakfast the next day, Daddy came with supplies, and some of The Hill's hired hands, to repair cracks in the walls and floors; this helped the heat from the fireplace warm the air and kill the dampness.

Clifford Yetter also came 'round, looking for his daughter. He was no different than anybody else; the sight of the ailing children tugged at his heartstrings. He worked as hard as the next person to set things right.

At dusk, Emmer and Newt Faulk came riding into the yard, doubled-up and barebacked on his dilapidated, chestnut-colored horse. Fawn leaned my way and whispered, "Chickens always come home to roost."

Emmer remained atop his horse as he stared at the small army of people standing on his porch and in his newly cleaned yard. I watched

Newt's father repeatedly clench his fist, his face beet-red. Unruffled, T.H. walked over and stood next to his angry friend, ready for action. What happened next became a permanent part of local history... Mamau Maude cleared her throat, a subtle call for silence. My grandmother issued her declaration with an expression of disgust: "Emmer Faulk, hear me and hear me well! If I *ever* find your home, or your children, in such disgrace again, I will personally hold your scrawny little neck, so that my friend can slice off a good-sized chunk of your flea-bitten scalp."

With a twinkle in her eyes, Badgerwoman lifted a grubbing knife from the holder that hung on her waist sash. The same kind woodworkers use, the draw knife had two handles, one at each end, set perpendicular to a sharp blade. She tautly pulled the rawhide strap that hung on the porch rail and began to sharpen the malevolently gleaming scalpel. "Cream always rises to the top," Badgerwoman hissed between clenched teeth.

Newt sat wide-eyed and mute while Emmer Faulk blanched the color of death. He groaned—curious, non-human sounds—as he fainted and slid off his horse.

SIX

Most of the animals that lived on The Hill were named, but we didn't name our hogs. Occasionally, I'd reach down into the muddy pig pen, petting them in response to their grunted greetings, but I never let myself forget that the doomed swine were just killing time 'til "Killin' Time."

Early on, the smell of raw blood made a permanent imprint on my memory. The reddish leaves of autumn and the annual rite of hog slaughter are forever linked in my mind. After years of rehearsed dialogue, Daddy and Uncle Finas had honed a polished script, mental preparation for the dirty task.

Uncle Finas would begin the one-act play. "It's bad luck to kill a hog durin' a new moon. If you do, it's hard to cook. It'll just shrivel in the skillet. Pop like corn."

Daddy would take his cue. "Yep, as the moon shrinks, the meat'll shrink."

"Uh-huh, that's the balance of it, Brother. There's always more lard if it's done at Full Circle."

"Right on the dot, Finas. But our market porkers should move on the quarter. For a heavier weight. Better for us."

Back and forth they'd go for several minutes. The unyielding, seasonal ritual of words could drive an unsuspecting visitor to the loony bin in Tuscaloosa.

That particular full moon brought with it my favorite holiday, Halloween. Seven Sisters always gathered to tell their scariest ghost stories. I was happy to trade the shrill screams of suffering swine for the thrilled shrieks of my friends. That afternoon, as Fawn and I rode to Horseshoe Cave together, something happened that can't be readily explained in the normal way.

It'd been a wet October. The mud on the road was deep, hard on our horses, slow going at best. We'd gone a short distance down Bear Meat Cabin Trail when we spotted an old woman walking toward us. A gray, wool coverlet was wrapped around her, enshrouding the top of her head. A pale, skeletal hand held the blanket closed. She moved hesitantly, in a shuffling manner, but more than her gait was out of kilter. The woman appeared whole from the front, but like a picture from a magazine, there was little depth to her form.

Suddenly, any sort of movement—hers or ours—seemed measured; the air felt as syrupy thick as the mud and just as hard to pass through. As we drew closer, I could see that the person who stood her ground was an Indian. Remarkably, her face appeared more withered with each passing moment, shriveling right before our eyes, until she looked like a toothless, dried apple doll.

"That's got to be the oldest person I've ever seen," I said. An abrupt, unnatural quiet heightened my unease. My next words were a whisper, "Listen, the birds stopped singing. Not a peep to be heard. Strange."

Fawn appeared not to hear me. As if talking to herself, she muttered, "As far as I know, there are no other Indians livin' around here. I've never seen her before. She looks out of place." Fawn sounded as perplexed as I felt.

The woman hobbled to Fawn's side of the road and stopped, clutching the blanket ever tighter. Her wizened expression conveyed distress.

Fawn's nervous greeting cut the heavy silence. "Good afternoon, grandmother, are you all right? Have you lost your way?"

The old woman purposefully lifted her arm, pointing her gaunt forefinger directly at Fawn. At first, it seemed like her lips moved to form words, but no sound came forth. Then, we heard a swishing noise, as if the old lady's voice and the sudden rustle of nearby leaves were joined somehow.

Transfixed, we leaned forward in our saddles as she spoke. "Listen child. The Grandmother of Time speaks to you with the voice of your ancestors. Beware the secret storm! Goblins of the night, conceived in darkness, cloaked in brotherhood." The frightening words echoed in the treetops, as if they'd been shouted across a boundless chasm.

With painstaking effort, the venerable elder made a cross in the wet dirt with her toe and spat into the center of it. Then she said, "I've completed my journey of the bloods. I go home now to rest." A fiery spirit was reflected in the old lady's eyes.

Unsure of what to do or say, Fawn and I guided our horses forward. The aged stranger's stare made me shift uncomfortably in my saddle, and as we rode past her, I focused my gaze farther down the trail. After a few moments, I managed to push aside my fear, forcing reason into my mind. I decided the poor, old thing had gone senile and shouldn't be left to wander alone, but when I turned and looked behind me—she was *gone*.

Simultaneously, ordinary woodland sounds returned, and the air felt lighter. Fawn and I turned our horses around, then explored the area where the old Indian had stood. There were no footprints in the mud, nothing to prove she'd been there. Even the cross in the earth had vanished. She'd disappeared without a trace. In that wet ground, a person would have had to leave tracks—unless she was a phantom.

We continued our ride without saying much. The uneasy silence was punctuated with Fawn's repeated question, "Are you *sure* she was real?"

Fawn asked this at least three times. I repeatedly dipped into my shallow reservoir of patience and answered, "I think so."

My mind kept going back to what Daddy had told Azberry at breakfast: "That's right, my boy. Stand at a crossroads at midnight on Halloween and listen to the wind. If you're brave enough, you can hear the whispered messages of loosed spirits that are roamin' the earth."

Azberry's eyes had grown as big as saucers by the time Uncle Finas added, "And don't forget, son, if you hear footsteps behind you on All Hallows Eve, don't turn around. They're the footsteps of the dead. If you meet their eyes, you'll die!"

I'd laughed at the good-humored taunts, but they no longer struck me as funny. For the hundredth time, I looked over my shoulder.

"Stop doing that, or I'll ride off and leave you to go the rest of the way by yourself!" The look in Fawn's eyes told me that she meant her threat.

I coaxed Blue to go faster; soon, we were on familiar ground. Horseshoe Cave was a welcome sight. Everybody got to the Seven Sisters' meeting early that evening. All of our families were distracted by the same bloody task of hog slaughter, making it easier to slip away.

When we told the others about the old woman, they accused Fawn and me of conspiring to conjure a Halloween prank. Fanny said it had the earmarks of a Pug Sheridan tall-tale. No one believed us until we took the Seven Sisters secret oath. Then, *all* of us were as jumpy as chicks hatched in a thunder storm.

The mood now properly set, Fawn began to speak in a low, monotone voice. "Badgerwoman says there's a lot more to the world than most folks know. She talks about four different kinds of *little* people livin' around here. They've learned to fear big persons like us. Some live on the tops of mountains, others burrow in brookweed, or in laurel thickets; she's also seen little sprites roamin' deep in the woods."

"What are they like?" Ruby asked.

"Their world is sort of catawampus from ours," Fawn continued. "Where our fire is hot and red, theirs is cold and blue. The fires of the little people are wet while they burn, but they still give off light. On summer nights, you can see them glimmerin' all over the valley."

"Maybe Azberry's not as crazy as I thought," I said. "One night, he was walkin' past a burnt-out tree trunk when he saw a large crack in the charred wood, running deep into dead roots. He claims a funny-lookin' light was shinin' out of the openin'. There, he saw a hidden world, all aglow. He swears he heard music and merriment comin' from that place; one wingding of a good time was goin' on down below.

"Azberry shouted a greetin' to those livin' beneath the tree, but he got no answer. When he returned the next night and peeked inside the ruptured trunk, there was nothin' left but darkness. As though it'd been sealed closed at the base. Afterwards, that boy rattled on about fairies and elves for weeks. Maybe, he was tellin' the truth."

Newt's voice quivered. "But what about the old woman you saw today? Do you think she was a ghost? I don't believe dead people can ever come back. Our minds play tricks on us when it comes to spooks, especially if we knew 'em when they were still alive."

"Maybe our feelin's bring them back to us. Perhaps true love is a bridge between life and the grave." Violet's remark gave me goose bumps.

Fanny chimed in, "The Bible preaches that dead folks don't know nothin' at all. They stay in the ground, where they belong, until they're called on Judgement Day."

"I don't believe you can see a spirit; I think you can only hear 'em. Especially where somebody's been killed; there's always a noise to be heard." It was Ruby, putting in her two cents.

Then, Fanny went too far. "I think a ghost is really the Devil after somebody, makin' 'em see things for some lowdown meanness they've done. Along with that, *certain* folks will claim banshee 'vexation' where there really ain't nothin' to see. For them, Dr. Buttinsky's nerve pills might come in handy!"

"Fanny!" I was shaking with anger.

"We took the oath!" Fawn's voice was filled with dismay.

"I didn't mean it that way!" Fanny said in retort. Then more softly, "I believe you're sayin' what you *thought* you saw, but sometimes such notions have a way of gettin' addled in the mind."

"We weren't *both* bumfuzzled, Fanny!" I didn't try to hide my disdain.

Violet was all aflutter; she hated discord. "Somebody tell us another story! We came here to share ghost legends, didn't we? Halloween's supposed to be fun. Pug and Fawn helped get things started, that's all. Look here, Ruby and I brought some treats!" With Violet supervising, crackling bread, molasses, and peach fritters were carefully arranged atop our communal picnic blanket.

Egypt began to talk for the first time that night. "Granny Essie says that if a rooster crows after dark, it means somebody's gonna get hurt or die. A few years back, one of our peckers crowed in the dead of night. Woke me up twice with its racket. Two days later, Pug got snakebit. Because that cock-eyed bird crowed when he did. So, I killed that old rooster deader than the hammer I hit it with. I buried him, tail deep to a tall Indian, in the compost heap. Granny thought a fox got him. Nobody's known the truth 'til now."

It was a side of Egypt I'd never known. My funny bone was tickled; I fell onto the cave floor and laughed for a long time, then the others joined in like dominoes. The dark cloud of dissension had been appreciably lifted by the time Ruby sputtered, "Let's all go to Crybaby Bridge!"

The bridge's legend was a sad one. Supposedly, a long time ago, a woman had a baby she didn't want. She killed the child by throwing it off the high span into the Locust Fork River. Local residents claimed that, sometimes at night, while standing on the infamous archway, they could hear a crying infant. I didn't believe that old wives' tale, but I was in no hurry to leave the coziness of the cave.

"Are you afraid to go there, Pug?" Fanny challenged.

The last thing I wanted was more fireworks with Fanny. I glanced at Fawn, and she nodded, "Let's go."

"Damn right by me," I said as I stood, showing more confidence than I felt.

Since Fawn and I were the only ones with horses, we decided to leave them tied near the cave's entrance. The seven of us made the hour-long, uneventful hike along the wooded path that looped around Warnock's Peak, reaching our destination around midnight.

The covered bridge looked pretty—bathed in moonlight—surrounded by gauzy mist rising from the water below. It had stood a long time and served the county well. Crybaby Bridge spanned ninety-five feet, boasting a fourteen-foot-wide passageway; the impressive, white-washed structure rested eighteen feet above the water. The river's banks were enveloped with overgrown, luxuriantly wild shrubs; moss-covered boulders dotted the landscape.

Our noisy tromping across rough planks broke the stillness of the night. Ruby complained, "Everybody be quiet or we won't hear nothin'!"

For a few moments, we listened to the tranquil splash of rushing water. Then, from beneath the wooden arch, there came an unearthly, pitiful racket.

"Somebody's cryin' and moanin' down there!" Violet shouted, on the verge of hysterics.

The wailing sounds were soulful, yet familiar, similar to those I'd heard at Mt. Hebron Church. The realization of what they *really* were hit me like a thunderbolt. My friends didn't need much convincing when I yelled, "Run!"

My warning came too late. Grady Holt and his five buddies had already blocked off both ends of the bridge. We were trapped.

"Evenin', ladies." Grady tipped his hat to us. "This ain't a good time for a bunch of pretty gals to be slinkin' about. Don't you know that the Angel of Darkness makes his evil rounds this night?"

Grady's friend Toad joined the sarcasm. "I'll bet they came hopin' to see a *baby* angel, the kind with little, flutterin' magic wings." Toad's real name was Wilburn Crowe. He was a small, wormy-looking teenager with dark features. He always walked like he was stalking something. A slight deformity of the face made Toad's jaw appear misaligned. When he was younger, he'd been cruelly teased by other children. Some still called him Whomper-Jaw, but his *current* nickname aptly suited *Toad's* personality.

Ollie and Odus Crowe, Toad's cousins, stood next to him. Except for striking, carrot-colored hair, the two boys had the look of albinos, with colorless eyes and milky skin. Ollie and Odus were harmless enough, but between them, they possessed the same amount of intelligence God gave the average grasshopper.

Grady put on a show, bellowing his words like an actor performing on London's Royal Stage. "Hey Mookie! How much white lightnin' have we got left?"

Moose and Mookie Gaither, twin brothers, helped Grady guard his end of the bridge. They were so alike, it was commonly believed the siblings could read each other's mind. Unfortunately, neither one thought much about handkerchiefs. Long strings of snot could regularly be seen, yellow and caked, on the twins' upper lips. The drooping, mucous mustaches, along with their enormous body size, made them look like bug-eyed walruses. It was just as well they shared a brain.

Compared to most fifteen-year-old boys, the sorry excuses facing Seven Sisters were three bricks short of a load, proof positive that people can grow stupider with age. Grady grabbed a large, earthenware crock from Mookie's massive hand. He leaned back, taking a good, long swig of the rotgut whiskey. Grady winked, then held the jug out, offering me some.

In the velvety darkness, something about Grady's face looked false, mask-like; it was unnerving. The other boys continued to gawk, like they were seeing girls for the very first time. I said nothing in response to Grady's unseemly offer. Instead, I glared a look of disapproval in his direction.

"Come on, Pug," Grady cajoled. "Come close and taste it. This is real Alabama moonshine. Tastes so good, it'll make you slap your grandma!"

Wicked chuckles came rolling in toward us from each end of the bridge, colliding and exploding somewhere near my spinal cord. Our female coterie found itself, as Mamau Maude would say, "between a rock and a hard place." We continued to hold our position, all clumped together in the middle of the bridge, waiting to see what would happen next.

Nervously, Egypt began to dance in place, like a chicken on a hot stove. That's when I realized the danger that she, in particular, was in. I shook the nagging doubts from my mind. *These boys are just havin' themselves some harmless fun. Still, this is an awful mess. Why did I let Fanny talk me into this? If anything bad happens, it'll be my fault. I've got to find a way to divert Grady's attention, then maybe they'll leave us alone.*

"All that boy likes to do is show off and aggravate somebody!" It was Fanny. She'd been unusually quiet while her older brother ran his mouth off.

Grady's next comment made Fanny's reticence understandable. "You'll stay shut-mouthed, my contrary little sister, or I'll tell Daddy about all the nights you go slippin' off at ungodly hours. I don't think he'd approve if he knew you were runnin' around with niggers and Injuns, do you?"

"Oh, I think *lots* of folks would be interested in this curdled bunch of playmates." Toad's tone was threatening.

Grady spat through his teeth. Each boy, as if on cue, did the same; the scene was almost comical.

"We'd like to go home now," I boldly announced.

"Well," Grady replied while scratching his chin, "Seein' as we got here first, it's only right that we collect a toll as you pass by…on your way home to Mama. Ain't that right boys?" His face was one big smirk.

"I'd like to see a silver-spoon-fed, Southern belle named Sheridan take her first itty-bit of mountain dew," Toad said. Then, as he devoured Fawn with his eyes, he added, "I'm partial to brown sugar with mine."

Suddenly, my body turned icy cold, and I involuntarily shivered. *Somebody must be walkin' across my grave,* I thought. *I wish I could wake up from this nightmare. How am I gonna get us out of this?*

Mookie and Moose looked at each other, then Mookie whispered something to Grady. Grady smiled. "Six boys, six girls, six kisses on the toll bridge," he announced.

"The nigger can pass for free. In fact, we'll pay *you* to keep Miss Big Lips as far away as possible," Toad croaked, his tone caustic. "Now, behave yourselves and give us what we want, or you'll be the main piece of gossip at Marsh's Grocery tomorrow." To emphasize his point and unnerve us further, Toad made an obscene gesture with his genitals.

Calf slobbers slid down the sides of Mookie's mouth as he snickered at Toad's "wit." Moose's laugh was a series of nasal grunts. Their "mustaches" grew.

"We'd rather kiss trolls than any of you!" I yelled.

"Pay the toll, or stay here all night!" Grady's grin mocked me.

"Root hog or die," Fawn mumbled under her breath.

Each boy called out a girl's name, like he was choosing sides for a game of King on the Mountain.

"I take Violet!" Moose hollered.

"Fanny," said Mookie.

"Give me that fair-skinned Injun," Toad said, licking his lips. "I'll bet this pretty little thing tastes mighty sweet."

"That leaves Ruby for Ollie, Newt for Odus, and of course, I get Pug." Grady's words were a slurred mess of drunken syllables.

"Grady, why don't you lie down, so you won't have to bother with fallin' on your face? You've all had too much bellywash. You know my daddy would box your ears if he found out what you tried to do tonight!" My words were futile. I was talking to a bunch of walleyed fools.

Grady snickered and pooched out his lips, waiting for a kiss; his face turned crimson with the affected effort. He looked like a half-wild, mongrel warthog.

Expectantly, eleven pairs of eyes focused on me; Grady had his closed. Cautiously, I moved toward Grady Holt, making him think I was giving in. As I leaned forward, my lips were close enough to touch his. Then, with lightning speed, I bit Grady's bottom lip. Hard. He hollered like a stuck pig.

Slipping past Moose and Mookie, I ran like the Devil was after me. I called over my shoulder, "Head for Horseshoe!"

But my friends ignored their chance to escape in the opposite direction. Grady, along with everyone else, gave chase. His chums wanted to see what he would do once he caught me; they were deriving some sort of depraved, vicarious thrill from the unfolding events.

I scraped my face as I plowed through some scuppernong grapevines. Excitement, mingled with fear, gave me a surge of energy. As I ran, the night felt magical. I fantasized that I'd transformed myself into a deer, swift and sure of foot—until I tripped over a cow patty. My body soared in the air before it hit the soft, slippery ground with a thud.

Grady caught up with me as I attempted to stand. He managed a quick dive that pinned me to the ground. His stout body straddled mine. My nemesis raised his hand to slap me, then hesitated as he stared into my face with an expression of intense fierceness. His lip was still bleeding; he wiped it with his shirt sleeve, breathing hard.

Shock immobilized my limbs and filled me with dread. With the others still out of earshot, Grady's demeanor softened. "Pug, you've always acted so persnickety with me. Ain't I good enough for you?"

"Get off me! Have you lost what's left of your feeble mind?" If I'd had a gun, I would've shot him right then and there. I was livid.

Grady used his weight to keep me pressed against the earth. Though his subsequent tone was tempered, his words sounded ominous. "I want to tell you something. You'd better pay attention 'cause things are gonna be changin' around here. It's a kind of secret. Something I can't name. When I'm solidly joined, I'm gonna be important, good enough even for you. You'd better come 'round to my way of thinkin' because I'm plannin' for us to be together."

Slowly, tortuously, Grady leaned down and kissed me. His mouth was wet and sour-tasting. The disgusting image of a sloppy stew made with whiskey, saliva, and blood flashed in my mind. A scream of protest began in the back of my throat. The world around me became a cauldron of convoluted emotion, everything happening at once, all blurred together.

An impressive war cry sounded as Fawn bounded from behind in an attempt to knock Grady off me, but he pushed Fawn away with one hand. Then Ollie grabbed her, holding her tightly by the arms.

Toad viciously tripped Egypt as she ran past him in an attempt to help. When she fell, she bloodied her nose on a rock. "Leave her alone!" I screamed. "Touch her again and you'll be sorry!"

Odus, Moose, and Mookie corralled the other Seven Sisters into a small circle of flailing arms and kicking legs. Our group resembled a giant hornets' nest as the situation escalated out of control. I heard myself scream louder as panic took over my mind. It was a moment or two before I realized that I wasn't the only one screaming; I'd become part of a mixed chorus of shrieking and screeching.

Everyone, girl *and* boy alike, was suddenly scared senseless. Even Grady howled like a wounded animal; the look on his face was one of stark terror. He still straddled me, but his wide-eyed gaze was focused farther down the trail, a direction I couldn't see.

Grady was able to squeak three original words before he and his pals ran away like frightened jack rabbits…"Bloody Hell, Medusa!"

I stood up and faced my six comrades. They made no move to join me, keeping a safe distance from whatever was behind me. Turning slowly around, I found myself standing five feet from Rola Moon, the self-proclaimed sorceress of Pine Bluff County.

Up close, Rola appeared to be my Mama's age. She wore a long, burgundy dress, made from some kind of uncommon bulky material. It'd been sewn in a quilted pattern with designs of stars, crescent moons, birds, spirals, and other things. A thickly woven, rope-like belt was tied at her waist. She held an impressive walking stick, carved from mahogany, with a shiny stone set into it at the top. White shafts of moonlight streaked Rola's face, giving her a savage appearance.

The witch wasn't very tall, but she posed a formidable figure that night. Rola made a complete circle around my rigid body, but came no closer as she carefully looked me up and down. I dared not move or speak. My imagination raced ahead of my wits. *This is my choice? The witch or Grady? Please God, let me wake up!* I was so scared, I could feel my kneecaps knocking together.

When Rola finished surveying me, like some specimen in a jar, I heard her make a "humph" noise. It was as if she was saying to herself, *"Just as I suspected…"*

Then the witch came 'round to face me again. In a strong, clear voice she declared, "The veil is thinnest between the worlds this night." Rola was silent for a few moments before she added, "Go home!"

Seven Sisters ran for the cave like bees storming back to the hive. Later, Fawn, Egypt, and I rode home together. Egypt's nose was slightly swollen, but I could tell she'd be all right, at least physically. Grady's gang had badly frightened her, but her deepest wounds were the kind that couldn't be seen.

"I don't care what those boys say about me," Egypt repeated, as if trying to convince herself. "The only difference between those stupid buffoons and me is that they sunburn easier. All those bad names they called me, I double right now and send back. I don't give a damn they didn't want to kiss me. I really don't."

As our horses cautiously made their way along the dimly lit trail, Egypt changed the subject to our confrontation with Rola Moon. Though she tried to act cheerful, it was just a brave front. "Isn't it amazin' how she came out of nowhere like that? Didn't it seem like real magic?" Egypt pondered the experience for a few moments, then added, "Don't you think Rola looked different than before? Prettier I mean."

"She *did* look younger," I said. "Witches can do that, you know." My friends laughed at my teasing joke, an inept attempt to brighten the mood.

Then Fawn said, "Well, one thing's for sure, Rola saved our butts tonight." She paused before turning to Egypt. "I know you don't want to talk about it now, but if anybody can understand how you're feelin', it's me. Those ignorant boys don't deserve the satisfaction of makin' you cry. Their squirrelly, little minds aren't worth the salt."

"They're idiots," I agreed, feeling frustrated. "I could kill them for what they did. I'm sorry things got out of hand, Egypt. We should've never left the cave."

Egypt managed a slight smile, then touched her tender nose. "Don't worry about me. I'll be fine. But I'm worried. The problem with rotten apples like those is that they grow more smelly with time. I'm tired. I just wanna go home."

All three of us were bone dry by the time we made it to The Hill. Nothing quenches a thirst better than cool water drawn from a deep well and drunk with a gourd dipper. We helped ourselves to the bucket that was sitting on the porch.

"What are we gonna do about Grady and his goons?" Fawn slurped.

"I don't know," I answered. "But I'm sure of one thing. I'm never gonna let 'em push us around like that again."

Egypt's response was surprisingly adamant. "Y'all better listen to me. We've gotta keep to ourselves. The way we always have. Those boys have pea brains and stony hearts. That can mean bad things happenin' to anyone in their way. Don't ask for more trouble. Especially on my account." It was clear that Egypt wanted no further conversation right then. She whispered a hurried "goodnight," then made the short walk to her house.

Fawn and I clambered into my room. Another short climb, and we were on my bed. "Poor Egypt," Fawn murmured. "What they did to her tonight was beyond harsh. It was depraved. We all got a dose of their meanness, but she felt it the most."

My own, unspoken thoughts tormented me with guilt. *Egypt looks to me to watch out for her. I let her down. Seven Sisters can't venture out of the cave again. Not without some form of self-defense. I can't make that kind of decision alone, not for the whole group. But the club was my idea. I'm responsible for the consequences.*

As if she could read my mind, Fawn answered, "Egypt doesn't blame you for what happened. And you shouldn't blame yourself. Egypt's strong. She'll sort this thing out. And I'm sure those devil's sons will learn; every dog has its day." Fawn yawned as she spoke; we were both exhausted, and she was already dozing off.

I smiled at Fawn's mixed metaphor, but inside I felt sad and anxious. "All together, those boys couldn't count to ten," I said. "I don't think they'll tell anyone about what happened tonight. They'd be too afraid of T.H. findin' out. Still, they need to be watched. Grady and Toad are the only ones with any smarts, a good reason to watch *them* the closest."

Fawn didn't hear me; she'd already fallen asleep.

Even though I believed that being more careful would take care of things, it didn't change the fact that our secret sorority was no longer a secret. We'd been found out; the ante was upped, and much was at stake. I shivered, then slipped under the covers and fell into a sound doze.

I remember one dream from that night's slumber. A head, disembodied, floated next to my pillow. I recognized the visage of Rola Moon. "Witches are born, not made. But a test must be passed. And this you have already done," she whispered. Then, the ominous specter faded away toward unknown realms.

SEVEN

"**H**ow can a black cow eat green grass, then give white milk that turns into yellow butter?" Azberry asked me this poser the morning after my fifteenth birthday, five days before Thanksgiving. At the age of ten, he could befuddle me with the most confounding questions ever imagined.

A young boy is the smartest and laziest person in the world, and my brother was no exception. He was a cute little booger. You know—the kind you can't quite shake off your finger.

Azberry didn't expect answers to his riddles. He was thinking out loud, a Sheridan trait I was all too familiar with. "I've been figurin' on it for a few days now," he announced, "and I'm here to officially inform you that it takes pretty-near four hundred squirts into that gallon bucket to top it off."

I sighed loudly, then aligned my little stool alongside the next available teat. I was in a grumpy state of mind, and Azberry felt like a second shadow. "I coulda gone all day without knowin' that," I snapped. My brother took his cue and hushed.

With the approaching holidays, life on The Hill became one giant bundle of chores. Though it was just past six A.M., I'd already milked our three Shorthorns: Martha, Marie, and Margaret. I always put Maddie off 'til last. She was a sizable black and white Holstein; a broken horn from a fight with another cow attested to her orneriness. Much larger than our regular milkers, Maddie was a monster in other ways, too. Sometimes, she appeared to suffer from demonic possession. That morning, the look in her eye made me trust her even less.

Azberry sat in the loft munching a persimmon, watching nonchalantly as I washed Maddie's milk bag with warm water. "I'm in no mood for your meanness, so behave yourself," I muttered to the wild-eyed bovine. She looked as if she planned to trample me as soon as my back was turned.

A gentle squeeze on one of Maddie's enormous teats was enough to bring the milk down; the creamy elixir began its familiar, rhythmic splash into the metal pail. Maddie swished her tail and hit me directly in the face. She turned to look in my direction as her tail came 'round again. I loudly scolded her, then slapped Maddie on her side, hard. The crack-brained cow promptly fell over sideways onto the ground, seemingly dead.

I heard Azberry's cry as he scurried down the ladder. "You've killed her, Pug! You've killed Maddie!" Azberry adored all The Hill's animals, even that one. He panicked whenever he saw one of his pets hurt or sick.

My head spun as I gaped at the inanimate form, wondering how I'd explain what had happened to our most expensive milk cow. There was a throbbing sensation in my right hand, the guilty one. I stared at it in disbelief.

Maddie had knocked over the bucket in her downward topple. Milk was splattered everywhere, including the front of my coveralls; the warm, uncomfortable stickiness added insult to injury.

Azberry, though fearing the worst from his sister's brutality, began shaking the cow, sweetly coaxing her to get up. Long minutes passed; Maddie finally stirred, shaking her head with an angry snort. My brother and I breathed a sigh of relief. It was a struggle, but we eventually got the infernal creature to stand upright again.

"She-devil!" I hissed as we led her to the nearest stall. Maddie defiantly kicked at the post nearest me as I walked away.

After things calmed down, my brother and I climbed into the barn loft; the hazy light of morning transformed it into a magical haven. Azberry quickly recovered from the "near tragedy," and he cunningly demanded that I tell him a story, a bribe for not squealing on me.

I pondered my impromptu fairytale as Maddie happily chewed hay. "You may've won the battle, but the war's not over," I yelled down at her. "By supper time, you'll be beggin' me to milk you!"

Turning to Azberry, I looked at him with all the seriousness I could muster. "Do you know where the first eatin' tools came from?"

"Nope. Where?" He sounded bored.

"To tell you the truth, it has something to do with that persimmon you've been suckin' on."

"No foolin'?" he asked, eyes widening.

"Why, sure! Folks would still be sloppin' up food with their bare hands if God hadn't put a notion inside every persimmon seed. The pulp's so delicious that, for centuries, nobody thought about the crusty kernel in the center. Long ago, everybody would eat their fill, throw down the pit and walk on. Then one day, somebody split the seed in half, down the dented middle where it's put together. What they found inside gave them the surprise of their life!"

Azberry gasped. "What was it?"

"Well, they discovered that each pit has a different shape at its center," I said. "Sometimes, it shows the outline of a knife or a spoon. Every now and then, you see a fork."

Azberry squealed with delight as he hurriedly pried open his persimmon seed; there, to his utter amazement, was the perfect etching of a miniature spoon. I laughed at his wide-eyed innocence and enjoyed showing my brother a phenomenon I'd discovered on my own.

As I continued to fondly gaze at my sibling, it occurred to me that something was wrong. "Come here," I said. "Let me get a closer gander at you. You look funny. Are you feelin' all right?"

Azberry wiped his runny nose with the back of his hand. "My eyes are itchy; I've been stayin' inside 'cause the bright sun hurts 'em. And, if you must know, I've got little red ants growin' on my arms. Maybe, I'll add 'em to my collection." The spunky little runt rolled up his sleeve and held out his arm, pointing out the small eruptions on his feverishly warm skin.

Understanding finally dawned on me. "Come on, baby brother; it's time to go find Mama," I sighed. There was no doubt about it; Azberry had the measles.

✳ ✳ ✳

Within three days, I had a tell-tale rash too; I was forced into quarantine inside a darkened room, bored out of my mind, allowed to see nobody. To make matters worse, I knew the Strawbridge brothers were returning home for the holiday break, their first visit to Village Springs in several years. I was one, body-sized, open sore of disappointment, but my family was too busy to give me sympathy.

"Take a potato and wait," Mama grumbled as she helped me into a fresh gown. She sounded exasperated and tired.

"What does that mean?" I yelled as she, and her layered skirts, swooshed out of the room.

Uncle Finas stuck his head inside my doorway. "It means give it a few days. Let nature run its course. Be patient and let it cool. Okay, Puglet?" I giggled as I threw my pillow at the easy, balding target.

Doc Self came to our house every day; he happily gave his stamp of approval to Mamau Maude's herbal treatments. In addition, Badgerwoman conjured up some home-made salve; Fawn waved to me from the window when she brought it over.

On Thanksgiving Day, Doc Self ungrudgingly made his normal rounds. I was surprised to see that Arious was with him, acting as his assistant. Mamau Maude was liberally basting me with Badgerwoman's concoction when they walked into my room. I quickly stretched the gingham squares of my nightie over my knees, feeling embarrassed.

"Hello, young lady." Doc's smile was warm and friendly. He was the spitting image of Abraham Lincoln—sunken eyes, beaked-nose, and all; everybody said so. All he needed was the stovepipe hat to complete the picture.

The doctor looked me over, paying close attention to my ears and lungs. I had a fever and was sweating like a racehorse. I daintily patted myself with a yellow handkerchief, enjoying my natural flair for dramatics.

Doc turned to Arious and explained, "The key to success with these herbs is to cover the patient with several blankets. Perspiration's the body's way of breakin' a fever. A temperature like hers is a good thing. It's nature's way of killin' the disease."

Arious said nothing as he intently listened to his teacher. They walked to the other side of the room while writing notes on their respective pads. Doc continued talking in a low voice, mistakenly thinking he was out of hearing range. "There are several other youngsters in

Village Springs with similar symptoms," he said. "All seem to be farin' well, save one. It's Azberry I'm worried about. His fever has been unusually prolonged and high. I'm goin' to prescribe quinine water to bring it down. He should have his first dose now."

As Doc headed for Azberry's room, he called over his shoulder, "See you tomorrow, Pug."

Arious stopped at the foot of my bed. "I'm sorry to see you feelin' so peaked, Miss Sheridan."

"Yeah, it looks like I'm in a piddle," I cracked. "Did Alton come to The Hill with you?"

"My brother stayed in Maryland to work on his ministerial thesis." Arious's voice was matter-of-fact; he couldn't have known how the words stung me. "He sure has enjoyed all your letters and poems. Alton asked me to give you this." Arious bashfully laid a small, wrapped gift and a letter on the bed.

"I have to go now. I'll be studyin' with Doc for a couple of weeks, so I'm sure I'll see you again soon." Arious turned to follow in his mentor's footsteps.

Alton and I had regularly written to each other since that rainy day he'd waved good-bye, five years earlier. We'd become good friends via smelly, leather mail satchels. Mr. White delivered those cherished letters in a horse-drawn buggy, regardless of rain, shine, or the Second Coming.

I hastily opened my present, laughing aloud at the rounded turkey staring back at me. Alton had carved it from a block of solid milk chocolate. Then, I ripped open the neatly printed letter. The news in the last paragraph made me leap for joy:

I've been in contact with Reverend Tidbow. He'll be retiring from Old Bethlehem Methodist in a few years, and has recommended me to the Overseer's Board as associate pastor under his tutelage. This appointment will begin in the spring if I make the grade here at Boylston. I hope that God sees fit to grant my approval. Pray for me, Miss Sheridan, as I pray for you. My best regards to you and your family—Alton

I gave thanks to the United States Postal Service and chomped down on my turkey sculpture, biting its head clean off. As the chocolate melted in my mouth, I opened my Bible, closed my eyes, and pointed. I was in the habit of doing this whenever confused or bored. With a foreboding, restless shiver, I realized that my finger punctuated Verse 1, Chapter 27 of Proverbs: "Boast not thyself of tomorrow, for thou knowest not what a day may bring forth."

Thanksgiving passed without the traditional, Sheridan fanfare as Azberry's condition worsened. He refused all food, even his favorite ambrosia dessert.

On Sunday, I awoke in the middle of the night to an alarming chorus of sounds, composed of my brother's alternating coughs and moans. My mother's soothing voice was in the background. The cold floor pressed against my feet as I tiptoed to Azberry's room. I peeked inside and saw my mother holding my brother in her arms.

Mamau Maude was lighting a second lamp. As the shimmering gleam caught the darkened corner, I glimpsed Badgerwoman sitting in a straight-backed chair; it was long past midnight, but the aged sage had appeared at our back door as though she'd been expected. Badgerwoman had an uncanny way of knowing when she was needed on The Hill. This night, she was deep in prayer; her eyes were closed, and she held a black hawk feather in each hand. As I studied her placid face, I wondered where Fawn was.

Badgerwoman's eyes flashed open, startling me. She stood and calmly said, "There's life in heat. Death is fonder of cold arrows." Fawn's granny advised Mamau Maude to heat rocks in the fireplace, wrap them in cloths, and put them in Azberry's bed. "This boy chokes with his own sickness," Badgerwoman continued. "Put hot, wet towels on his chest; make him drink warmed water 'til he finds his lost breath."

I thought about the menacing words, "chokes with sickness," as I looked at my brother's diminutive frame. He had the shaking chills. As he tried to breathe, Azberry clutched his side with the most horrible look of pain in his eyes, as though he were being ripped apart by a butcher knife. I saw a shadow pass over my brother's face; the sight made me gasp.

Mama heard my convulsive intake of breath. "Sadie Lou Sheridan, step on back to bed now. It's too late and chilly for you to be prowlin' about." Mama sounded unlike herself, her voice tight and high-pitched.

I stood there, planted to the floor, as tears welled in my eyes. Never once had I considered the possibility that death might visit my own family. I knew my brother had one foot in the grave; the other wasn't far behind.

I heard the sound of Daddy's brisk walk. Before I knew it, he'd whisked me into his arms. "I'll carry this one to her room, Cora," he said in a quiet voice. "Then I'll ride over and get Doc."

I'll never forget how gently T.H. tucked me into bed that night. "Is it late?" I asked, searching for something to say.

"It's later than I've ever known it to be in my life. Go back to sleep, darlin'." With a few giant strides, Daddy was out of my room and down the hall, headed for the back door and the stables.

As T.H. passed Azberry's room, I heard Mama call out, "Tell Doc his fever's worse, and he feels warmer by the minute."

Doc Self arrived and diagnosed the illness as bronchial pneumonia, a complication of the measles. After acknowledging the wisdom behind Badgerwoman's ministrations, he and Arious set to work to save my brother's life. They bundled Azberry in a quilted pneumonia jacket to keep him warm while applying poultices of flaxseed and corn meal to his chest.

When that didn't help, Badgerwoman suggested a red pepper and mustard poultice. Doc was open-minded enough to try this, and sure enough, it eased some of the discomfort. That pair of country healers soon formed a mutual admiration society, but Azberry's condition remained desperate.

Meanwhile, Doc declared me no longer contagious; the next morning, Fawn was allowed to visit. I found comfort in her quiet presence while a grim stillness blanketed our house. There's something about secluded silence that sums up a situation. At first, Fawn and I sat soberly together, saying nothing while staring at the grape patterns crocheted into my bedspread. Then, we locked hands and played Hull Gull until our thumbs wore out.

Essie did her best to keep us cheerful. Over the fire in my chimney, she made waffles with a long-handled iron. While we ate, I felt a strong need to talk about Azberry.

Fawn patiently listened as I told her about the day he was born. "Other kids told me where their brothers and sisters had been found," I said. "Supposedly, one siblin' was pulled from under a brush pile, a second was plucked from a hollow log, and another was uncovered in an alfalfa field."

"And you believed them?" Fawn laughed.

"I didn't know any better," I answered, grinning. "When Mamau Maude said a baby brother was comin' that day, I started lookin' in every nook and cranny in the woods. Later, I heard his first wee cry, and I thought it was a cat! He sounded just like a baby kitten…" My words trailed off with worry.

"Remember when we taught him how to use a Tommy Walker?" Fawn forced an optimistic note into her voice. "His legs were so bowed on those stilts, a young hog could've passed between 'em."

I was feeling sorry for all the times I'd teased my only brother. "Azberry was real scared of gopher rats," I confessed. "Sometimes, we'd be in the crib, shuckin' corn; when it got spooky quiet, I'd grab a small ear of corn and throw it under his feet. 'Look out, there's a rat!' I'd yell. He'd scurry up a mountain of grain to get away."

"You talk like he's already dead." Fawn's words allowed me to cry; she held me tight while I let go of my grief. During that short time together, I realized Fawn and I would be friends for life, ready to do anything for one another. Anything. It was a comforting revelation.

Later, we walked past the hall cupboard where Azberry kept his collection of worms, bugs, bats, and other creepy crawlers. As we turned the corner, we collided with Arious Strawbridge. "I'm sorry, Miss Sheridan, I didn't mean to bump into you. I was on my way to your room to see how you're feelin'." Arious was talking to me, but his eyes stayed glued on Fawn.

"I'm fine, almost back to normal," I said.

"You were *never* normal," Fawn muttered.

"Arious, this is my friend, Fawn…Fawn Storm."

"A pleasure to meet you, Miss Storm."

Time stopped as breathless moments floated, then waned in the wintry air. While Fawn and Arious stared into each other's searching eyes, four generations of deep Southern living passed by. The intensity of their gaze made me squirmy and uncomfortable. As I watched them, the first two lines of my next poem raced into my mind: *Taste the roses and hear the passion flower bloom. Remembering floods my soul like rivers of waters.*

Someone had to break their romantic reverie. "How's the little clod-hopper?" I clumsily asked.

Arious replied without answering my question. "Doc and I just finished makin' a breathin' tube. It'll help him rest easier."

I looked into the next room and saw what Arious was talking about. The physicians had fashioned an inhalation apparatus out of a metal coffee urn and an elderberry branch. By forcing the pitch out of the limb, they'd made a tube through which Azberry could breathe inhalants from hot vinegar poured over various herbs.

Still, my brother looked terrible. I trembled as I watched Azberry struggle to breathe with a rapid, unnatural rhythm. The air he craved defied capture.

Doc looked troubled as he reached into his black bag and removed some medicine, packaged in a square piece of newspaper cut to size. Doc Self measured a portion of the yellowish powder with his pocket knife. He mixed it with a spoonful of jelly and stuck it in Azberry's mouth.

Mama sat next to her son's bed, looking haggard and drawn. She'd kept her vigil for forty-eight sleepless hours while T.H. paced up and down the hallway. Exhausted, they both looked ten years older. Doc answered my parents' unspoken question with, "All we can do now is wait and see."

It pained me to see my mother's sad expression, so Fawn and I hightailed it to the living room. There, Mr. Hudson, a hired hand, had spent the day cleaning the main chimney. Finas was there too, keeping Mr. Hudson company.

My uncle camouflaged his worry with his mouth, a habit he and I had in common. Finas talked up a blue streak, and the poor chimney sweep was getting an earful. "Yes sir, the draw from that fireplace feels good now. It'd suck a hat right off a feller's head. Hey, did you know the signs are forecastin' a bad winter?"

Before his captured audience could respond, Finas babbled on. "Our horses have coats as thick as I've ever seen. You'll find most trees this year with bark, dense as barnacles, on the north side of their trunks. Most squirrels are flauntin' bushier tails, too. Mark my words: The comin' season is gonna be rough."

Yep, Uncle Finas is crazy worried about Azberry, I decided.

Fawn and I marched back to my room. "I've made a decision," I announced when we were out of earshot. "I'm gonna visit Rola Moon tomorrow and pay her to conjure a spell to make Azberry well."

Fawn was so shocked, her mouth gaped open.

"I'm not afraid. And I don't see what I'd be doin' wrong," I added, my tone defensive.

Fawn continued to stare me down. After a full thirty seconds ticked by, she finally blurted, "Pug, I know Azberry's in a bad way. But they say Rola Moon's in league with the Devil. Black magic! Bad spirits and such!"

"We don't know diddly-squat about Rola Moon, except what's rumored around Village Springs," I shot back, my voice louder than I'd intended.

I'd heard the gossips refer to Rola as the "Straw Woman." According to them, she never appeared the same way twice. Some swore she rode broomcorn and conversed with animals.

Fawn could see that my mind was made up when I declared, "I'm goin', Fawn. You can't talk me out of it. But you *can* help me slip away."

My friend eyed me with an expression of intense concentration and awe. A slight grin creased her face as she said, "I double-dog *dare* you."

Together, we hatched a simple plan. I'd sneak out early and steal away on Blue. She'd pretend I was still in my room, fetch our breakfast, and keep up the ruse that I was home. Willing to accept the consequences if my sick-room escape was discovered, I knew Azberry might die if I didn't do something drastic.

However, there's no denying I had second thoughts as I made my night's rest under soft flannel sheets. Fawn sensed this, and the mischievous side of her nature surfaced as she whispered a wickedly impish chant:

> Darkish night and dancin' moon,
> Listen to the witches' tune.
> East and South and West and North,
> Hear! Come! I call her forth!

EIGHT

Rola's house was located a mile south of The Hill, past Slippery Rock Canyon. She lived smack-dab in the middle of nowhere, a wilderness ignorant of the ax. As I neared her place, I had to help Blue up a steep ravine; the cabin appeared as I crested the rim. Built beside an old beech tree, it was a small, one-room structure, entirely self-contained. From the outside, the house appeared neat and tidy, but there was no sign of life.

I'd heard that the witch-of-the-woods always halted people at the makeshift gate that guarded her place. Visitors were required to speak their names aloud. If she liked them, they could enter her yard; otherwise, they were quickly turned away. While dawdling apprehensively at the notorious gateway, I saw a flock of wild ducks fly overhead…and longed to join them.

When I looked back at the little porch, Rola was standing beside a white clay churn, replacing its stone lid. The witch barely glanced up. "I thought you'd be here sooner."

"Excuse me, ma'am…What did…Is it all right if…" I stammered like a simpleton, unsure of what I'd heard her say.

"Come in, child, before they rename Fool's Day in your honor." Rola seemed wary, yet approachable.

In the light of day, I could see that Rola's eyes were unusually colored—magenta eyes with tropical hues. As I stared into their purplish haze, I felt an unexplainable kinship with her. I cautiously opened the squeaky gate, gathered my courage, and walked up the stoop steps. Without another word, Rola Moon turned and went inside. I hesitated, then followed.

The cabin was ingeniously arranged to accommodate the odd collection of items that adorned its walls and ledges. Tiny burlap parcels hung from the ceiling. Large and small earthenware cylinders, all containing mysterious contents, sat on shelves attached to every bare space. Mason jars, filled with assorted fruits and vegetables, were neatly stacked in orderly rows on the floor; I noticed that most held wild varieties like crabapples, chokecherries, blackberries, and possum grapes.

There were dried roots, berries, and leaves everywhere, as well as the infamous broomsage. The dry, wild straw was wrapped and fastened with twine. It hung or lay in all four corners of the house. The only decorative item was a basket set upon her table. It was filled with painted hollowed eggs, the ones Seven Sisters initiates had left in her yard. The eggs were *supposed* to guard against witches and curb their power. I smiled, embarrassed.

As I moved inside the doorway, I observed a large cluster of brushbroom on the far wall. It moved. A grass owl had happily made its nest there. Like me, it stared and blinked with wide-eyed curiosity.

There was enough room in the cabin for a wood stove, a tiny bed, and a table with two chairs. Rola had a hickory stick for stoking the embers of her fire; she used it to point me toward a chair. Rola sauntered across the room and sat opposite me, looking somewhat different than she had on All Hallows Eve, slighter and more compactly built. Still, there was strength in her walk and posture. She folded her hands and waited.

What has she lost? I wondered. Then I asked myself how I knew she'd lost *anything.* We hadn't spoken a word to each other since I'd stepped inside. If somebody was gonna speak first, it'd have to be me. "Do you know a sure cure for pneumonia?" I blurted out.

"Have you ever used a divinin' rod?" Rola shot back.

I couldn't imagine what that had to do with anything, but decided I'd better answer the question. Most residents of Pine Bluff County were dowsers, and some had a special knack for it. While holding a forked willow branch in both hands, they'd search for underground wells. If water was beneath the stick, it turned downward, seemingly on its own. I'd done my own fair share of dowsing. But, instead of looking for water, my sights had been set on finding Indian gold and silver. To Daddy's delight, I'd found a few treasures. Rola's smile was coy when I told her this.

"Had visions yet? The 'third eye' kind? Seen any souls livin' in the world beyond ours?"

I shivered as I shook my head.

This response annoyed my hostess. "You will," she assured me. "Are you gonna be like the old lady who fell out of the wagon," she asked, "or are you wantin' to be on the inside?"

"The inside of what?" I responded, confused. Everybody in my life talked in riddles; my brain felt like it was twisting back on itself.

"The truth, sister, the truth," was all she'd say. "When you're ready, you'll know."

Then she added, "I want to give you what you came for. A sureshot cure for pneumonia is black cat tail tea. Now, listen carefully. Find the blackest cat you can and cut some fur off its tail, about a thimbleful. Make a tea out of it. Mix the tea, about half and half, with good red liquor and have it hot. A generous dose, a small cupful, should do the trick. The only time I've known this spell to fail was when the cat wasn't black enough." Rola pounded the table for emphasis, then walked outside to resume her churning.

As squeamish as it made me, I had what I'd come for. I found the silver dollar I'd buried in the pocket of my topcoat. When I reached the porch, I offered it to the silver-blond sorceress. "No, pay me after the spell has worked its magic," she said. "Besides, you never hear a hen cackle 'til she's finished her job."

"That sounds like something my grandmother would say," I mumbled as I waved good-bye.

I'd just mounted Blue when Rola called out in a voice rich with color, "Be sure to tell your brother that the potion came from me."

I was halfway home before I realized two things. Number one, it was common knowledge that the witch *always* asked for payment upfront for services rendered. Also, never once had I mentioned that it was my brother who was ill.

Blue happily trotted back to The Hill, carrying me past some Roosterhead Violets. As cold as it was, some of them were still flowering. Their reddish blooms looked like miniature roosters, hence their name; it was common for young boys to have pretend cockfights with them.

However, that particular Roosterhead bush was making strange noises. I pulled on the reins and swung off my pony. When I walked behind the bulky plant, I couldn't believe what I found. A live rooster had been buried, with its head left above ground. It looked pitifully from side to side as it clucked and tried to crow.

I'd already begun to dig the bird out with a stick when Egypt stepped out of hiding; she had a spade in her hand. "Oh, Pug, I'm glad it's you. I didn't want anybody to see me!"

"Egypt—come help. Somebody's buried this poor little thing and left him here." I was breathless with disbelief.

"*I'm* the one that planted him. I was gonna root out the pecker myself when I heard somebody comin'." Egypt's voice was even and matter-of-fact.

Using her Seven Sisters secret name, I asked the obvious question. "Taygeta, why in Heaven's name did you *entomb* him in the first place?"

"Granny says if somebody you love is sickly, one way of knowin' if they're gonna die is to secretly bury a livin' rooster. If it's still alive after three days, then the person you love won't die either." With a sheepish grin that stretched to Gadsden, she exclaimed, "This is the third day!"

I bit my tongue as I swallowed a question: *Just how many roosters had Egypt sacrificed over the years to satisfy her cockamamie fetish?* In truth, I didn't want to know the answer.

Remembering where I'd just come from, I simply nodded and smiled my understanding. Then I enlisted Egypt's help in sneaking back to my room. The easiest way to accomplish this, without being seen, would be on foot. After promising to tell her about the witch's house at a later time, I asked Egypt to escort Blue to the barn.

It was misting rain by the time I reached my window. Fawn gave me the "all's clear" signal, and I tumbled in. As I dried off and changed my clothes, I told her what had transpired that morning. The kind of ritual described by Rola Moon appealed to Fawn's Cherokee instincts, and she faithfully offered to track down a fitting feline promptly.

Once Fawn had set off for the hunt, I feasted on Brunswick stew, a tasty combination of pork, corn, tomatoes, and okra, all cooked to-gether so that my mouth couldn't tell meat from vegetable. While I chewed, I daydreamed, glimpsing the silhouette of clouds with each flash of lightning. *Heaven's Gate stands at the ready,* came a worried thought; suddenly, I was no longer hungry.

Mamau Maude quietly ambled into my room and settled in the chair beside mine. "Your uncle is havin' a time of it, tryin' to keep the fires goin' in this raw weather," she began.

"Yes Ma'am, it's a bitter cold." As I wondered what she really wanted, I counted the beats between a lightning flash and the next round of thunder it announced.

My granny's eyes knowingly rested on mine as she said, "I don't suppose you want to tell me where you slipped off to this mornin'." Fawn and I thought our mischief had gone undetected. Most folks couldn't be in twelve places with one behind, but Mamau Maude could.

I stared at the floor while I answered her probing question. "No, Ma'am, I'd rather keep it a secret. That is, if you don't mind."

In a voice that blended vulnerability, strength, and kindness, she admonished, "Your daddy and mama are beside themselves...sick with worry. You shouldn't add to it. You promise not to venture out again for a couple of days?"

I smiled, then leaned across time and space to kiss Mamau Maude's wrinkled cheek; it was as soft as velvet. "I swear. I won't leave the house again until you say it's all right." With her business completed, my grandmother gently patted the top of my head, then meandered back to her chores.

Night fell before Fawn returned with the precious, pitch-black fur. Although she'd been in the freezing rain and was soaked to the skin, Fawn was jubilant, joking as she peeled off her clothes. "Remember what your daddy says when it's rainin' like this? 'Landsakes Cora, it's pourin' in the house and leakin' in the yard!'" It was a dead-on imitation of T.H.

"This is tail...not body fur, right?" I had to be sure.

Fawn rolled her eyes. "Damn, Pug! Have *you* ever tried to find a black cat on a whim? After I finished with the one *I* found, it had a tail that looked like it'd got caught in Granny's garden tiller!"

With a grateful sigh, I patted her on the back and said, "You did good, Calaeno—a fine job. I'll thank the cat, too, if it ever crosses my lucky path."

Determined, the two of us set to work to create the queer concoction Rola Moon had prescribed. With a good bit of trouble, we finally got the hot toddy prepared using Johnny Walker's Red Label Whiskey; it was the closest thing to "red liquor" I could find.

Mama and T.H. were pleased when I offered to sit with Azberry; it gave them a chance to have some supper. Once my brother and I were alone, Fawn crept into his room carrying the steaming brew. Azberry was drowsy but awake.

"We've brought you some special medicine, sprout," I whispered.

"What is it?" he wanted to know.

"It's fairy juice. Enchanted elf nectar with magical powers. It'll make you well in no time, but you can't tell *anyone* I gave it to you. Not even Mama."

Even in his weakened state, Azberry was suspicious of me. With a voice that wheezed from the mucus that threatened to strangle him, he asked, "Where'd you get it?"

"From Rola Moon."

"The witch?" Azberry was obviously impressed.

I nodded, quickly glancing at the doorway for any sign of an adult. "Now, you've got to hurry and drink it before the magic dissolves away."

"I'm scared." His lip trembled.

"Don't be a baby," I cajoled. "If it doesn't have teeth, it can't bite." I put the cup to my brother's lips and watched as he slowly downed all the warm liquid.

"Do you believe it'll work, Pug? Do you really think so?" Azberry's fear had surrendered to trust, tender and touching.

"If any squawk survives that, it's your friend," was all I could think to say. Azberry relaxed, closing his eyes as I lovingly stroked his cheek. Soon, he was fast asleep, boozily lulled into slumber by Johnny Walker Red, a slight grin sealing his lips.

✳ ✳ ✳

The next morning was the coldest ever recorded by local historians. The ground was frozen solid, hard as a lightard knot. However, a blizzard could've driven past and nobody in Sheridan House would've cared. Azberry's fever had broken during the night, and Doc Self affirmed that he was gonna be "just fine." It wasn't long before our home returned to its normal rhythm and relaxed mood.

Daddy believed that the twelve days before Christmas foretold the weather for the rest of the winter. As the holiday approached, snow-flakes the size of goose feathers fell on a frozen lake. On Christmas Eve, my brother spent the morning torturing his calico cat, making little paper boots and tying them to her feet. His expression turned angelic as he called out, "Pug, doesn't it look like Santy Claus has sprinkled sugar all over the ground?"

I put on the warmest clothes I could find, then loaded Blue's back with toys earmarked for Emmer and Newt Faulk's brood. The grab bag included English walnuts, candy canes, Christmas cookies, and canned preserves. The Faulk children saw oranges only on Christmas, if they were lucky; Mama made sure there were some juicy ones in my sack.

As I made my slow, slippery way to Newt's, I was careful to avoid broken tree limbs, cracked by clumps of ice that dangerously weighed them down. When I finally arrived, Newt and her stepchildren were having a late breakfast, a strange combination of tea cakes, quail eggs, and parched chestnuts.

As usual, Emmer wasn't home. Though he'd managed to keep his family fed and clothed, he spent most of his time gambling at Tin Top, a gin mill set in a pine thicket on the upper west side of Sand Moun-tain. Occasionally, I'd hear of a fight erupting at Tin Top, resulting in somebody getting their guts split open. For Newt's sake, I'd pray it wasn't Emmer.

Though his face had been busted up a few times, it hadn't stopped Emmer from going back to the squalid honky tonk, leaving Newt to fret as she fended for herself and their children. To keep up with all that had to be done, she stayed extremely busy, exhausted and miser-able.

My friend appreciated the hand-me-downs I brought her, though she was a genius at making the most out of every available scrap of material, even feed bags. Fawn had shown Newt how to dye burlap by burying it in the red mud near Scarum Bluff, an area the Cherokee considered sacred. The cloth came out of the ground colored a lovely, brownish shade. With it, Newt sewed beautiful quilts. Obsessed with the Wedding Knot motif, she believed that whatever one dreamed while sleeping under a new quilt would come true.

Newt also created many of her own dresses with the rough fabric of fertilizer sacks. Unfortunately, it was impossible for her to get all of the printing off the cloth. As she passed by, one often saw the letters "FERTIL" spelled out across Newt's back in faded green print.

During her first holiday season with Emmer, she'd been thirteen years old, and he'd given her a baby doll as her Christmas gift. At fourteen, Newt looked like a child grown too weary to play. That morning, she seemed sadder than usual.

"I'm pregnant," Newt factually announced as we boiled the molasses I'd brought. The jolting words hung in the steamy, sweetened air while she buttered ten little hands for a taffy pull. The children squealed with delight as the syrupy candy turned a delicate, pinkish-cream color, ready to eat. Soon, there was a hushed reprieve from the noisy chatter of excited kids while they gorged themselves with sticky sweetness.

Newt and I sat together on her spool bed. "Are you sure?" I asked, knowing it was a stupid question.

"Positive. I haven't had my period for four months. My belly is bloated." Newt lifted her dress to show me the swollen mound hidden underneath, and more pent-up feelings came blustering forth. "I don't want it, Pug. I don't like bein' married, and I swear I don't want a baby. Not now. Not with Emmer. He doesn't even care about the ones he's got!

"I wish I could leave him. But, I know Daddy won't take me back, especially with a newborn on the way. Besides, I love Emmer's kids too much to leave 'em now. They treat me like I'm their real mother. I don't know what to do, where to turn. I feel worn out." Newt wiped her tired tears with the handkerchief I slipped into her trembling hand.

I thought about the number of times I'd heard townsfolk say, "You've made your bed, now lie in it." All Newt ever wanted from Emmer was true love, but he appeared incapable of giving her even that. It was possible his attitude would change once he heard the news of her impending motherhood, but I doubted it. Newt's situation looked hopeless, and I refused to lie to her. Instead, I tried to make her smile. "T.H. says marriage is fine. It's havin' breakfast together that causes all the trouble."

My joke had the opposite effect of what I'd intended. Newt completely broke down; her heaving, helpless wails were so fervid, I became concerned for her unborn child. Holding her tight, I repeatedly promised what she needed to hear. "You're not alone. Remember the oath we made in the cave. You can count on your friends. Trouble is a sister to courage, that's what Granny believes. So do I. I swear to you Newt, we'll get through this together."

All five little Faulks came running into the room, alarmed by the sound of their mother's distress. To allow for privacy, I ushered them back to the kitchen. Newt's soft, reassuring words followed close behind. "Mama just needs a nap, children, that's all. Everything is gonna be all right. You mind Pug, now."

While my friend rested, I let the fidgety tikes stuff themselves with cookies, promising them a Christmas story. I patiently waited as they gathered at my feet. Amused, I watched their eyes grow big with wonder when I said, "Did you know animals can talk on Christmas Eve? Sometimes, when the wind's blowin' like today, you can close your eyes and hear their happy little voices carried on the breeze..."

After I ended the tall tale, I readied myself to leave. Newt was feeling better, busily preparing another meal of hot-water corn bread, wild winter onions, and turnip greens. "I'll see you at Horseshoe," she whispered.

"Yes, you will," I answered, smiling.

Blue and I had one more stop to make, so I pointed his cold schnozzle south. As I stared at the gray-toned, frigid landscape, I wondered why my elders stubbornly stuck to old-line principles, even when they made no sense. *If you're old enough to lie with a man and have his babies, you're at a suitable age to get married. Who made that rule? A man, I suspect. And who says it can't be changed?* I answered my own internal question. *The law. And who dictates that?* I screamed with frustration, and Blue bolted for several yards, confused.

I talked to my horse to calm him. "But what about a girl like Newt? She was attracted to legal matrimony like a moth to a flame, with the same result. Damn it, Blue, she's trapped. Marriages may be made in Heaven, but the raw materials for that one came from the depths of Hell." My pony nodded his agreement, then gingerly proceeded across the crusty earth.

By the time I reached Rola Moon's place, my teeth were rattling in my head; my nose had grown dead-numb in the shivery frostiness. The pythoness was in her yard, extracting cuttings from an alder shrub that grew beside her house. She nodded and waved me inside; her cabin welcomed me with its warmth and the smell of baking bread. Without thinking, I sputtered, "It's colder than a witch's tit out there!" My face warmed with embarrassment.

Then, something wonderful and unexpected happened—Rola laughed. It was a sound that swelled above the clouds of morning and followed the Eastern Star. Its reverberation surely melted a good-sized chunk of the ice outside because it certainly thawed the cosmic barrier that kept me from knowing Rola Moon.

Between Rola's shifting moods, she was downright good company. Over the course of that afternoon, I got to know the witch-of-the-woods better than anybody in Village Springs. That's because I came to understand that her pauses were as important as her words. Rola communicated in symbols and allegories; maybe I was the first person who not only listened, but really heard her. We sat at her little table and ate "cat-paw scones" while warming ourselves with raspberry tea.

"Blackbirds are gatherin' on the roof," Rola said, her tone soft and smooth. I could tell she was purposefully trying to put me at ease.

I nodded. "They do that when it's cold." I paused. "Ma'am, have you always lived alone?"

"This is the night that honors mothers." Rola's voice was suddenly sad. "My turn is comin' around again. I can feel it. So much time already lost. I hear her cryin' in the silent darkness. Beyond my dreams." Neither of us spoke for a couple of minutes. Then she added, "I was loved once. Where did it go?" Her expression was tinged with the sweetness of melancholia.

"Miss Moon, lots of folks are scared of you. They say…"

Before I could finish my sentence, she declared, "I don't believe in the Devil. Satan keeps his own company. I know what the preacher men claim, but they're wrong. I've got to have strong evidence before convicting someone of bein' a Christian. Sayin' one thing, then doin' another—that don't serve. I try to remember that whenever I point a finger at someone, I still have three pointin' back at myself."

Rola looked at me with a studied gaze before continuing. "The Mystery in your heart burns strong. When you're ready, I'll teach you the Earthlove Song. You were born with gifts you've yet to know." Her words sounded like a blessing, an initiation.

Before I left, I gave Rola her proper payment for helping me with Azberry. I also offered her my own handmade gift of thanks. Inside the festive paper tied with a ribbon, she found the candles I'd made for her. They were formed with beef tallow and dyed assorted, bright colors.

In return, she gave me a good luck charm, "the left hind leg of a graveyard hare."

As I turned to leave, Rola spoke for the last time that day. "At night, give thanks to the moon. She's a kindred spirit, you know. I call her Lady Lodestar. The great Lady has the same cycle as us women. The ocean's tide is her heartbeat. Lady Lodestar gets lonely sometimes, but she never wanes when it counts."

I had a lot to mull over as I headed back to The Hill, passing many snow-covered gardens along the way. I thought about how beautiful they'd looked in the springtime when they'd boasted crepe myrtle, roman hyacinths, daffodils, jonquils, and narcissi. Some of the gardenia bushes had been so large they'd looked like delicate trees, refined and exquisite. But, like the old South, the gardens now lay dormant, their beauty suspended. Any future glory was contingent upon unforeseen factors. And, like the old South, the gardens remained in their element, exposed to parasites, fungus, and jungle rot.

For me, that day was the beginning of the end of my youthful innocence. *I've been livin' a store-bought fairy tale, a delusive lie,* I thought to myself. *Swimmin' upstream my whole life. But now I know for sure. The people in this town will go on treatin' each other the way they always have, right or wrong. Some form of defense, includin' the Bible, will justify their sins. It'll never change. There are fine, southern manners. And then there's the truth.* It was a lesson that would serve me well.

Pressing onward, I pushed aside my somber thoughts and headed home for Christmas. The blazing glow of a bonfire welcomed me, a preamble to the fireworks that would come later in the evening.

I helped Azberry decorate the giant cedar tree that Uncle Finas had placed in the living room, adorning it with a popcorn rope and paper lanterns. When Mama wasn't looking, Daddy let me sip some sillybub, a festive drink made with whole milk, sweet white wine, and sugar.

We opened our gifts right before dinner. I got the Stetson hat I'd been hinting I wanted; its coal-black color, high crown, and wide brim suited me fine. Supper was served as the clock chimed midnight. It was my favorite part of our family's Christmas tradition; eating that late tickled my fancy. We dined on roasted duck, brandied peaches, corn pudding, and pecan rolls.

When we finished feasting, Daddy and Uncle Finas played some fiddler's tunes. They stomped their feet until the wee hours of morning, playing such songs as "Sugar in the Gourd," "Turkey in the Straw," and "Shortnin' Bread." Appropriately enough, they ended their evening's jubilation with that age-old standard, "Too Much Rum's Made a Fool Out of Me." The precious memory of that time burns brightly in my heart. I loved my family more than life.

NINE

Uncle Finas had a topmost New Year's Day credo knotted within his confounding, mystical doctrine of life: "If a woman visits your house before a man does, you'll have bad luck." Thus, fortuitously, on January 1st, Sara Ledbetter came walking, awkward and stiff, up the frosty pathway that led to our kitchen door, the first visitor of the morning. The old maid was enamored of Uncle Finas, although he seemed oblivious. His behavior, as he greeted her that particular day, heightened her nervousness; the moment Finas saw Sara, he became convinced something bad was going to happen.

Forgetting his manners, Finas hesitantly opened the door to let Sara in, muttering under his breath, "Dear God, please don't let her comin' be a sign!"

* * *

An afternoon two weeks later found me hard at work on a light-hearted essay, based on my recent trials in the kitchen. The composition was titled "Congealed Deviled Eggs." I'd just finished considering the merits of such foods for false teeth wearers when I heard Finas scream. It was more of a warble than a shriek—a fluttering, tremulous sound that alternated between belief and disbelief.

A small, frenetic crowd carried my uncle into the house. They laid him on the first bed they came to, which was mine. The bloody scene was surreal. The blunt horror made my head spin. Finas's right leg was a mangled mess; a leather tourniquet rested high on his thigh.

My uncle, while tinkering with our newly-delivered grain thresher, had lost his balance. His leg wedged between the powerful, teeth-like gears. The monster machine chewed him up before spitting out what was left.

Finas's face was pallid, like that of a corpse, his breathing fast and feeble. He complained of extreme thirst and grew increasingly restless as he drifted in and out of consciousness. My mother brought a glass of strong whiskey, and my father gently lifted his brother's head, coaxing him to swallow the makeshift anesthetic.

When Doc Self arrived, he wasted no time on formality. "Finas will bleed to death unless the leg comes off," came the hurried pronouncement. Within seconds, our fancy dining table became an efficient operating surface, covered with a clean, white cloth. Once Finas was placed on the table, the doctor mashed a large wad of chloroform-saturated cotton into the bottom of a water glass, then held the inverted container over my uncle's nose. "Try to breathe normally, Finas," he coaxed.

With calm precision, the surgeon opened the leg all around the bone, five inches above the knee. Then he cut off Finas's injured femur with a hacksaw. A red-hot fire poker was used to cauterize the arteries that encircled the stump before the doctor wrapped his handiwork in a towel.

As a group, we helped where we could, aiding Doc in tying off the blood flow, passing him cotton cloths when needed. Our desire to contribute overshadowed any revulsion we felt. The experience seemed like a bad dream, but reality slowly set in; the nightmare was a waking one.

The severed limb was bundled in the bloody tablecloth and buried in our flower garden. Only then did I shudder, imagining the grotesque sprouts that'd be making their way to the earth's surface as the mutilated "spore" took root in the dirt.

The following spring, what actually burst forth in that patch of ground were May Pops; they came up green, about the size of goose eggs. Those particular flowers had the most exquisite blooms I've ever seen. As a rule, after the blossoms turn bright yellow and ripen, May Pops taste delicious; they have a gelatin-textured, sugary pulp that mimics soft candy. However, *nobody* dared eat the enchanting posies that grew over Uncle Finas's leg.

Within a few weeks, my uncle was active and well. Finas harvested the facts, then gleaned, culled, and plucked the particulars until he had a prized crop of amputation tales. He became quite popular at Marsh's Grocery as a result, entertaining folks all winter.

Sara Ledbetter insisted on nursing Finas back to health. He was as full as a tick from all the adoring attention Sara gave him. The crux of it is, they fell crazily in love. Those two proved to be a perfect match, with complementing eccentricities; they hastily planned a June wedding.

I'd often referred to my uncle as "a strange old bird." At last, he'd found his mate. The nest they'd make together would be a peculiar one—but as Daddy was fond of saying, "It's easier to kindle a fire on an old hearth!"

✴ ✴ ✴

May Day arrived; my first, uninvited clue to the way that entire Spring season would unfold appeared early that morning. I'd gone to where our designated bucket regularly sits to collect rain water. I planned to put a lump of coal in the bottom of the pail, then use the water to rinse and soften my unruly hair. I found the rain bucket just fine, but so did the cottonmouth viper that had looped itself over the edge to drink out of it.

Daddy chopped the serpent's head off with a garden hoe, and seventeen squirmy baby snakes wriggled out; they'd crawled inside their mother's mouth for safekeeping. The tiny reptiles raced away so quickly—and in so many different directions—that Daddy wasn't able to kill them all. Off they slithered to lie in wait for another opportune time to foster devilment.

"Cottonmouths like lakes and creek beds," I heard my father mutter. "Often seen 'em lyin' on roots in the sun, but I've never seen one so close to the house." I went weak-kneed when T.H. added, "Never known anybody to live after bein' bitten by one."

I stopped at Ruby and Violet's house on my way to a Seven Sisters gathering. Although it was always fun to walk together, I never liked visiting their home. As I stepped onto the Seay porch, I picked a blackberry from the vine that grew along the weathered railing; to this day, it remains the sourest fruit I've ever tasted.

The two sisters had a huge white dog named Cat. The colossal mongrel was the first one to greet me as I reached the front door. Poor Cat had no tail, and I assumed that's why he was always wild-eyed and grumpy. I made it a habit to keep a peace offering in my pocket on any day that promised an encounter with the temperamental canine; after accepting my bribe of leftover bacon, he reluctantly let me pass.

The Seay place was a pea-green six room frame house with hand-split shingles on the roof. There was no underpinning beneath the floor; instead, the house was set on rock pillars the size of boulders. The Seays were sharecroppers, and theirs was like most tenant houses, plain and functional.

Ruby opened the unpainted, plywood door before I could knock. As I stepped inside, I saw that countless flies buzzed in and out of the living room. The rickety, wooden windows were opened wide to encourage circulation of the heavy, stilted air.

Zine Seay, Ruby and Violet's mother, was a timid little mouse. She nodded to me as I haltingly entered. I watched Zine mindfully scrub the plank floors with crushed sand, as though her life depended on a job well done. As long as the rinse water was dirty, she'd sweep it out and scrub some more; her floors were as dead pale as her own skin by the time she was finished.

Zine was a recognized local artisan, known for her talent with handicrafts. Lying around the room were all sorts of works in progress. I saw tatting lace, knitted socks and caps—all dark colors—along with multiple, embroidered pillow shams.

Common "threads" bound Zine's latest designs; they were unified by a downcast, forbidding tone. The cushion covers highlighted sayings in chain stitch such as, "Let lying lips be put to silence" or "The curse of the Lord is in the house of the wicked." Responding to the edgy mood Zine's work evoked, the hairs on my arms stood and saluted with heightened wariness.

Zine's husband, Bosie Seay, was an uncouth specimen of a man—the kind that would pee in a river. I'd noticed, on previous visits, that the Seay women were extremely quiet when he was around. He walked with a swagger and wore his dirty blond hair slicked back, straight up from his forehead in a pompadour style. Bosie fancied himself a "ladies' man." I didn't like the way he'd try to touch me every chance he got; his mealy-mouthed behavior made me routinely uncomfortable.

I glanced uneasily around the room, searching for a place to sit. Bosie reclined on one of the three straight-back chairs in the small alcove serving as a parlor. Violet and Ruby had found some old nail kegs to perch on. I managed a determined stride toward a milk crate in the corner farthest from Bosie, and settled upon it.

Since he was a self-appointed know it all, there was no way to escape a pompous lecture when visiting Bosie's house. As he set his jaw to yapping about various uninteresting topics, I glanced at Violet and Ruby, signaling to them that we should leave.

Their father grasped our intention, and a look of sweeping indignation came over his face. As we proceeded out the door, he crudely yelled after Ruby, "Wipe off that lipstick, girl! Your mouth looks like a kid's behind at pokeberry time!" When I looked back over my shoulder, Mr. Seay, pock-faced and unshaven, was scratching his privates.

Situated ten yards from the Seay home was a small pond. As the three of us walked by the water, I could see that the fetid pool was a hotbed for the rapid growth and propagation of dragonflies. Hundreds of the strong, agile insects whirred in every direction as they fluttered on two pairs of narrow, net-veined wings.

Folklore dictates that a dragonfly can sew closed the eyes, ears, and mouth of a sleeping child, a superstition that lends to the insect's nickname, the "Devil's Darning Needle." I would soon discover that the dragonfly and Bosie Seay had a lot in common.

✶ ✶ ✶

We walked in unnatural silence for a long while. I figured Ruby and Violet were embarrassed by their father; I knew I would've been. Abruptly, Ruby turned to her sister and said, "I think you should tell Pug. Maybe she'll know what to do. And Pug can help us tell the others."

The rising wind blew Violet's velvety soft curls around her pretty face, making her appear vulnerable. After the three of us sat on the side of the road, she had trouble looking me square in the eye.

"What is it?" I asked, suddenly feeling jumpy, as nervous as bear bait.

Violet's mouth contorted with the effort of speaking. "I need help...Daddy said...I never thought..." I held my breath as something hovered between us, crystalline, like an unspoken prayer.

The L&N approached with a banging clamor, pounding nearby tracks. Violet said something more before putting her hands over her reddened face, but the train's grinding roar muffled the hurried words. By the time the caboose had passed, the spell was broken.

"I'm sorry," I sighed. "I couldn't hear you, Violet."

Violet hesitated a moment, then lied to me. "A joke. I was wonderin' if I should tell this ditty at the meetin' tonight. Daddy told it to me. It goes like this: A woman should be like a roast of lamb—tender, sweet, and nicely dressed with plenty of fixin's, but without sauce."

I tried to smile, but instead, tears welled in my eyes.

As we neared Horseshoe Cave, I could see thunderheads making their way toward us. The dark, billowy clouds appeared quite close to the ground; they whirled like puffs of smoke, moving fast. The Seven Sisters' roll call was complete with our arrival.

Newt's pregnancy stretched across its eighth month, but she still managed to squeeze through the cave's opening. "How's the little mama today?" I asked.

"I've got some backache. Other than that, I can't complain," Newt responded flatly, her eyes blank. "I like the moist coolness here in Horseshoe," she added dreamily.

"Well, I'm starvin'!" Fanny declared. "What did y'all bring to this Fa-So-La?"

Everybody contributed their share of potluck. We eagerly spread a decent supper on the red gingham tablecloth: ham, baked potatoes, pinto beans laced with cane syrup, coffee, and Essie's famous fried fruit pies.

As it had for the past few months, the conversation inevitably turned to the subject of babies—or more specifically, the numerous superstitions surrounding women having babies. Except for Violet and Ruby, who remained unusually quiet, everybody had a "granny tale" to share.

"Do you have a hankerin' for certain foods, Newt?" Egypt's words raced past without waiting for a reply. "If a pregnant woman wants something she doesn't get, it can cause a birthmark. See this lightish-colored strawberry on my leg? My mama must've craved 'em while she was pooched out with me. But, I don't mind the scar since it reminds me of her." Egypt's voice broke with unexpected emotion as she mentioned her mother.

"I don't know about foods and such," said Fanny, "but an expectin' woman shouldn't touch herself anywhere if she's upset." There was no stopping Fanny as she continued detailing her deformed theory. "Hattie-May Calvert was in a blown-out family way when she hung her arm on a barbed-wire fence. She worked it loose with her free hand. The following week, her son, Buck, was born with birthmarks that looked exactly like handprints!"

I felt uneasy, wondering if such tales should be told in front of Newt, but she didn't seem to mind. In fact, Newt didn't appear to be paying attention to what was being said.

Violet asked, "Is it true that if a pregnant woman wears a rope belt with lots of knots tied in it, the baby will stay in her forever?"

The question went unanswered when Newt murmured, "My back side sure does hurt, worse by the minute. It tingles like it's on fire."

"Maybe you're sittin' too close to the flame," I said.

We needed a small, open fire in the cave, even in warm weather, to provide enough light for our gatherings. Newt had rolled up her cotton shift, its hem gathered high on her lightly tanned legs. Newt's knees were turning pink from the nearness of the heat; she scooted farther from the fire, but grew more restless. Every ten or fifteen minutes, she'd stand and turn slowly around. In the flickering light, she looked like a pregnant wind-up toy, a Lilliputian figurine of motherhood.

When Fawn began to speak in a soothing voice, Newt settled down. "Badgerwoman's told me about birth among the Cherokee. Durin' her monthly periods, a woman wasn't allowed to live in her own home. Menstruatin' women were feared for their special powers, especially by the men. No man was allowed to touch a woman durin' her moontime; she was considered too magical. The strong medicine she carried in her body was a danger to the male chieftain's potency and authority. Every female was forced by tribal law to stay in a menstrual hut, imprisoned until her bleedin' stopped.

"That same lodge was where the babies were born. At the onset of labor, the mother was attended by several midwives. She knelt durin' her pains while holdin' on to a stick driven deep into the ground. As soon as it was born, they dipped the new baby in river water; in winter, it was rolled in snow. The whole tribe would chant in welcome: 'Ho! Ye

Winds, Clouds, Rain, and Mist. A new life has come! The Great Spirit smiles on us this day…'" As Fawn finished the ancient birth chant, the storm broke outside—and so did Newt's water. Newt's labor had started.

We'd been mesmerized by Fawn's story, but now we were terrified. We had no horses; outside the cave, an impressive wind was bending full-sized trees. The ongoing rain delivered enough water to strangle a toad. There was no way of moving Newt, no way to go for help.

Fanny went outside to check the weather for the hundredth time. Her wet clothes dripped, spattering the cave's dirt floor as she took me aside and whispered, "I don't see that gully-wash breakin' anytime soon. We're on our own with this."

Fawn held Newt's hand as she squirmed and moaned with animal-like panic in her eyes. Seven Sisters made her as comfortable as we could on my sleeping mat, then discussed what to do next.

"I helped Uncle Jasper deliver a calf once," Fanny volunteered. "How different can it be?"

It occurred to me that Newt's baby might be born with finger-prints around its neck if its mother saw me strangle Fanny.

Fawn was the only one in our group who'd seen a human baby born, so we followed her lead. She and I took turns pulling on Newt's arms to help her through the contractions. During the worst of it, Fawn told Newt to pant like a heated-up dog.

The storm was deafening as it stubbornly raged into the night; it seemed like a thing alive. The wind droned and Violet sobbed, crying for hours as Ruby held her. The two sisters appeared detached from the unfolding crisis. They huddled in a private, unseen world of their own.

In contrast, Newt's labor evolved as a violent process, an impression accentuated by the sticky darkness enveloping us. As her time neared, Newt became a groaning bundle. Once in a while, she'd cry out, "I don't want to do this! It's a bad idea. I want to go home!" But with each contraction, the words turned into a bellowing wail that lasted until the long cramp was over.

Throughout it all, Fanny and Egypt sang Sacred Harp hymns. Their voices were easeful and sweet, though their song selections were curious. The melodies that echoed off the cave walls that night included "There's Power in the Blood" and "Throw out the Lifeline." As delivery neared, they offered up a nice rendition of "Heaven Is Nearer Since Mother Is There."

"Badgerwoman would give her some sulfur and wine of cordial now." Fawn's voice remained composed. "We don't have any, but tell Fanny to go outside and collect some rainwater to boil. We've got to be as clean as we can. Granny says that's most important."

In the final stages of labor, squatting on her haunches gave Newt the strength to bear down on the pain. Still, the worry must've shown in my eyes, for it was then that Fawn looked at me and said, "With anything that's born, the mothers have to suffer. Nothin' will prevent it 'til the birthin's complete. She's gotta work to spread the bones down there so the baby can come out."

We waited until the last possible minute to light our lamps, making sure that the extra light would be there for us when needed. The Aladdin kerosene lantern fired right up, but I had trouble with the old carbide standard. The same kind coal miners used, there was water at the top and carbide on the bottom; the water would drip down, and the mix formed a gas that could be ignited with a match.

Fawn placed her hand on my shoulder to calm me, and finally, after several tries, the lamp flamed to life. I watched as the shadows of our group lengthened, thin and misshapen. The ghost-like images of our shadow selves danced with the flickering lights.

That night, Fawn and I were linked together by an unseen force, a common impulse. However, several times during that long vigil, uncertainty would take hold of my mind, and I felt like I was made of bone from the neck up.

"It's time!" Newt screamed.

Fanny and I held Newt's knees while Egypt clasped her hand. Violet's sobs reverberated in the background as we moved into action. "Ruby, make Violet stop," I yelled. "She's upsettin' Newt!" In truth, Violet's unending wails were flustering *me*.

"Badgerwoman always says a certain prayer before she births a baby. It's her own secret—she never taught me the words!" It was the only time during that ordeal when it appeared Fawn might panic.

"It's comin'!" Newt's voice was a grizzled growl.

"Oh, sweet Jesus!" Egypt and Fanny cried out in unison.

"Well, make one up!" I hollered at Fawn.

"You do it!" she begged. "I know you'll say what's right."

"Ughhh!" Newt pushed harder.

What blessin' would Badgerwoman give? I thought to myself. *For that matter, what would Rola Moon say?* For a few seconds, I was able to force blankness into my bustling brain. Then, an implausible chant spewed out of my mouth:

> Heavenly Bodies and the Seasons,
> sea-beasts and birds of repose,
> clay, wine, wool, and blood.
> Supreme Ruler from on high,
> please sanctify and bless…
> this night's division of waters. Amen.

Fawn smiled. Newt yowled. That's when the darkly crowned head came out. Fawn calmly guided it by the shoulders until the rest of its body came through. But there was an obvious problem: *Newt was still pushing!*

"There's another one in there, Pug. You're gonna have to cut the cord on the first. I don't have time to help you." Fawn knew better than to look at me as she said this.

Without a word, Fanny fished out the knife and string from the kettle of boiling water, then shakily handed them to me. A million thoughts raced through my mind, but a primary one held fast. *Mamau Maude calls the birth cord the "silver thread." She says it's a baby's lifeline to God. Only part of it can be seen. That's the part to be cut.* I hesitated, then used my left hand to stop my right hand from trembling.

Fawn shot me a fiery look.

"What if I don't slice it right?" I whined.

"Do it!" she yelled.

I got it done, snipped and tied. Afterwards, I took a deep breath, the first in what seemed like hours.

Newt's second son was born as black as tar. Fawn picked him up and gently shook him. The boy wasn't breathing; he looked dead. Fawn deftly pulled his dainty, little mouth open and blew inside, giving him delicate, precise breaths, gifts from her own beating heart. To this day, that sight remains the most amazing one I've ever seen.

"Tap the bottom of his feet!" Fawn's spirited instructions prompted action.

A few seconds later, the little body began to make squeaking sounds, its color gradually turning a healthy, pinkish tone. Like his brother, he was quite small; and like his brother, he would live.

Fawn acted as though she'd been performing such miracles all her life. But her words belied her calm disposition when she said, "I feel like I've reached into Heaven and pulled down a star."

"Two stars," I smiled. It was the kind of moment that captures the soul of friendship.

Newt managed to whisper, "Thank you," while we made her, and her babies, as cozy as possible. Soon, the new mother lay sound asleep, exhausted, with a baby in each arm.

The rest of us sat around the fire, listening to the distant thunder; it now sounded like a fast running waterfall. Fawn and I felt powerfully pleased with ourselves, and as a group, we sat upon the backbone of the earth.

Even so, Violet's tears continued unabated. Though the birthing was finished, something indelible hung in the moist air, too close for comfort. Anxiety crept up my spine and held firm. Tense, I sat stone still, waiting for the answer to an unspoken question.

"It's all right, now," Egypt assured Violet. "Newt's gonna be just fine."

For several moments, the cave remained guardedly quiet. Violet was breathing hard, like she'd tried to outrun a wildebeest and failed. "I'm happy for Newt," she said between choking gasps, "but it'll never be *all right*."

The two sisters stared into each other's eyes before Violet spoke again. "Our daddy's been messin' with me. I'm pregnant."

My brain buckled, paralyzed by the words Violet had spoken. The others silently sat, mouths open, like newly landed fish. Except for Fawn, who began to rock her entire body with agitated movement. I'd seen her grandmother do the same thing, whenever she communicated with Cherokee "nature spirits."

Fawn's swaying motion soon gave way to utterances that sounded unlike herself. Her voice was a howl, wolf-like, as she shouted, "His reason became nothin'. Now and again, what he held would shake. Always, his hands enclosed it. But his reason became nothin'!"

Fawn wept as she chanted, and all her sisters cried with her. Our tears descended like dewdrops borne by the wind—then flooded over the world.

TEN

Every member of the Seven Sisters Society passed that wearisome night in Horseshoe Cave as well as she could. Violet sat uncommonly still while Ruby nervously plaited and unplaited her sister's long, brown hair. Violet's face was a fixed mask, a study in emotional numbness.

Ruby filled in the ugly details. She explained that their father had, throughout the years since they were five, touched and fondled them inappropriately. Bosie hadn't bothered Ruby since she was ten, but he'd recently managed to get time alone with fifteen-year-old Violet while she recovered from a prolonged bout of whooping cough. Bosie told Violet that a red-blooded man like himself suffered from the need to demonstrate his feelings for the women in his life. He also suggested that, if she'd cooperate and keep the secret, he would find a way to leave Ruby alone.

When Violet tried to talk to her mother about Bosie's advances, Zine responded as though her daughter had merely commented on the weather. "Come on, child! Company's comin'. You *must* comb your hair. Now, dry your eyes, and I'll help you change into that pink cotton shift I sewed for your birthday."

Zine was guilty of the ultimate betrayal—passive abandonment. Both girls were tossed from their mother's heart like a couple of puppies dumped in the woods. Zine could not face the truth; it was easier for her to believe Bosie's lies.

✳ ✳ ✳

We went for a wagon, Fanny and I, as soon as it was light enough. Newt and her babies were wide awake by the time we returned with a buckboard piled high with blankets. My weary friend had a suckling child at each breast and looked content enough, considering what she'd been through.

When we arrived at The Hill, Seven Sisters faced unified, resolute interrogation regarding the birth of Newt's sons. It proved impossible to explain things without giving away the existence of our secret sorority. That revelation resulted in uncounted raised eyebrows, but my family said nothing about it right then.

Essie was amazed when she heard that I'd helped Fawn with the deliveries. She shook her head and laughingly declared, "Girl, you can't even burn toast! How is it you knew what to do? A riddle it is, and a puzzle you'll always be!" Tears of pride flowed with her words as she poured me a third cup of coffee.

Fawn helped me arrange a bed for Newt with soft, fresh linens. When we got her settled into her room, Newt surprised us both by divulging the names she'd chosen for her boys. She'd named them, she said, after her "midwives." The firstborn would be called Storm, and his brother, Sheridan. "Aunties" Fawn and Pug glowed proud.

Mama showed the new mother how to keep the babies' navel cords greased with castor oil. Mamau Maude gave Newt a big dose of paregoric tincture and admonished, "Eat anything you want, hon, except for sauerkraut and pickled beans. Those foods will make your milk bitter tastin' and give your babies colic."

My granny thrashed it out with Emmer Faulk when he attempted to collect his wife and babies. She impatiently listened to his nasal whine of complaint about how hard it would be to manage his other children without Newt. Mamau Maude explained to Emmer, in no uncertain terms, that his wife would remain on The Hill, in bed, for at least ten days. Then she slyly patted Emmer's exposed scalp, reminding him what was at stake if his young ones suffered from neglect, with or without Newt to help him.

Ruby and Violet didn't want to go home; reluctantly, they gave me permission to tell my family why. I asked Mama if I could talk to her alone. When I'd finished telling all I knew, Mama called Daddy into her sitting room; he came quickly, responding to her urgent tone. Mama made a considered, conscious effort to calm herself, then turned her focus back to me. "Inform your father about what you've heard," Mama softly encouraged. Her eyes radiated comforting support.

My face turned the shade of red sassafras root as I stammered, "Violet's daddy has been hurtin' her."

"Bosie was never one to spare the rod. I'm sorry to hear he's been hard on his girls. Nobody should get a whippin' severe enough to show marks."

"No, Daddy. You're not hearin' me. Violet and Ruby are up against it with Mr. Seay. He's defiled Violet, and now she's in a family way." My words buzzed around the room before swooping down to sting my father. His body literally jerked from the raw, one-two punch of understanding. T.H. and I stared at each other, eyeball to eyeball. He looked mad enough to fight a circular saw.

Daddy turned to Mama for confirmation, and her words were succinct. "I wouldn't put it past him."

As a U.S. Marshall, T.H. could arrest wrongdoers as the need arose, but it seldom did. Fifteen years of experience had shown that most folks in Village Springs towed the line of the law fairly straight, but being a high sheriff was serious business, regardless. The first thing T.H. did was talk to Violet. Alone. Then he talked to Ruby, also alone. Dusk was setting in by the time all the questions had been asked, the answers given.

The two sisters found sanctuary in the guest room that was now theirs as long as they wanted to stay. Their bodies literally drooped, shattered with fatigue, sadness, and fear. They were sitting together in awkward silence when Fawn tapped at the window. After I let her in, Fawn handed a bouquet of flowers to Violet, the first Indian Violets of spring. Violet held the blossoms close to her breast as she curled into a fetal position, then drifted into listless sleep.

During the weeks that followed, the two sisters and I grew ever closer. Most evenings, Fawn and Egypt would join us for a lively card game. Late at night, Ruby and Violet often asked me to read aloud to them. Ruby would inevitably doze during these stories, leaving Violet and me time to talk.

An oft-requested tale was the legend of Lady Godiva's naked ride through Coventry. Violet loved hearing about the "fine lady on the white horse." She'd nod enthusiastically whenever I came to the part that described what happened to Peeping Tom; he dared to catch a glimpse of Godiva's nakedness and was stricken blind for it. Violet proclaimed Tom's fate a "divine punishment."

As for her father, Violet found creative ways to doubt Bosie's culpability, at least in her own mind. One night, she looked at me and sweetly said, "Daddy's always been an incautious eater. Perhaps he ate some undercooked meat."

It was easier for Violet to believe that Bosie merely served as a vessel for some unruly, evil tapeworm. I never expressed it to her, but I knew that if her father *was* possessed, his demon was the cream of Hell's celebrities.

Around Village Springs, critical, condemning words regarding the existence of Seven Sisters spread like wildfire. Floyd Molely's attitude typified the views of most. Floyd, who had been a good friend of my father's when they were young boys, came to The Hill determined to drive home a point. The two men sat down to coffee in our polished library while I secretly listened outside the door.

"T.H., you know as well as I do that certain people are determined to stir things up around here. Your daughter's unseemly behavior is addin' fuel to the flames. The fact that her daddy is a U.S. Marshall makes some folks think you're askin' for a showdown."

"That's funny, I thought I was sworn to *uphold* the law." T.H.'s voice was calm and steady. "As far as I can see, my girl hasn't broken any statutes. Nor has she hurt anybody with this club she's cooked up. It's an innocent thing, Floyd. Let it go."

"It's an insult to community values. You can run your own home any way you want to. Adopt a *hundred* niggers for all I care. But your daughter has corrupted several young girls, with no remorse to show for it. Have you any idea what's really gone on, T.H.? It's rumored they chant like Injuns. It ain't Christian. Those girls are actin' like heathens, a bunch of little witches! Thanks to Pug, they've even turned against their families; she's the ringleader, you know. Pug's bad influence caused Ruby and Violet Seay to make horrible accusations against their own father!"

Floyd stopped talking and waited for a polite response. When none came, he continued his ill-informed argument. "For Christ's sake, T.H., I hear Fanny Holt openly cussed her daddy—and him a preacher! Vigil had to punish Fanny for her own good. Your girl's ruffled the feathers of some devout, hard-workin' people, and it has to end." Mr. Molely took a breath, a sip of coffee, then added, "Our committee believes that you should send your daughter away to school. There are some fine ones in Virginia for headstrong misses like her. They'll teach Pug how a well-bred young lady conducts herself."

Unyielding silence deafened the room. T.H. had shown remarkable patience, allowing Mr. Molely's diatribe to continue uninterrupted, letting him empty his whole mind. When my father finally spoke, his voice was strong and full of passion; he made no attempt to hide the boiling rage that had steadily stewed during this "conversation."

If he hadn't been a lawman, I'm sure T.H. would've decked the fellow he faced. "Floyd, I wish there was a school where you, and your so-called 'committee,' could go and learn how to behave. This used to be a carin' town. What happened? Did the war change us that much? Is this how we get even? If it is, then you, and those like you, are an embarrassment to the South. Get out of my house, you arrogant bastard."

Floyd stood to leave, but was undeterred. "No, T.H. *You're* the one they ridicule. This town has tolerated your pigheaded notions long enough. And you call yourself a Southerner? There's no denyin' we once were friends. I, along with certain people, have protected you and yours. But no more. Damn it all to Hell, Tyne…wake up! Before it's too late." Floyd marched to the door and flung it open.

I'd remained transfixed, unable to move—so we stood there, Floyd Molely and I, face to face. His expression was suffused with loathing and disgust. I felt dizzy. Multiple, agonizing questions spun in my head. *Am I a bad person? Is the town's upset really all my fault? Is Fanny all right?*

Floyd was about to fire more high-minded words in my direction when it happened. I didn't plan it. I couldn't stop it. I sneezed. The penetrating, copious spray covered the front of Floyd's stiffly starched, white shirt. He bounded out the front door before I could hurl another round of "weaponry" in his direction.

I meekly murmured, to no one in particular, "I guess that's the kind of thing they teach you not to do at those fancy Virginia girl schools."

My father walked me to a sofa, then sat beside me. "I'm sorry, Daddy," I said. "I never meant for this to happen. Everybody's so mad. Why can't they mind their own business and leave us alone?"

"This'll blow over, darlin'," T.H. reassured me. "Those same folks will be talkin' about something else a week from now. Wait and see."

"But Mr. Molely threatened you, Daddy. Threatened us all if I heard right," I whispered.

"Pay no attention to Floyd," he answered. "He's always been a puffed-up bag of hot air. Never got over bein' so short."

I pretended to laugh, then turned the discussion to another troublesome man. "Emmer tried to forbid Newt from continuin' in our…" I stuttered over the words, "…'special club.' He changed his mind, though, when she threatened to leave him."

"Emmer's like an old dog." T.H. managed to keep his voice upbeat. "He'll always remain loyal to the one who feeds him."

"It's Fanny I'm worried about," I said. "None of us has heard from her for a couple of weeks. I've been over to the Holt place a few times, but nobody answers the door. Mr. Molely said she's been punished. I think something's wrong, Daddy."

My father held me close. "Ah, my girl. I wish everyone could see your pure heart as clearly as I do. Stand tall, lassie. It'll all turn out for the best." Then he added, "I've got to take care of some business in town. It shouldn't take long. How about we ride over to Fanny's together this afternoon?"

After Daddy left, I found a quiet place to ponder the meaning of recent events. I decided the uproar over Seven Sisters was just an excuse to light a fuse; the explosive charge had been set long before.

Now, battle lines were being drawn. A local war was imminent. As the unhappy conflict neared, even my mother's cousin showed her true colors. Because she was family, Mama had long tolerated Janet's candy-coated prejudicial slurs, hoping that, over time, patient education would change her. That is, until Janet's last and final visit to our home. On that day, she'd brought my mother a "gift," Thomas Dixon's novel, *The Clansman.*

"Keep your mind open, Cora," Janet admonished as she handed my mother the package. "For your own good, for your family's, you need to read this." The book was an enormously popular publication, not only in the South, but in the North as well. Its jacket cover proclaimed the author's grand intention: To reveal the "true story" behind the Civil War, Reconstruction, and the defeated South's "redemption from shame by the white brotherhood."

Annoyed, Mama opened the novel, flipped to the middle section and read aloud, "For a thick-lipped, spindle-shanked Negro to shout in derision over the hearths of white men and women is an atrocity too monstrous for belief. The issue isn't whether the Negro shall be protected, but whether Society is worth protectin' from barbarism." Mama loudly snapped the book shut and tossed it back into her cousin's lap. "Janet, this is a racist sermon in the guise of fiction." Mama's words were an angry hiss.

I'd been sitting on the edge of the porch, serenely watching them drink jasmine tea from teeny china cups. I'd considered the social visit a self-imposed lesson in the genteel art of feminine, southern sophistication, wondering if I'd ever measure up. My mother's reaction to Janet's "gift" made my jaw drop; I'd never seen her so angry.

"Don't be a fool," Janet retorted. "The author's been called a twentieth-century Homer!"

"It's the work of the Devil. And if you agree with it, that makes you his handmaiden!"

Made furious by the insult, Janet savagely upturned the tea tray. Mama's fine porcelain shattered into multiple, sundry pieces, reflecting the ill-defined division of our once tranquil village.

Exhausted by the memory, consumed with worry, I made my way to bed. I curled into a ball and prayed for peace.

Later, T.H. and I arrived at the Holt residence to find the curtains drawn tight. Daddy's determined knocks echoed about the tiny yard. He stopped banging and pressed his ear against the door. "I can hear you movin' around in there, Mrs. Holt. I'm askin' you, officially now, to open up and let us in."

The click of a latch was followed by a loud squeak when the pine door slowly swung open. Glacie Holt, Fanny's mother, stood before us, apologetic. She kept her troubled gaze focused on the brightly-varnished hardwood floor as T.H. got right to the point. "We need to see Fanny."

Glacie nervously shook her head, "She's bein' punished. My husband is the head of this house, and I honor his wishes. For now, he's allowin' Fanny no visitors." She stubbornly added, "Vigil knows what's best for the girl. He's away, visitin' sick parishioners. Y'all come back later and ask *his* permission to see Fanny. Only he can give it."

T.H. placed his big hands upon the woman's tiny shoulders. "We have to make sure she's all right. It can't wait. We can do it together, as friends, or I can ride into town for a court order."

Glacie turned to me and said, "Vigil was furious when he found out what y'all have been doin'. His own daughter, mockin' him behind his back. He believes sorcery's at work here, African voodoo and pagan rites. Grady told his father that he saw you girls with Rola Moon, sometime around Halloween. We won't let you taint Fanny anymore." Glacie sniffed, smug and self-satisfied.

A cold, clammy wave of apprehension washed over me. "Where is she?" I demanded.

Glacie refused to address me further. Instead, she turned back to T.H. and said, "Follow me." Glacie led us behind the house to a small shed, bolted shut and secured with a heavy lock.

"Fanny! Fanny are you in there?" My call was answered with punctuated silence. I shouted again. I pounded the shed's metal door and walls. Still, there came no sound from within. I panicked, pacing around the steel-framed prison, mumbling furious thoughts to myself.

"Daddy, do something!" I begged.

"Do you know where the key is, Glacie?" T.H. spoke with a controlled calmness I'd come to recognize as a sign of anger. On edge, Fanny's mother shook her head and backed away. My father walked to the other side of the Holt yard and retrieved a crowbar. With unyielding brute force, he pried the steel lock open.

When I first peeked inside the windowless shed, I could see nothing; it was too dark. My eyes slowly adjusted to the nightmarish scene that came into focus. Scanning the hut's interior, my mind registered a bowl of water, a small piece of stale bread, a used chamber pot, and countless flies. An engulfing, malodorous stench tickled my gag reflex. In the corner, Fanny lay on a thin, bare mattress. She was wrapped in a soiled blanket. Though her eyes were open, she appeared not to see us.

For me, the sight of her like that was akin to a violent, unexpected blow to the head. I threw myself upon my friend and shook her. I cupped her face, staring into her eyes as I repeated her name. I tried everything I could think of, short of hitting Fanny, to elicit a response. None came. Her stare remained vacant.

"Daddy, what should we do?" I cried.

Glacie's soft chant of "Lord have mercy, I had no idea," was repeated as Daddy gently lifted my friend, then carried her to his horse. Ignoring Glacie's protests, T.H. and I departed at once, delivering Fanny to the safety of her maternal grandmother's house. Grandma Terrant was a woman my family knew well and trusted, the only relative Fanny had who could stand up to Vigil Holt.

Doc Self lived next to the Terrant place; he hurried over when he saw us arrive. He quickly determined that, other than a broken finger and a few big bruises, Fanny was physically fine. "From the look of her injuries, I reckon she acquired them tryin' to free herself," he announced.

Still, Fanny remained mutely limp. Like a baby bird, she'd reflexively open her mouth whenever her Granny or I spoon-fed broth into it. Otherwise, she looked and acted like a rag doll.

After further talks with the Holts, T.H. and Doc put the puzzle pieces together. Vigil had tried to exorcise "demonic possession" from Fanny with a starvation diet of bread and water, along with solitary confinement in total darkness.

In Doc's words, "Such harsh treatment must've been a severe offense to Fanny's sense of propriety and decency. Especially comin' from her own father. Her mind has all but disappeared. There's nothin' more I know to do, medically, to help her. She needs lots of love, rest, and time."

With her physician's permission, I was determined to pull Fanny back into the world. I tried a number of things in my attempt to reach her, to get her to hear me, to recognize my voice. Daily, I'd make my way to Fanny's bedside. I read her poetry, including verses from my own work, such as, "We are the Web. We find our center by comin' closer. It's heart is our truth."

I also serenaded my friend with music boxes, singing to her as they played. I focused on two of my favorite songs, "What a Friend We Have in Jesus," and "Give the World a Smile Each Day." I even tried singing more off-key than usual, hoping she'd beg me to stop. Still, no response.

The other Seven Sisters wanted to visit Fanny, to see if they could help. I asked Grandma Terrant, and she replied, "Under the circumstances, I think it best you visit Fanny alone."

So, for six straight days, I sat with Fanny as I read to her, brushed her hair, and held her hand. She slept a lot. When she wasn't sleeping, she stared at something I couldn't see.

On the seventh day, patience gave way to frustration. "Damn it, Fanny," I cried. "You've gotta snap out of this! If you give up, they've won. Your father, Mr. Molely, and the rest. I know you don't want that. You're a 'Daughter of Atlas,' Fanny. You're Alcyone, the brightest star in the Pleiades. The kingfisher. You can soar as high as anybody. Fly home. Fly home now!" My tears pelted her pillow as my words met hollow ears.

I left Fanny's bedside, headed for Rola Moon's place. When I arrived, she was sitting quietly in her front porch rocker, waiting. I sat on the top porch step and took a deep breath. "My friends and I have done something lots of folks don't like."

"What's that?" Rola's tone was casual.

"I'm not sure I understand it myself," I softly answered. "We decided to be buddies and meet often. A harmless enough thing. But that simple fact has woken up a wasps' nest. We've all felt a stingin' bite, to one degree or another. But one of my friends got stung bad." The enormity of Fanny's plight, along with the fear that she might never recover, pressed hard on my heart; my chest felt tight with the weight of it.

Overwhelming sorrow gripped my spirit and held firm. I broke down completely, weeping as I spoke, garbled words and syllables that Rola was somehow able to understand. "I feel like I caused her pain. It was me that brought us all together, me who's to blame for what's happened. While my friend, Fanny, has been sufferin', the others have considered disbandin' our group. We love each other, and it's hard to let go. They've left it up to me. I want to do what's right."

"A friend's eye is the best mirror," Rola answered. "To give that up would be like erasin' part of yourself. As for those who criticize you, just remember—no two persons ever lit a fire in this town without disagreein' about which match to use." She paused, then added, "You have another question. What is it?"

I worked at calming myself, then gave her a summary of what had happened to Fanny. Rola listened with caring concern. After I'd finished explaining it all, she asked no questions. I sat very still while Rola silently rocked to and fro.

Suddenly, she stood, crossed the porch and sat beside me. Rola whispered, "Your friend was denied light for too long. She's lost harmony with the natural rhythms—the sun, the moon, that which coincides with the cycle of all livin' things. She needs flower magic."

"I'll pick some right now," I said, my response one of hopefulness.

Confusion was added to my jumbled feelings when Rola answered, "No, she needs to eat a flower salad. See, God's blossoms turn their heads to follow the sun. They'll help Fanny do the same. What is her birth sign?"

"Cancer, I think," I managed to answer, incredulous.

Rola nodded. "Daughter of the moon. We'll start with water lilies."

Like a dutiful servant, I followed Rola around the wooded hillside, obeying her strict orders to pick this flower, then that one. We gathered seven "shooting stars," the fanciful name for the American cowslip. They had an interesting shape; with their petals bent backwards, the pistil and yellow stamens formed a pointed tip that seemed to shoot out of the flower toward the sky.

We also pulled borage, which I tasted; it had a mild cucumber flavor. Petals of lilac, calendula thistles, scented-leafed geraniums, and "johnny-jump-ups" were added to our bouquet feast. After we washed the buds and blended them all together, Rola produced a beautiful, homemade wooden bowl.

The final result was an enchanting array of color and fragrance. We topped the salad off with some nasturtium petals; their rough, heady scent was bitter, almost peppery, with a vague smoky sweetness. "Like life," proclaimed Rola as she generously sprinkled them on.

I carried the witch's remedy back to Fanny, along with some iced tea made with anise and hysops. As I carefully spooned the delicate blossoms into her mouth, some deep, innate part of her responded eagerly. She'd chew quickly, swallow, then open her mouth wide. Throughout the meal, Fanny's vacant eyes still stared straight ahead. After she'd eaten every bite, she fell fast asleep. She slept for ten long hours without moving a muscle, her breathing slow and shallow.

As I sat beside my friend, doubt crept into my mind. *Have I poisoned her?* I wondered, alarmed.

Late in the evening, I decided to go to Doc Self and confess all. As I stood to leave, Fanny finally awoke. I knew she was really back when she winked at me while managing a slight grin. "You came to the shed. You found me," she whispered. "I knew you would."

"You're safe," I promised.

Even so, Fanny would never know how far I'd had to go to find her. Within the ruddy glow of candlelight, we sat together, comforted by our mutual trust and our transient moment of gladness.

Time proved to be an impartial judge. T.H. helped Fanny with the legalities of making a permanent home with her grandmother. But she refused to press criminal charges against her parents. I overheard T.H. tell Mama that Fanny's decision was just as well. The court would've ruled her external injuries "self-inflicted." Also, the "southern code" allowing parents to govern, thus punish, their children was an unyielding, ruinous tradition.

Unfortunately, Fanny's deepest wounds were invisible to the naked eye. Only the grace of God could heal them. Even so, a dense, hard layer of scar tissue would remain, covering the place in her heart where unwavering devotion had once resided. Thankfully, Fanny's spirit brightened whenever I repeated the flower salad recipe. She asked to hear it often, and it always made her giggle with delight.

"Ecclesiastes is right!" I'd grin. "There's a time to be born, a time to croak, a time to seed, and a time to pluck up that which is planted."

I was sure that Fanny had regained her strength when she responded to the fiftieth telling of the flower story with a quote of her own. The words were from the Song of Solomon. "For, lo, the winter is past. The rain is over and gone. The flowers appear on the earth and the singin' of birds is come." That's when Fanny shyly asked the question I'd been dreading, "When's the next meetin' at Horseshoe?"

I shifted the weight on my feet, trying to appear nonchalant. "That hasn't been decided," I softly answered. "We're gonna lay low for a while. And think it over."

Fanny didn't challenge this answer. She knew me well enough to know that would be a waste of time.

I'd been doing some studying since my last talk with Rola Moon, reading up on Greek myths regarding mirrors. I agreed with her belief that "a friend's eye is the best mirror." But I now knew a further truth, one I'd painfully witnessed. To break such a mirror, thereby shattering the image, is to endanger one's soul. How could Seven Sisters ever risk that again? Until I had the answer, there could never be another meeting in Horseshoe Cave.

✶ ✶ ✶

A cornfield in June is like the opening of summer, its arrival confirmed with the whistles of blue jays in sweet gum trees. Quite a fuss was being kicked up at Sheridan House that particular morning; it was Uncle Finas's wedding day.

I was assigned the task of keeping tabs on Azberry and getting him ready for the ceremony at Old Bethlehem Methodist. My brother raced me to the lake and won. As I played in the water with him, trying to splash as much of the crusted, caked-on mud from his thin form as I could, I thought about what a difficult month it had been.

Daddy had arrested Bosie Seay. He was out on bail, awaiting trial. Bosie moved back in with his wife as soon as he was out of jail. Neither he nor Zine had anything to do with their daughters after that. In fact, they acted as if they'd never had daughters.

My family had done its best to smooth things out for the Seay girls. However, Violet's pregnancy had begun to show; the mound in her belly was a reminder that some things just couldn't be "smoothed out."

Both sisters often appeared depressed, especially Violet. Like Red Oak ooze, her sadness seeped out, opaque and cloudy, incurable and catching. The wedding would, at least for a short time, eclipse the hazy, empathetic despair felt by the rest of us on The Hill. We were thankful for a joyous occasion to celebrate.

The hour for the marriage rite finally came, and all invitees appeared on time except the bridegroom. I followed when Daddy slipped away from the church to look for his brother.

Finas had been in a nervous twitter all day, with superstitious notions knocking about inside his head like so many loose marbles. "Did you know bridal veils come from medieval times?" My uncle had posed this question over breakfast. "Yep, a bride's veil protects her from evil spirits; they hate happy times, weddings most of all," he added.

Finas held his head in his hands and moaned, "What if I drop the ring? If the groom drops the weddin' band durin' the ceremony, the marriage is doomed!" That's when I noticed he was taking an occasional swig from the cask that contained the homemade sage wine Essie used for her fancy sauces.

Daddy and I found Finas—snockered—humming the wedding march to himself in the bowels of our storm pit. I picked up the wine keg; it was bone dry. My uncle's slurred words were a rambling mess. "Hey, Puglet, did you hear about the old woman who didn't have to brush her teeth no more after she married a feller with a mustache? By the way, does mine look all right?"

Daddy looked at me, perplexed and peeved. "What in the hog-headed cheese is he talkin' about?"

I smiled in answer, then shrugged.

Daddy lifted Finas by his shoulders while I grabbed his leg. We were flustered with the effort of moving dead weight. "One way or another, I'm aimin' to get you to that damn church!" T.H. vowed as he pulled, heaved, and groaned.

Eventually, we managed to drag Finas out of the underground shelter and lay him on the grass. Daddy shot me a cross look when I mumbled, "At least he's not nervous anymore."

From across the yard, we heard a familiar voice say, "Red Chank Root will sober him a little. Nothin' will sober him complete." It was Badgerwoman, right on time, as usual.

Making our way to the church, I managed to propel a significant amount of herbal tea down the bridegroom's sotted throat while Daddy drove the wagon like a bat out of Hell. Surreptitiously, we helped Finas enter a side door. He drunkenly staggered—on his crutches—to the front of the altar, then Daddy stood next to him as his best man.

The bridegroom was swaying ever so slightly, not quite parallel to the hitching post, still humming the wedding march, eyes half closed. Finas had his thumbs stuck in his suspenders while standing with his belly thrown out, like he was gearing up to tell a big yarn of some kind. When he leaned back a little too far and almost fell backwards, Daddy reached over and rescued his brother, grabbing him by his spruced up collar. "I swear in my time!" I heard T.H. mutter under his breath. I suppressed a giggle.

Reverend Tidbow entered, and to my utter amazement, Alton came in right behind him! Now *my* head was swimming with a drunken kind of glee. I'd known Alton would be returning to Village Springs, but he hadn't told me when he'd arrive; he'd planned this surprise and was obviously savoring the moment. As the new assistant pastor, he took his rightful place in the Amen Corner, grinning at me the whole time.

The wedding march began, and Sara Ledbetter made her tentative entrance. *Never* was there a more flustered bride. She had the hiccups, and I wondered if she, too, had dipped into somebody's cooking sherry. Sara wore an enchanting gown, Copenhagen blue with black accessories. With squinted eyes, Finas watched her adoringly as she came down the aisle, though he continued to rock tipsily to and fro.

The ceremony wasn't the disaster I was afraid it would be, although Daddy had to nudge his brother when it came the groom's turn to respond to such questions as "Do you or Don't you?"

I held my breath when Finas put the ring on Sara's finger; he did it kind of slaunchways, but at least he didn't drop it. Finas missed the target, though, when he kissed his new bride, ending up with her nose in his mouth. She didn't seem to mind, and they both laughed it off. The ceremony was finally over, and everyone heaved a sigh of relief.

An outdoor banquet was held on The Hill. Essie prepared an extra long table, covered with blue linen and delectable victuals. The wedding dessert was, appropriately enough, a fruitcake.

Alton and I found it difficult to spend time together at the party. Both of us had to answer to other demands. It was dark outside when the celebration wound down, and we readied ourselves to see the newlyweds off. As the decorated nuptial carriage departed, Alton stood beside me, then took my hand in his. We laughed for a long while as several pounds of rice were thrown, carried on the warm breeze like tiny pearls.

Alton turned to look at me, his gaze seeking what I gladly gave. His words were spoken in a voice sweet with deliberation. "Pug, one of the oldest and most charmin' of versifiers once wrote: 'Mirth is the medicine of life. It cures its ills, it calms its strife. It softly smoothes the brow of care, and writes a thousand graces there.'" Alton purposefully lifted my chin as he recited the last verse. Then he kissed me, ever so tenderly. His caress carried me to another world, where sorrows and weeping are vanished, and the wheat is pure and white.

* * *

Two weeks after their wedding, Egypt and I were drafted to help Finas and his new bride make syrup. It was hard work, labor that began in the humid river lowlands with the gathering of sugarcane. Indians had once built villages within the dense thickets and tall grasses, finding shelter in the cane break from the winds of southern storms.

The work gave me an opportunity to get to know Sara. It wasn't long before I learned that *she* had a few things to teach *me*. After we'd gathered the cane, Finas took it to be mashed at the mill. Sara, Egypt, and I waited for him on their porch while sipping iced mint tea and savoring a slight breeze.

Sara cut to the heart of the matter. "A lot of folks are talkin' about your girls' club that delivered Newt's babies in a cave."

Egypt gave me a knowing look. I coughed, smashed a fly with my shoe, then asked in a resigned tone, "Uh-huh? What are they sayin'?"

"The usual. That such behavior ain't proper. That nothin' good can come from it. Some even claim that y'all have broken the law."

My face was feeling hot. "What do *you* think, Sara?"

"Me? I think you girls are wonderful! You remind me of happy times I had at your age." She glanced at Egypt, then back at me. "I had a secret friend, too, but my daddy sold her to a man in Mississippi. Was the saddest day of my life when she left."

"What was her name?" came Egypt's shy question.

"Martha Banks. Best friend I ever had." There were tears in Sara's eyes. "Some folks around here are just plumb full of meanness. You go on with your business, and don't pay them any mind."

When Finas returned, we boiled and strained the cane. As the sticky juice moved from vat to vat, it reluctantly became syrup. Sara's next revelation came as we were finishing up. She looked me straight in the eye and said, "You may think your association with Rola Moon is secret too, but it ain't. The town's abuzz with the gossip of it."

Egypt giggled nervously. I was speechless.

"What's more," Sara continued, "a few of us don't hold with treatin' Rola like she's evil. Some have taken her food and other essentials for years, includin' your own mama and granny. We leave our baskets in the woods, close enough to her house to be found." Sara beamed with self-satisfied delight as she added, "Y'all ain't the *only ones* with a secret club!"

Sara and Egypt enjoyed a belly laugh at my expense. The dumb-founded look on my face was all they needed to amuse themselves for several minutes.

"Tell me more, Sara," I sighed, recovering.

"Well, I was deliverin' a vegetable basket to Rola last week when I saw her outside, tendin' her garden. I hid behind a forsythia bush and watched her. She was actin' stranger than usual. Rola rocked an empty bassinet while she talked and cooed to an imaginary baby. Then she called out to a man, also invisible. It was a queer name she addressed him by, sounded something like Dolphin."

"Dolphins live in the oceans," an entranced Egypt chimed.

"Yes, I know. It was odd," Sara answered, nodding. "As I was about to slip off, I saw her pick up a bow. She dipped the tip of an arrow into something, then speared a movin' possum clear through. Quick as lightnin'. Where do you think she learned such a thing?"

Where indeed? I wondered.

As we poured the sweet, dark liquid into barrels and sealed them, I thought about Sara. She'd shown herself to be a kindred spirit with unexpected tidings; the sum of it would take some time to soak in. I felt like a juggler who, after successfully launching several balls in the air, gets hit in the head with them, one by one.

Luckily, my new aunt's frank words knocked some sense into my indecisive state of mind. The elder females in my life had more gumption than I'd imagined. They'd followed their convictions despite the obvious obstacles. My shrewd mother and grandmother had let me keep my own "secrets," though they'd known them all along. In this way, they respected my inner spirit while nurturing my developing backbone.

Disbanding Seven Sisters would mean giving into villainy, letting down my female kin…betraying all those who'd gone before, including Sara and Martha Banks. *Seven Sisters would continue,* I decided, *come Hell or high water.*

I swore to myself that I'd find a way to protect my friends. But, as Egypt and I traveled home, I glanced at the sky above us; the tempestuous clouds looked angry, dark, and full of rain.

ELEVEN

O n my sixteenth birthday, I stood alone and watched as sporadic, patched sunlight created angelic halos above nearby treetops. I'd gone to familiar woods to cry; it'd begun to snow, but I hardly noticed the beauty around me. Disheartened, I stared transfixed at the dead caterpillar curled in the palm of my hand. Out of season and out of time, the hairy critter had fiercely clung to the frost-covered log I plucked it from before succumbing to the cold. My tears fell upon the corpse that would never be a butterfly. Some folks think it's unlucky to hold anything while it's passing away from this world, but I believe every dying creature should be comforted.

Caring people are like porch pillars in one's life, supportive and sure while maintaining the illusion of being freestanding. Sometimes they hold you up, sometimes you lean on them, and sometimes it's enough just to know they're standing by.

Violet had gone from pillar to post to survive the last few months of her pregnancy. She was now in agonizing labor. I'd watched her suffer for sixteen hours. When I could no longer stand to see her pain, I'd escaped to the serenity of the forest to compose myself.

After burying the caterpillar in the cold, hard ground, I followed life's morning march back home. Mama met me at the door. As she spoke, her eyes welled with tears. "The baby was lodged in her side. It took all your granny and Badgerwoman could do to turn him. Even so, he was stillborn."

Before I could recover from the shock, Mama swallowed hard, then continued. "Violet's bleedin' from her womb. Badgerwoman gave her some Black Haw tea, but there's nothin' more that can be done. We've sent for Doc…" There was a long pause before she added, "…and Reverend Tidbow." More silence. "She's been callin' for you. You'd better go to her now."

When I walked into Violet's room, Ruby was holding her sister's limp hand. Badgerwoman and Fawn quietly sat in straight-backed chairs that had been moved to a far corner. Newt, Fanny, and Egypt stood near the doorway, still as statues. A collective numbness permeated the air.

Mamau Maude was extremely upset; she didn't even look up as she methodically gathered bloody linens, scissors, thread, cloverine salve, water basins—tools of the trade, all no longer needed.

The atmosphere in Violet's room was shrouded by a hazy incandescence, bringing the dim grayness of that winter day into soft focus. I moved to the bed, the side opposite Ruby's, and took Violet's other hand in mine. Violet moved her mouth to speak, and Ruby and I leaned closer. She smiled and said, "The game is done. I've won. I've won."

At first her words made no sense to me. I would later realize that Violet knew she'd maintained her dignity in the shadow of evil. Her soul had triumphed, and she told us so. "Sing to me," Violet sighed, her eyes half-closed.

"What song would you like to hear, Maia?" I whispered.

"*Monks' Garden,*" she softly answered.

Violet slipped into a coma as we sang to her of eternal life.

Doc Self arrived. After examining Violet, he shook his head sadly. "Some people are just too good for this world," he murmured. The doctor hung his head, then sat silently on the little bed for several minutes. Later, Doc opened the black bag he always carried and took out a small wooden box with a drum in it. The ingenious design served as a crude stethoscope. After listening to Violet's heart, Doc Self looked at Ruby and said, "She's slippin' away. I'm sorry."

Ruby lifted her sister and wrapped her arms around her, holding on tight. Ruby began to rock and moan, low and raspy, like a wounded animal. She'd been the strong one in spite of all circumstance. Now, already abandoned and betrayed by both parents, she faced the black void of Violet's loss, a dark abyss that separated her from any understanding wrenched from such a cruel twist of fate.

Badgerwoman motioned me to her side. "There's none can die peacefully in the arms of a loved one sorely wishin' them to stay. Take your friend outside." Her words were soft-spoken, yet direct. There would be no magic potion for Violet; her time had fast run out. I led Ruby, weeping and childlike, to our living room.

Alton arrived with his mentor, Reverend Tidbow. I motioned them to Violet's room. One look at my face told the ministers all they needed to know. Alton later told me that, upon Violet's death, Fawn and her granny flung both bedroom windows wide open, their way of helping the young woman find Heaven.

Though it was freezing weather outside, Badgerwoman insisted that the windows remain open while the body was laid out. Mama and Mamau Maude took charge of bathing Violet's corpse, dressing it in the prettiest gown we could find. One of mine, it was made from a deep-indigo taffeta weave.

I heard Mama discuss with Doc the necessity of putting coins over Violet's eyes to keep them closed. I shuddered when he said, "I don't think it's needed, Cora, but if you do, make sure they're silver. Copper pennies will turn her skin green. The younger they are, the quicker it happens for some strange reason."

Violet's body looked beatific by the time my mother and grandmother finished their task. They'd combed her silky hair, then placed a winter aconite over her left ear; the dainty, yellow flower was one of the few species that bloomed in frosty surroundings, solitary and still.

Mama lovingly wrapped Violet's stillborn son in a freshly-washed blue flannel blanket; she laid the child's body in his dead mother's arms, so they could be buried together. Daddy, Azberry, and Finas worked feverishly to construct the pine box that would serve as the satin-lined casket.

During the wake that was held for Violet, the remaining Seven Sisters bunched up together like a litter of kittens. Alton helped Reverend Tidbow set her funeral for the following day. I agreed to compose a poem for the graveside burial.

We gathered at the cemetery to say good-bye one last time. Alton spoke reassuring words at the solemn ceremony. "This earth was not where she belonged. Violet's home is now in Heaven, the land of rest, where saints delight, God's place prepared for her."

Throughout the funeral, images flashed before me. Past and present met in glowing, fleeting moments. I thought of our cherished meetings, of all we'd shared. *Young girls laughing. Violet's gentle eyes. "Maia," always the peacemaker. Had Violet's mother been hunkered down in the back pew?*

"Pug…uh…Pug, are you ready?" Alton nudged me to get my attention, snapping me out of my unconscious reverie.

Daddy, Finas, Azberry, and Violet's Uncle Ralph had already lowered her coffin into the icy hole in the earth. It was time for me to recite my poem. As I looked up to begin, I saw Violet's mother, standing by herself a fair distance away. Zine shivered uncontrollably as heavy breath trails encircled her face, like a cloudy veil of frigid air. Resolutely, I willed my heartfelt words to travel to her soul:

> I trace the rainbow through the rain,
> My heart restores its borrowed ray.
> If it would reach a monarch's throne,
> Seven-fold gifts would be imparted.
> A light to shine upon the road,
> Though the cause of evil prosper.
> As Mother Earth holds the roots in place,
> *Maia* quenches her roar with waters wild.
> She is a wonder, origin unknown,
> From the flower of Eve, Atlas's Daughter.

Only Seven Sisters recognized Violet's secret name as it was spoken. We formed a circle around her grave and silently mouthed the Seven Sisters pledge, then I dropped the handwritten poem into the yawning gulf in front of me.

* * *

Zine Seay, Violet's mother, had always been a tightly-strung instrument. With Bosie's trial, her emotional cord stretched to the breaking point.

The hearing took place in the Pine Bluff County Seat, located in a little town hall near Low-Water Bridge. It was where the most serious offenses were tried—in this case, the statutory crime of participating in an incestuous relationship. There were many, including me, who believed the charge should've been murder.

Judge Rayford Foreman had purposely postponed Bosie's case until Violet gave birth. That decision was based on the recommendation of Doc Self, who knew the unbearable strain such an ordeal would've caused his pregnant patient. As it turned out, the consideration had been for naught.

Bosie's lawyer wasted his time with the fool he called a client; good advice was useless unless one had the wisdom to follow it. In the face of overwhelming evidence, Bosie continued to proclaim his innocence, even as several of Violet's friends were called to testify.

Levi Grit, the prosecutor, made witnesses of Daddy, Mama, Doc Self, Reverend Tidbow, and me. We told what we knew regarding the disgraceful way Bosie conducted himself as a father and as a person. We also told the court what Violet had confided to us. However, Bosie's lawyer objected, calling it all "hearsay" and inadmissible as evidence. The judge, reluctantly it seemed to me, agreed.

As each of us did our duty on the witness stand, Bosie mocked us with his smirk, like he was enjoying the attention. Mama leaned toward me and whispered, "There's anger in the open smile of a dishonorable man."

Ruby's testimony was more damaging; she told her *own* story regarding his un-fatherly actions toward *her*. Then, under cross-examination, Bosie's lawyer brought Ruby to tears when he got her to admit that she'd never actually *seen* Bosie touch Violet in an unseemly way.

"Hearsay once again! The witness is dismissed."

Sobbing, Ruby made her way to where our family was sitting.

Zine was the sole witness for the defense, claiming she knew her daughters regularly "sneaked away" at night. "I figured they were trampin' off to see boys," she said dryly.

"Mama, that's not true!" Ruby blurted out. Judge Foreman politely admonished Ruby for interrupting the questioning.

Zine had learned about our Seven Sisters meetings when Newt's sons were born, yet she consciously thought the worst of her own flesh and blood. As I watched her answer the defense's questions, I decided that there's nothing as sorrowful as a mother without her children.

Bosie's lawyer started down an unknown path when he stepped up the interrogation of his client's wife. "Your husband is a God-fearin' Christian man, isn't that right Mrs. Seay?"

"No worse than some," she answered.

"A good provider, is he?"

"We've never gone hungry."

The attorney for the defense then brought the Bible, and its verses, into his questioning. "Proverbs 4 begins: 'Hear ye children the instruction of a father, and attend to know understandin'. For I give you good doctrine; forsake ye not my law.' Your husband's only transgression was to be misunderstood, ain't that right? Your daughters simply misinterpreted their daddy's lovin' gestures, got him confused with the young men they ran around with. Right, Zine?"

"I guess that's so." Her voice was softer, less confident.

"'Let lyin' lips be put to silence,' warns the Bible. Your girls haven't told the truth, have they?"

All color drained from Zine's face as she asked, "What did you say?"

The graceless lawyer repeated the Bible verse. It was then that I remembered the numerous needlepoint sayings I'd seen in Zine's house. "Let lying lips be put to silence" was one of many.

Zine began to tremble; her breathing came rapid and deep, more of a gasping for air than a taking in of breath. "The curse of the Lord is in the house of the wicked." Zine choked on her own words. She looked at her husband, whispering, "Oh my God..."

"I beg your pardon, ma'am?" Bosie's lawyer was stumped.

"Ye are of your father the Devil, and the lusts of your father ye will do," she continued as though trying to remember something long forgotten. "'Wives, submit yourselves unto your own husbands, as unto the Lord,' Ephesians 5, verse 22."

A hush fell over the courtroom.

"Are you Satan's son?" Zine angrily asked her husband from the witness stand. The baffled lawyer tried to calm Zine, but she stood and fought him off.

"What have *I done?*" Zine screamed, anguish bitterly twisting her delicate features. That's when the final thread snapped. Zine crumpled into a heap onto the floor.

Bosie was convicted and sent to the state prison in Montgomery. The other inmates didn't take kindly to having a child molester in their midst. They stabbed him fatally in his own cell nine months later.

As for Zine, she never spoke another word. She existed as a helpless infant, lying in a fetal position in a bed of the state hospital's mental ward, to be bathed, fed, and diapered by nurses until she died.

✳ ✳ ✳

After Violet's death, Ruby and the rest of us found refuge in hard work; it kept us from choking on bitterness and grief. Ruby's favorite job was beating soiled clothes with a battling stick—to remove excess dirt before washing. She pummeled those clothes with frightening ferocity. Blisters formed raw and red, erupted then bled, but she kept pounding.

During that cold, colorless season, Mama spent many days in the smokehouse. Made from hewn logs that enclosed an earthen floor, it had a shallow pit in the center; there were no windows, allowing total privacy. Any dim light came from lanterns, a small fire, or a partially opened door. My mother did chores in the cozy shed, but it was also her thinking place. I'd find her atop our huge, old pickle barrel in a misty-eyed daydream. Sometimes, I had to touch Mama to get her attention; she'd hastily wipe tears, then stand and smooth out her dress. Embarrassed, she'd say, "The smell of dill and brown sugar makes my eyes water every time I come in here."

I found Mama secluded in the smokehouse one particularly gloomy afternoon. She held a large, leather-bound book in her hands; I was amazed that she could focus her eyes in such hazy light. I turned over a bucket and sat near her.

"Good readin'?" I asked.

"It was under Violet's bed," came Mama's subdued answer. "She must've found it in the library."

The book, which concerned the Great Inquisition of the Middle Ages, was titled *The Slaughter of Innocence*. Together, Mama and I read the sections that Violet had underlined. She'd marked many passages, but one in particular struck a chord: "Exchange the punishment of the heart for divine salvation. Forgiveness is a salve for the soul. It will lead you home."

"I think Violet knew she wasn't long for this world." Mama's voice sounded weak and heavy-hearted.

"I miss her, too," I said.

"I know," she whispered. "It's gonna be a hard winter." Mama reached into her oversized apron pocket and pulled out a package wrapped in plain brown paper. "I've been waitin' for the right time to give you this."

I hurriedly unwrapped the gift. It was an exquisite hard-bound journal, embroidered with beautiful, gleaming threads. The design was like none I'd ever seen before. A brown-skinned maiden stood in a noble pose; she held wheat in one hand and a piece of elaborately decorated pottery in the other. The moon, along with many stars, had been sewn in gold on a dark blue background. Mama must have noticed something in the simple scene that reminded her of my true nature.

"Begin again." My mother's words were delivered with a kiss atop my head. Then, she quietly resumed her inventory of smoked meats and dried fruits, a clear signal she needed more time alone.

Insomnia became a way of life for me. Out of sheer boredom, I learned the art of stargazing. Those December nights were pristinely clear. Sometimes, Ruby would join me at my window.

"Fawn says that every star is a soul." Ruby's words rang true on an evening when the heavens sparkled like diamonds. She directed her question skyward: "Are you there, Violet? Can you hear me?" As if to answer Ruby's fervent wish, a shooting star danced across the sky in an acrobatic display of brilliant light.

In late fall, Ruby's grandparents arranged for her to travel to Boston to live with them, and she was ready to go. We met in Horseshoe Cave, six of us, the night before she boarded the train. It was a sad farewell, made bittersweet by memories shared of happier times.

Our sorority agreed that, in spirit, we would always be *Seven* Sisters, regardless of the actual number of girls gathered around our fire. We said our good-byes to Ruby with the understanding that sadness, like the early morning, waxes lighter with time.

The arrival of Christmas was an antidote to our grief. During the height of the festivities, Alton took my hand, and we stole away to the front porch, the only place it was possible to be alone. We settled on the portico's double swing, rocking together for a long time, hand-in-hand, saying nothing. Until that night, our relationship had been circumspect. However, something changed that Christmas, and we both sensed it.

Alton took an object out of his shirt pocket, then held it over my head. I looked to see what he dangled, quickly realizing that the sprig above me was mistletoe. The passionate nature of Alton's subsequent kiss startled me at first, but I gradually relaxed. When our lips finally released, Alton moved to my ear and whispered, "As long as water flows, and the green grass grows, will I love you, Miss Sheridan." It was the first time he said aloud what I had known all along.

Afterwards, Alton and I became masters at a cool kind of flirting, but in all honesty, we yearned and burned for each other. As hard as it was, we followed the challenging rules of decorum and southern propriety, but it became increasingly difficult to do so. Such rigid behavior went against the unwavering, physical laws of Mother Nature. I had impure thoughts even while Alton preached his sermons!

There's an apt Irish proverb that counsels: "The paving stones on the road to Hell have the weeds of lust to bind them." Naked truth. All are not saints that go to church, and Alton and I were living proof. By spring, we knew we'd better get married, or it would be a rocky road to Heaven for us both.

My love for Alton had softened my own, cynical ideas toward marriage. "You're not Newt, and I'm not Emmer Faulk," he reminded me when we finalized our plans. As a couple, we knew what we needed to do; but first, Alton had to undertake an extraordinarily brave errand. Custom required that he ask T.H. Sheridan for my hand in marriage. It was a good thing my sweetheart had God—and an army of resourceful angels—on his side.

My beloved planned to talk to Daddy early one Sunday morning. Alton was scheduled to preach later, a fact that would help the task at hand because Alton needed to present himself as a man with a livelihood. On that momentous day, my hopeful fiancé came to our door looking his spit-shined best. Still, there was worry in his expression when he said, "Could I speak to you in private, Mr. Sheridan, sir?"

"What time is it by your watch and chain?" T.H. calmly asked.

"Just past eight, sir." Alton's voice gave a little squeak as he said this.

"Go on, Tyne," Mama coaxed. "It'll be a while before the cornbread's ready." If Mama suspected that Alton was about to pop the question, she didn't let on.

"All right, but when it's time to put the feed bag on, call me. I'll be ready for it." T.H. was obviously hungry.

As Alton and Daddy headed toward our library, my head swam with anxious anticipation. I went outside for some fresh air and found myself sitting under the open library window.

"It beats all how picayune some folks are 'til they get in church," T.H. was saying, "then they try to make you think that sugar wouldn't melt in their mouths."

Alton kept clearing his throat, unable to say a word.

"Got a frog in there, son?" Daddy asked as he vigorously slapped my lover on the back.

It was as though T.H. knocked the question right out of him. "May I have your permission to marry Pug?" Alton croaked.

You've got to butter him up first! I thought. I scrunched down farther, expecting the ground to quake with my father's temper.

On the contrary, Daddy acted as though Alton had said nothing out of the ordinary. In fact, Daddy acted as though Alton had said nothing at all. "Son, have you ever had a Kentucky breakfast?" My beloved shook his head "no" just as T.H. handed him a glass containing a half inch of water, a lump of sugar, and a spoon. "Now, the only other thing we need for our Kentucky breakfast is a big beefsteak, a quart of Bourbon, and a hound dog."

"What's the hound dog for, sir?" Alton meekly asked.

"To eat the beefsteak," T.H. answered with a tone that dared defiance.

At that point, Alton would've been a fool to refuse any suggestion Daddy made. Frowning with concern, my paramour attentively, and warily, measured the Bourbon as it was generously poured into his spotless, Waterford glass. Daddy downed his first dose of brew, then waited for Alton to do the same.

While pouring another round, T.H. soberly barked, "Alton, do you believe that you are called by God to preach?"

"Yes, sir."

"Well, I can't deny the value of religious instruction. However, it seems to me that it doesn't encourage goodness as much as it fosters the confession of badness. Most do-gooders lead lives that end up being fiction in excellent disguise. As for me, I just lie enough to enjoy myself."

There was a long silence before Alton responded. He stammered and stuttered, but finally found his tongue. "I had a professor at seminary named Dr. McAllister. After a full year of demandin' studious theological excellence from his pupils, he gave a dynamic lecture entitled, 'The Secret of Success in Preaching.' Dr. McAllister advised us not to bother makin' our sermons full of spiritual truths that regular folks would comprehend, because when all was said and done, they just weren't interested. My professor declared that the best way to hold a job as pastor of any church is to feed the congregation long sentences filled with confusin', religious platitudes.

"That way, nobody's ever insulted, intimidated, or misled. It'll have merely been another good sermon. 'A white mule never dies,' my teacher said. 'But when he gets to be fifty years old, he turns into a Methodist minister!'"

To my ultimate relief, Daddy and Alton shared a rollicking belly laugh. T.H.'s temperament had been softened by a master. "I've been called a horse's ass myself more than once," my father chuckled. "Mind if I try my hand at preachin' for a few minutes? Maybe you could judge whether or not I've the knack for it."

"It could make for an interestin' mornin'," Alton answered with a smile.

I suspected that my betrothed was being set up for something. And I was right. Daddy waited until they'd both downed a respectable portion of the whiskey. While refilling their glasses for the third time, T.H. proceeded to give a long-winded sermon of his own.

"Pastor Strawbridge," he began, before embracing a long dramatic pause. "I now stand before you to point the narrow way leadin' from a vain world to the gold-paved streets of heavenly bliss.

"The text I shall choose for this occasion is in the pages of your Bible, somewhere between the chapters marked Chronic-Ills and the

Gospel accordin' to I-say-so. You'll find it reads: 'And they shall gnaw a file, and flee unto the mountains where the lion roareth, and the unicorn mourneth for his firstborn.'

"Remember, the text says they shall gnaw a *file*. As you know, there's more than one kind. There's the accounts-due file, the hand file, you could file for Congress, single file, double file, or if you're a Republican, defile. But the kind spoken here is a figure of speech, and it means goin' it alone without gettin' beat." I smiled with understanding. Daddy was telling Alton, in his own grandiose way, that giving me up was mighty painful. T.H. sounded sad when he finally asked, "Are you up to it, son?"

"I love her, sir."

Daddy sighed deeply before speaking again. "Pug was born under a new moon. It was a good time for a child to come into the world, because as the moon gathered strength, so did she. I've never told anyone this, but I chose a name-tree for her that day.

"If you take on the serious business of selectin' a name-tree for a child, it should be done right, or bad things can happen. It must be an early sprouter, but most of those have a rough bark, which makes for a mean temper. The oak, though strong, is a late bloomer and a slow grower.

"I settled on a straight elm saplin' for my girl; a quick budder, it grows fast, stayin' tough even as it bends in the wind. I watered it with her first bathin' water. Son, I know you don't believe in the 'signs,' but it's better to do wrong tryin' to do right, than it is to do wrong not tryin' to do anything at all. Old folks, they know."

I crept away from the window and went back inside. I strolled into our library to find my besotted betrothed smiling indulgently; he looked both amused and amazed.

I sat on my father's lap for the last time and told him of a "dream" I'd had. Mama came into the room as I began to speak. "In my sleepy fantasy, I was standin' alone in a cotton field," I said. "It was night, but I could see the soft flower heads as they blew. A gentle breeze carried the white, downy fibers right toward me. What might a vision like that mean, Daddy?"

T.H. sighed once more, resigned. He grinned slightly as he looked knowingly toward Mama and said, "That, my sly daughter, is the sign of a weddin'."

Alton's parishioners uniformly commented on the uncommon fervor made manifest in his sermonizing later that day. I teased him mercilessly about how much of his inspiration was due to having won my hand and how much was owed to the fiery brimstone he'd found in a certain bottle of Kentucky Bourbon.

TWELVE

"Wake up, Sadie Lou! My Lady Bugs are dancin' in their collection jar like the party's already started!" Azberry stood outside my open window; he peeked over the edge to make sure his boisterous yell had its desired effect. Every freckle on his impish face grinned at me; *it was my wedding day.*

Many myths and legends had been avidly recounted in Horseshoe Cave as I'd celebrated with my friends the previous evening. One of those yarns, a grisly one, found its way into my dreams. With her piquant flair for storytelling, Fanny shared a saga she called, "The Tale of the Headless Maiden." "*It happened a long time ago in a nearby village…*" came the opening words.

The heart of Fanny's story involved a young Chickasaw woman who wanted to marry a white man. Her father opposed the union and summarily killed her before the wedding could take place; he murdered his daughter by slitting her beautiful, swan-like throat. Now, so the legend goes, one can sometimes see the sorrowful ghost of the Indian maiden standing by the dark, copper-colored waters of Coffee Pond, holding her head in her hands, moaning dismally for her lost and forbidden love.

In my unsettling dream, the face of the Indian girl resembled Fawn's, with deep-set eyes. Her shining hair was so black it had a purple tinge, reflecting the starlight. I brushed my own locks one hundred strokes as I shook off the nightmarish feeling.

Glancing beyond the open space behind our house, I spotted Fawn, assuredly traipsing across mossy, wet ground toward me. My maid of honor was right on time to help me ready myself for the coming day. As planned, she'd arrived early so we could quietly sip ginger tea while listening to the field lark's morning song.

When we'd emptied our cups, Fawn acquainted me with Indian wedding ceremonies, describing how the bride and groom were led through the ritualized four cycles of life by the tribal medicine man. "In Cherokee tradition, the woman has the final say in *all* affairs of love," Fawn concluded. Laughing, we both agreed that was the way it should be in every marriage.

Soon, Mama joined our revelry. "Mrs. Sheridan, what's the essential secret to a good marriage?" I grinned as I asked my mother this question, half teasing.

Without missing a beat, Mama answered lightheartedly, "Havin' the common sense to give in to your husband's persuasions once in a while, without keepin' score."

"You know your daughter well," Fawn playfully chimed. The three of us twittered like schoolgirls for much of that azure morning.

As I was slipping on my wedding gown, Mamau Maude shuffled into my room. She nodded to Fawn, an unspoken message that she wished to speak to me alone. As we sat on my tall, lacy bed, my beloved grandmother cupped her wizened hand over mine. The persuasive emotion behind her words permanently emblazoned them into my heart.

Mamau's missive went something like this: It's not possible for any *one* person to unlock every discernable chamber of another's heart. And while we've all been conditioned to hunger for that special someone who can give us *everything*, we should acknowledge the fact that life doesn't consist merely of people. It's also made up of key, individual moments, twinkling instants in time that are gifts you can pick up and hang like pearls around your neck. But no one can gather these moments for you; your own heart must supply the dulcet string if you are to hug them to yourself.

When she finished speaking, Maude pressed her wedding ring into my hand. Never before had she taken the treasured band off her finger, not even after my grandfather died. "For luck," she whispered as she kissed my forehead.

We were married at sundown. I became Mrs. Alton Strawbridge a few weeks shy of my seventeenth birthday; he was not quite twenty-one. I wore a maize-colored silk dress that Mama had trimmed with cambric and lace. Though still a virgin, I didn't agree with being forced to wear a traditional white gown; such a garment would've seemed too colorless against my pale complexion and red hair.

I'd also changed the wedding vows, one in particular. Alton chuckled when, during our rehearsal, I demanded that Reverend Tidbow take out the line, "Your husband is, by the laws of God and man, your superior; do not give him cause to remind you of it."

"Lick your calf over," had come my angry response. "In other words, try again, Reverend." The minister, after a quick glance at my irate, red face, took out the offending line—despite having used it in every other wedding he'd performed during the past thirty-five years.

For the actual ceremony, the church aisle was carpeted with hundreds of exquisite African violets. Double lilacs decorated the sanctuary's darkened recesses, illuminated with high, lavender candles.

Uncle Finas had tried to dissuade me from an evening service. I laughed at his assertion that bad luck follows a wedding where the groom sees the bridal dress by candlelight. When the designated time came, Finas lit the ceremonial candles, reluctantly and without enthusiasm.

Sara took me aside and said, "I love him more than life, but that man can be a silly old coot. Pay Finas no mind. This is your honored day. Cherish it." We both snickered when she added, "Men are like bagpipes, no sound comes from them unless they're plumb full of hot air."

I took Sara's advice and ignored my uncle. For me, the evening was bewitchingly enchanting; my romantic spirit soared to lofty spheres and a feeling of hallowed, heavenly bliss poured through me.

Daddy regally held my arm while I glided, as if on gossamer air, to my proud and handsome bridegroom. Alton wore a stylishly dapper navy blue suit. Mama had pinned a yellow sweetheart rose to his lapel, and a golden-colored bachelor's button on to Arious, who stood as his best man.

When we exchanged rings, Alton pushed my grandmother's antique golden band onto my finger. The ring I placed on Alton's hand was a Strawbridge heirloom; one of a kind, it had belonged to his father. The family crest was patently engraved upon the ring's inner rim. Alton and I sealed our union with a passionate, unhurried kiss. Reverend Tidbow tactfully cleared his throat, reminding us that our exultant embrace should find an appropriate conclusion.

Afterward, we had an elegant, refined supper on The Hill. When it was finished, I threw my bridal bouquet to Fawn. She and Arious spent most of that evening laughing and dancing together, exclusively. Amused, Alton whispered, "Looks like the right person caught the bouquet!"

Alton and I danced to a few favored tunes, but tired early. When the clock in Sheridan Hall chimed midnight, my groom and I strolled, hand in hand, to the lakeside cabin that would become our home. Daddy spent several months remodeling the little guest house. He'd expanded it to four nice-sized rooms, augmented with ivory paint and lots of wooden beams that added warmth.

After dutifully carrying me from the rose-covered gate, up the porch steps, then across the threshold, Alton plopped me onto the high, four poster bed with exaggerated effort.

"I'm not *that* heavy!" I playfully protested.

Alton smiled nervously, like a Cheshire cat, in the dappled light. A full moon was once known as a Rose, Flower, or Honey Moon. From that concept sprang the idea of deflowering a virgin on her wedding night. As Alton took me in his arms, I gazed at the brilliant circle framed against our window.

"What were you thinkin' as I walked down the aisle?" I whispered.

"About faces," he answered.

"Faces?" I giggled.

He nodded. "If we tried to draw a thousand faces, eventually they'd all look alike. Yet, our Creator molded millions, each one a distinct form. In all the world, with a vast multitude to choose from, I'd never find a bride with a face more perfect than the one I'm lookin' at. When you came down that aisle, you were the embodiment of an angel. You still are, and I'll always adore you."

We melted into each other, heart and soul. Alton was a patient lover; sparks flew and a rumbling blaze was raised. Nothing in my life had prepared me for the intensity of feeling I could now express for my lover, my husband. I took my grandmother's advice and kept those moments close to myself, like pearls around my neck.

Our passion spent, Alton and I fell asleep to the soft strain of delicately refined music. Its origin remained unexplained; the melody was carried upon a sweet breeze from the hidden, wooded darkness. Like a mermaid's refrain, it rose from the depths of the nearby lake, then floated over us.

"The angels are singin'," Alton whispered, before nodding off.

We were abruptly awakened in the middle of the night to another, very different noise. It was a frightening sound, one I didn't recognize. We ran outside in our dressing gowns to see water spewing in high, mushroom-like eruptions. Somebody was dynamiting Sheridan Lake! The carefully orchestrated detonations were discharging quite close to our cabin. Alton quickly pulled me away from the lake's shoreline, out of harm's reach.

Through the woods, I glimpsed a speck of white on the other side of the water. It looked like a wraith among the trees, cloaked like a ghost in moonlight. It vanished in a flash of shadowy motion.

Daddy came running to our cabin, making sure Alton and I remained unharmed. My weary family stayed awake the rest of the night, consuming countless pots of thick coffee. I was furious, hotter than a bog fire, with rising suspicion regarding the culprit behind the explosions.

Dawn's light showed us the damage that'd been done. There were hundreds of dead fish, some floating on the cloudy water, others lying bug-eyed on the bank. Full-grown trees had been uprooted, and there were small craters along the lake's edge. It was a bloody, smelly mess; the water was dark with death. Somebody had scrawled "nigger lover" on the side of our barn with heavy, red paint.

In the days that followed, my new husband habitually shook his head, smiling as I blew off steam. I felt helpless, and that made me madder. "Whoever did this has nothin' but a bull's pistle for a brain!" I ranted. "Mountain-grown mule tinkle runs in their veins!"

The rest of my family took the setback in stride. "You never miss the water 'til the well runs dry," my grandmother remarked. "Misfortune sends no warnin'."

The well didn't go dry, I thought to myself. *It was blown bloody to Hell!*

Daddy searched for evidence pointing to the perpetrators, but found none; he patrolled the unlit, inky lake late at night, as did I. T.H. gave me a suitable gun to wear during my obsessive strolls around the water. It was a German-made .38 caliber derringer two-shot, light and easy to aim.

Though I had no proof, in my heart I knew that Grady Holt was responsible for blowing our lake to smithereens. Fanny had warned me that he was het-up about my impending marriage, and might pull a prank. He'd done other things—little annoyances over the years—but Grady crossed the line on my wedding night. Still, I kept my unfounded belief to myself.

* * *

Two months later, a diabolical conspiracy revealed itself in a consecrated church. It was a cool, drizzly morning, and Alton was ten minutes into his Sunday sermon. I was comfortably settled in the front pew when, from somewhere behind me, I heard four bugle notes that sounded like whistles. They were followed by one long bugle's wail.

A male voice announced, "Enter the Knights of the Ku Klux Klan!" Then, eight disguised figures marched ceremoniously down the aisle. The silent, parading men wore white sheets with matching hoods to hide their identity. At first, I thought it was a Halloween gag—I wasn't alone in this misconception; amused snickers and chatter erupted throughout the congregation.

Finally, the KKK leader delivered a commanding discourse. The voice was that of an older, seasoned man: "The Cyclops has arrived in Pine Bluff County! You'll find it a good thing to keep peace in the neighborhoods. We consider it our sworn duty to preserve law and order, to protect the Democratic Party, and to keep niggers down. We're ambassadors from the ancient tombs, come to warn you of impendin' doom if you do not hear us." A pregnant pause was followed by, "Our purpose is to maintain harmony throughout the land, the lifeblood of all nations. This message is sent to you from Atlanta, Georgia. It was written by the Commander of the Cross Roads, Joseph Simmons."

"And recorded by Hell's clerk," I mumbled under my breath. Mamau Maude pressed her hand hard upon my shoulder to silence me.

The leader walked to the pulpit and handed Alton a note, accompanied by a generous monetary contribution. Another bugle tone was sounded, and the ghoul squad marched heel-toe out of our house of worship.

My husband was visibly upset, but he finished the lengthy service. Later, Alton told me about newspaper articles he'd read regarding a resurgence of the Klan in Georgia; he'd thought it was an isolated phenomenon.

"I'd hoped that dark, cruel monster was dead and buried after the KKK trials of the 1870's," Alton remarked as we continued the discussion over dinner at Sheridan House. "But they've reunited, patternin' themselves after the courtly knights of medieval Scotland. They've used Sir Walter Scott's book *Demonology and Witchcraft* as their ceremonial guide. It's gone into its second printin'."

"They can carry around all the spooky books they want," Daddy answered, "but they've got no business totin' those guns on Sunday." His voice sounded strained.

I reminded Alton that my Grandfather Sheridan had died because of shots fired from the guns of Klansmen. Palpable tension and anxiety permeated our dining room. Nobody showed much of an appetite.

"What did the note say?" It was the first time my grandmother had spoken since church. There was concern in her voice, stubbornness as well.

"It was addressed to Pastor Tidbow and me," Alton replied. He pulled the officious letter out of his pocket, then read it in a matter-of-fact tone. "We sympathize with you preachers over risin' crime rates and the evils of bootleggin'. The KKK can stand behind you by encouragin' an increase in church attendance. We are the one force equipped to deal with the deterioration of society. Our members honor Christ as the Klansman's sole Criterion of Character. We seek at His hands divine cleansin' from sin and impurity which only He can give."

Mama said, "It's frightenin'; that sounds like it was written by an educated man."

My family remained mute with subdued dread. Finally, Mamau Maude bluntly declared, "We must never forget history, or it might repeat itself." Her sad gaze remained fixed on Alton.

* * *

I began to lead a double life. One part reflected the dutiful, devoted wife of a Methodist associate pastor; the other was fascinated by the teachings of Rola Moon. I experienced an internal, spiritual evolution that left me dazed and confused.

During a recent lesson, Rola had explained that the *first* Holy Trinity was based on a female—a Goddess, not a God. The Trinity had three aspects: a young girl, a birth-giving matron, and an old woman. The combination was called the Virgin, the Mother, and the Crone.

Reading on my own, I discovered that Rola was right. In our own culture, the female trinity was still alive within the marriage ceremony, represented by the flower girl and the matron of honor, though the crone figure had vanished from modern weddings. In medieval times, the female trinity also symbolized what women want most from men— respect, love, and kindness.

Alton was aware of my "stabilizing" friendship with Rola, but he didn't know how deep it ran—that she sometimes taught me subjects she called "*the secrets of women's mysteries.*"

The feminine mystique of housekeeping continued to elude me, but my new husband didn't mind that either. There were three parts to my credo regarding housewife matters: a drop of oil or a little spit works wonders, leave a dead fly and others gather, and a good wife always has lemons in her ice box.

When those basics were accomplished, I often visited Rola Moon. She knew a lot about the history of other cultures, and much of what she shared made excellent research for my stories, though I was amazed at what she was able to talk about. She even taught me about some remarkable people living in Australia called *aborigines*.

When I told Rola about the blasting of our lake and what had been painted on our barn, she replied, "The evil eye, you need to ward it off. Those aborigines I mentioned, they know."

"The aborigines know about my barn?"

Rola ignored the joke. "What you need is an amulet," she announced with an urgent tone. "Garlic works pretty well." She proceeded to tie some around my neck. "Hang this in your house while you sleep."

I was relieved to hear that I didn't have to wear the garlic necklace; it wasn't the alluring aroma I had in mind for newlywed encounters. I returned home, looked up the term "evil eye" in my encyclopedia, and discovered that the idea existed in virtually every culture in the world, dating back to ancient times. It was believed to be the result of envious looks and the ultimate cause of illness or misfortune.

Alton walked into our house as I sat, alone, laughing out loud. My husband asked me what had tickled my funny bone, and I didn't know how to respond. I'd just finished reading a passage in the text that stated, "Even today, in some parts of the world, particularly Italy, it is common for men to grab their genitals as a defense against the evil eye, or anything unlucky."

I decided to risk telling Alton the truth about my conversation with Rola Moon and my subsequent research. Rather than chide me, my amused husband seemed truly interested. He hammered a nail into the kitchen wall from which I could hang my garlic braid.

"Don't expect more from people than they're capable of giving," my family has always said. Though I never told Alton about *all* that transpired between me and Rola, it was good to know that he was capable of understanding part of it.

In actuality, my saintly husband understood me uncommonly well, warts and all. Alton's spirit was consistently tempered and caring. He didn't complain when I continued to spend every Sunday night with Seven Sisters while he preached his evening service.

Certain people gossiped about me—or more specifically, about the *lack* of me—at Alton's church, but they were of little consequence to my self-understanding. As long as the rumor mill didn't detract from the Bethlehem congregation's love of Alton, I let judgmental attitudes fall away, like ashes on snow.

✳   ✳   ✳

I'd been married three months when I found myself alone and bored on a rainy, humid afternoon. My family had departed before dawn, headed for a two-day shopping expedition in Roebuck. Alton was visiting sick parishioners; Fawn had gone grubbing for roots with Badgerwoman.

Fanny stopped by, and we decided to visit Newt and her growing brood. When we arrived, they were jubilantly baking pecan squares; the confections disappeared faster than they could be made. Storm and Sheridan, now tireless two-year-olds, toddled toward me, wrapping themselves around my knees. I was a happy captive.

Fanny lifted Storm, swinging him around like a whirling dervish while he begged for more. Sheridan showed remarkable strength as he clambered up my body like an orangutan. I held him in my arms while he began the little game we'd developed. Sheridan's expectant delight was infectious as he peeked into my pockets, checked under my hat, and motioned for me to open my mouth. There, my godson saw the lemon drop expressly meant to tease him.

The boy knew to expect a surprise whenever I visited. I pulled a small bag of candy from beneath my belted shirt, and he grabbed his treasure before sliding down my leg. His precocious squeal echoed about the room as he ran away.

"Remember, Sheridan," I laughingly admonished, "you have to share fairly with your brothers and sisters."

Fanny shook her head as my godson's siblings gathered around the precious booty. "In all my time," she announced, "I've never seen a more spoiled child."

Newt chimed in, "Except Storm. You should see the deer moccasins Fawn made for him just last week. She and Pug have set into this godmother business with more muster than hens have eggs."

As the three of us settled in for some good-natured tittle-tattle, a wagon rattled into the yard. We hurried to the porch in time to see two grimy-looking men unceremoniously rolling Emmer Faulk onto the ground. "Shot in a brawl," the taller one mumbled before hastily driving the team of horses forward.

Newt jumped over four steps to get to Emmer. "Oh my God, he *is* shot. His shoulder's bleedin' bad."

"Let's get him into the house." Fanny seemed calm as she said this, but I saw unreserved panic in her eyes.

Emmer groaned with real pain as we carried him to his bed. Newt brought scissors, and I cut away his shirt. "We've got to get the bleedin' stopped," I said, forcing my voice to a level tone.

"I'll go for Doc," Fanny volunteered.

"No, send Darlene; she can take my horse. You're needed here."

Fanny was about to argue with me, but stopped herself. I knew she hated the sight of blood; nonetheless, Newt was borderline hysterical, and there was nobody else to call upon.

I heard eleven-year-old Darlene gallop away as I applied a compress to Emmer's wound. "I want something to kill the pain," he whined.

"We'd better wait for the doctor," I coaxed.

"No, goddamn it. Give me something now!" Reluctantly, I gave Emmer some essence of peppermint, but that didn't work. Soon after, he took a large dose of sweet oil, which also had no effect. He rolled from side to side as the pain increased.

"I can't stand it. I swear I'd rather you just cut off my damn arm!" Emmer pleaded. I relented, offering him spiked apple cider; he drained the jug. It came as a blessed relief to all when he finally passed out.

Two hours ticked by without any sign of Darlene or the doctor. Newt cried and fretted while she attempted to distract her children. Sheridan kept sneaking into the room; he'd tip-toe to the bed, climb into my lap, then put his arms around my neck with dramatic affection. Slowly, he'd turn to gaze at his father with the most pitiful look of concern. "Daddy fall down?" he'd whisper.

My godson grew suspicious each time I confirmed his question with coded double-meaning, "Uh-huh, Daddy tumbled *way down,* that's for sure."

Somebody rode into the yard, and I breathed a sigh of thankfulness—but Darlene had returned alone. "Doc's deliverin' a baby in Pinson," she announced. "Nobody knows when he's comin' back. His wife said it might be tomorrow before he gets here."

Emmer was perspiring with fever, and his body jerked with agonizing spasms. I glanced at Fanny, then spoke to Newt. "We can't leave him like this. I don't think it can wait; somebody's gotta cut the bullet out."

Fanny groaned, then put her head between her knees to keep from fainting. She sat up, squinted at me, and promised, "I won't go back on ya. You've my permission to slap me if you see that happenin'. Let's do what needs doin'."

As a team, Fanny and I barked orders at Newt and her oldest children. The bed was too soft for what we were about to do—what country folks called "hunting knife surgery." Emmer's family placed three long planks on top of the kitchen table while Fanny and I gathered iodine, a needle, and some of Newt's durable, scarlet quilting thread. I made a fire in the stove, then held some tweezers and the blade of a suitable knife over the flame.

We carefully lay Emmer, still in a drunken stupor, on the wooden boards. I poured the dark, iodine tincture into his open wound before dipping the tip of my knife into a bowl of the acrid antiseptic. On my signal, Newt took all of Emmer's children into another room.

"How are you gonna see what you're doin'?" Fanny questioned. "It's too dark to focus by the light of day and too light for candles."

"I'll manage. You just keep the blood soaked up with those rags. You ready?" I was hoarse with anxiety.

"Damn. I guess. Go ahead. Hack away." Fanny's voice was strong, and she held firm while we worked to save the life of our friend's husband.

I removed not only the bullet, but fragments of clothing as well. As I worked, Emmer's mumblings sounded mostly like feverish, jumbled nonsense. But they also held the essence of something notable. "No more. No horny-mouthed blisters. Lyin' spots on my tongue. Don't you insult my wife. A real man doesn't hide behind a sheet. You wanna take it outside? I'll fight. I'll…" Emmer passed out again.

While I sewed him up and dressed his wound with strips torn from a clean shirt, I thought about Emmer. He'd been knee-to-elbow deep in trouble since I'd known him, making one too many trips to Tin Top. I also suspected there was more to why Emmer was shot than he'd ever admit. Around town, Newt had been consistently bad-mouthed since the birth of her sons, when she'd openly flaunted her friendships with Egypt and Fawn. In my heart, I knew Emmer had defended his young wife in the only way he knew how. Maybe, when all was said and done, he truly loved her.

Darlene fetched Alton, and he took a turn sitting with the ailing man during the night. By the time the doctor arrived the next morning, our patient was sitting up. Newt lovingly spooned beet soup into Emmer's mouth as seven energetic youngsters entertained themselves by keeping stinging flies away from their father's sickroom.

Doc jokingly offered Fanny and me jobs as nurses. I'll never forget the look of gratitude on Newt's face, or the show of pride on Fanny's. As for me, self-perception shifted, ever so slightly, with the discovery of a new possibility. Perhaps I, like Badgerwoman and Rola Moon, could be a healer.

THIRTEEN

The late autumn air was brisk on the Sunday evening that found Fawn, Badgerwoman, and me having dinner in their little cabin. We'd dined on zucchini squash, kidney beans, and flatbread. Badgerwoman was serving apple fritters for dessert when we heard riders drawing near. We stepped onto the front porch, disbelieving our own eyes at first. In the Storms' yard, seven costumed men, like those who'd interrupted Sunday service at Old Bethlehem, sat upon their hooded horses. It was a surreal sight.

Revolvers hung from red belts sashed at the riders' waists. A patch had been sewn to the white sheet each man wore, approximating the heart; the panel was a white cross surrounded by a scarlet circle. The same blaring insignia appeared on the torsos of their horses; on the animals' flanks, one could see three menacing letters painted in red—KKK.

A whistle was blown from somewhere among them, and they formed a semicircle around the cabin. A wild dog, roaming nearby woods, answered the call of the whistle's high-pitched whine.

The horses snorted and tried to shake off the makeshift hoods as I addressed the men. "Who the Hell are you? What do you want?"

"We're true friends of hardworkin' people," came the deep, booming reply, a familiar voice. "We've come in answer to a call for action and Divine order. We're the Invisible Empire, the Knights of the Ku Klux Klan!"

A rebel yell echoed about the yard. The leader added, "Our fellowship rides across a broken South, raisin' up a dead Confederacy by spreadin' the Almighty's Holy Word that white Christians are the true Israelites of the Old Testament. They're pure and virtuous, God's chosen few!"

The spokesman for that band of hoodlums delivered his speech with ceremonial pomp, as though he were giving a king's proclamation. "This county must be cleansed of all coloreds, Negroes *and* Injuns. Therefore, you two standin' before us have forty-eight hours to be gone, or we'll burn you out! So says the Grand Dragon!"

A small cross, drenched with smelly kerosene, was pounded into the Storms' front yard, then set on fire. The blazing image struck me as bizarre; in the blink of an eye, a universal symbol for brotherly love had been converted into an emblem of hate.

By then, I'd heard and seen enough. I drew the gun Daddy had given me and fired over their heads. A younger voice yelled, "You can't shoot us—there's a law against it!"

"No, what *you're* doin' is a crime!" I furiously screeched.

There was taunting laughter among the masked mob until their bellwether spoke again. "Silence! Be still all of you! You will ride with respect for the Knights' Code, or I'll be damned if you'll ride at all!"

I shot in the air once more as they spirited away in double file. "Get out of here!" I screamed and spit and kicked. "And don't come back, or my aim will get better!" I was so mad my vision blurred with the defiant attempt I'd made to exorcise the demon riders from my sight.

The Storms, on the other hand, stood impassively by my side. Neither woman showed fear or anger. Instead, Badgerwoman spoke softly, her words shaded by placid tones, as though she were praying. "When Turtle Island was born, the Ancient Ones gave their council: 'Remember that you come from the place of the Seven Dancers.' The white man calls that piece of sky *Pleiades*. At its center stands the Great Tree of Peace. Every livin' person is bound to it by many roots."

Badgerwoman turned to Fawn and added, "Carry that truth for my great-grandchildren, unto seven generations. Someday, the sacred fire will also burn in the white man's heart."

Fawn nodded her promise.

Badgerwoman looked at me, and I seconded the motion. How-
ever, the only fire I could see right then was blazing in the front yard. "I
don't think y'all should stay here tonight," I announced. "Those no-
goods might come back. Let's ride to The Hill and talk to T.H."

Daddy wasn't home when we arrived; he'd been called away, doing
his best to calm things down. The Koo-Koo Klan, as I began calling
them, had carried on with their foolishness throughout Village Springs.
They'd "visited" the homes of several colored families, ordering them
to get out of town or else. Scared the bejeebers out of every man, woman,
and child they "crossed."

Daddy returned to The Hill, mad and frustrated. He'd learned
from a local judge that there was nothing to be done, law-wise. No
charges could be made, much less proven, since nobody was hurt, no
property destroyed, and no positive identifications could be made. It
was the beginning of profane, tense times for Pine Bluff County.

Mamau Maude talked Badgerwoman into moving to The Hill for
safety. Fawn and her granny gratefully settled into a guest cabin, across
the water from mine and Alton's.

We tried to keep to our normal lives after that, but the goal proved
impossible. Fewer colored families made their way to The Hill; despite
T.H.'s assurances of protection, they were fearful of Klan retaliation.
For those visitors who did come, Sheridan Resort remained a place to
relax, a needed oasis. Guest activities were more closely monitored than
before, but our customers liked the fact that T.H. guarded their back-
sides. At night, The Hill turned into an armed camp, patrolled and
protected by the extra men Daddy hired for that purpose.

From then on, whenever I looked at a male neighbor, I wondered
if he'd been in the Storms' yard, hiding under a sheet. The more I
learned about KKK philosophy, the less I understood; there was no
honor in their words or deeds.

However, I remained certain of one notable fact, the identity of
the Klan's local leader. The invader with the booming voice, the one
who had done all the talking in the Storms' yard, was none other than
Vigil Holt—Fanny and Grady's father, Mt. Hebron's preacher, the man
who'd baptized me seven years earlier.

✳   ✳   ✳

"I keep havin' the same nightmare; in it, I'm crossin' muddy waters. Every time I reach dry land, I'm swept into the stream again." My words bounced around Horseshoe Cave; it was our first gathering since the KKK's campaign to gain control of Village Springs.

"Ever since you told me that Daddy and Grady are mixed up with that bunch callin' itself a Brotherhood, I've been havin' bad dreams too," Fanny answered. "I fall off cliffs, crashin' on the rocks below. I clutch at ledges, grab at trees, but after feelin' the terror of tumblin', I die every time." She gave a shiver, then pulled her legs up close to herself, and gathered her body into a protected ball.

"I don't understand why they're doin' this," Fanny continued, her voice subdued. "I know Daddy and Grady can be mean. I haven't forgotten those nights I was locked in the shed, but there's good in Daddy. Grady, too. My brother's weakness has always been his parrot, the one he named 'Tennie C.' Not all the words he's taught that bird are repeatable in church, but he loves her." A slight grin appeared on Fanny's face. "I'll never forget how mad Daddy was when he came home one night, years ago. As he opened the door, Tennie C. screeched, 'Oh, Hell, here comes that damn preacher!' She must've heard Grady say that a few times."

Fanny loudly blew her nose. "Somehow, my father's won Grady over with this night-ridin' men's club." Fanny's tears flowed freely as she added, "Daddy is what's called a Primitive Baptist, believin' in God's Elect Family on earth—the only ones who'll be saved come Resurrection Day. Accordin' to him, I'm headed for Hell. He's disowned me before God in Heaven." Fanny's words made me shudder. She lay her head in my lap to cry.

For several long minutes nobody knew what to say. Finally, Egypt expressed what we all felt. "Lies buzz like flies. You just gotta wait your chance." Egypt pounded the cave's dirt floor for emphasis. "Then swat 'em."

The five of us soundlessly stared at the blaze of our fire for a time. I thought about the flames of Hades and what a surprise it'd be when certain persons found themselves there. "Most folks are walkin' human riddles," I murmured.

"When I lay down at night, everything goes black," Newt declared. "I'm so tired, I don't even turn over. But I *have* woken up once or twice, thinkin' a hood's been put over my head to smother me."

As the night progressed, we discovered that *all* of us were having trouble sleeping. When the talking stick passed to Fawn, she told of a recurring dream in which she observed a white buffalo pushing hard against a dam of large stones, placed in the river to prevent flooding. In her dream, the noble bovine struggles to keep the dam from crumbling. "The scary part comes when I watch that poor creature grow tired." Fawn shivered while hugging herself. "I jolt awake as Buffalo falls to his knees, because I know the flood's comin'. There's nothin' I can do to help him or stop it. I wake up with the sound of ragin' water still roarin' in my ears."

It didn't take a genius to detect the ominous nature of the visions we shared. When I returned home, I told Alton about the worrisome nightmares. My husband's sober response made the tiny hairs on the back of my neck rise up, ready for battle. "Pug, you and the others must be very careful from here on. You're up against everything those Klansmen stand for. Stay alert. Don't deny you've made troublesome enemies. Remember your daddy's motto: If you stick your head in the sand, best look behind you first; there's a good chance you'll get your butt kicked."

Stars continued to cross paths, and sometimes collide, as time swiftly passed. It felt like the world was holding its breath, waiting for something dark and inevitable.

Arious finished his studies at Johns Hopkins and returned to Alabama. His plans included permanently remaining in Village Springs as Doc Self's intern and eventually taking over his practice when his mentor decided the time was right.

Arious and Fawn came together with a magnetic compulsion that defied the laws of gravity. Their attraction was tangible; occasionally, I'd receive an electric shock while sitting between them. Alone, each existed in an emotionally secluded place, but together, they drew each other out. Like the secret ingredient of an alchemic recipe, their love affair changed each of them consummately.

Alton and I would stare in mute, bemused astonishment at the transformation we witnessed. Gone were the quiet, shyly reserved brother and "sister" we'd grown up with; they were utterly carried away by love.

One afternoon, at a church picnic social that the locals called an "All-Day Singin' and Dinner on the Ground," I asked Arious why he'd become a doctor.

"I wanted active learnin' that wasn't just about absorbin' facts and figures," he answered. "I realized early on that the world hasn't given a carefree promise to anyone. We have to help each other; there's no worse feelin' than powerlessness. To be honest, I guess I became a doctor out of sheer inadequacy."

"Maybe, that's why anybody does anything," I laughed.

"Except for those who'll carry your basket only because they want to see what's inside," Fawn chimed.

"He who *recognizes* sickness is the *true* physician," Alton joked with his brother. "The ministry stomps out disease before it spreads!"

"Who's called first to the sickbed, the doctor or the preacher?" Arious chuckled in retort.

"Dear husband, is this what you mean when you preach brotherly love?" I teased.

Fawn took advantage of the lighthearted moment and presented Arious with a cross-stitched wall hanging for his new office that read: *Every young doctor will succeed if he only has patients.* Contrite smiles rested on both brothers' faces after Fawn added, "Why do men, even the good ones, insist on havin' peein' contests? All you manage to do is kill any small creatures that happen to be in your watery way."

Alton raised one eyebrow and declared, "That's one wise lassie you've got there, Doc. Consider yourself lucky she'll have you."

Arious stayed rigidly silent, his face fire-red with irritation. Something hadn't set right, but it remained unclear who or what had stirred his anger. An awkward uneasiness hung in the air for the rest of that afternoon. It wasn't the first time I'd noticed a sudden shift in mood when my brother-in-law was around.

Over time, a nagging concern made its way to my mind, one I'd avoided putting into words. "What does Badgerwoman say about you and Arious?" I asked Fawn during one of our Sunday evenings together.

"She says I've never acted happier, not since I was a child." Fawn smiled as we huddled near the wood stove that sat in the front room of her cabin.

That night, Badgerwoman retired earlier than usual, subtly announcing she wasn't feeling well. I'd offered to fetch Arious, but the old Indian wouldn't hear of it. "These tired, old bones will feel better in the mornin'," she'd answered, turning toward her bedroom. Fawn and I decided we'd better stay nearby in case she needed anything.

Fawn poured hot cocoa into mugs. "I don't know what would've happened to me without my granny in this world," she murmured. "I have a hazy memory of Mama. When I think of her, she's standin' in a rickety old boat that floats away, farther and farther from the shore. I cry, but she only smiles and waves good-bye, like nothin's wrong. It's not as if my mother came up missin' one day; it's more like she slipped away in plain sight."

Fawn sipped her drink, then asked, "Have you ever had a bad cold you tried to ignore? Then, it wasn't until you got better that you realized just how bad you'd been feelin' all along?"

I nodded.

"That's how I feel, Pug. Bein' in love makes me realize how sad I've been most of my life."

My voice kept catching, forcing my words to sputter, squelching needed emphasis. "It's good to see you so happy. But, there's something we haven't talked about."

Fawn averted my gaze. She knew what I was getting at. Arious's jealous outbursts. His possessive nature was much in evidence. At a recent barn hoe-down on The Hill, he'd cut in tempestuously whenever another man tried to dance with her. Even Daddy and Finas were denied Fawn's kind attention. The scene served as fodder for gossip. When I'd approached Alton with my concern, he simply dismissed the issue, believing it would pass with time. I wasn't so sure.

Fawn gave a frustrated sigh. A stubborn strength suffused her forthright words. "In the beginnin', I thought he wanted to spend time alone with me purely for the sake of love, and that was partly true. Then, I decided that Arious feared KKK retribution toward us both, and that may still be true. But you're right, there's more to it. I can't even *look* at another man without him noticin'; he's even jealous of his own brother." When my friend glanced up at me, uncertainty showed in her eyes.

I nodded my sad understanding. "Go on," I murmured.

"Something happened, perhaps when he was small, that made him feel unworthy of love. But I know I can change that, give him his confidence back."

Was it ordained at the beginning of time that all women should believe such a thing? I wondered. Tactfully, I admonished, "Arious must choose to change himself. Otherwise, I'm afraid he'll break your heart."

"I can't lose him. I don't think I could bear it." A dam of emotion burst forth. Fawn's long-diverted tears began to wash her clean. "Think about it, Electra. There's already been so much pain, real sufferin'. Badgerwoman grieves for an entire tribe. She tells me she can hear the whispered sorrow from their Trail of Tears.

"The willows weep when the wretched sound passes through the darkness on windy nights. Sometimes, I hear it too. The worst pain is the guilt of bein' saved, of not dyin' with the others. That's an ache that never goes away. My family was spared the march simply because my mother was white, and the officer makin' the decisions thought that fact mattered. Love hasn't come easy for me 'cause I fear losin' what matters most. My love for you and Granny, that's made me strong enough to love Arious." My friend and I sat quietly after that. Together, we listened to the rustling branches of restless, melancholic willows.

✳ ✳ ✳

The emotional upheaval wrought by the Klan had caused my husband and me to postpone our honeymoon. We'd been married four months when Alton and I boarded the L&N for Mobile. We rented a cottage by the bay, within a stone's throw of gentle waters cradled by the Gulf of Mexico. When we weren't frolicking in the soothing wetness, we sat on the shore, basking in the sultry sunlight while reading aloud to each other.

Each morning, as he'd done since the day we'd married, Alton presented me with a sweetheart rose. How he was able to do this unfailingly was a mystery. He always woke before me, placing the fragrant blossom near my nose until its syrupy, sweet scent caused me to smile, then open my eyes. My husband would kiss me and gently lay the long-stemmed, sensuous flower upon my breast.

One day, while reading the *Mobile Herald*, Alton announced, "Look here, Pug, a woman named Bessie Stanley won $250 in an essay contest for answerin' a simple question."

"What riddle might that be?" I asked.

"The newspaper challenged its readers to describe what constitutes success. The winnin' entry is printed here on the front page." Alton drew out a dramatic pause.

"Well, read it to me!" I cried, feigning frustration.

"The winner wrote: 'He has achieved success who has lived well, laughed often, and loved much…who has left the world better than he found it, whether by an improved poppy, a perfect poem, or a rescued soul…whose life was an inspiration, whose memory a benediction.'" Mrs. Stanley had titled her piece, *Success;* it later became famous in the annals of American poetry.

The affecting words of the poem brought tears to my eyes. "Sounds like Bessie Stanley met you somewhere along the way," I said.

"I was thinkin' she must know my red-headed angel," Alton grinned. The moment was locked in time.

Alton believed in my gift for writing; his intent was to plant a seed, a spark of confidence. By pointing to the recognition of others, he hoped I'd find trust in my own talent…the faith that, someday, I too would be acknowledged for my words.

Later, I read to Alton from *The Housewife's Almanac.* The article was entitled, "A Recipe for Cooking a Husband." Alton recovered from acute spasms of laughter long enough to inquire, "Speakin' of cookin' husbands, and cookin' *for* husbands, I've been meanin' to ask why you always sing 'Nearer My God to Thee' whenever you boil our mornin' eggs?"

I looked sheepishly at my baffled mate before I replied, "Three verses for soft, five for hard."

During that blissful time, we had one significant spat. It involved a knotty, theological argument regarding the sex of God. "Why do all preachers see the Almighty as a man?" I'd demanded. "Why not a woman? Or a bird, for that matter. If God created the whole world and the stars, who's to say what the Divine looks like?"

My husband was clearly frustrated by this conversation. "Jesus taught that He was created in *The Father's* image. The Savior's words were plain and simple."

"Perhaps the Lord was speakin' in symbols," I countered. "Like poetry conveys an intangible feelin' for things there are no words for. The language of the wind. Plainsong with an ocean of meanin'. Interpretation is a different matter."

"Don't let your creative fancy flaw your faith in the Bible," my husband admonished. "The rich details are its truth. To see our Creator in any other way borders on blasphemy."

That's when we both got angry. "How can the desire to see the Divine reflected in my own body be a sin?" I was aware that my voice was rising in tone and volume. "Compassion and mercy are hallmarks of the Almighty *and* of the feminine creatures placed on this earth. That can't be a coincidence. My Creator has kneaded me like a loaf of bread. I'm tryin' to rise to the occasion in spite of the presumed shortcomin' of bein' a woman!"

Alton chuckled at my irreverent metaphor, and the tension between us eased. "My darlin' Pug, it's your passionate curiosity that St. Peter will be unable to resist when you stand before His Pearly Gate. Your shinin' spirit touches my heart in so many ways. To me, you're every woman that's kept a hearth, planted a garden, nursed the sick, or gazed at the moon. But sometimes, my dear wife, I worry for you. That your stubborn, fiery nature will lead you astray and prevent your spiritual needs from bein' met."

"We're livin' in a new century, Alton," I countered, my voice softening. "I'm not sayin' the Bible is wrong, or that Jesus was. But I've got this gnawin' feelin' that part of what the Lord said was left out, either wasn't recorded or wasn't passed on, for whatever reason. Especially regardin' women. It's a knowin' that reaches way down into my soul. I don't mean to insult you, or God, or anybody else. Maybe, all my questions can't be answered until I reach Heaven. But why can't I start askin' them now?"

After that, nothing more was said about the face of God. In fact, we consciously avoided the subject; it was a hot coal neither of us wanted to toss into the other's lap. The beauty of that particular evening was hypnotic; the ocean glowed green, as if lighted from below. We held hands and let the smell of the Gulf, along with our mutual affection, carry us forward until we found our way to bed. While the stars burned around us, we came together, bonded by the oneness of sanctified love. I thanked my Deity, whoever She might be, for the source of my delight, then pulled my lover to me once more.

On our last night in Mobile, I awakened with a start, drenched in cold sweat. My drowsy scream woke Alton; he held me until I found my voice. Trembling, I haltingly recounted the nightmare. "I was lost in an endless bluebonnet patch," I explained. "You were there, Alton. I sensed your presence; I could even hear your voice. But for the life of me, I *couldn't find you*. The bluebonnets were too tall to see over." Words eluded me after that; I sobbed like a small child.

Alton firmly grasped my shoulders, earnestly staring into my tear-stained face. Abruptly, he looked off into the distance. "I was havin' the same dream," he said.

My heart skipped a beat.

Turning back to me, my lover appeared overcome with bewilderment; his complexion had noticeably paled. "I could hear you callin', Pug, but I couldn't guess the direction. I was runnin' in circles tryin' to reach you. It was maddenin'."

"What do you think it means?" I managed to ask between nervous hiccups, trying not to sound worried.

Alton managed a reassuring smile. "I guess we're really married if we even dream together."

When we packed our bags for home, the cooling air twirled wildly across the water; tiny cyclones appeared, then vanished within moments. It was the last vestige of the fall season—when, according to Rola, supernatural forces held sway over the Earth.

FOURTEEN

W hen I told my mother about the shared dream mystery, she cocked her head and said, "I once heard a word that's never made sense until now. It was in a book of Celtic verses. *Soultwin.* People joke about spouses bein' each other's second half. It sounds like you and Alton really are."

"So, you don't think we're crazy, Mama?"

"Far from it. God has given you a marvelous, astonishin' gift. Count your blessin's." Mama's reassurance felt like a misty rain, soft and complete.

My mother also believed that one's sleep sense goes by contraries: "Dream of a funeral, hear of a weddin'. Dream of a death, wait for a birth, and vice versa." I didn't tell Mama, but I prayed she was wrong. I'd been dreaming of an awful lot of births.

Since moving to Boston, Ruby had religiously written to Seven Sisters from the College of Saint Rose, the Catholic women's school she attended. We cherished her letters and read them aloud at our meetings. That fall, we received one from her that was disturbing. Her letter began, "I guess you've heard the rumblings of war making their way across the country. It's the main topic of conversation in the city. Many are concerned that our boys will be called to fight and die in a foreign land. Granddaddy says war makes people crazy. Maybe that's why those hooded men are acting so queer and mean back home. I miss you and the others every day. Don't forget me…"

I soon discovered that Ruby was right; it would be a year of change—of loss and gain. Its tumultuous race was quickly run.

In early November, Alton and I traveled to a spirited gathering at the Holiness Church of the Brethren. I forced myself to attend, but I didn't like going. The favored practice of handling snakes as part of the Holiness worship service went against my God-given sensibilities.

The Brethren's leader, Brother Watkins, was barely five feet tall, but his size didn't detract from his charismatic charm; he had an exceptional ability for winning the devotion of large numbers of people.

Egypt, forever grateful to the pastor for finding her under his porch step, regularly attended his rebuilt church. That night, she planned to sing a solo part with the small choir; she'd invited Alton and me for support.

Egypt's alto voice was smooth and sweet as she sang the hymn's quick verses with energetic feeling. When her song ended, Egypt glanced in my direction. Alton and I had settled in the corner of the farthest back pew, as far away from the snakes as one could get. I nodded an approving grin. Egypt's face was one proud smile as she walked forward and sat in the front row.

Following brother Watkins' brief sermon, the narrow, brick sanctuary pulsed with animated music; some of the worshipers eagerly plucked their own guitars and banjos. Others danced and clapped to the hypnotic rhythm. There were those who wept and wailed, and even gnashed their teeth, as the excitement mounted. When the assembled flock had reached an impassioned frenzy, Alton and I watched with guarded interest as Brother Watkins opened a large, wooden box. On one side of the container, the words "IN JESUS' NAME" were printed with white paint. The preacher swiftly reached into the box and pulled out six rattlesnakes; they quickly slithered up his bare arms and around his body.

I'd seen Brother Watkins "take up" snakes before, and I could tell right away that something was wrong. The reptiles were extremely agitated, as was evident from their noisy rattles. Their heads moved differently than usual, snapping to and fro in a blur of rapid convulsions.

It was expected that, as he'd done hundreds of times, the pastor would immediately pass the snakes among the awaiting congregation.

But this time was decidedly different. He was clearly in a dire situation.

In the blink of an eye, Egypt was in the middle of that reptilian fog, fearlessly ripping snakes off Brother Watkins and throwing them to the floor. The vipers were united in their attack as they repeatedly bit the bewildered man; they struck at Egypt as she attempted to help him. Instinctively, I ran past the mute and shocked worshipers.

An unusually long rattler was tightly wrapped around the preacher's neck; another coiled stubbornly as it clung to his upper arm. Egypt held their heads firmly to keep them from biting while I uncoiled them. As each serpent was dropped to the floor, it curled itself into a protective ball.

In a matter of seconds, Egypt and I snatched the remaining creatures from Brother Watkins' body. Using the curved part of somebody's walking cane, Alton gingerly deposited them back into their box. The reptiles didn't struggle; their fighting nature had been spent.

I frantically examined Egypt to see if she'd been bitten, and she did the same for me. We were both spared, but the preacher had collapsed in front of his pulpit. He'd lost consciousness by the time we could attend to him.

Within a minute, Brother Watkins' face bloated and turned a frightening bluish color. Reflexive spasms seized his body, causing it to twitch all over. I counted nine bites on the preacher's arms and face. Punctures in his clothing indicated more on his stomach and back.

Alton yelled for a doctor, but the deacons of the church acted like he'd poured kerosene onto a smoldering fire. "Belief in God's mercy is the creed of the faithful, brother Alton! All doubt must be cast aside." As Deacon Stough spoke, he and a few others began the "laying on of hands" rite, thought by them to be the only prescription Brother Watkins needed to live.

"Without medical attention, this man will surely die!" Alton was furious.

The assembly ignored Alton and continued praying. I pressed my hand upon my husband's shoulder; the argument was a moot point. Brother Watkins was already good as dead. Alton realized it, too, as we helplessly watched the man's body slow its writhing agony.

For the pastor and his followers, there'd always been *one* church and a single set of doctrines to follow. The foundation of their faith was built on four particular books of the Bible: Matthew, Mark, Luke, and John. The Holiness sect adhered to strict guidelines interpreted from those scripts. One's true faith was proven by victory over fire, poison, snakes, or a combination thereof.

The minister's death was the first in three decades of snake handling, though many had been bitten over the years. One worshiper claimed he'd suffered over two hundred bites, but not all at one time. The anointed faithful either fully recovered to handle more snakes, or they changed faiths, one of the two.

Alton and I stayed with Brother Watkins' followers until the emotional upheaval died down; then, the preacher's body was wrapped in a blanket and taken, by wagon, to relatives.

By late evening, Alton, Egypt, and I were the only ones left in the somber house of worship. I glanced around to locate Egypt and, to my horror, spotted her peering into the crate containing the guilty serpents. She'd taken the lid off and was bending down dangerously close, within striking distance of their venomous fangs. "Egypt! What in the name of all that's Holy are you doin'?" I shrieked.

My friend stood perfectly still as she calmly gazed inside the box. "These snakes have holes in 'em." Egypt's words held no emotion; she was numb with grief. Brother Watkins had been like a father to her.

I decided that Egypt was out of her head with sorrow, unaccountable for words or deeds. "Alton," came my plea, "I can't get near any more serpents today. Close up the box. We'd best take Egypt home."

Alton put his arm around Egypt, gently pushing her down onto the nearest bench. As he moved to replace the crate lid, Alton suddenly stopped. My stomach nervously rumbled as I watched *him* lean perilously close to the rattlesnakes, examining them just as Egypt had done. "She's right," came Alton's surprise announcement. "Look here, Pug. These snakes have been stuck with something."

I inched my way toward the carton, stood behind my husband, and hesitantly peeked over his shoulder. The snakes looked exhausted; I don't know if snakes sleep, but they looked like they were united in peaceful slumber. This made me braver. I deliberately bent down until I could see what Alton and Egypt had noticed. Pinpricks, up and down scaly skin. The small holes were quite obvious between the snakes' markings. "Looks like they were poked with a hat pin," I whispered, afraid of waking the sleeping reptiles.

"What do you make of it?" Alton asked, perplexed.

"It beats all I've ever seen. Strange. I actually feel sorry for 'em," I answered, my words sincere.

When we arrived home, we told T.H. about the grisly death. "If you're right, this wasn't an accident," Daddy sighed. "Don't tell anyone about the evidence until I can look into it."

For the next two days, I ministered to Egypt, coaxing her to eat and taking her for walks. She and Essie cried piteously at the preacher's open-casket funeral. It didn't help that the corpse was unrecognizable as Brother Watkins. During the forty-eight hours it'd taken to prepare the burial, his body had turned into a grotesquely swollen mass of darkly discolored flesh.

As the pastor was lowered into his grave, I overheard two of his parishioners exchange words of faith. "Brother Watkins had a glorified look on his face when God called him home," said one.

Nodding agreement, the other replied, "I don't think there could be a better way to go."

After the post-funeral reception, I wrote in my journal, "Faith in immortality encourages belief in the right ritual, limited only by our imaginations." Then, I went to find Egypt; she hadn't attended the post-burial meal, and I was worried. I finally found her at the Brethren's church, diligently scrubbing the threshold.

I sat near my friend and waited for her to speak first. "I know this looks silly," Egypt began. "But some things are too important to leave to chance." Egypt explained her grim mission timidly, to help the preacher avoid becoming a ghost. "Granny says coffins are always carried out feet first so the dead person won't return. Washin' the exit is further insurance they can move on to be with Jesus."

After she'd finished swabbing the steps, Egypt and I walked along the river, gathering wildflowers. We took them to the cemetery and entwined the stems to form a wreath; Egypt lovingly laid the colorful garland on the fresh grave. "I wouldn't be here if it wasn't for you," she whispered to the dead clergyman. "Thank you for savin' my life."

Days later, it came as a surprise to everyone that Brother Watkins had left all his worldly goods to Egypt. This revelation fueled recurrent gossip that the preacher was her real father.

Though Egypt received a noteworthy inheritance from Brother Watkins, much more had been withheld. Three weeks after the preacher's funeral, Daddy asked Egypt, Essie, Alton, and me to join him and Mama in the library. A calming fire was burning in the hearth as the six of us settled ourselves.

T.H. seemed nervous, uncharacteristically tongue-tied. Mama nudged him, and he began to speak in short, deliberate sentences. "Egypt, hon, there's something you're old enough to know. You deserve the truth. Now that Brother Watkins is dead, there's no reason you shouldn't be told." Daddy hesitated, then continued. "When you were a baby, I set on findin' out who your parents were. Why you were…uh…that is…left at the church."

A chill passed through my father. Shivering, he moved closer to the fire. "My investigation led me in circles until, one week after you were found, Brother Watkins sought me out. He took me to the home of a widower white man named J.L. Youngblood. It was there that Brother Watkins told me about the gruesome find he'd made the day after he brought you here. Awful events had taken place at the Youngblood ranch. I hate havin' to describe the details to you. But, like I said, you deserve the truth."

I crossed the room and sat next to Egypt; she'd grown pale and was nervously fidgeting. My own heart was pounding in my chest, anticipating what was to come.

"J.L. had killed himself with his own shotgun," T.H. continued, his voice quivering. "Brother Watkins found another body floatin' in the pond behind J.L.'s house, that of a young colored man. Egypt…J.L. Youngblood was your granddaddy. The colored man, Ezra Rooker, was your father."

Egypt blinked, again and again, trying to absorb the vast implications of what she was hearing. She gripped my hand as though it remained her lifeline to all known truth.

Before anyone could speak, T.H. forged ahead. "You see, darlin', this is a sad but simple story. Ezra was a drifter, without family. He worked for J.L. as a ranch hand. Ezra fell in love with J.L.'s daughter, your mother. Her name was Ila Fay."

"My mother," came the soft words, the echo of Egypt's longing.

"Yes, darlin'," T.H. answered. "The Youngbloods kept to themselves. J.L. didn't care for social occasions. Most folks thought him a hermit. He had one close relative; his brother Hexter lived in Elkwood, near the Tennessee line."

Daddy held onto the hearth mantle for support as he took a couple of deep breaths. "Ezra and Ila Fay talked Brother Watkins into secretly marryin' them. They made the preacher promise to carry their secret to his grave. Your mama and daddy were savin' their pennies, with plans to move someplace up North where they could be together. But, before they'd saved enough, your mama got pregnant."

Tears the size of raindrops rolled down Egypt's cheeks, then splattered onto my arm. Her slender frame shook as she struggled to hear the rest. Daddy handed her a clean handkerchief, then sat at her feet. T.H. tenderly touched the top of Egypt's left foot as he said, "When Ila Fay refused to tell J.L. who the father of her child was, he kept her hid away at home. Nobody else ever knew she was pregnant…except Brother Watkins, whom Ezra secretly visited, askin' for guidance. The good reverend tried to help your folks get away before you were born. However, they miscalculated, and you came early.

"I'm sorry, Egypt, but your mama died right after your birth. When J.L. saw you, he put it all together. He went crazy. It's unclear what happened next. Perhaps Ezra tried to console him with the truth about the marriage."

Egypt pleaded with her eyes. Some part of her was asking Daddy to stop, but another part begged him to tell it all. T.H. was on the verge of tears himself. After a deep sigh, he told the worst of it. "J.L. went berserk with rage and grief. He buried your mama, then killed your daddy. That's when he carried you to the church."

Daddy's voice softened even more. "You know about that night, about bein' brought here. The fire was meant to destroy evidence, which was you. J.L. also wanted to kill his enemy, the preacher that aided his daughter's betrayal. Brother Watkins knew whose child you had to be. He went to the Youngblood place to confront J.L., but ended up buryin' his corpse instead, along with your father's. Then, the preacher came to me and confessed all.

"To protect you, I helped the reverend spread the word that J.L. and Ila Fay had died of the flux. It was an easy lie, even when your Great-Uncle Hexter showed up to claim his brother's estate. Since he was fond of whiskey and stayed drunk most of the time, Hexter was never suspicious of the story we told." T.H. paused before he added, "Unfortunately, there was no relative to look for Ezra. Except you."

Egypt sat still, stunned and mute, so I spoke for her. "Why haven't you told Egypt this before?"

"That question has many answers," T.H. whispered before choking up, overcome with emotion.

That's when Mama took over. She said, "Brother Watkins was a man of his word. He'd made a promise to take a secret to his grave. He was also concerned about how the truth would affect Egypt, should she learn it too soon." Mama sighed, then added, "I think the main reason was one Pastor Watkins never admitted. He was afraid Egypt would hate him for his part in the sad tragedy. Though he helped Ezra and Ila Fay all he could, he still felt responsible for their deaths. He carried that remorse to his."

T.H. knelt on one knee, proposing forgiveness. "We lied to protect you, hon. But, based on recent events, we can protect you best by divulgin' all. You see, there are bad people in this world. By understandin' that, you can stay out of harm's way."

Daddy looked at Essie. "I hope you're not mad at me for keepin' the secret from you, too."

Essie's smile was one of reassurance. "I'd already scryed it in my glass ball. I had all those dreams, you know, before my child came to me." Essie turned to Egypt. "I think it was your mama that visited me while I slept. All those nights, years ago. It was her vision that promised my cradle would rock with the innocent breath of a sweet child. Yes, it must've been your mama."

There was nothing more to say. Egypt buried her head in Essie's bosom. That was how Essie cushioned her grandchild's pain and heartfelt sobs. Then, she and I readied ourselves to walk Egypt home. As we stood to leave, Alton stayed silent. Like the rest of us, he'd been deeply moved by the poignancy of truth. My husband also understood that the news was keenly distressing to Egypt's mind. No words of comfort would've helped right then, not even from Alton, whom Egypt adored.

I helped Essie put Egypt to bed. My friend buried her head in the pillow, whimpering like a lost kitten. I picked up the book that lay on Egypt's bedside table; the biography was based on the life of a charismatic Negro evangelist, a woman. It was entitled *The Narrative of Sojourner*

Truth, with a preface by Harriet Beecher Stowe. In the most calming tone I could muster, I read aloud. "We must obey a supernatural call to travel up and down the land. There we'll find God's goodness, and the brotherhood of man…" Soon, Egypt quieted—then fell asleep.

It was very late, but Alton was waiting for me when I arrived home. Immediately, I lowered myself into his lap. "It had to be told sometime," he murmured, "but even in all that darkness, there was a miracle. *Egypt lived.* And, I believe Essie was given the gift of grace. Maybe, some people are more receptive to the mystical powers of God."

"I think I'd die of fright if I ever saw a vision," I said, my tone serious.

Alton began to tease me, but there was something odd about the way he did it. His ribbing carried an earnest undertone. "My darlin', grace is simply that state of bein' that transcends Heaven and Earth, by the favor of the Divine. Now, does that sound like something to fear?"

I shook my head, bemused and sleepy.

Later, I awoke during the night to find Alton gone from our bed. I shivered, fumbling for my robe. I found him in the living room, sitting quietly by himself in the dark. Alton was staring out the window into a starless night. He knew I was there, but said nothing for several seconds. I jumped, startled, when he finally said, "They killed him. I didn't want to believe it, but it must be true." Alton's voice trembled with emotion.

I abruptly sat down, shaking with dread and cold. "They?" I mumbled.

"The Klan. They threatened him, you know, when he refused to join. 'Our defense is of God; it is He who hath prepared the instruments of death.' Psalms 7:11. It was included in the letter."

"What letter?" I said, my voice full of fear and loathing.

"The letter Brother Watkins showed me a month ago." Alton's softly spoken words fell like a quiet thud. "The letter he and I *both* got."

✳ ✳ ✳

Alton and Brother Watkins, each in his own way, had avidly preached against the Klan and its vile doctrines from their pulpits. Their words held strong admonishments, warnings relating to the KKK's deceptive tenets and its claimed affiliation with "gospel truths."

T.H. confronted Vigil Holt, accusing him of being a ringleader and a murderer. But once again, he came home frustrated; strangely, Daddy was also perplexed. An excellent judge of character, my father had a sixth sense when it came to knowing if somebody was lying. He was certain that Reverend Holt was genuinely shocked to hear that criminals deliberately agitated the Holiness Church's rattlesnakes.

With the murder of the Holiness preacher, Alton changed. From then on, he waged his own contentious, personal campaign against the Klan's gross outrages, his crusade a vendetta. Daddy tried to settle him down, and so did I. For my husband to lambaste the Klan repeatedly was dangerous. Soon, Alton received a second letter, short and to the point: "Reverend Strawbridge, your name is before the Council, HEAVEN! We will attend to you. You shall not call us 'villains'—damn you. KU-KLUX"

Worshipers at the Elam-African Sunday night services in Pinson were regularly raided. The Ku-Klux carried a particular grudge against their plucky Negro preacher. The first time ruffians disrupted a service, Preacher Frazier reached under his pulpit, pulled out his pipe case, and shook it at them. The Klansmen broke down the doors trying to get out, thinking it was a gun. The incident remained the joke of the county for many days and, in the minds of the Klan, Reverend Frazier caused them to "lose face." They wouldn't soon forget such an embarrassment.

During the latest intrusion at Elam-African, several church leaders were rawly beaten while Reverend Frazier was pistol-whipped about the face. When he came to our door that same night, I didn't recognize the parson at first. He asked Alton and me to speak to T.H., to find out if anything could be done to protect his parishioners. "All we ask is to be allowed to pray freely," he said meekly.

Alton and I decided that Pastor Frazier should consult with T.H. himself. I walked to the main house and awakened my father. T.H. got out of bed, wearing only his long johns. He staggered to the bedroom window and flung it open; he stuck his head outside for several chilly seconds, muttering to himself. Daddy's hair stood crazily on end, blown by the heavy breeze, making him look somewhat deranged. Eventually, the frigid air awakened his senses and sobered him up. He dressed and found his way to the kitchen. Mama followed close behind.

After reviewing the preacher's story while examining his wounds, T.H. spoke for us all. "Has common decency and humanity been lost in the South? How about old-fashioned Christian civility?" The uncertainty in my father's voice surprised me; I'd never heard it there before. Mama laid her delicate hands upon her husband's broad shoulders. "Nothin's been lost," she tenderly replied. "It's been misplaced, but it's not lost. I know of no better man to find it and bring it home. That is, if respect, esteem, and earnestness count for anything."

Daddy gazed up at Mama and smiled. Then, he looked at Reverend Frazier, eyeball to eyeball. There was no doubt T.H. meant every word when he promised, "I swear to you I'll give this attack the weight it deserves. If the Ku-Klux doesn't hold its peace, Hell will be its portion."

Except for Daddy and his small band of deputies, there seemed to be no intention, or desire, by our community to bring the "blackguard" to justice. Fear played a part in this collective failing, but it was more than that. Many regular, upstanding citizens saw the Klan as outlaw heroes, affectionately viewed as former Confederate champions of the Civil War, decent people with the South's best interests in mind. The author of the southern way of life, proclaimed the Ku-Klux, was God Himself.

In other parts of Alabama and nearby states, the KKK was supported, and even joined, by many sworn to uphold the law; with their blessing, the Klan intensified its rampage. Word soon reached us from bordering regions.

I was near the sugar bin at Marsh's Grocery one frigid, gray day when talk turned to the Ku-Klux. Berna Loggins announced that she'd heard some news. She told us that southern schoolmarms who dared teach black children were subject to obscene pictures and narratives via the U.S. mail; some were forced to watch their schoolhouses burn.

As the gossip continued, I learned that "kluxing" helpless victims had other, baser forms of expression. There was even an official name for such depravity: "Dark Lantern Tactics." The scandal included blacks, Indians, and even sympathetic whites being brutally raped or castrated. Others were burned at the stake or lynched for trespassing on the patience of Klan leaders.

Some sort of sick excitement was present within those who eagerly related the stories of perverted behavior. Jacob Nabors energetically reported "on good authority" that a Georgian schoolteacher, a Yankee, had her clothing torn off by a group of Kluxers. They bound her wrists and ankles, poured warmed Karo syrup on her, then laid her naked body atop a huge, rounded nest of biting red ants. The vicious act drove her temporarily insane.

I desperately held onto the sugar barrel for several moments, then made my way outside. I vomited into a bed of winter gladiolas as my body shook from the inside out. I left my unpaid groceries and returned to the comforting warmth of my cabin. I sipped mint leaf tea and cried for people I'd never met. My tears fell into the earthen mug, creating a satisfying, salty broth. Mamau Maude had always taught, "Leave bad news where you find it," but this time the "daily telegraph" was impossible to ignore.

After the recent violence in Pinson, Daddy stepped up his detective work, setting out to learn about the dark-minded fraternity. He collected posters that'd been nailed to fences, doors, and trees, designed to intimidate and frighten. Interestingly, no such placards had been found in the vicinity of Rola Moon's place. I smiled with understanding; even the KKK was afraid of a *real* witch!

While patrolling the county, T.H. and his deputies watched for signs of the secret Klan handshake, made with the forefinger extended against the other's wrist, along with the covert gesture of recognition, achieved by sliding the right hand down the left lapel of one's coat.

Even so, the local band of the Ku-Klux eluded justice. After each unsolved incident, my father would pound his fists and roar, "The constitution *guarantees* the Negro shall not be denied protection! What's happenin' is a crime, damn it, a *Federal* one for Christ's sake! Congress better wake up and send us some help!" Daddy emptied many bottles of Kentucky Bourbon during those somber nights. He couldn't understand why multiple telegrams to the U.S. Attorney's office went unanswered.

As we neared the end of 1916, a movie titled *The Birth of a Nation* swept the country with unheard-of popularity. It extolled the "virtues" of the *Nightriders of the South*. The film was even shown in the White House with favorable response. After that, T.H. came to understand that our northern government believed the reported Klan atrocities were mere rumors and gossip, an over-reaction by those who transmitted claims and subsequently asked for help. Corrupt southern officials cleverly manipulated the truth, perpetuating the deception.

A small circle of trusted friends aided Daddy's uphill battle, including Alton and me. One starless night, my husband and I kept the owl's watch with the Frazier family at their home near Sulfur Springs. The KKK had left threatening, "final" notices at the gates of blacks across the county, including the Fraziers. Many chose to head for the safety of major northern cities, but others elected to stay. T.H. assigned volunteers to safeguard these households during the darkest hours.

While we visited, Reverend and Mrs. Frazier repeatedly thanked Alton; they acknowledged him for things I hadn't known he'd done. He'd given money to a Negro family forced to sell their only cow, worth one hundred dollars, for fifty cents during a terrifying KKK night raid; they bought another heifer with Alton's gift, providing their small children with needed milk.

Alton regularly tracked down books and supplies for the local black schoolhouse. Also, in his own remarkable way, he'd stopped countless fights between black children and white. One particular skirmish over a stolen watermelon had ended in a bawdy seed-spitting contest, the adversaries forced to laugh together in spite of themselves. Alton's positive effect on youngsters was obvious to everyone; teaching them came naturally.

Now, as we waited out the night, it was heart-wrenching to watch the brave Fraziers interact with their own little tikes. They soothed their brood with lighthearted games while masking the fear behind a mother's smile, a father's caress.

Our little group challenged the sluggish mantle clock, singing hymns and drinking rich, warm cider. Dorothy and John Frazier enjoyed teaching us old Negro gospels. I entertained the kids, young and old, with a humorous tale titled, "Two-Toed Tom." Alton held his own in a game of checkers, three against one, using Chinie-Berry beads as board pieces. By midnight, everybody under the age of twelve was tucked into bed and sound asleep.

At two A.M., without warning, the house sustained attack from the relentless pelting of large rocks; the resounding clamor upon the tin roof was enough to wake the dead. The sleeping children awoke, terrified. Alton motioned for everyone to stay inside before walking to the door.

Glancing at Reverend Frazier and his family, huddled in an unlit corner of the tiny farm house, I regretted letting Alton talk me into leaving my derringer at home. "If anything happens, the gun will only make it worse," he'd argued. Alton had made sense at the time, but now we were unarmed and surrounded, with the accursed fraternity waiting outside. As if he could read my mind, Alton assured me with a wink, "Don't forget, we have the Lord's brigade on our side." When my husband moved onto the porch, I followed.

There were eight of them, "haunts" atop their horses, more regimented than before. Signals for the movement of flanks were tooted on a pea whistle, four notes in all, the last one a long, low, pitiful wail. The misty night air carried another disquieting racket as well, eerie and unfamiliar, like the sound of bones rattling together; it made me shudder.

The Klansmen positioned their horses about the yard to form a wide half-moon. A snarling voice announced, "Behold! The far-piercin' eye of the Cyclops is upon you—flee the wrath to come!"

Alton stepped forward. "I see nothin' but a bunch of misguided men, sittin' on their tired horses, all dressed up in funny-lookin' clothes!"

Another voice cried out, "Step back, preacher. Our business isn't with you or your wife, nigger-lovers though you might be!"

A running commentary emanated from the ranks. "Hell, that wife of his was suckled at an amply-sized, black breast! I'll bet she shared a pacifier with that nigger girl of hers!"

I cleared my throat for a comeback but stopped when Alton shot me a fervid look. My husband's voice remained passive as he pleaded for reason. "How about you boys ride on and leave this family in peace. You're scarin' these little children half to death."

"We'll leave," came the response, "as soon as we find that black preacher's still. Vile whiskey is made and sold behind this house. The Devil's mistress peddles her debauchery in firewater such as that." This report was punctuated with sips taken from the various flasks that hung from saddles, canteens that no doubt contained inebriating grog.

Reverend Frazier stormed onto the porch, enraged, holding a large shovel. Alton tried to calm him, but there was no stopping the insulted man. "Liars!" John Frazier screamed. "You'll find no whiskey here. This is a God-fearin' home! Get off my land!"

"It's you, nigger, who'd better hightail it. You've stirred up enough trouble. You have forty-eight hours to get your black ass out of Village Springs!" came the returned shouts.

"You expect me just to pick up and abandon my church, my home, and twelve acres of cotton?"

A Ku-Klux answered the Reverend's question with a question. "How'd you like to see your length measured on the ground?"

Before Alton could stop him, John Frazier used his shovel to attack the goading Klansmen. The moment was exactly what they were waiting for. The Night Riders swung off their horses in a flash of white and grabbed the preacher from behind. His wife and children screamed as he was savagely pounded with raw fists.

Events happened very fast after that. When Alton attempted to free his friend, he was restrained by two Kluxers. Two more pounced onto the porch, eagerly manhandling me and Mrs. Frazier. I kicked and squirmed but couldn't get free. I felt a grimy hand grab my breast; furious and fearful, I bit the molester, hard, forcing my jaws into a vise. My captor cried out in pain, then savagely wrenched my arm while he continued to fondle my bosoms.

Alton shouted, "No! Leave her alone! If you want to harm somebody, let it be me. But please, for the love of God, leave the women alone!"

Orders were barked from somewhere in the scuffle. "Number Five, stop it!" (I'd noticed that the Klansmen referred to themselves with numbers to keep from revealing incriminating names.) My wrist was twisted painfully tighter, but the molesting stopped.

Before my disbelieving eyes, a shallow grave was dug, and the unconscious black preacher was thrown into it; they intended to bury him alive! As the hooded men covered the limp body with dirt, three more henchmen ripped Alton's shirt from his back and tied him to a hitching post. I panicked when I saw a whip removed from a nearby saddle. I intensified my fight with the brute that held me, but he covered my desperate pleas and shrieks with his sweaty palm.

Alton coolly stared into the foggy night, his demeanor serene, his flesh incorporeal, a mystical look in his eye. My lover communed with something great, something unseen, as each Klansman in his turn punished my husband with a single, ferocious lash.

The man that constrained me was relieved by another so that he, too, could strike a marking blow. The torture was shared; every member participated in the "entertainment." And the crime. Thus, brotherly loyalty was ensured within the Klan's den.

Alton offered them little satisfaction. His body flinched reflexively; otherwise, no reaction to the flogging showed on his face. He gave no sound, no cry for mercy. The Klansmen were angered, yet bewildered, by Alton's courage. I believe they were also frightened by it.

When the whipping was over, the Night Riders' leader stood in front of Alton and stared at him intently, not speaking. My husband slowly raised his head to meet his tormentor's gaze. With a voice as clear as crystal Alton said, "God will punish you, Vigil. He will condemn you *all!*" As if acknowledging a Divine decree, a bolt of brilliant lightening struck nearby; it was followed by the rhythmic beat of galloping steeds, headed our way.

Another clap of deafening thunder sounded as the cowardly Klansmen ran for their horses, just as the tree nearest their mares was cut in half by a second spear of penetrating light. All managed to mount and ride, save two. I watched as they frantically chased their horses into the gloomy woods.

Alton collapsed, and I ran to him. "No," he gasped. "Help John first."

Dorothy Frazier and her children remained too terrified to move; they stood frozen with shock as I grabbed the shovel, then dug as fast as I could. I gasped; the Reverend was wildly clawing his way out from inside his suffocating tomb.

T.H. and his deputies rode into the yard just as John Frazier sat up in his grave. All were struck speechless by the sight. During those few harrowing minutes, the buried preacher's hair had turned completely white, rendered the color of hoarfrost.

T.H. managed to catch the two men who'd lost their horses. Bevis and Clyde Walpole were neighbors my father knew well and had grown up with. They owned Preston's Granary, where we'd sold our surplus corn for decades. If Bevis and Clyde were involved with such degeneracy of spirit, *anybody* could be culpable.

Several "friends" came forward with alibis for the Walpoles, supporting the brothers' claim that they'd just discovered their stolen horses when they were apprehended; the matter never made it to court.

Within days, Reverend Frazier and his family packed their meager belongings onto a dilapidated wagon and headed for sanctuary among relatives in Missouri. Alton bought their farm for twice what it was worth, knowing how badly the money was needed. The raw stripes on his brother's back were diligently treated by Arious. It pained me to look at Alton's open wounds; his suffering was my own, but he stubbornly resisted any pampering. He also resented being called a hero by his parishioners.

On Thanksgiving Day, Alton preached a memorable sermon: "The Klan claims that its colors are mystical flags, white robes, shiny bugles, and polished swords. But, hatred is the greatest liar in the world. The *true* colors of the KKK are mud, filth, and blood." A stunned and rapt congregation listened to their young pastor describe what he'd witnessed upon Brother Watkins' death by snakebite. My husband dramatically revealed the pattern of threatening letters, leaving nothing out. Alton concluded, "I truly believe a black-hearted master is served by the Klan, a Spirit of Evil so malevolent I will not speak his name in this Holy place. Think on this as you gather with your dear ones and give thanks to God today."

After the service ended, I was in a quandary. "How can I be so angry, yet proud of you at the same time?" I declared as Alton guided our buggy toward Thanksgiving dinner at my parents' home. "What you said today was like wavin' a red flag in front of a bull." I trembled with fear and dismay. "You've accused the Ku-Klux of bein' in league with the Devil, blind followers of Satan! You've signed your own death warrant!"

"Somebody has to take a stand, Pug, no matter the risk!" Alton yelled back. "God knows I've done what's right."

It was a serious argument. After our shouting match, we journeyed in vexed silence, riding past numerous flower gardens tended by poor black women. Even as the petals withered, the rich hues drew the eye; the softly-colored blooms cast their spell and cooled my anger. I said, "I love you, Alton. I don't want to lose you." I was awash in an emotional wave of sentiment.

A winsome smile crossed my husband's face as he guided the buggy to the side of the road, took me in his arms, and kissed me. "It's far and away what God sends," he whispered, "and He fits the back to the burden."

"You're beginnin' to sound like my uncle," I replied as he snapped the reins and steered us forward.

Once on The Hill, we left worry at the door. Uncle Finas made the traditional Thanksgiving proclamation while chewing on a fat drumstick. "If the fowl bone be thick, so will the winter be. If the turkey bone be thin, so will Mr. Frost."

Whereupon Azberry answered, "If a cuckoo sits on a bare thorn, you may sell your cow and buy some corn. But if she sits on a green bough, you may sell your corn and buy a cow." Amusingly, my brother and uncle went back and forth, exchanging their favorite seasonal ditties for several minutes. As I piled my plate high, I decided their silly verses made the holiday official.

The party died down in the late afternoon, stuffed and spent. Before Badgerwoman meandered the few paces to her cabin, Maude offered another medicine to treat the old Indian's persistent cough; with a grateful nod, the Cherokee elder accepted the little jar of syrup.

Alton was expected to solo preach that evening's service at Old Bethlehem. The citizens of Village Springs took the words "Thanksgiving Day" to heart, treating the holiday as if it were an extra Sunday in the Calendar year. While escorting Alton to his horse, I noticed the moon was already in the sky; there was a dim, but distinct, orange ring around its outermost edge.

Fawn and Arious were following a few steps behind us. "I've heard that's a sign the world's about to end," said Fawn, pointing to the hazy orb, suspended among the clouds like a faintly lit beacon.

"Don't let Finas hear you say that," Alton jokingly chided.

The two brothers planned to ride together partway, then separate at the first fork in the road. Fawn and I kissed them good-bye, waving in unison as their horses trotted away.

Suddenly, I glimpsed a smoky light around Alton—like fine, glowing lace. I squinted, but when I focused again, it was still there. Like the moon, my paragon was enveloped in a translucent mist. I watched his departure until I could no longer see him. "The sun's playin' tricks on my eyes," I murmured, panting for air.

Fawn looked into the distance, concentrating hard, searching for something too far away to see. The temperature was unusually warm, at least seventy degrees, and I was having trouble breathing. My wheezing gasps rang in my ears; the air smelled musty, heavy with humidity.

Fawn nudged me onto soft grass, conjuring reassuring words until the smothering spell passed. After I'd composed myself, she cautiously remarked, "I've never seen a November day like this. There's a greenish look to the sky, and the clouds are hangin' real low."

"Heaven does seem close up," I mumbled, still feeling dazed as we walked to Fawn's cabin. When we arrived, Badgerwoman was resting in her rocker. She sat dead-still with her eyes open, listening to inaudible voices.

"She's havin' a tappin'," Fawn whispered.

An hour passed before Badgerwoman spoke. "The sky spirits are restless." A look of compassion came over the old woman's face as she gazed into my eyes and added, "Nothin' more needs tellin'."

"Is it a storm?" I asked.

She nodded.

"A bad one?"

Another nod.

"Oh my God! We've got to get everybody to the pit." Then, I remembered. "Alton. I've got to go after him!"

Fawn and her grandmother exchanged a glance. "There's no time," Fawn said, her tone gentle but firm. "Those at the church will find their own cover."

The tornado came from the southwest, turning counter-clockwise. There was a deafeningly-quiet, powerless lull as we watched the monstrous funnel move closer.

Everybody made it to the storm pit, except Finas. We couldn't find him in the house or the yard. Sara didn't want to give up the search, but Daddy forced her into the cellar. She loudly wept, repeating her husband's name. I knew how she felt; I squeezed Sara's hand.

The twister arrived with a roar and an enormous amount of water; its hum sounded like a hundred freight trains.

My family stayed secure in our man-made shelter, an artificial womb built into the hillside, waiting for the storm to roll over us. We seated ourselves on discarded railroad crossties, rough and damp.

"This one looks like it'll blow on quick enough; no need to fret. Shouldn't last as long as last year's barrage…probably won't even touch down." T.H. spoke rambling words of reassurance, sounding uncertain, even desperate. The rest of us nodded in unison, a blessing upon Daddy's assessment of the situation; all except Badgerwoman.

In the unsteady light of the flickering kerosene lamp, I could see that a bullbat fluttered in a far corner. As guarded wings stirred stale air, my nerves were stretched to the breaking point. Uncle Finas was missing. I wanted to be with Alton. My imagination worked overtime as I worried about what might be happening outside. A growly kind of warble began deep within my gullet as I fought the urge to scream.

FIFTEEN

Hail the size of walnuts covered the ground when our little group tentatively emerged from the shadowy safety of our storm cellar. Within minutes, the tornado had cut its path, a half mile wide and ten miles long. The Hill's main structures had been spared damage, but part of the barn's roof was gone. We heard a man's panicky yell coming from the orchard, begging for help. "That's Finas!" Sara hollered, her voice hoarse with fear.

When we finally found my uncle, we couldn't believe our eyes. He'd been awkwardly trapped in the outhouse when the swift storm struck. The potent winds had launched the little pine building, and it gleefully sailed hither and yon. After a hard, hasty landing, the privy precariously perched itself within the sturdy limbs of a large crabapple tree. Indeed, an impressive sight to behold!

Stunned, my speechless family clustered beneath the oval-shaped hole at the structure's rear side; blue sky shone straight through the opening of the toilet's wooden seat. As we slowly traced a tiny circle to the outbuilding's front door, I made a mental note to title my next rhymed verse, "Latrines and Flying Machines."

Finas rapidly lost patience with our dumbfoundedness. "Get me down from here, T.H.! Dab-blast it all to Hell! I barely got my pants pulled up when me and this stinkin' thing went sailin' off. Rose up like an accursed kite!"

Our reflexive snickers were barely suppressed, a response that set Finas into a fury. "Stop laughin' damn you; climb up here and help me down!" As Finas howled, his torso flailed wildly while he daftly gestured with both arms and his one good leg.

Daddy stopped chuckling long enough to say, "Sit tight brother while I go hunt a ladder."

Tolling bells at Mt. Hebron and the Holiness Church began their urgent call. Everybody within hearing distance knew someone needed immediate help. An alarming realization struck me as I instinctively ran for my horse. "The bells aren't ringin' at Old Bethlehem!" I yelled, panic-stricken.

As I headed down the road, Fawn and her mare were right behind me. From atop the hill, I heard Mama call out, "Tell Alton we'll gather some supplies and meet you there!"

As we rode, the dreadful scene unfolded around us like successive, nightmarish photographs. Huge sections of land had been torn open. The earth sacrificed hundred-year-old oaks to the coiling twister. The trees lay on their sides; the upturned roots looked like skeletal claws pleading for mercy. To control my fear, I focused on riding fast and straight. When we reached the site of Old Bethlehem, dismay gave way to dread. The church was gone.

"Oh my God. Dear Jesus, *no!*" My own jagged, terrified screams echoed around me. "Alton!" I scanned the desolate scene, but couldn't spot him.

Bodies lay everywhere, some alive, some not. Those that survived were hurt badly. I knew them all and wanted to comfort those that lived, but any rational capacity left within me focused its unyielding beam on the search for my husband. "Lie still, darlin', I'll find you!" I repeatedly yelled. I blinked hard, fighting the persistent dizziness that clouded my vision.

In a moment of clarity, I turned to Fawn. "Go get Arious! Bring him back, as fast as you can, with every medical tool he has! And send word to Doc Self."

Fawn stubbornly shook her head. "No. I'm gonna help you find Alton first," she argued.

"I'll find him by myself. Look around! We need help! Please go, Calaeno," I wailed, begging. "I'll be all right. Hurry!"

Fawn turned her horse, looked back at me sadly, then galloped away. Shakily, I slid off my skittish stallion to explore the horrific sight before me more carefully. Numerous people were trapped in the structure's rubble; others had been thrown a fair distance away. They looked like rag dolls, tossed aside on the playground. Despite their pleading moans, I couldn't stop moving until I found Alton.

My miserable search ended in the same place I first saw him. My true love had been thrown into the wall of the Amen Corner. The rich, coffee-colored panel now lay on its side, its boards torn asunder, but recognizable. Mahogany lasts forever, you know.

Alton was tautly pressed, unmoving, beneath the heavy hardwood. With strength I didn't know I possessed, I lifted the massive weight off him. Whimpering sounds escaped my lips as I gently cradled my husband's head. There was a bluish bump along his hairline that subtly distorted his facial features. No other injury was evident, but I knew that Alton was dead. The realization deprived me of any anchor that might moor me to sanity.

For a time, stunned and completely immobilized by grief, I remained a desolate statue. I don't know how long I sat with my husband, oblivious to life, before a baby's piteous cry drew my attention. Finally, instinct overtook my body, isolating my mind the way an abscess walls itself off, inflamed while teeming with agitated tenderness.

Nearby, a two-year-old child lay atop some splintered planks; her tiny left arm was broken, snapped like a twig. I recognized the little girl as Winona Crenshaw. The bewildered toddler was in pain and shivering with cold.

I covered my husband's body with my tunic, then kissed him for the last time. Sobbing, I pulled the prayer cloth from beneath the toppled pulpit and somehow managed to wrap it around Winona. She was crying for her mother; I tried to soothe the babe with gentle words, but when I opened my mouth to speak, no sound came forth. Every time I tried to talk, my windpipe closed up, choking off air. Ultimately, Winona and I shared a mutual, unspoken yearning. The child frantically clung to me as we walked from body to body, listening and feeling for life.

We made a quick search for Winona's mother, but didn't find her. The toddler's deep, rapid breathing broke the eerie, unearthly quiet. Trance-like, we drifted with ethereal breezes, as if in a slow-motion dream. Baby Winona and I walked in shadows until I felt the child purposefully lifted from my arms. It was Mama; she patiently passed Winona to Fawn, then cradled me while I convulsed with soundless sobs. When my weeping was spent, my mother carefully propped my limp form against a tree and covered me with a blanket.

Someone took my cold hands into his own; it was Arious. Behind his gaze lay positive proof that sorrow is supped from a humble spoon. Gradually, the familiar Strawbridge stoicism re-emerged. Arious stood and wiped his tears, veiling his sadness long enough to help those in dire need of a healer.

There'd been fifty people at the service; twenty-nine were confirmed dead. Daddy worked among those who pulled tumbled concrete and storm-blown debris off the living. Many were impaled with long nails, as though they'd been crucified. Some cried for Jesus; others simply cried.

I was swept along by the ghastly current of images. Mellie Gafford had been scalped by a tree branch, yet she lived. The sight of Doc Self sewing her back together was the most gruesome thing I'd ever seen. The wind blew Mellie's fine, strawberry-blond hair in pretty patterns as he stitched. For Mellie and the rest of the injured congregation, pain was eased with skullcap tea or sage wine. When she found time, Egypt brought me some of both.

Arious applied poultices of spirit turpentine and brown sugar to stop bleeding. Badgerwoman used, among other things, pine resin or a mixture of chimney soot and lard. I watched as the Cherokee healer pulled a spiderweb from her medicine bundle and laid it across a gaping wound. "Spiders bring good luck," she informed her patient with absolute certainty.

Sometimes, the claw end of a hammer had to be used to pull out a nail or piece of wood before the wound could be cleansed of infection. The punctures were treated with wool rags smoked in a kerosene flame. Small billowy clouds carried accidental messages to God. Born by the wind, the primitive smoke signals conveyed primal pleas for mercy.

Using axes, countless men tirelessly cleared the roads, so that the wounded could be transported to their homes. Periodically, a family member would arrive on the scene and ask about a loved one. Bad news was met with another anguished wail; it was a language that was spoken for five mortal hours.

Baby Winona ran to me when Arious tried to set her fractured bone. She'd permit no other person to hold her while he worked. The child fell asleep on my lap as Arious splinted the petite arm, then cast it with a mixture of red clay and water, finally securing it with a white satin, gossamer sling.

Soon after, Bernard Crenshaw came to take his daughter home; her mother had been confirmed dead. Winona's father wept as he tried to lift his only child, stubbornly enfolded across my bosom. When he fell to his knees with anguished grief, Winona fiercely clung to me with her one good arm around my neck, screaming, "Mama! Mama!"

I resolutely carried the hysterical child to her father's buggy and sat down. Fawn came along on the ride to the Crenshaw home, and Daddy followed behind with extra horses. With delicate care, I placed Winona in her warm bed, staying near her until she fell asleep. When I stood to leave, I kissed Winona's forehead as her mother might have done.

When I tried to walk, I found I could not, so Daddy carried me to my horse. Numbly, I returned to the blessed peacefulness of my old room at Sheridan House. Fawn and Egypt stayed with me; for many days, they kept constant watch, attending to my basic needs while exchanging troubled, knowing looks. My friends intuitively knew that woeful sorrow edged out the appropriateness of words in my presence. During that wretched week, whenever they were near me, they merely hummed. Most of their songs were velvety tunes I didn't recall hearing before, born of loyal constancy and soulful need.

Alton's burial was held at the Holiness Church of the Brethren. Mourners overflowed to the outside. I'm sure it was the hardest liturgy Reverend Tidbow ever gave; his associate pastor was like a son to him. With his final words, Reverend Tidbow made eye contact with me. "We are forever changed by knowin' him. His loss has left us seized and shaken. But in truth, our loved one has merely traded this world for another. The time will come when we'll see him again."

I nodded to the minister, my old friend. His words told me that he understood what was impossible to express fully. Alton had become my lifeblood's essence; no deeper or more essential part of myself could fate have found to pilfer. He'd been my compass, my raft, and my oar. When my husband's coffin was lowered into the ground, a part of me went with him. Sullen, and still unbelieving, I gazed at the words Finas had carved into my husband's tombstone: *His Life Was An Inspiration, His Memory A Benediction.*

✳ ✳ ✳

Upon returning to live in the house I'd shared with Alton, I recovered my voice. But I dreaded the evenings, the coming darkness. Nightly, I began to sleepwalk, my response to a recurring nightmare, identical to the shared dream that had revealed itself on my honeymoon: Over and over, Alton was lost to me as I frantically searched across an infinite, bluish maze of blossoms. My picturesque Hell was a bluebonnet field. I always awoke calling my sweetheart's name, fiery tears stroking my cheeks.

I suspected that Rola Moon was routinely surveying my cabin. Upon waking in nearby woods, I often found myself with her. The witch would patiently escort me back home, then securely tuck me into bed. When I visited her during daylight hours, my self-appointed guardian would suggest ways to cure my unwanted, nightly strolls. "Straw magic is what you need," Rola announced one sunless, dusky afternoon. "A hay-filled mattress will hold you in place." She threw a reed-thin piece of dry straw into the wind for emphasis.

When that promised antidote didn't work, Rola insisted I rearrange the positioning of my bed, sleeping with my head to the magnetic North and my feet to the galvanized South. "Strong currents rush through the earth," she whispered, as if telling a treasured secret. "They're good for eliminatin' impurities."

Three days later, the hapless witch found me at midnight, roaming Mama's overgrown flower garden in a restless sleep. I shivered in the cold as I listened to Rola's exasperated pronouncement. "I know just one more thing to try."

My witch-friend walked me home and watched silently as I crawled into bed. Then, Rola tied double-looped crochet string to my heavy clothes iron, placing it on the cold floor; she tied the other end of the slap-dash cord to my wrist, securing it with an impressive sailor's knot. I never walked in my sleep again after that, but the nightmare—the bluebonnet patch—continued to plague me.

My mood remained melancholic and self-absorbed. I wore my heart on my sleeve and I felt physically ill, especially during the wee hours of morning. I wasn't good company, even at Seven Sisters meetings. It didn't help that the main topic of conversation at our gatherings centered around tornado tales. News of our local disaster had made the front page of several big-city papers.

I listened to my friends' stories, told again and again, but said nothing until an evening in mid-December. With a taut and icy voice, I abruptly announced, "I've got a riddle. One you should all memorize."

"Tell us," my sisters answered in unison, surprised but pleased by the rare interlude to my sullen withdrawal.

As I spoke, I tasted anger, hot and acrid upon my tongue:

> Ever eating, never cloying,
> All devouring, all destroying.
> Never finding full repast,
> 'Til I eat the world at last.

Suddenly, I lost my battle with deep-rooted rage as wrathful tears threatened to drown me. "Forget it. I've gotta get out of here," I moaned through my fury, though I had no idea where I was going.

When I climbed out of the cave, I heard someone follow me. Then I heard Fawn say, "No Egypt, let her be. She needs time alone." Relief passed through me. Fawn was right. Fervent grieving requires privacy. A swaying division of spirit threatened to blacken my heart; its pace was keen.

After running, stumbling, and falling for more than an hour, I was there. I stood over Alton's fresh grave and wailed like a banshee. It was the first time since his death that the anguished veil was fully lifted. Denial gave way to the tormented suffering of one lost in despair. I clawed the earth like a madwoman, desperately searching for a way into his muddy tomb. I wanted to be with my love again, to feel his body, to reassure myself he'd lived, to have proof that what I'd lost was real. At that moment, my single desire was to join him where he lay.

Kindred to an animal whose jaws do not release its prey until its quarry has lost consciousness from the pain, bereavement seizes the soul with undisguised wretchedness. It compresses its raw grip until a miserable cry can be heard in the wilderness; only then can the healing begin. Eventually, exhaustion overtook me, and I collapsed to the ground to empty my tears, securely burrowed into the depression I'd hollowed out of the graveyard mire. Sometime later, I returned to Horseshoe Cave.

"We should've known all our silly talk was upsettin' you," Newt cooed.

"You don't need to go somewhere else; you can cry right here with us." Fanny's tone was sweet and maternal.

"Are you all right?" Egypt and Fawn asked in unison, searching the spent core of me with their insistent stares.

My silence was their answer; my friends' own, determined quietude echoed back at me.

Nobody knew what to say or do next. With attentive thoughtfulness, Fawn laid out the materials she'd brought to teach us basketry. Split reed, willow, corn shucks, grasses, pine needles, and white oak covered the cave floor. Seven Sisters planned to use our workmanship to transport everything from eggs and seeds, to babies and firewood. As we plaited or coiled our chosen material, somber feelings became part of the weave.

"After losin' Alton, it's hard to care about anything," I said, forcing the words out of some inner, twisted confine. "Like I no longer matter, like nothin' does."

Egypt placed her hand on my shoulder. "Findin' out how my parents died was like losin' them all over again. I never knew 'em, but that didn't stop my love, or theirs. I now know I can't give up on livin'. And neither can you. Alton would want you to stay strong, to carry on. I'm sure of *that*."

Newt added, "Egypt's right, Pug. No man ever loved a woman more."

Fanny's soft words echoed about the cavern. "Sometimes, faith in love can be taken. Like a thief in the night, it's stolen to a place that's hard to find. What's happened to Pug isn't fair. Nothin' can change that."

My raw hands bled, staining my basketwork as I pushed my cross-grained feelings upward. "I feel guilty for not bein' with him when he passed over," I said. "Alton loved me. But it didn't matter. He left anyway. He chose God over me. He's gone. I cry. I beg for it not to be true. But nothin' changes. He stays in Heaven with his precious Lord." I dug my broken nails deeper into the earthen floor.

Fawn finally spoke, "No Pug, you're wrong. He didn't choose one over the other. Destiny chose *him*. Alton met his unhappy fate bravely. You couldn't ask more of him than that. You're bein' too hard on Alton. And yourself."

I nodded. But it was still a struggle to breathe. As the five of us said good-bye to each other, Newt nudged me. "Pug, you can't leave without tellin' us the answer."

"The answer?" I'd forgotten.

"The endin' to your riddle," came Fawn's gentle reminder.

"Oh yeah," I choked. "All devourin', all destroyin'—the word is *time*."

When we reached my cabin, Fawn hesitated before walking toward her cottage. She started to say something, then changed her mind, slipping soundlessly into the night. Fawn must have stayed awake until dawn to complete the embroidered pillow she left on my doorstep the next morning. White thread formed the even-handed words, sewn upon a black background: *Time Leaves Sweet Memories.*

* * *

The next evening, I made my way to Arious's house, where he and Fawn waited dinner for me. The coziness of a simple meal, set beside a brilliant fire, helped winter become a bonding time. Even so, as alluring as they found each other, Fawn and Arious struggled with the subtle symmetry of love. He was the hard-working perfectionist, deemed infallible by most acquaintances. However, Arious was also like his father, a man readily disappointed by any moral lapse in those around him. His Cherokee valentine was a more humble giver, a virtue contrasted by a seductively willful nature.

As lovers, that which kept them from unmitigated intimacy could be summed up with a single word: pride. A thorn, a hound's tooth, a proud word—it's said that these are the three sharpest things. Sometimes, Fawn and Arious pricked each other with bloody sentences. On that winter's eve, the dialectic involved the advantages of scientific versus traditional knowledge.

"The power of the *healer* is most important," Fawn insisted. "A strong medicine woman can hear across centuries, rememberin' what works and what doesn't."

"No, my darlin'. Science holds the *real* power to change lives with new medicines and advanced biology," Arious countered. "Studies are comin' about that prove the necessity of balancin' the blood. How many hoodoo doctors know that?"

Oh God, I thought, *he's thrown down the gauntlet now.*

Fawn took a deep breath. "How about the balance between good and evil forces?" She knew her words were a challenge to an old argument.

"You can't categorize illness accordin' to natural or unnatural causes," the doctor scoffed. "The existence of disembodied spirits, degenerate or otherwise, has yet to be proven. Even then, I'd have to see evidence with my own eyes to believe such nonsense."

"Granny says there are unseen specters that affect the body as well as the mind. They're as real as you or me." Fawn's face turned bright red, flinching with the backwash of righteous indignation.

"As usual, you're both right," I sighed. "I've seen Badgerwoman confer with phantoms only she could see or hear. They told her the tornado was comin'." I looked at Fawn before I conceded what had never been openly acknowledged. "Somehow, those same spirits knew that Alton was goin' to die that day." I took a measured breath. "Arious, you also have a point. We're enterin' an era in which any healer can combine new remedies with traditional roots."

The deadlocked lovers' quarrel ended when I impatiently added, "No physician or sorceress, no medicine or herb, can cure death. Each of you has a lot to teach the other, if you'll only listen."

* * *

Christmas arrived the following week, and I dreaded its coming. Like Scrooge, I wanted to cancel all festivities. The prospect of facing the new year without Alton added to my sinking cheerlessness. For weeks, Azberry had hinted that my Christmas present would be a happy surprise, but I didn't believe any gift would bring me pleasure.

On Christmas morning, there was a knock at my door. I opened it to find Seven Sisters standing there with silly grins. My extended family joined them, all crowded together on my little porch. Nobody said a word. They were hiding something behind their bunched-up gaggle of bodies. One by one, each person moved aside so that I could see my present.

"Merry Christmas," said a familiar voice, one I hadn't heard in a very long time. It was Ruby. I couldn't speak; I could only weep. My emotions were a jumbled mess. So much had happened since Ruby went away. Entire worlds had been divinely created and destroyed during her absence. Because of her university studies, Ruby hadn't attended my wedding or Alton's funeral. As my old friend embraced me, the soft squeeze expanded into a rollicking group hug. Even T.H. was drying his eyes when the corny scene was over.

My family returned to Sheridan House to prepare the holiday meal while Seven Sisters gathered in my comfy cabin for coffee and flapjacks. For me, the reunion was a dream come true. Everything seemed clearer when Seven Sisters were all together, whole and complete, with Violet's memory safeguarded.

"Who would've thought our little sorority would last this long?" Ruby said after the excitement died down.

"I did," answered Newt.

"Me too," chirped Egypt.

"I think fate brought us together," said Ruby. "Divine Providence. I've got a big announcement in that regard. I want my sisters to be the first ones to know." Anticipation filled the room. I braced myself. Something about her pert manner gave me pause, made me realize a profoundly changed Ruby had returned to us.

"Well, tell us!" cried Fanny. "The suspense is killin' me."

Ruby took a deep breath, then blurted out her news. "I'm gonna be a bride of Christ."

You could've heard a pin drop in that animated room. Sunlight met swirling air to form illusive dust bunnies that danced around us like fairies perfecting pirouettes. Silent confusion reigned.

Egypt spoke for all when she said, "I don't understand. You're gonna marry Jesus?"

"In a way," Ruby giggled. "I'm gonna be a nun."

One by one, jaws dropped. Nobody knew what to say.

"Aren't you pleased for me?" Ruby's voice reflected her heightened nervousness.

"Of course," I finally managed to say. "We all want what makes you happy. You'll have to give us time to get used to the idea, though, to sort out what it means."

Fawn was the savior of the day. She took Ruby's hand and said, "It means she's found her callin'."

We took turns congratulating our faithful friend, but I felt off-balance. I babbled, stuttering like a young child until, mercifully, the excitement of the holiday carried us further forward. When Finas and Sara came to summon us to Sheridan House, relief washed over me.

The holiday dinner was served in the formal dining hall; all three crystal chandeliers glowed with candle flame. The table sparkled with engraved silver and gold-plated Bavarian china. The six remaining Seven Sisters, Emmer and the Faulk children, and the entire extended Sheridan family celebrated with us. Finas and Sara dressed like Mr. and Mrs. Claus to the delight of the children. Merry distractions enveloped me as I floated on a wafting draft of faltering joy.

Late that evening, Ruby and I found time to be alone. We wrapped ourselves with woolen shawls, settled near the small fire burning in my cabin's hearth, and gratefully cupped steaming mugs of honeysuckle tea.

My friend had blossomed in Boston; Ruby radiated energy and self-confidence. There was a sparkle in her eye when she said, "You think I'm makin' a mistake by joinin' the Order of Saint Rose."

"To tell you the truth, I'm not sure what I believe," I answered. "The notion of you becomin' a nun has stirred lots of feelin's. But the muddle has more to do with me than it does with you."

"What do you mean?"

I found it hard to meet Ruby's eyes. "Even with all that's happened to you, you've chosen to embrace God. You're so good, so brave." I swallowed hard and sputtered, "I'm not like you, Ruby. Since Alton died, I've been *very* angry with the Lord. It's a burnin' sensation, vague and lingerin'. The heat smolders through me. Sometimes, it feels like my skin's on fire."

A loud pop of erupting sparks sounded in the fireplace, and we both jumped. I quickly recovered, then added, "I've lost my center of knowin' about the Almighty. The abiding trust I once had is gone. He's betrayed me." My head fell with my words, heavy upon Ruby's narrow shoulder.

Ruby hesitated, then spoke so softly, I was forced to raise myself up to hear her clearly. "I know Alton's death hit you hard. But I'm learnin' that God's divine plan is too grand for us to understand. Sister Margaret told me that, sometimes, we misinterpret His mercy."

I shook my head, downcast and unmoved.

Ruby left the room and returned with a glass of water. "Maybe, our Creator took Alton to spare him a more painful death, Pug. You wrote to me about what the Ku-Klux did to Brother Watkins. You said yourself they also threatened Alton. Perhaps the tornado was part of God's all-seeing mercy…Here, drink this. You look as pale as milksop."

"Other people died that day, too," I sighed, accepting the water, still unconvinced by her argument.

"Yes, I know," came her patient reply. "Like I said, it's a grand plan."

We sat in silence for several tense minutes. Finally, I gathered the courage to ask frankly, "What about Violet? Why did *she* have to go so soon?" My voice sounded like a grating, squeaky gate.

Ruby's eyes glistened. The lines of her face plotted the map of pain etched upon her heart. "I miss her more than words can say. I think Violet was sent to this earth to give Mama and Daddy a chance at salvation. A chance they didn't take. I'm hopin' my daily prayers are favorable to Heaven, so that my parents won't have to burn in Hell forever."

I murmured, "They say every knot has an angel to unravel it. Maybe, given time, one of God's own will unbind your parents."

"They must do that for themselves," she smiled, thankful to see shades of "the old Pug," even for a brief moment.

I couldn't imagine how hard it'd been for Ruby to resolve her parents' sins in her young mind. She wanted them to find their way to Heaven, to follow the signposts, even though the markers on earth had been badly lit for Bosie and Zine. I believed Ruby's wish for their redemption played no small part in her decision to become a nun. Still, I couldn't accept her conviction that God doesn't make mistakes.

"My world has turned upside-down," I said, stiff-necked with defiance. "My spiritual devotion isn't won with the rampant brutality I see around me. How can I worship a God that condones such madness?"

My words hurt Ruby, but she never judged me. With the forbearance of a budding saint, she answered, "Maybe, the Divine teaches with sufferin'. With it comes wisdom. The choices we make after bad things happen are our own. Perhaps, there's truth in His justice that we simply can't see. I'm hopin' someday it'll all make sense."

Ruby and I huddled together, eating angel cookies until the fire died out and there was nothing left to say.

The next afternoon, Seven Sisters gave Ruby an early birthday party in Horseshoe Cave. Since she'd be turning seventeen in January, we decided it would impart a nice sendoff. "What do you give somebody who's about to become a nun?" Fanny had expressed our dilemma as we planned the celebration.

"Anything that reminds her of who she is," Egypt responded, composed and collected, wise beyond her years.

I gave Ruby a framed picture that'd hung in my room since birth, depicting a guardian angel protecting a young girl as she crossed a covered river bridge. Egypt presented her with Brother Watkins' Bible. Newt's homemade gift included white candles with shiny stars glued onto the outer edges. Fawn gave her friend several green braids of sweetgrass incense to burn during prayer time.

Ruby's delighted face glowed with rosy hues as she shyly held open the lacy box containing scarlet-colored panties with black polka dots, a gift from Fanny. "So you never forget you're a red-blooded woman!" Fanny declared emphatically while squeezing Ruby's knee. Fanny's penchant for showmanship never failed to spice things up with the promise of carefree gaiety.

Ruby returned to Boston three days later. The night she took the train home, I dreamed of happy times with Alton. At dawn, I awoke and wrote Ruby a letter of thanks for her supportive counsel. I began with the vivid, encouraging words Alton had spoken in my dream: "Walk the path we began together. Let your heels touch the earth in a way that matters. Begin at the end."

I took the visionary message as a guiding sign, one that meant I should continue Alton's fight against the Klan. The original path, the one my husband and I trod together, had come to a fork in the road. I'd have to decide which way to go on my own. But that was the problem; I'd misplaced my compass. The loss of Alton led me down a trail that swiftly sank into a valley previously unknown—a bloodless place, arid and ashen.

SIXTEEN

By February, there was no doubt; I was pregnant with Alton's child. "Glory be to God!" came the unified chorus of my mother and grandmother.

Essie, hardly missing a beat, began planning the celebration. "I'd better go kill me a hen and make dumplin's!"

T.H. was so moved by the news, he couldn't speak. Instead, he hitched up the wagon and made an unscheduled trip to Robinwood. When my father returned, I saw he'd brought me a surprise. His wagon was completely filled with just two items: red snapper packed in ice and stalks upon stalks of bananas—my favorite foods. There was no way I could eat it all, but I had fun trying.

Seven Sisters presented me with a handmade cradle. My friends worked together to shape it from the green wood of a young willow tree. "Granny says the willow has a soul that speaks in music," Fawn murmured as I floundered for adequate words of thanks. "You're supposed to give a new cradle a name blessin'. So it knows you welcome its embrace of your baby."

The others grinned, enjoying the moment. I felt silly as I searched my mind, scrambling for the right note of praise. I'd never named an inanimate object before; plus, the moniker I chose would have to please Fawn. In the waning, reflected light of late afternoon, I closed my eyes. And then it came to me. "Greetin's willow," I began, my manner demurely respectful. "Hereafter, you shall be known as Starleaf." I relaxed when Fawn nodded her approval.

My other friends were charmed by the engaging ritual, especially Fanny. She clapped her hands together and promised, "I'll carve a small nameplate. We can attach it right here, in front."

Thereafter, throughout my pregnancy, one or another of my sisters would occasionally cheer me with a modest gift: a whittled rattle, knitted booties, or a crocheted blanket. For me, each treasured item was symbolic reinforcement, reminding me that my babe was nurtured within a sheltered circle—as well as a broader destiny.

Rola Moon wasted no time in giving me the witch's required list of do's and don'ts for a mother-to-be. "This is what the owl announces," she said in a voice reserved for her most serious advice. "Rock an empty cradle, your child will know it's wanted. Avoid burnt foods, or your womb will hold onto the child overlong. And at all costs, don't let a rat, mouse, or weasel leap upon your stomach!"

I responded with an obedient smile.

"Wait, darn it, I'm forgettin' something." Rola squinted as she struggled to recall a final warning. Like a dutiful apprentice, I stayed quiet, waiting for her to finish the unorthodox lesson. "Oh, I remember now," she announced with a darkening mood. "If a woman with child looks upon a dead body, her baby will be born of pale complexion. You might hatch-out an albino. Best not risk it."

An uncontrollable giggle escaped me, but Rola's tone remained earnest. "I know you still mourn the child's daddy. The twilight of sorrow now blooms inside you. The wee one will have his smile. The angels' tower has endless ways of sendin' comfort. Don't forget, you carry the link." Rola lovingly patted me on my head as I walked away.

Any fool, given nine months, can diagnose pregnancy. Still, Arious insisted upon a doctor's official examination and confirmation. I knew what he wanted to rule out, and what the professional gossips of Village Springs initially whispered. It wasn't uncommon for a newly-widowed woman to exhibit "hysteria" in this fashion, manifesting a false pregnancy in an overwhelming desire to have her dead husband's child.

Arious had many personal questions, and I answered them all with resigned understanding. Finally, he was able to say delightedly, "I'd stake my reputation on the fact that I'm gonna be an uncle." Arious touched my cheek, emphasizing his parting promise. "No worries, I'll be here for you when the time comes."

During those next few weeks, a veil of peaceful acceptance enveloped me. I felt an uncanny connection to countless generations of my foremothers, stalwart women long passed from this world. I prayed to them for their courage and strength.

One night in early spring, Vigil Holt appeared at Sheridan House and asked T.H. to arrest him. Before my father could reply, the reverend shouted his revelation. "I'm bein' haunted by God!" Vigil zealously proclaimed. The bluish veins in his neck looked like they might explode.

Our cold supper went uneaten; we sat around the kitchen table, glued to our chairs, numb and dumbfounded while the preacher's confession proceeded. "I've known about Reverend Strawbridge's last sermon at Old Bethlehem for many months now," he began. Vigil paused, looked at me, and added, "I'm sincerely sorry for your loss, Mrs. Strawbridge."

I nodded, grim-faced.

Vigil continued, "Reverend Strawbridge preached his final message mere hours before God's Wrath brought that twister to Village Springs."

I shifted uncomfortably in my seat, then felt Mama's comforting touch upon my shoulder.

Vigil lowered his eyes, inspecting his hands like they weren't his own. "You're right about me, T.H. I've been the local leader of the Ku-Klux for a year now. I thought I was bein' a true friend to the people of this county. I now realize I delivered misery and ruin instead."

Vigil held out his arms, looked at me, and admitted, "I couldn't control the boys in my charge, and people are dead because of my shortcomin's. There's innocent blood on my soul. Only God's forgiveness can wash it clean." The reverend held his head high as he spoke, his back ramrod straight. With what seemed like one continuous breath, he declared, "The Lord has spoken. He told me I've been guided by passion and prejudice. That I stole the robes of justice. The twister was a sign, proof that the Almighty Father took Reverend Strawbridge to sit at His right hand.

"I was spared to set things right. Satan was an archangel before he became the Devil, you know. God has been unrelentin', seein' to it that I keep my promise to mend my ways. It isn't easy; the set penalty for divulgin' Klan secrets is death." Vigil gamely stared at T.H. for many long, tense moments before moving closer. "Marshall Sheridan, as the Cyclops for Pine Bluff County, I surrender myself to your protection."

The next morning, Vigil Holt boarded the L&N with a federal deputy at his side. They rode the train to Birmingham, where the prisoner could be protected until he was arraigned and tried. Vigil was sentenced to one year in prison for the double charge of arson and disturbing the peace.

✳ ✳ ✳

Subsequently, with their leader's arrest, the local band of the KKK dispersed, except for a small, renegade bunch. Most of the gang's mischievous pranks were harmless—until a misty night in late March.

Restless that whole evening, I channeled my excess energy into a compilation of poems. My favorite was one I'd written for Ruby:

> When twilight's passed away and
> The scream of the Sky Lark has died,
> Truth shall sound the alarm.
> Then Phoenix-like from Parent Dust,
> She'll soar to Heaven beyond a Harvest Moon
> To find that Truth and Justice are one in the same.

While fumbling to turn off the lamp, I heard a thump on my porch, like the dead weight of a body. A quick glance at the clock told me it was half past eleven. My holstered derringer hung on a three-inch nail next to the front door. I grabbed the loaded gun and held it ready in my free hand before noiselessly turning the knob.

An unconscious man was sprawled, face down, at my threshold. Using all my strength, I turned him over and gasped. It was Grady Holt; he'd been stabbed in the right shoulder. He wasn't hurt bad, but he was bleeding enough to notice. I dragged him inside, then tore some clean rags to use as compresses. Grady came to when I wiped his smudged face with cold water. He sat up, and I automatically reached for my gun. Grady's expression was frantic, not aggressive. "Hurry, Pug. You've got to help her," he panted. "It got out of hand…I couldn't stop 'em."

Grady lost consciousness again; I cushioned his head as he dropped back to the floor. Several mild slaps brought him around once more. "Grady, stay with me, tell me what happened. What are you talkin' about?"

"Me, Toad, and the others, we cornered Fawn in the woods," he said. "I swear, Pug, I didn't know it'd go past teasin' fun. You've got to find her. Right now. Before it's too late." Grady's trembling, blunt, terrifying words were delivered with pain-wracked moaning.

A shrill cry rose out of me as I fought against hysterics. "Damn you to Hell, Grady Holt!" I wrenched the collar of his shirt hard enough to jerk his head away from the floor, then screamed, "Where is she?"

"The hollow on the other side of Crooked Creek Cemetery, near Old Keene Mill." Grady passed out again.

In a blind rage, I saddled a horse and rode west, the derringer strapped to the bulging mound of my expanded waistline. I don't know why I didn't wake T.H. I was thinking of only one thing—find Fawn, find her fast. But visibility was poor in the murky darkness. I was as patient as I could be with the slow, careful footing of my horse. When I finally reached Crooked Creek Cemetery, the only living things I immediately detected around me were countless crickets and frogs.

The gate to the cemetery swung back and forth, menacingly, as if beckoning me to enter; I noticed the wild pillar roses that tightly twined around its single, creaky post. Then, I heard something else, a woman's cry—muffled, velvety weeping. I felt a hard quickening in my womb as I awkwardly dismounted and rushed across the graveyard toward the creek. Instinctively, my right hand pulled back the hammer of the pistol I carried.

Another distinctive sound, that of male laughter, was carried on the swelling breeze; it bounced off the nearby water like an echo. Someone coughed, and I made a complete circle where I stood, searching for the right direction. Any hint of which way to go dissipated like pixy dust.

I was Fawn's only hope of rescue, and I'd lost my bearings. A piercing pang wrenched my heart with the sudden, vivid recall of my nightly vision—Alton lost in the bluebonnet field. Only now, it was Fawn. I doubled over with anxiety and whispered a hurried prayer. Slowly, I raised myself up, then closed my eyes tight with stiff determination, willing my ears to hear, to guide me forward.

"Say you love me," I heard a man snarl. I recognized the voice; it was Toad's. "Say it! Maybe, this knife will loosen your tongue. Speak, damn you."

They were upstream, about a hundred yards away. With effort, I quieted my crazed fury. *I mustn't alert Fawn's captors,* I thought. *My only chance is to catch them off guard.* I waded into the icy water, knowing its rippling, chirpy sounds would mask all movement. While I raced upstream, the unfolding horror ahead of me became clearer. I pressed on, pushing my bulky pregnant form ever harder as I listened to Fawn's screams. "I love you. Please, stop! I love you. No, don't! No!"

Then, for what seemed like an eternity, there was utter silence. I stopped, listening intently, but the only thing to be heard was my own rapid heartbeat pounding in my ears. Then, there came a sickening recognition. I detected grunting, similar to that heard on a farm, like the rutting of a bull. Fawn was being raped.

Caution was no longer an option. I climbed ashore and hurriedly made my way through the dense briers that lined the creek, ignoring the scraping cuts that ripped my face and arms. Soon, I found myself on the edge of a grassy clearing. And then I saw them. Fawn lay on the ground, the blade of a six-inch knife pressed against her throat. She no longer struggled; her stare was fixed and vacant.

Two men wearing brown hoods watched the violent act with silent, single-minded interest. No one noticed me until I yelled, "Get off her, or I'll shoot you through!" The hooded men turned and ran like frightened deer, but Toad kept violating Fawn; it quickly became apparent he hadn't heard me. I fired two bullets to get his attention. They hit the soft dirt, coming within inches of my target, stirring multiple swirls of dust and grime. I was about to fire again when Toad jumped to his feet. I hesitated, realizing the shot might hit Fawn instead. Even at close range, I was too unsteady, shaken with fear and loathing.

Toad inched himself backward, sliding his feet in the dirt like a cold-bellied lizard. "I'm done anyway," he sneered. I walked forward, putting myself between him and Fawn. By now, I had clear aim. Using both hands, I pointed the barrel of my pistol at the space between his eyes and pulled the trigger. The sound of Toad's jeering laugh followed an empty click; I was out of bullets.

I heard a noise behind me; when I turned to look, Fawn was gone. Toad used the moment's distraction to make his escape. Soon, I heard horses galloping away. I headed in the opposite direction to find Fawn. I didn't have to search far. She stood in the middle of the stream, splashing cascades of pure, river water—trying desperately to wash Toad's seed away.

Fawn's hair was dirty and matted. The delicate curves of her inner thighs were bleeding, rubbed raw by the rape and her frantic scrubbing. She was in shock and didn't seem to notice me. I took Fawn's hand and coaxed her, as one would a child, out of the creek. Her homemade dress had been ripped at both shoulders; I tenderly lifted and tugged the damp, corduroy material, covering her as best I could.

Somehow, I managed to get us home. During that long ride, we said nothing to each other; our nonstop tears served for words until she lay down on my bed, exhausted. I was relieved when Fawn finally spoke. "Pug, Arious must never know. *Never.*"

"You're hurt. You need a doctor. And somebody has to sew up Grady," I answered.

"Granny can do all that's needed. Please, Pug, Arious can't find out!" Her eyes beseeched me in the yellow, dim lantern light. Reluctantly, I agreed to keep Fawn's secret. I thought I knew her chief reason for not telling Arious; she feared he would go after the rapist and be killed himself.

I briefly left my friend, returning with Badgerwoman; the old sage quickly determined that Fawn was in no immediate physical danger. She then turned her attention to Grady, keeping an impassive expression as she expertly stitched his jagged wound. After the task was completed, she made him a mysterious brew to drink. In between sips, Grady confessed more, filling in certain details.

The renegade fragment of the Klan, convinced that her romance with a white man was "unsavory," had conspired to scare Fawn into breaking off her relationship with Arious. The plot had gone grievously awry, or perhaps Toad knew what he wanted all along. It didn't matter. The crime was the same.

Grady eyed me nervously. "Are you gonna tell your daddy?"

I glanced at Fawn. She shook her head. I pressed my finger against Grady's sore shoulder. He winced, but I stood firm. "I'm warnin' you, Grady. *You're* the one who'd better stay quiet about this. Keep your trap shut, or else." I escorted Grady outside and watched as he gingerly climbed onto my horse.

"I'll return your mare in the mornin' without nobody knowin'. And, I'll make up something to tell Mama about the cut." Grady sighed, surrendering to unbridled sentiment before whispering my name. "Pug?"

"Yeah?"

"I tried to help her 'cause…well, you know how I feel about you, how I've always felt…" Grady had second thoughts about completing his bold, intimate avowal. As he rode away, he mumbled, "I'm sorry."

I found a clean gown for Fawn in my chifforobe; it smelled of fresh, sweet lilacs. After slipping it on, she talked about what had happened, speaking as if she were watching the scene from a distant, separate part of herself. "I was walkin' home," came the agonized, hesitant words. "It seemed like such a lovely night to do that. I was enjoyin' the soft moonlight. Arious and I had a wonderful evenin' together before I left…"

Fawn's broken sentences persisted, even as her granny bathed and soothed her wounds. "They came out of nowhere, hidin' in the graveyard, waitin' for me to pass. 'Dark meat shouldn't mix with white,' said one. 'But ya gotta admit, boys, it's a mighty pretty piece.'" Fawn winced while recalling the hateful words, then continued. "They had their hoods on. No faces to put with the voices. One of 'em grabbed me. When I tried to run, he held me in a headlock."

A sudden tremor shook Fawn, but she caught her breath. "The man that held me rubbed his dirty hand over my body. That's when Grady fought with him. Durin' the struggle, they pulled each other's face masks off. I realized it was Toad that touched me. He pulled a knife and stabbed at Grady, then Grady ran off. Another hoodlum guarded me while Toad and the third one chased after Grady. But, it wasn't long before they came back madder than before."

Fawn held her stomach, rocking to and fro as she finished telling it all. "When Toad put himself inside me, he said, 'I'm havin' Doc's leftovers.'" Fawn paused and covered her face with both hands, moaning with tormented suffering. She shook off the appalling memory with another reflexive shudder. "The next thing I remember, Pug was leadin' me out of the water."

Badgerwoman sat upon the bed and held her granddaughter; then, she spoke for the first time that night. "You are Cherokee. You are God's child, and His medicine is free. Give Him your flesh pain. You're still pure in your body and your soul. Spirit flows through you like sacred wind. The world is a better place because you are here."

Fawn and I fell asleep in my bed while Badgerwoman played her rawhide drum. She pounded an ancient, soulful rhythm, one synchronized to the beat of our hearts.

* * *

"Who would've thought Grady Holt a hero?" I muttered to myself as I stood on my porch, watching him slowly ride into the yard. The sun had just come up, and it was a turbid dawn. Grady sat on his own horse while holding the reins of Blue, trailing behind. Grady's wounded arm was in a sling. He held it steady with his opposite hand while he dismounted in one swift motion.

I noticed that Grady's clothes were badly rumpled, his hair a tangled mass. He walked toward me with his head cocked sideways, like he had a bad crimp in his neck, then stopped at the bottom of my porch steps. Grady kicked the dirt for several seconds as if tongue-tied. When he finally spoke, his voice was thick and husky. "That tub of rainwater out yonder is crawlin' with wiggle tails." Grady spat through his teeth to emphasize the point. "Gonna be a mess of musskeeters if you leave it like that."

"You're stirrin' around mighty early," I said, ignoring his advice. "I see you're also totin' a gun."

"I wanted to bring your horse without bein' seen. The Smith and Western is a simple precaution against who I might meet."

I smiled at his blunder, a common, country way of saying Smith and Wesson. "I'm beholden to ya…for what ya did last night." A hesitant smile met my stern gaze. "But don't think for one minute, Grady Holt, that last night's gallantry made up for all the wrong you've done!"

Grady twitched with understanding. His blushing complexion deepened an angry red, and his tone turned sarcastic. "You don't have to throw all that up to me, *Mrs. Strawbridge*. I'm mending my ways, so let it ride."

"All right, under two conditions. I'll keep quiet if you do. You'll never tell another livin' soul about what happened to Fawn. If Daddy knew of evidence linkin' you to the Klan, he'd fling you in jail, ready rolled." Then I added, "I think one Holt in the hoosegow is enough, don't you?"

Grady's eyes flashed with fury.

Making sure my tone remained placid, I continued, "I also want to know who else was with you last night and where I might find Toad."

Grady eyed me suspiciously. "Pug, what have you taken a notion to do?" There was real concern in his voice.

"That's none of your affair. Tell me, or I'll fire my pistol and roust Daddy out of bed quicker than you can spit."

Fanny's brother knew I had him against a wall. "The other two were Moose and Mookie Gaither," he answered. "They'd follow Toad into Hell. Since his grandfather died, Toad's been livin' in the old man's shack near Coppers Gap, on the banks of Mardis Falls."

"That's all I need to know. You can go now."

"Pug, don't go off half-cocked and do something stupid."

"Thank you, Grady. Like I *said,* you can go." My jaw remained stubbornly set, hard as stone. My not-so-secret admirer had no choice but to make the halfhearted walk to his wretchedly thin, tired horse.

As soon as Grady rode out of sight, I checked on Fawn. She was sleeping, though fitfully; Badgerwoman dozed in a nearby chair. I jotted a quick note for them, strapped on my gun, and mounted my mare—then headed north toward Coppers Gap.

I left my faithful Tennessee Walker tied to a tree on the south side of Mardis Falls. A makeshift foot bridge had been placed across the rushing waters; I warily inched my way across the slippery boards to the other side. When I stepped onto land, I saw a clearly marked trail winding up a gently sloping hill. Carefully, quietly, I made my way forward. I could see Toad's cabin through the swaying trees.

Suddenly, Toad appeared at the door and sauntered outside, stretching as though he'd just gotten out of bed. I quickly stepped behind a large hydrangea bush, then peeked around its outer edge in time to see water arching high into the air. Toad was peeing off the stoop's right side; he hadn't even bothered to step off the porch. I heard him cough as he shuffled back inside and slammed the door.

I crawled a few yards west, surveying my target, then quickly ducked for cover when Toad's door reopened. He was kicking a large, black Labrador in the rump. "Damn you, Nigger Dog! You've chewed shoes for the last time. To Hell with you!" The quaintly-named mutt ran for the safety of nearby woods and, thankfully, didn't notice me as Toad's door banged shut again.

Meadow muffins—large piles of cow dung—spread across the yard. I crept among the maze-like droppings, inching my way to a window. I cautiously peered inside and saw that Toad was alone in the one-room shack. The cabin's interior was disgustingly filthy. Dirty dishes and unwashed clothes lay everywhere; maggots feasted on decaying food. Dried mud covered the floor, the furniture, even the bed. Toad sat at a dilapidated table, having breakfast. The dish was a local one—hogs' brains and eggs, popular with the poorer residents of the county. The way it looked, heaped upon a steaming plate, made me want to retch.

It was the perfect time for a surprise attack, so I squelched my nausea, then hurled my misshapen body through the narrow front door with such violent force, I almost fell. Toad had no time to react before I recovered my balance and pointed my derringer straight at him. The tip of the barrel was five feet from his ugly face. Toad casually pushed back his chair; his deformed jaw accentuated the smirk that overshadowed his face. "I might've thought your fine family would've taught you better manners," he said, his voice cool and contemptuous.

"You're not worth the salt you've sprinkled on those eggs, you whomper-jawed pig."

Toad flinched at the reference to his disfigurement as he methodically poured milk into a glass. "A lot of folks don't like buttermilk, but I'll take it over the sweet kind any day." He looked up and added, "Care for some?" Toad took a big gulp; the thick, creamy liquid formed a foamy mustache over his upper lip.

"Why'd you do it?" I demanded. "What's she ever done to you?"

Toad feigned surprised ignorance. "Who?"

"Fawn, you son-of-a-bitch. I saw you rape her!"

His tone remained matter-of-fact, like I'd just commented on the weather. "That Injun girl, she's a friend of yours, ain't she? I hear tell she's been keepin' company with young Doc Strawbridge." Toad exaggerated a gasp, then added, "You reckon there's anything to it? The gossips say he's the jealous type. If that's the case, he'd be mighty mad if he knew how she flirted with me."

Toad took another swig of buttermilk. "Our midnight rendezvous was her idea, ya know. When we came together in the dark, we got carried away…" His voice trailed off as he gazed at my drawn gun. The only sign of fear was revealed by a nervous habit; Toad swallowed repeatedly. His Adam's apple rode up and down his skinny, pimpled neck as his tone turned defiant. "Who are you to be my judge and jury? I answer to only two masters, the Klan and God."

"You're a liar, Toad. You hurt her bad. Which 'master' taught you how to hate? Which one inspired you to violate a woman?"

Toad blew an impatient, exasperated sigh. "There's a new game in town, Miss Sheridan. Or haven't you noticed? The Klan is destined to rule the South. We have our rights and our own code. We're makin' a claim to this land. All Niggers and Injuns have to leave." Toad paused, gave me a knowing look, then added, "Or else."

He noisily wiped his nose on his shirt and kept talking. "As for hatin', all right, I'll give you that. I'm a happy hater. It comes from pride in my own kind. It serves the Cause. Unlike some people, I'm honest with myself. I see hate in your eyes too, Pug. You can't deny it. There's no difference between you and me. Except, the name you give your shadow side. What do *you* call it, the righteous superiority that allows you to take the law into your own hands? What is it with you high and mighty Sheridans, anyway?"

"I've heard enough, you piece of cow shit. I let you talk this long just to be fair," I said. "The final words of a condemned man. I didn't come to hear your side. I came to settle the score. I came to kill you."

"Exactly my point," Toad smugly answered.

Toad's words made me uncomfortable, but I ignored his biting comment. "I know the Gaither boys were with you last night," I hissed. "I have a witness. I can prove it all. If I were you, I'd find myself a healthy sense of shame, especially knowin' I was about to meet my Maker."

My murderous intent finally registered with my adversary. Astonishment and dread clouded Toad's features. His body jerked with sudden comprehension and the realization of how much I knew, especially the fact that Moose and Mookie Gaither had been involved in the rape. "You'll ruin your own life if you do this," he gulped. "I have friends. The Klan doesn't forget an enemy."

"I'll take my chances," I said with indignant contempt. I wiped cold sweat from around my eyes with my sleeve. *What are you doing?* came the internal question, my voice of conscience. I winced as I pulled on the trigger, all thought foggy confusion. Abruptly changing my mind, I snapped my hand painfully to the right, but my bullet found its target anyway.

Though Toad was still alive, I'd blown off a significant part of his cheek, the one on the healthy side of his head. Now his entire face appeared deformed and disfigured. Toad fell to the floor, squirming and bleeding like a stuck pig. I could see that the wound was shallow; he was in no immediate danger of dying, but permanent scarring was a certainty.

I was a bundle of nerves while my spirit wavered. I shakily pointed my gun at Toad again, and he desperately begged for his life. "Pug don't...please don't shoot again."

My voice did not betray me; it held firm as I threaded together unyielding words: "You and your brainless, evil-minded friends leave Village Springs—in fact, I want you out of Alabama. *Today.* Make tracks as far as your mangy horses will go." I paused to make sure Toad was looking at me. "If I ever see you again, I swear on my husband's grave I'll blow your whole head off next time." Toad was still wallowing on the rough-planked floor as I turned and followed a little stream of blood to the exit.

They say that a person with a bad name is already half-hanged. I later heard that Toad and his gang were being hunted by Texas Rangers for crimes they'd committed in that part of the country. I hoped that would spell the end of the trail for my sworn enemy. I never told anyone about shooting Toad, and only Seven Sisters knew about the rape.

It was a secret we vowed to take to our graves—even after Fawn discovered that she was pregnant.

With the passing weeks, my Cherokee friend grew more withdrawn. It became a daily habit for Fawn to seek out broken birds' nests, repair them, then replace the bundled twigs where she'd found them. Sometimes, the tree limbs were quite high, and I lived in constant fear that she would fall during one of these excursions. Fanny took it upon herself to shadow Fawn as her self-appointed bodyguard. Because of her brother's involvement, Fanny suffered untold guilt for what had happened to her friend, though Fawn never blamed her.

Becoming Fawn's protector helped to compensate for the heavy yoke of family sins Fanny now insisted upon carrying. I'm sure Fawn was aware of her friend's presence as Fanny concealed herself in the forest. Any self-respecting Cherokee would know when he or she was being spied on. Fawn let Fanny be, remaining emotionally aloof, even from Arious and me. Her physical symptoms of pregnancy were as classic as mine, with fatigue and constant nausea while she missed two periods.

Though Fawn and Arious had been longtime lovers, she felt certain the child was Toad's. Together, we decided what she should do. It was a heart-wrenching dilemma, an impasse no woman should face alone. Upon Fawn's request, Badgerwoman concocted an herbal mixture that included the poisonous addition of bloodroot and tansy. The drink's intended purpose was to cleanse Fawn's womb.

Fawn took her first dose of the brew at noon. Within four hours, she complained of mild pain. By early evening, her uterus commenced cramping, forceful and severe. For several, fearful hours, Fawn moaned, squatted, and pushed. Around midnight, she began screaming, the way a rabbit howls while being devoured, a ghastly sound. Delirious from fever, Fawn no longer recognized her friends and family; her pulse raced dangerously fast.

Badgerwoman realized we were in deep waters. "Get Arious," she said. "Hurry." The old woman's voice crackled, filled with apprehension.

I rode with reckless abandon, borrowing a track horse Daddy planned to run at Birmingham Downs. I pounded on Strawbridge Mansion's heavy door, making good use of the brass knocker. After several minutes, Arious finally appeared, still fighting sleepiness. "Come quick," I said. "Fawn's sick; there's no time to explain."

Once he'd saddled his own horse and joined me, Arious, looking anxious, insisted, "What are her symptoms?"

I looked straight into his tired, non-comprehending eyes and answered, "I think she's miscarryin'."

"She never told me she was pregnant." My brother-in-law's tone sounded strangely flat, yet his words reflected a peculiar combination of worry, anger, and dejection.

By the time we arrived at Fawn's bedside, the bleeding had worsened. She was wrapped in several blankets, shaking with a bone-dampening chill. Terror seized me by the throat. Fawn was hemorrhaging. All color drained from her face and her lips turned blue, then purple. I held onto my friend's hand, willing her not to die.

Arious reached into his black medical bag and pulled out a curette. He used the long, spoon-like instrument to remove a bloody mass from Fawn's womb, emptying the wad of soft tissue onto a piece of newspaper.

Then, Arious held a small vile of amber-colored liquid to Fawn's lips, carefully ensuring she swallowed it all. When the bleeding slowed, Arious told us to put icy packs on Fawn's abdomen to reduce the fever and pain; his voice was as cold as the prescription he ordered. Then, to my surprise, he abruptly left the house without so much as a nod.

I followed Arious into the yard. His manner mirrored a soul in limbo, like somebody dead inside. Arious formed a tight fist around his colt's mane, stiffly gathering the long, coarse hairs in his wide hand as he struggled to speak. Then came the frustrated, beclouded words I couldn't counter. "I've often wondered if she truly loves me. She's been actin' distant for weeks. There's no use lyin', Pug. I know this wasn't a typical miscarriage. Fawn doesn't want our child because she doesn't want me." Arious's pronouncement washed away all reason with the tearful words, "Tell her it's over between us."

After he climbed on his horse, I obstinately held onto the reins. I pleaded, "No, it's not what you think. Fawn *does* care deeply. There's more to this than you realize!"

"What? Tell me if you can how killin' our child proves her love for me."

I was mute. Befuddled. Exhausted.

"Well, I'm waitin'!" Arious's stoicism seasoned into impassioned anger, his spirit ablaze; the nearness of his fiery wrath scorched my skin.

I wanted desperately to explain, but I'd vowed never to tell Arious about the rape. Conflicted loyalties created a squirmy restlessness within me; the puzzle could not be solved in that moment.

"Your silence speaks volumes," he hissed. Arious impatiently slapped his horse and rode away—impetuous, headstrong, and stupid.

I considered going after my sap of a brother-in-law, but as long as my quandary remained, nothing more could be said. I placed a protective hand atop my burgeoning stomach as I sadly climbed the porch stoop.

After making sure Fawn was asleep, I curiously examined the bloody blob that lay upon the smooth newspaper. Like Toad, it looked like something malformed. I wrapped the fetus in a scrap of pink satin before burying it in fecund earth at the first sign of dawn. When I started to walk away, saying nothing, the growing child inside me kicked vigorously. I registered my baby's protests with a sigh. *What could be said over such a grave?*

"May you meet a white lamb in the early mornin' with sunlight on its face," I whispered. I patted the dirt with my shovel, then made my way home.

✳ ✳ ✳

For the next few days, I fretted over Fawn and Badgerwoman. My friend could barely raise her head, and her weary granny often napped beside her. Consequently, it was several days before I found time to visit Arious, to explain that, no matter how it appeared, Fawn needed him.

When I arrived at the Strawbridge house, Aunt Caroline answered the door. Age lines criss-crossed her pale face, and she looked more fragile than usual. She expressed sincere surprise when I asked for her nephew. "Didn't you know? He's returned to Maryland. I'm sure he'll write as soon as he's settled."

I shook my head in disbelief. "When's he comin' back?" I stammered, still in denial.

"He's not, dear. Arious accepted a wonderful position at his *alma mater*. Johns Hopkins answered his telegram, one he sent to Baltimore in the early part of the week. Didn't he tell you? An *excellent* opportunity. He left this mornin'."

As Caroline innocently rattled on about her nephew's "bright future in the world of medical research," my head reeled with sick comprehension. Jumbled feelings of sadness and outrage were drowned out by a pervasive disappointment that suffused all thought.

Love is like sun to a flower, I finally decided. *It invigorates the strong but wilts the weak.* On the way home, I pondered the task of telling Fawn about Arious's faithless departure. "Remind yourself that you are brave," I would begin. "Remember, you are a daughter of Atlas."

SEVENTEEN

The Klan continued to gain ground and political popularity in Village Springs. Seven Sisters reached a sad conclusion: The Ku-Klux survived because a large number of local citizens wanted it that way.

In response, our sorority launched a naïve crusade, spearheaded by me, aimed at changing public opinion. Together, we removed or marked-up the growing number of Klan posters, replacing them with our own garish tag lines—"Remember. Every criminal, every wife beater, every moonshiner, every BLACK SERPENT is a member of the Ku-Klux. Think it over. Which side are you on?"

In our spare time, Seven Sisters sewed multiple skull caps, atop which we attached large donkey ears. It was fun forming the dark brown, cotton beanies, then securing the coarse, red flannel ear pieces. We pinned a note to each sardonic hat which read, "What a KKK ass you've made of yourself." During the dead of night, we delivered our "gifts" to the darkened porches of local, suspected Klan supporters. The names on our list came from inside information, unwittingly provided by T.H.

The number of dire incidents within our community was growing. Black men were whipped nightly, their mouths lacerated by the gags that silenced them. When the beaten body of Jeremiah Jones was found floating in the Locust Fork River, colored families that still remained started vacating the county with heartbreaking regularity. Only a handful stayed, bold and stubborn—daring rebels who defied the Klan's repugnant beliefs with their lives.

Each injustice fed my growing obsession. Finding ways to defeat the Ku-Klux's schemes consumed my every waking thought until my frustration reached a boiling point. During the next meeting in Horseshoe, I was emphatic. "Let's up the ante. We'll see how *they* like it." I knew I was talking too loud, that I sounded maniacal, but I didn't care. "If they paint 'Niggers Belong in Africa' on somebody's barn, we'll paint 'KKK Villains' on theirs! I've got ideas that'll scare the livin' blazes out of the bastards. Make 'em choke on their own spiteful venom."

Fawn and Egypt appeared confused, but there was no mistaking the disapproving looks of Fanny and Newt. Before they could argue, I continued, "What's wrong with showin' 'em a mirror? Let 'em drink from the same nasty trough, sip their own poison. By God, it's time to really fight back!" Stunned silence followed my passionate plea, but I didn't give up. "If we don't commence with some dirty tricks of our own against them, they'll never stop!" I challenged, arms crossed, my expression absolute.

"Jesus, Mary, and Joseph. Listen to yourself, Pug," Fanny scolded. "We'd only be addin' insult to injury. What you're suggestin' means stoopin' to their level. We *can't* do that. It goes against the creed of this club!"

"Fanny's right," Newt concurred. "Why add fuel to flames? Somebody could get hurt! What's gotten into you? You're so preoccupied with this thing, it's eatin' you alive. Besides, what would your daddy say to such a harebrained scheme?"

I lost my temper. "T.H.'s hands are tied by stupid laws," I yelled. "I don't need his help, and I sure don't need yours! I can fight my own battles. This one is for Alton. If you can't see that, then stay the Hell out of my way!"

Hurt and angry, Fanny and Newt stormed out of the cave.

During the argument, Egypt and Fawn remained quiet. Since the rape, Fawn always followed my lead, like a docile puppy. After the three of us were alone, Egypt tentatively asked a pointed question: "They say that lizards can change colors to match what's around 'em. Do you think some grow up to be crocodiles?" Egypt gave me a cursory hug before purposefully taking Fawn by the hand, leading the way home.

That night, fuming and alone, I spent the first of many late hours fashioning hateful, anonymous letters. "The *true* lower race of human beings can be found among yourselves, Klan followers," I wrote, feeling passionate and powerful. "The face of the earth would be much improved by your hastened disappearance. You reveal yourselves as bushwhackers and desperadoes, a plague of locusts spawned by demons."

The Klansmen patterned themselves after the courtly knights of medieval Scotland. To take full advantage of folksy superstition and custom, they actively strove to appear as spooks on nightly rides. Fighting fire with fire, I sent suspected Ku-Kluxers original curses. I stuffed my vexations into black envelopes; I also added the bones of small animals I found decomposing in the forest, along with spiders and bugs. I got disturbingly good at this.

The Klan believed they were backed by the restless ghosts of the Confederate dead. Thus, my damnations promised, "Every Kluxer will *become* the *Living Dead.* By the powers of Earth, Air, Fire, and Water, your skies will blacken. A single, heavenly star shall shine upon your horrible deeds, and you will know fear. You'll drink tea made of distilled Hell, stirred with the lightning of angels, sweetened with the blood of those you've harmed. May this be the fate of all who plummet into that unholy abyss, the vile soul of the Ku-Klux!"

As time passed, my wicked work improved. One day, I bragged about my clever curses to Rola Moon, and she was uncommonly alarmed. "You're breakin' the rules," she angrily warned. "Weavin' a tangled web, you'll only trap yourself. I taught you the 'Three-Fold-Law of Mara'—from the 'Ancient Law of One.' Have you conveniently forgotten this?"

Obstinate, I stared coolly at the ground while Rola hotly admonished me. "A witch's work must go accordin' to free will. With none harmed. *None.* Without exception. Everything comes back to you three times as stated in the Invisible World. Includin' curses. You're treadin' on thin ice, child. Over dangerous waters. And the tick-tock of time is against you."

When I attempted to argue, Rola silenced me with a raised hand. Overcoming great agitation, she searched her cabin for a pencil and paper. She hastily scribbled many words, scratched upon a yellowed, lined sheet while I held my determined breath. Rola folded the note and said, "Don't read this until you've seen her guiltless eyes. Her fear is your own. You'll know when you see her, whose eyes I mean. Until then, don't open this. Put it under your pillow and sleep on it." She shoved the note into my hand and walked off in a huff.

Somewhere deep inside, I justified my "eye for an eye" principles. *Rola doesn't understand what's at stake,* I told myself. *The tyranny must end, no matter the cost. Otherwise, how can I bring my babe into such a heinous world?* For me and my unborn child, each day heralded an advanced loan held by an unseen banker. My heart beat with rote habit, devoid of feeling or devotion. My thoughts were like half-written notes, and nothing was guaranteed.

The day after Rola's warning, I overheard a conversation between Mama and Mamau Maude. "Pug's voice has taken on a monotone that's downright frightenin'. Her inner world is secret, unreachable," my mother anguished. "Words of comfort fly past her ears like distant echoes. I give her a sizable portion of my love, and she politely hands it back to me. I worry; how will she care for a baby in such a state?"

My mother started crying, and I walked away; the sound of her despair made my head hurt. I was still within earshot when my grandmother responded to my mother's tears. "Pug is in a one-sided fight with life, especially the essentials of hope and joy; her sufferin' increases in tandem. To find wholeness, she needs our prayers more than ever."

That night, another house was deliberately burned; it belonged to the Buckalews, longtime Negro friends of my family's. This event inflamed me further. My anger made me brittle; one little fall and I'd snap like driftwood. Still, I truly believed the Kluxers could be forced to see the wrong of their ways.

The following week, I organized my own team of nightriders, complete with mocking disguises and costumed horses—it was my ultimate plan. My "comrades-in-crime" included myself, Egypt, Fawn, and two colored girls, Desiree Buford and Rainey Jowell, long-time friends of Egypt's. We wore gloves and put white paint around our eyes, covering traces of tell-tale skin under the white sheets that hid our identities.

At half past ten on a dry, April evening, we rode boldly into Clyde Walpole's yard. He'd been part of the gang that'd cruelly whipped Alton and terrorized Reverend Frazier's family by burying the preacher alive. Clyde had participated, but remained a free man because of perjurious testimony. I despised him.

"Let me do all the talkin'," I announced after we lined up our horses in a horizontal row.

I'd previously mail-ordered a small megaphone, adjusted not only to amplify, but to distort one's voice. Cocksure of my intent, I put it to my mouth. "Clyde Walpole," I cried, "You are hearby ordered to present yourself before the Alliance of Medusa. The gorgon speaks! Obey her now, or be turned to stone for your disobedient and ungodly ways!"

Clyde stepped onto the porch in his underwear. His timid wife and children stood behind him. Confused, he blinked several times while he registered the scene. My friends and I exchanged baffled looks when Clyde broke into laughter, falling to his knobby knees with merriment. With bemused inquisitiveness, Clyde asked, "Bevis, Orbin, Stein, is that you? My birthday's not 'til tomorrow. Is this the joke you've been plannin'?"

Clyde's smile slowly vanished when I answered. "I assure you this is no joke, Mr. Walpole. The Alliance of Medusa accuses you of outrageous offenses against innocents, the worst crime bein' your picayunish cowardice. You must answer to the sword of justice we carry in her name!"

"Who the Hell are you? I demand you show yourselves!" Clyde's mood metamorphosed into rage.

"Who are we, you ask? What do you answer when asked that question by those *you* trespass? I'll bet you lie, you craven flincher." I swallowed hard, forcing down the bile that kept climbing to my throat. "All you need to know, Mr. Walpole, is that the Alliance of Medusa is here to burn a cross in *your* yard, as a warnin'. And, to let you see how it feels to have your character torched."

I nodded to Egypt. She got off her horse, walked to the center of the yard, then pushed the cross we'd made into the damp earth. When Egypt set it ablaze, Clyde went berserk; he bounded off the stoop and rushed toward her.

Hurriedly, I pointed the long, steely barrel of my derringer at the irate man. "Stop where you are!" I screamed. "Get back on the porch, or I'll shoot. I swear I will." Unfortunately, I'd dropped the megaphone when I drew my gun; the warning was given with my own, undisguised voice.

Still acting like a rabid animal, Clyde returned to his family. Foam gathered at the sides of his mouth, his response to the perceived indignity. When Clyde's wife whispered something in his ear, he suddenly stopped ranting and stood still. Clyde calmed himself. With a smug, self-assured smirk, he said, "That's you, Pug Sheridan. Ain't it? You and your simple-minded, brownie friends. It's rumored you're behind recent shenanigans. You've gone too far this time. Get on home now, before I lose my temper and do something I regret."

"*You've* already done plenty to repent for," I countered. "Unfortunately, it can't be proved in court, no more than what occurs here tonight can be. You align yourself with evil, Clyde. If anyone deserves to have a cross remind them of that, it's you."

Clyde replied with a loud, offensive, condescending roar. "First of all, Missy, you've bitten off more than you can chew! When you threaten one Klansman, you threaten all, with no idea what you're up against. Our power covers six states. With more to follow. A goal no less than Democratic supremacy. Not you, your nigger friends, or your highfalutin' daddy can stop that!" Clyde spat a big wad of phlegm at the fiery symbol. "And second, Miss High-On-Your-Horse Sheridan, Klansmen don't burn the cross. We *illuminate* it, shinin' a sacred light on ideals we hold dear."

Having my identity guessed was beginning to undo me, affecting my self-confidence. Steadfast, righteous indignation took over. I angrily yelled, "Is that so? Well then, how about we *illuminate* your house?"

Clyde blanched with fear. His eyes mirrored the loathing in his heart, filling me with a kind of depraved pleasure. I'd gotten to Clyde, found his Achilles heel. He knew I could carry out my threat and get away with it. T.H. would never arrest me, not based on the testimony of Clyde Walpole, a man he now detested. The enemy I faced understood that. And so did I.

At that moment, Clyde and the Klan became one entity in my mind. I could burn them out, end the nightmare once and for all. I felt unabashed hatred wash over me. *Why not do it?* I asked myself. *God knows they deserve it. I can throw this torch, and they'll burn in Hell forever. All of them, the sons-of-bitches.*

That's when I saw the frightened stare of five-year-old Cyndy Walpole, Clyde's youngest child. Struck to my marrowed core, I became transfixed by her unusual eyes, the color of ball lightning—hazel orbs that jolted my apathetic soul. Cyndy's shimmering eyes beseeched me as they unraveled the mysteries of my heart. Her thin body shook with paralyzed dread in the chill of the stinging night air. But she never looked away; she'd have held my gaze until the end of time, her fear frozen in amber.

The little girl truly believed I was going to burn her house down. I'd seen that petrified look before, in the faces of the Frazier children as their daddy was buried alive. Now, *I* was the cause of such dread and panic. Cyndy's angelic face, uncorrupted by evil or malice, her sweet innocence, brought me to myself. I felt stunned, gutted by embarrassment and shame, the depth of which I'd never before known.

Those passing moments allowed Mrs. Walpole to slip a Winchester rifle into her husband's hand; Clyde eagerly grabbed the barrel, then fired over our heads. Our horses bolted in five different directions, unnerved by chaos, screams, and gunfire.

Eventually, our little band of outlaws regrouped where we started, in Sulphur Springs. To my surprise, Newt and Fanny were waiting for us. They wore concerned expressions as they stood tall, but said nothing. A tense silence reigned as we hid our costumes and washed our stained faces.

Downcast, I walked to the bank of the Springs and gazed at the reflection of stars. Soon, Fawn joined me, absently moving the water in a circular motion with her foot. Newt and Fanny seated themselves on the other side of Fawn; I could hear their heavy, nervous breathing.

For several minutes, Egypt, Desiree, and Rainey bunched together near a small tree. Egypt eventually gathered her courage, approaching me with a determined stride. She said, "I speak for all of us when I say we *never* want to do that again. It didn't make us feel better about anything. It made us feel even worse." Egypt trembled as she added, "Fanny and Newt were right, Pug. Treatin' meanness with meanness makes two hornets' nests where before there was only one."

Slowly, tearfully, I stood. Everybody huddled 'round, encircling each other. Seven girls, fourteen arms, seven hearts. "I'm sorry I put y'all through this," I said. "Maybe, the biggest victory is knowin' when to quit."

I arrived home exhausted, shaking with fatigue and remorse. Approaching the unlocked door, I noticed an oil lamp burning within, one I knew I'd snuffed out. Once inside, I found T.H. in my overstuffed chair, fuming with vexed outrage. "An anonymous rider left this at our door," he said, holding up my megaphone. With his jaw tightly clenched, Daddy was so mad he could barely speak. "A note was inside, addressed to me," he managed to add.

Showing obvious effort at self-control, my father read the written message aloud. Without mentioning any names, other than mine, it described the night's misdeeds in detail. Daddy gathered his wits, then asked, "Is it true? Were you part of some foolish attempt at vigilante justice tonight?"

"No, I wasn't part of it," I said. "I was all of it."

I gasped, startled, when T.H. pounded the side table, breaking it in half. "You could've been hurt, or worse!" he yelled. "You might've lost your baby. Have you lost your mind?"

I swooned, grabbing a coat rack for support. T.H. rushed to help me onto the sofa. He put a cold cloth to my forehead, but it took a while for the vertigo to pass. My father's tone softened. "You want me to get your mama?"

"No, Daddy," I whispered. "I'm just tired, that's all."

T.H. sank to the floor beside me, looking helpless, bereft. There was desperate emotion behind his next question. "What were you thinkin', daughter?"

"Sane reason doesn't apply. I'm several bushels short of a peck in that regard," I replied. "I have no excuse. Except lunacy. It's a relief to admit I'm crazy. You should lock me up, Daddy."

"Daffy people don't admit the fact," T.H. assured me, smiling.

"Then, what's wrong with me?" I cried. It was no excuse for what I'd done, but I knew that grief had indeed driven me slightly insane. My father held me while I sobbed with contrition. "Alton must be so ashamed of me," I wailed. "I've become everything he despised. He was right to leave me! I'm not good enough to be loved by him…"

T.H.'s voice was soothing and sweet as he attentively wiped my tears with his handkerchief. "You've forgotten your connection with Higher Powers, darlin'. That's true enough, but easily fixed in a heartbeat. You are high-spirited in the surest sense. By remembering that God cannot fail, the selfless warrior wins the biggest victory of all— heavenly peace." Daddy continued to hold my gaze for emphasis.

It was the most honest and open statement my father had ever made concerning the Almighty. With effortless care, T.H. carried me to my bed, then tucked a quilt tightly around me, a childhood ritual re-enacted and appreciated. Standing above me, he asked, "You put up those posters? Sent letters and donkey ears all over the county?"

"I'm through with all that, too," I promised.

"I'm near if you need me," he said before quietly closing the door.

I warily reached beneath my pillow, retrieving the folded paper Rola Moon had given me, and read it for the first time. She'd written, "Heed the words of the Great Mother, She of Old, also called many other names by those who know her: 'Listen, ye who are ready to learn magic, yet have not won its deepest secrets. Remember, my law is love unto all beings. I am the Nurturer of children. The Comforter of women. The Giver of mercy. With pure intent, strive toward your highest ideal. And remember, I have been with thee from the beginning, and I'll be with thee to the end.'" I meticulously re-folded the paper along its deep, immutable seams before slipping into the best night's rest I'd had in months.

Fawn continued to slumber day and night. Her misfortune had no voice, and her suffering couldn't speak. To survive the bitterness of loss, she immersed her soul in nature. During her daily excursions through the woods, Fawn searched for wounded animals, then carried them back to The Hill where she fed and healed them. Soon after Arious's departure, Sheridan Resort boasted a menagerie of wild creatures that rivaled the Birmingham Zoo.

Fanny helped Fawn build the makeshift enclosures needed for veterinary ministrations. The pens were of all shapes and sizes; the critters included whitetail deer, lost dogs, wild pigs, two owls, and a snapping turtle. The two friends displayed a stewardship toward the animals that found expression through patience and empathy. It was a tender reverence, vibrating with the cycle of life and death.

Azberry was also good company for Fawn. She didn't feel the need to talk when he was around, and my brother had a gentle knack for getting her to relax. He was always there whenever she released, with ceremonial care, one of their recuperated "pets" back into the wild.

Frogs outnumbered the other animals Fawn rescued. This was due to a local, night-time entertainment called frog gigging. Carbide lamps blinded the reptiles with light, then huntsmen would impale each frog with pronged sticks. As the creatures lay skewered to the ground, their back legs were cut off; the meat was considered a delicacy, pan fried and eaten. The mangled animals often survived, crawling off by way of their front legs. That was the condition in which Fawn would, inevitably, find them.

One night, after viewing several "gigged" frogs that she'd brought home, I had a bad dream. I found myself alone in a dark forest, surrounded by hundreds of crippled frogs, hobbling around me as they croaked in pain. I awoke from the nightmare to the sound of my own muffled moan. That was bad enough. But, what I saw after awakening made me scream.

A silvery, spectral light floated at the foot of my bed. I focused on the glistening figure of a woman as I sat straight up and rubbed my face, forcing my eyes to see more clearly. *It was Violet.* She was dressed in the same blue gown she'd been buried in, but her form was outlined by a brilliant, whitish glow. Violet's face beamed serenely, and she wore a knowing smile. "I told 'em there was no way to do this without scarin' you to death," she said, giggling at her own joke.

"It's just a dream…I'll wake up any minute now…It's just a…" I repeated this affirmation aloud as I sleepily stared at the ghost, spellbound. Soon, I was wide-eyed and quite awake, more convinced than ever that my mopish mind had gone around a final bend.

"You know you're not dreamin', Electra," came Violet's voice, easeful and sweet. "It's not easy to do this, to come back this way, but I've something important to tell you."

"Something…tell me," I parroted, a slack-jawed simpleton witnessing a miracle.

"Badgerwoman was supposed to cross over weeks ago, but she's holdin' onto a weighty secret. It's keepin' her earthbound. Denyin' the old woman the rest she's earned. Soon, her confidence can be passed on. When that far-reaching day reveals itself, you'll know your part."

I nodded, dumbstruck.

Violet smiled indulgently. "Also, you *must* contact Arious. Convince him to come home to the truth about Fawn. Her spirit rests between our two worlds, and she's in danger of comin' over to the Light World too soon." Violet seemed so wise; she patiently waited for me to absorb her meaning.

"I understand, Maia," I finally answered, knowing my words were whispered to a real angel.

"Good. I must go now, spirit sister."

"Wait!" I cried, startled by the loudness of my own voice. "Is Alton with you in Heaven?"

The question appeared to sadden Violet, and she didn't answer. Instead, her inner glow blazoned majestic as compassion filled her being. It suffused the room and touched my heart. Gradually, like the dimming of a lantern, she slowly vanished before my weeping eyes.

At dawn, I discovered that a foxhound, an old stray, had settled under my porch during the night. She'd given birth to five puppies. The aging canine shook from fatigue, hunger, and the early morning chill. I built a little fire in the chimney, put a ragged quilt into a nearby box, and brought the new mother and her pups inside. When offered leftover eggs and bacon, the scrawny hound ate like she'd been starving for weeks. I named her Olive Kate.

That afternoon, I set in motion a relentless, daily letter-writing campaign to Arious, imploring him to return home. I wielded every argument I could think of, reminding him of his promise to be with me when his niece or nephew was born.

Repeatedly, I assured Arious there was an issue that desperately needed discussing. In person, face to face. "The truth is not evident," I pleaded, "*but it will prevail.*" In spite of my effort, letter after letter, and even three telegrams, went unanswered.

A few weeks after Violet's ghostly warning, we convened a meeting in Horseshoe Cave. Olive Kate accompanied me there; she'd begun to follow me everywhere, leaving her pups safely inside my cabin.

The Secret Society of the Seven Sisters was almost a decade old, and our gatherings had profoundly changed. The childish cackles and contests were supplanted by a growing interest in the rites and virtues of womanhood. The surviving members of our group now ranged from seventeen to nineteen years in age.

I wasted no time revealing some good news to my friends. I'd received an important notice from a national magazine, *The Ladies Home Journal*—a formal announcement of intent to publish several of my poems in its "Summer Romance Number." The signature was that of Fiona Mills, editor-in-chief.

With theatrical aplomb, I stood and read the postscript aloud. "We at *LHJ* would be quite pleased to receive more of your work. Evidence of your talent has stirred the stale air of our boardroom, bringing with it a long-awaited breeze." A check, in the hefty sum of thirty dollars, accompanied the editor's elaborate, peach-colored stationery. Whoops, hollers, and Indian war cries resounded in the cave. Olive Kate howled her approval. I was a published author, at last!

"Don't let this go to your already-fat head," Fanny loudly teased.

Once I'd composed myself, Newt handed me the talking stick. Anticipation permeated the air, bringing with it an ethereal chill. I moved closer to the fire, deciding the time had come to enlighten my friends about Violet's ghostly call. Entranced, they listened as I carefully related the fantastic details. I didn't include *all* that Violet suggested, but I emphasized her admonition that Arious be persuaded to come home. "She insisted on complete truthfulness about the unhappy events that led to Arious's departure," I said softly.

The strong emotions I'd felt during Violet's visit came flooding back while four gaping faces stared at me, their expressions reflecting unreserved belief. I lowered my eyes for a moment, then turned my questioning gaze to Fawn.

"Violet said we have to tell Arious everything?" Fawn's voice was not one of protest, though it did betray fear and apprehension.

I nodded, then took Fawn's hand in mine. I'd been taught that true courage involved suffering. I now understood that just being alive sometimes requires a special kind of bravery.

EIGHTEEN

Rola Moon suggested a way to guarantee an answer to a letter. "Hang a hairpin as high as you can in a pine tree. Cedars work the best," she coaxed. "You'll hear something within the week."

"Can't Arious count to nine?" I grumpily mumbled as I struggled to hang the designated comb. My bulging belly got in the way, and I was breathing hard after repeatedly jumping. I slumped down to rest, discouraged. I wanted to return to my bed, pull the sheet tightly over my head, and secure it with the damn hairpin. I flung the wretched comb as far as I could, feeling guilty after cursing loud enough for my baby to hear. Olive Kate retrieved it, then doggedly pushed the pearly pin into my lap, insistent that I try again. After several tries, I finally reached the right limb.

I griped to Olive Kate as we marched home with snappy steps. An excellent listener, my dog kept her ears pointed forward in earnest concentration. However, she gave a little yelp of protest when I lamented, "Maybe Arious really doesn't care!" Olive Kate made me laugh; the sensation of joy felt good, yet unfamiliar—like the taste of exotic fruit.

Badgerwoman was waiting for me on my porch; we planned to grub for birthing herbs during the coolness of late afternoon. In Cherokee tradition, the head midwife and the expectant mother completed this ritual near the end of pregnancy, within days of the birth.

Since that fateful day when she saved my life, Fawn's granny had supplied me with a variety of herbal remedies. After Alton's death, she'd offered me a tea, infused with the petals of a passion flower, promising it would heal my broken heart. For my labor herbs, Badgerwoman insisted they be freshly picked and include valerian root, blue cohosh stems, and false unicorn leaves.

Before we left, I slipped my gun belt over my shoulder. I no longer had a waist onto which I could strap a holster, but I never left The Hill without my derringer. For unknown reasons, Klan activities had abated in Village Springs, though surrounding areas sometimes reported problems. T.H. insisted we not let our guard down. He was especially fearful for Essie, Egypt, Fawn, and Badgerwoman because they lived with us as part of our "white" family. That made them coveted targets of prejudice, especially to our enemies.

Badgerwoman figured our quest would take only two hours, so we decided not to tell Daddy, fearing he might stop us or insist on coming along. As we headed down the trail, Fawn waved us off, knowing her granny and I meant to be alone. With Olive Kate and my gun as added security, I looked forward to our mission. Time with Badgerwoman always proved interesting. For me, she was an adopted grandmother, and our souls knew each other well.

As we entered the quiet solitude of nearby forests, my footsteps were noticeably noisy. The elder Cherokee's boot-styled moccasins, fashioned from soft deer leather, made little sound even as she stepped on dry leaves. We soon reached the heart of lush woodlands, teeming with an abundance of flowering fruit trees, woody stems, and richly-colored leaves. Badgerwoman, clearly content in these surroundings, stopped to sit on an old tree trunk. The wise Cherokee senior leisurely stuffed some dark tobacco into her Indian-head stone pipe; she carefully lit it, inhaling slow and deep, before blowing a few perfect smoke rings. A quick nod and a rare wink affirmed her pleasure in the simple act.

Then, with casual attentiveness, Badgerwoman began the expected lesson. "Most folks don't understand how precious plants are," came the modulated, knowing words. "God created them for man's use, to help us help ourselves. The sacred secrets, the power they contain, mustn't be forgotten."

According to the aging sage, Cherokee shamen who drank special herbs and saw the future were called diviners; such men were revered for their bravery because they never knew if the foretellings would be good or bad. Sometimes, a diviner went insane after seeing visions of prophecy, unable to speak about the ominous portents, supernaturally revealed. Suddenly feeling a little depressed, I asked, "Did anyone ever divine the meanin' of life?"

Badgerwoman smiled and answered, "Yes. Our life's purpose is to *remember* who we are. Life's meanin' is to *become* that. We're not just animals. We're not just spirit. We're something more."

Eventually, we traveled farther from The Hill than we'd intended; even Olive Kate was panting, in need of a rest. We settled into a cool, aromatic grove of oversized mountain laurel trees. Badgerwoman picked the evergreen leaves and small blackish berries from the laurel while I searched for the ham and baked bean sandwiches I'd stuffed into my pouch.

We were on a little piece of land called Shadescrest, so near the river we could easily hear the sound of water as it clamored and spilled over rocks and other obstacles. After we'd eaten, my mentor played the homemade flute she kept tucked inside her waist sash. Its high-pitched, melodious sounds were so soothing I nodded off, letting the music's charm carry all cares and worries to the clouds.

I slept for several minutes before Olive Kate's wary growl awakened me. The deep, coarse rumble was the most threatening sound I'd ever heard her make. My foxhound stayed near me, turning in alert circles, as though the detected danger might come from any direction.

A skinny man stepped from behind nearby bushes, scratching his unshaven chin as he thought out loud. "Looks like it's time to play cowboys and Injuns, fellas," he snickered. Three other slovenly men, also with guns drawn, showed themselves. I didn't recognize any of them.

"Who are you? What do you want?" I asked, hiding my growing fear. I lay my hand atop Olive Kate's head, but she refused to relax.

"We're part of a midsummer night's crusade," answered one.

"To reclaim what's ours," replied another. "Up to now, Village Springs hasn't shown the white brotherhood much of a welcome. In fact, we've heard you've even locked up some of our friends."

We were trapped, surrounded by babbling lunatics. These Ku-Kluxers weren't wearing hoods or robes. They talked among themselves, discussing what to do with us as if Badgerwoman and I weren't there. I noticed that the vigilantes referred to each other with nicknames rather than numbers; this nuance signaled paramount danger. Within my womb, my baby stopped moving; it lay very still, as though guarded, listening for clues.

Reining in my temper, I asked, "Where are you boys from?" I hoped a friendly question, requiring a civil answer, might diffuse the situation.

"We are the law itself, Missie. Actually, we're here to do what the law can't…or won't," sneered their leader, the one called Rattler. With his angular face, hollow jaws, and beaked nose, he looked more like a bird of prey.

"We come from Pulaski, down around Kettle Creek," volunteered Mush, who appeared to be slower than the others; the dim-witted man nervously snapped his pudgy fingers to a silent beat only he could hear.

Rattler viciously jabbed his flustered comrade, hitting him in the ribs with the butt of a rifle. "You've already forgotten the three rules I gave you, Mush. First, keep your mouth closed. Second, don't talk. And third, shut up."

The heavyset, simple-minded man curled into a pain-filled ball and groveled at Rattler's feet. "I'm sorry, Rat. Mush won't talk no more. Don't tell Tangle-Eye I talked. Please Rat, don't tell!" Mush had let important information slip; Pulaski and Kettle Creek were both in Tennessee.

The men I faced were evidently part of a larger group now invading the woods and back roads of Village Springs. The quiet of previous weeks had been part of the plan, a teasing lure, that bewitching moment before the trap is sprung. As understanding filled me with dread, the name Tangle-Eye tweaked my intuitive sense with foreboding. I somehow knew that he and Toad were the same person.

"The scum is back," I muttered to myself.

"Shut up!" Rattler's malicious warning was directed toward me, but I ignored him, lost in thought. I almost fainted with the realization that Fawn was in danger; Toad would try to get to me through her.

The two men with Rattler and Mush were called Jabbo and Catfish. They appeared restless. Without warning, Jabbo moved toward me. Before I could respond, he shoved his hands under my breasts and lifted them, snorting, "My, these are nice. They feel like ripe, juicy melons—soft flesh and hard rinds."

I fought panic long enough to slap Jabbo. I smacked him hard, leaving my handprint on his pale, pock-marked skin. With trepidation, I watched as Jabbo's anger surfaced. A smirk crossed his face before he returned the slap, knocking me to the ground. I lay still, dazed and stunned.

With amazing ferocity, Olive Kate leapt onto Jabbo and sank her teeth into the space between his neck and shoulder. He shrieked in terror as her strong canine jaws clamped down, then tore away a sizable portion of muscle.

I screamed, "No!" when Rattler took retaliative aim. My protest and the rifle's blast sounded simultaneously. Olive Kate fell to the ground with a heartwrenching, inert thud. Fighting panic, I searched for my gun but couldn't find it.

In contrast, Badgerwoman sat in unperturbed meditation, remaining motionless as she stared into space. She'd laid aside her pipe and was holding her precious eagle feather with both hands.

Rattler purposefully lifted my dress with the barrel of his rifle, his expression raunchily carnal as he tortured me with the slowness of the act. The sight of my full-term belly, the bulging mound, had the opposite effect from that which he'd hoped for. Rattler didn't find my pregnant condition erotic; with evident disappointment, he let my dress fall.

"Moral degenerate!" I cried. My tears flowed freely with unleashed fury and relief.

The Klansman's attention turned to Badgerwoman. "Mongrel Injun," Rattler grunted. He spat in the old woman's face. Still, she didn't move or acknowledge his presence. "It's time you learned who owns this land." Rattler's tone was a hateful snarl. "There seem to be more coloreds around here than fiddlers in Hell, but we'll fix that."

Mad hysterics took over my mind when I realized what the Ku-Klux planned to do. Mush held onto me as I squirmed, kicked, and clawed at him. As Jabbo helped Catfish gather and stack inordinately large pieces of wood for a fire, blood seeped through the kerchief he'd tied around his dog bite.

I watched in horror as Rattler removed a branding iron from his saddle pack and began heating it over the open flame; the insignia on the end of the metal rod consisted of three K's enclosed by a double circle.

Badgerwoman must've known they planned to mark her with the evil seal, yet her expression remained passive, neutral. She appeared to be waiting for them to do their deed and be done with it; her hand clenched tighter around the brown power feather.

Once the wrought iron rod's brand was red hot, Jabbo and Rattler walked to the stiff old woman. Jabbo ripped the front of her dress with savage, bloodthirsty zeal. Without hesitation, Rattler pressed the fiery metal onto the softest part of Badgerwoman's skin, over her left breast-bone. The putrid smell of burning flesh permeated the air. Then, with delayed reaction, came the grievous, prolonged wail. The lamenting cry of unbearable pain. The elder's mournful protest subsided when she fell backwards, unconscious, onto the ground.

Mush released his hold, leaving me to my misery. As I crawled toward Badgerwoman, my hand touched cold metal; it was my derringer. Without my noticing, the gun had landed in a pile of leaves. I felt the furious pounding of my heart as rage coursed through my veins. I picked up the pistol, dead foliage falling away, and pointed the barrel.

Rattler laughed when he saw my intent. "I wouldn't try that if I were you," he scoffed. "You might get one of us, but I guarantee you won't shoot us all before the last one shoots you—right in the stomach."

It was a risk I couldn't take. I fell to my knees with the gun still in my hands as they rode away. Wracked with sobs, I moved to attend my injured friend.

Badgerwoman's eyes were still closed; the offending burn was deep, and the old woman's body trembled with shock. The skin around the brand's mark, as well as the underlying tissues, had been utterly destroyed. The sign of the KKK, with its double-edged circle, could be distinguished by charred and blackened skinless areas.

I whined, gently poking Badgerwoman's arm the way a puppy might nudge its injured mother. Her answering moan was piteous. I felt dizzy as I ran to the river, ripping wide pieces of cloth from my skirt and hurriedly dipping them in the chilly water. As I put the cold compress upon Badgerwoman's wound, I gasped at the sight of filmy vapors, rising like steamy clouds. Fawn's granny grimaced, then opened her eyes.

"They're gone," I whispered.

"Olive Kate?" In the midst of her own terrible pain, she was reminding me to check on my dog.

"I think she's dead," I murmured. But when I turned to look, I saw that the foxhound was gone. She'd crawled away during the commotion.

Badgerwoman tried to sit, and I encouraged her to lay still. "No, help me up," she insisted.

I made the old matriarch as comfortable as I could. She gingerly reclined upon my knapsack, propped against a nearby log. "I'm gonna get help," I assured her. "I'll leave now, and try my best to run. I'll come back as quick as I can."

Badgerwoman fervently shook her head, her eyes pleading for understanding. "You have to stay, child; there's something you must hear."

I comforted my hurt friend by dripping cool water upon her forehead. As I stroked her long, gray hair affectionately, her panic subsided.

"There's something I need you to do," she beseeched. "I'd do it myself if these twisted hands worked right…" a pause, and then, "…and if Grandmother Time wasn't callin' me home."

"All you have to do is name it, and it's done," I said.

"Make Fawn a feather bundle to wear when she's off by herself. To keep her from harm." The old woman's voice was low and serious. "You'll need three feathers to make it right. One of them should be soft, with smooth lines. The other two must be stiff, so use my eagle feather for one of those; its power will give the bundle fire and wind. The hardness brings balance to the tender touch. Tie the bundle at the top with the longest sides of the feathers pointin' outwards."

"I'll make it right away," I murmured.

"You won't forget?" Her voice carried a pressing, urgent tone. The elder Cherokee's unusual request raised my anxiety; I wondered if she sensed danger for Fawn. I felt a headlong, critical need to return to The Hill.

"I promise, Grandmother," I said as I touched her cheek. It was the only time I'd ever called her by that name, and she was obviously moved by the gesture.

"I must tell you a story." Her words belied intense physical agony.

"Stories can wait 'til you're better. This burn needs to be tended right away. You've *got* to let me go for help."

"Hear the story, then go get Maude." She tried to move, then winced with the effort. "Promise you won't go before I finish?"

Never before had I heard Badgerwoman beg. "All right," I finally conceded, camouflaging my own desperation.

After a deep sigh of relief, she said, "I once knew a young white woman who had a wanderin' spirit. A college teacher who wrote about people livin' in far-off places. In time, she came to live with the Cherokee. The woman fell in love with a young man from the tribe. Their bond was strong, and it brought forth a girl child."

Badgerwoman coughed repeatedly; the spasms increased her pain. I put a water-filled canteen to her lips, and she sipped from it before continuing. "Soon after the child was born, the woman fell from a cliff and hurt her head. She slept for many days. When she woke up, she had no memory. She didn't know anyone—her friends, her husband, not even her own baby.

"After the fall, the woman acted strangely. Yet, her new visions were pure. The tribe's Elders called her gift the 'second sight.'" Badgerwoman struggled for breath, forcing the words with stubborn determination. "Many moons passed, but the woman's mind was lost. She wandered away from the village. Again and again, she was brought back by search parties. Her young husband grew sadder. Then, after the poor woman drifted away for the last time, his heart was broken. He held his child and cried for days. That child grew up happy, raised by Dolphus—her father—and her father's mother.

"The young man never stopped lookin' for his lost love. He found her, ten years later, livin' alone in the wooded hills of another state. He wanted to move his family there, to watch over her from afar. He died of the flux before the trip could be made."

Badgerwoman stopped, swallowed hard, then went on. "The child and her granny did as the man would've done, makin' the journey to be near the woman. The girl believed her mother had died. The lie was told to keep her from longin' for something she could never have, a mother who knew and loved her."

From somewhere nearby, a barn owl hooted; odd, considering the time of day. Fawn's grandmother didn't seem to notice. "The girl's granny kept the secret for two more reasons. She was afraid the child would hate her for tellin' such a fib, though it was the only lie the granny ever told. She also feared the growin' girl would try to talk to her mother, causin' the woman to spook and run, never to be found again."

Badgerwoman concluded her story, saying, "Doin' one's best drives away regret. That's why I must tell the truth now."

She waited for me to unravel her riddle. My lips grew numb as I pressed them tightly together. The owl hooted again. Proverbs 3:3 rattled my brain: "Let not mercy and truth forsake thee. Bind them about thy neck. Write them upon the table of thine heart."

Without blame or judgment, I asked, "Is Fawn the child in the story?" Badgerwoman was exhausted, but she managed a nod. "And the woman? Who is Fawn's mother?" My whole body tensed.

"Her mother is the woman you know as Rola Moon. Her real name is Nora Storm." The elder's words were barely a whisper, but they were unmistakable. A satisfied smile crossed the old woman's face before she drifted into blessed, anodyne sleep.

I quickly formed a makeshift blanket using my slip and a layer of leaves, covering Fawn's granny as best I could. I stood upright, but felt weak. During Badgerwoman's confession, I'd noticed several abdominal pangs, the beginning of labor. Bewildered and distressed, I again made my way to the river, headed for help.

We'd been gone over three hours. It would take almost that long to make it to The Hill, if I could sprint. I soon realized that would be impossible; my labor pain intensified rapidly, prompted by agitated excitement. The mounting contractions harmonized at regular intervals. In between the sharp cramps, I experienced ongoing lightheadedness.

Never slowing, I stumbled across exposed tree roots and immense boulders that bordered the river. Sobbing, I held onto my distended, aching stomach; my other hand caressed my gun belt.

The struggle to walk grew increasingly difficult. My imagination conjured a terrifying image. I saw myself, alone in pitch-dark woods, having my baby with nobody to help me. Disappointment and despair overwhelmed me when, after an hour, I'd progressed less than a quarter of the distance I needed to cover. I lay on the ground, exhausted.

"In every lifetime there's a moment when *any* wish will be granted. Yours is now! Pray, Pug. Pray like never before!" The familiar voice resounded inside my mind. It was Alton, speaking to me from an unquiet grave—I was no longer alone. Persuaded by that belief, I raised my head and saw that I'd fallen beside a small rowan tree. According to

Rola, its narrow limbs could be hung over a child's bed to keep away evil spirits.

I held onto a rowan branch and prayed, "Dear God, please guide me and my baby to safety. Aid me in doin' what's needed to help Badgerwoman. It's a heavy load; I can't carry it alone. Send Your lovin' angels to my rescue. I ask this with a grateful heart."

It was then that I saw it. I blinked hard, doubtful at first; but there it was, acting as a compass card. The flower lay upon a patch of scattered pine straw a few yards away, apart from any other greenery or blossom. The single, red sweetheart rose glowed with a purplish tinge in the dim afternoon light. Such roses do not grow in the dense shade of deep woods. Its sudden appearance was a miracle, proving to me that, even in death, Alton hadn't abandoned me.

I knew that even God's brigade couldn't help me if I didn't help myself, so I broke off a small tree branch and used it as a walking stick. I made my way to where the rose lay and picked it up, no longer feeling crippled by the expanding contractions. Instead, I kept moving, taking strength from knowing that the pain heralded the arrival of Alton's child.

Ten minutes after leaving the rowan tree, I heard horses approaching from the north. I hid behind a Douglas Fir and waited to see who the riders were. Heaven had sent three angels in the form of Fawn, Azberry, and the last person I expected to see—*Arious.* I immediately stepped into view, and they jumped off their horses. I collapsed into my brother-in-law's arms with a weak-kneed sense of relief.

"When Olive Kate limped home with a bullet in her back, we knew something was wrong!" Azberry excitedly announced. "I've been helpin' to guard The Hill 'cause Daddy and his deputies have their hands full," my brother added. "They've been gone the whole afternoon. Kluxers are causin' trouble all around, like an invasion!"

Arious had arrived on The Hill shortly after Badgerwoman and I left. He'd been looking for me, but found Fawn instead. I could tell that she had told him about the rape, about everything. The renewed bond between them was apparent, stronger than ever.

"How'd you know where to find me?" I sobbed.

"Fawn knew." Arious's astonishment was reflected in his voice.

My friend leaned over and whispered, "I think it was Violet."

After Azberry and Fawn assured me they were armed, they rode toward Shadescrest, to find Badgerwoman and return her to The Hill. Arious lifted me onto his horse and spirited me home, carefully placing me upon my bed.

Doc Self saw to Badgerwoman's wounds while Arious took care of me, but every able body looked in on the old woman when they could. Throughout my labor, my family assured me that Fawn's granny was resting comfortably.

The physical efforts of childbirth were more difficult than I'd imagined. As I labored, I sweated a pint of fluid. The overall agony lasted twelve long hours. Arious helped me through the final, screaming stage by keeping me in a "twilight sleep." This was accomplished with intermittent doses of chloroform, just enough to ease the pain but not render me unconscious.

When the time came for my baby to be born, I lay with my feet elevated upon homemade leg rests. A small pillow was substituted for my regular one, then Mama draped the rest of me with sheets. I smiled with excited joy when Arious announced he could see the top of my baby's head. He grasped my child under the chin and guided his niece into the world. At the moment my child uttered her first, hesitant cry, my dead husband's photo tipped over on its own accord.

Arious laid my little girl, with her umbilical cord still attached, upon my flattened belly; he immediately swabbed her mouth. Mamau Maude expertly tied off the birth cord—then cut. I felt a brief pang of regret as I was permanently, physically separated from my daughter.

Mama gave her grandchild a sponge bath, then wrapped the little whelp in a warm blanket and placed her in my arms. I cannot describe the intensity of feeling that washed over me as I held my baby for the first time and sensed the promise of her future. She'd inherited my blue eyes, but her hair was dark like Alton's. Her lips were shaped like a perfect, tiny heart.

"Have you thought of a name for her?" Arious's smile was a red-letter grin.

"Uncle, I'd like to introduce you to Piper Cora Strawbridge." Mama gave a startled, throaty sound upon hearing her own name, and I could tell she was pleased.

"Piper was *my* mother's name," Arious murmured, subdued by emotion.

"I know," I whispered, "This one will carry the torch of those that love her, near and far."

Arious continued to sit with me while my mother and grandmother returned to Sheridan House for something to eat and a change of clothes. The moment gave us the chance we needed to talk privately.

"Why didn't you answer my letters?" My voice was free of anger, but I punched him hard on the shoulder for emphasis.

"Pride," Arious replied with an embarrassed shrug, grimacing while rubbing his new bruise.

"Pride goes about as far as one can spit," I countered.

"I know," he chuckled. "At least I know it now."

"Are you and Fawn gonna be all right?"

Arious's face streamed with tears. "I literally pulled some of my own hair out when she told me. It'll take a while to forgive myself for actin' like such a horse's ass. It helps that she already has. Forgiven me, I mean."

"What made you decide to come home?"

"I'm not sure you'd believe me if I told you." Arious's face reddened.

"Try me," I responded with a sly grin.

Arious scrunched his forehead. "Well, this one's a doozie. I don't want to upset you, but you deserve to know sooner or later. In this case, sooner is better."

I held my breath as he solemnly reached into his pocket and pulled out a ring. "This lay on my bureau when I arose for work earlier this week. It wasn't there the night before."

I didn't recognize the significance of the ring until Arious placed it in my hand. It was then that I saw the inscription, the Strawbridge crest. It was Alton's wedding band, the one he'd been buried with.

$$* \quad * \quad *$$

The following morning, Fawn brought me breakfast. She wore a coy smile, like a Cheshire cat that'd swallowed the pet parakeet, wordlessly waiting until I'd settled Piper onto my breast. Then, with a gleeful giggle, Fawn asked, "Will you be my matron of honor?"

"Of course!" I squealed so loudly I startled the baby; Piper let out an earsplitting, high-pitched cry.

"I believe she has her mother's temper," Fawn joked.

"God's fury has nothin' on the wrath of a newborn, Irish girl-child," I replied, laughing with indescribable joy.

After eagerly discussing preliminary wedding hopes and wishes, our merriment settled into a comfortable silence. It was then that Fawn haltingly murmured, "I also have some bad news."

I knew what was coming. Until that moment, I'd been afraid to ask. "Olive Kate?" I whispered.

Fawn nodded. "Fanny and I tried our best to pull her through, but she died durin' the night. I'm sorry. There's comfort in knowin' her pups will make it. That is, with a little help."

While Piper nursed, I held onto the makeshift necklace that now encircled Alton's wedding band and cried. Olive Kate and I had a special bond; my grief cut deep. She had proven her devoted attachment and affection to the end. "God only knows what would've happened if she hadn't crawled home. Tell Azberry to bury her next to his fairy tree. It's pretty there, and Olive Kate liked smellin' the wild strawberries that grow along its trunk."

"I'll help him," Fawn promised. "We'll do it this mornin' while the ground is still wet."

✳   ✳   ✳

As Piper was being born, T.H. arrested three unidentified Klansmen, but not before five Negroes were branded and their homes burned to the ground. Alabama's Attorney General, a Klan sympathizer, ordered my father to send his prisoners to Montgomery to stand trial, but there the case was whitewashed.

It was the last straw for Daddy. He made plans to travel to Washington, to storm his congressman's office. He was so mad, Mama worried he might blow a gasket and have a stroke. Thankfully, T.H. calmed down every time he held Piper in his arms.

In contrast, the wound I'd given Toad so long ago would never heal. He and his black-hearted friends posed an ongoing threat, to me and the community as a whole. That fact became clearer one week after Piper's birth. While visiting Alton's grave, I found a note lying on my husband's tombstone, held in place by a heavy rock. I rolled the large paperweight over, then picked up the childish scrawl:

Pug, Do you feel a pebble in your shoe? It's you who'll someday be stepped on. I'm willing to bide my time, even if it takes years to settle the score. If I were you, I'd keep one eye in the back of my head and the other on anybody I cared about. Speak to the Devil and you'll hear the clatter of his hooves...Toad

Someday, I'd cross paths with Toad again. When that time came, only one of us would continue down life's road.

NINETEEN

Our family took turns sitting with Badgerwoman. Day or night, one of us was always at her bedside. Increasingly ill with a bronchial condition and a persistent infection from her wound, she accepted her fate with forbearance and unruffled grace. Arious's medical prognosis was bleak. "She's plain worn out," he sadly announced, whispering the grim outlook to those of us holding an understated vigil on her porch.

Between naps, the old Indian rambled; her words usually made perfect sense, but sometimes they didn't. Occasionally, she had conversations with people only she could see, including her dead son.

Desiring time alone with the Cherokee elder, I left my week-old baby sleeping contentedly in Mama's arms. When I arrived at the Storm cabin, Badgerwoman was drowsy, but awake. Azberry had been with her since midday; he welcomed me with a sad smile.

As soon as my brother left, my aged friend asked how I'd spent my afternoon. While arranging a bouquet of red canna in a vase that sat near Badgerwoman's bed, I said, "The baby and I planted Daylilies on top of Alton's grave."

She nodded her understanding, grasping the symbolic meaning of my flowery choice; the golden petals bloomed for one day only, then each beautiful blossom died. Long spans of time passed before another bloom took the place of the dead one. "Don't water them with bitter tears," she tenderly admonished.

"I won't," I whispered as I kissed her forehead, then slid into a cane-backed chair. Badgerwoman wasn't appeased; she knew I was lying. The stinging wound left by my husband's death was as plain as day to her. We'd *both* been permanently branded.

"My people learned about bitterness the hard way," she murmured. "It muddles the mind. Turns cold hearts to ice. You've every right to feel as you do, child. But only for a while. Someday soon, you must go on livin'."

As our eyes communicated our emotions, the sun broke through an overcast sky and warm, pink light filled the room. "Fawn showed me the feather bundle you made," she said, changing the subject. "She's real proud of it. As she should be. You did fine." The accolade made me smile. I knew what was coming next, so I waited. "You're keepin' our secret?" Badgerwoman's eyebrows raised expectantly, though she already knew the answer.

"You don't need to worry," I reassured. "Here, let me fluff your pillow—you look uncomfortable."

"Careful," she quipped, "if you move old furniture, it might fall to bits."

"I'll remember that," I said, joining in the joke.

As I stood to leave, Badgerwoman's voice grew weaker. "I'm sorry we didn't get to use our birthin' herbs."

"That's all right," I answered. "Arious took good care of me."

"Try to remember all I've taught you?" The undercurrent of resolute will went far beyond mere words.

"I promise I won't forget," I said, my voice breaking with emotion. I kissed my friend on her leathery cheek, making our final good-bye complete, then returned to my baby.

The next morning, my family gathered in and around the Storm cabin, huddled together as Badgerwoman lay dying. Doc Self was there too, helping Arious when he could. Uncle Finas, Sara, and I sat on the little porch steps, shaded by the pale, peach-colored flowers of a dogwood tree. My uncle leaned in close and whispered, "There's a dove sittin' on the gate. He's come for her."

What followed was a lesson about dying with dignity—which, according to Mama Maude, means dying in character. As the end grew near, my grandmother and Badgerwoman actually *joked* with each other. "Maude, it won't be long now. How about comin' with me?"

"I'll walk that red road with you as far as I can," came my grandmother's calm, knowing answer. She gently massaged her friend's feet, smiled, and added, "I'm sure I'll be catchin' up soon enough."

For those two, the process of death held no fear; the lamp was merely running out of oil, the way it's supposed to. As Badgerwoman put it, "I'm happy to shed this old winter coat for a new one."

In contrast, Fawn sat speechless, pale and rigid; she'd held her granny's hand since dawn. Fawn was losing the last of her family, or so she thought.

Badgerwoman's final words were whispered to her granddaughter. "I'll be with you, my child, as you trace the path to Spring."

With honored reverence befitting a medicine woman, we formed a loving circle around Badgerwoman's bed. Her last few breaths were labored, but there was no struggle. She simply closed her eyes, then followed the setting sun.

An unassuming burial was held on a venerated patch of Strawbridge land called Oneona, an old Indian word meaning "end of the trail." Fawn liked the area's rolling, sage-covered hills and babbling brooks.

Once the coffin was lowered into the ground, Fawn knelt and dropped her granny's precious medicine bundle into the grave. As Badgerwoman requested, she was buried in a plain, pine box. There was no minister, just family and friends. Fawn stood, then touched my shoulder, beseeching me to give the eulogy. I nodded, handed Piper to Mama, and composed myself.

With arms outstretched I said, "The past lives on in our memories. Those we've loved and lost are there, too. We're reminded of this whenever we look at a star at dawn." I pointed to Badgerwoman's final resting place and continued, "A good and wise person sleeps here, one that never disturbed the wind. She taught us the most important lesson of all: *The oneness of God equals the total of all there is.*"

When I finished speaking, I raised my head in time to see a mysterious, lone figure standing in the far-off distance, amid fog-enshrouded trees. I wondered if I was seeing another deceased spirit, come from the Beyond to scrutinize the burial. Then I saw the figure move as a living person does. No one else seemed to notice the uninvited guest.

When the funeral ended, a simple marker was placed upon the burial mound, an epitaph that read, "The Storm of Life Echoes Still." Badgerwoman's final secret lay buried in my heart. I intended to tell Fawn about her mother's identity, but the right time hadn't come. Fawn needed to be stronger; her reconciliation with Arious would help in that regard. With added confidence, Fawn would gain the fortitude required to accept the truth. That was my reasoning—before fate intervened.

Two weeks after Badgerwoman's passing, I gave Piper her midnight feeding, then fell into a sound sleep. An hour later, I was awakened by a series of fervent, frustrated screams. I sat up in bed, heart pounding. The distant calls for help were frequently interrupted by long moments of loud swearing. I threw on my robe and checked on Piper; she looked like a slumbering cherub. I left her safely tucked into her Starleaf cradle, then followed the unending trail of cuss words to Sheridan House. As I neared my childhood home, I was relieved to hear my father's deep, earthy laugh.

I rounded the corner on the southeast side and realized what had happened. Azberry, now fourteen, continued his life-long habit of prowling darkened woods. As he'd commenced this night's nocturnal stroll, he'd fallen from his window into the rain barrel. Immobilized, securely wedged in the stale, rusty water, as hard as he tried, Azberry couldn't free himself.

Embarrassment fed Azberry's panicked anger while he shivered in his watery pen. Ultimately, the only way to free him was literally to pour him out, headfirst. Laying on the ground, my brother looked like a shriveled bottle gourd. Pickled and rinsed, abashed beyond words, Azberry ran into the house and slammed the door.

Afterwards, as I approached my own threshold, I sensed another presence; somebody was inside my cabin. *Oh my God,* I thought, *Piper!* The corner of my eye caught the sparkle of a shiny object, reflected in moonlight. A mahogany walking stick rested against the porch railing. I breathed a sigh of relief; it belonged to Rola Moon.

I hurried inside to find the white-haired sorceress bending close to the cradle, examining my daughter with great care. When Rola saw me, she said, "I've brought her a present." Rola announced her intention nonchalantly, as though all my visitors delivered their baby gifts in the middle of the night. But, I couldn't be angry with her; I understood that she didn't want to be seen.

My witch-friend pressed a pearly, translucent gem into my hand. "It's a moonstone. It opens one's heart to inner knowin'. You can give it to Piper when she's old enough to know it's not candy."

"Thank you," I said. "I've never seen anything like it." I'd lost my desire to sleep, so I politely added, "Would you like something hot to drink?"

Rola gave a quick, appreciative nod, then asked, "Have you given your babe her weed yet?"

The little leaves of the Bittersweet Weed had been made into a tea and given to three-week-old babes for centuries, a preventative against contagion. The brew caused irksome hives; but, superstition held that a baby lacking such a skin rash wouldn't live.

"I'm not so sure that old wives' tale works," I mumbled.

Rola frowned, displeased with my halfhearted answer. She reached into her pocket and pulled out two small newspaper-wrapped bundles. "Here are some Bitters," she insisted. "If you won't use those, this catnip will work almost as well."

"All right, I'll give it to her in the mornin'," I reluctantly agreed. Mamau Maude had been pestering me for days regarding the same topic. She'd worn me down, and Rola finished me off.

"Good. You won't regret it," the witch replied. The night grew eerily quiet. It was unusual for Rola to initiate an extended conversation, but on that particular night, under the cover of darkness, she did.

"I've often had the feelin' that the time I'm livin' in isn't real," she sighed. Her lilting voice betrayed something I'd never heard before—a kind of wary expectancy, the way one might sound while opening a present with suspicious contents, knowing it could be a coiled snake or a diamond tiara. Rola cocked her head, then shyly said, "You seem jumpy. Beyond nervous. Tell me what's wrong."

For the life of me, I couldn't meet her gaze. "No, I'm fine. Really. Just sad about Badgerwoman's passin'. I miss her." I continued to stare, with fixed resolve, at the cuckoo clock on the far wall.

"You're lyin' to me, Pug, and have been for weeks. You've never lied before, so I guess there's a good reason. You even look at me different. Why? You grieve for your friend, but there's more on your mind. And I'm part of it. What are you holdin' back?"

"For your own good, Rola, don't ask me that." I was feeling flustered. Rola Moon was the one person I couldn't stall or mislead. Sometimes, I was sure she could read my mind.

Her next statement shocked me; with it came the realization that Rola and I were playing a risky game of cat and mouse. "Nothin' is so burdensome as a secret," she murmured.

"Sometimes, that's true," I answered with a raspy voice.

"Some confidences are like feet firmly planted in the past," she shot back.

"If a big trust is put in your hands, you can safely tell it to God or the wind. It's a kind of oath one takes," I countered. My ears began to burn.

"Nobody understood that better than my adopted mother," the witch whispered.

"Oh my God, Rola. Are you sayin' what I think?"

"I hope I am," she said, her voice low and cautious. "I'm livin' the dream of the watcher, with confusin' flashes inside my head, like lightnin'. Sketches of faces. Pictures of places. They stay clear for a moment, maybe two, but then blur again, disappearing into some dark hole I can't find."

Rola paused for my reaction, though I remained tongue-tied. She searched in quicksilver for more words. "I've deciphered who Badgerwoman was," she began, hesitant. "Kind of. It's a hard puzzle, a familiar knowin', like a rekindled fire that keeps burnin' itself out. It started a year ago." Rola clasped my arm with a firm, unyielding grip. "Pug, I need your help with the rest of it. I see it in your eyes; *you know more than I do.* Please tell me what I'm missin'."

With anxious care, I spoke the words Rola waited to hear. "You are Nora Storm, wife of Dolphus, now deceased. You are Nora Storm, mother of Fawn, my best friend." Rola clutched her chest, stood, then steadied herself with the back of her chair. "Are you all right?" I asked, fearing she'd bolt and run, never to be seen again.

Rola nodded, then stiffly walked to the window and stared at the blackness beyond the glass. "Deep down, I knew there was a bein' linked to me. A sweet child. Here, where my heart aches. She's been so close. And far away at the same time. I wish I could hold her in my mind. Remember her at my breast. But I can't."

My witch-friend finally turned to look at me with resignation and sadness. "I trust you. If you say this is true, then it is. I just don't know what it means. Where it fits into my head pictures." Rola rubbed her temple as she absorbed the enormous implications. I knew she'd moved into the second phase of understanding when she asked, "Does Fawn know about me?"

My words fell with a gentle thud. "She believes her mother is dead." I hesitated, then added, "I could speak to her. You could meet…"

For the first time that night, Rola looked as if she might panic. She vigorously shook her head as she inched away from me. Her back hit the wall. She wept with the words, "I can handle scorn. I'm used to it. But from my own child? No. That would break my heart."

Rola's mood slowly shifted to anger. "Lost years. Countless lies. Deceitful words. Badgerwoman kept my daughter from me. For all this time. Why? Maybe I did something bad. Something the old woman couldn't forgive. I can't be sure. So much is lost in that memory place. If the truth were known, my daughter might hate me, too."

My own deep, frustrated sigh filled my ears. Misunderstanding abounded; I was the only one who could set it right. "Badgerwoman wasn't angry with you, Rola," I began. "She held no grudge. In fact, she loved you like a daughter. She was sorely afraid of doin' the wrong thing, of scarin' you. Her biggest worry was that you'd run away again."

I risked moving closer to my friend, though the look in her eyes remained wild and fearful. "Rola, Badgerwoman watched over you from afar, in the same way you watch over me. Withholdin' your identity was a heartache she carried to her grave, to protect you and Fawn." I lightly touched Rola's shoulder. "Badgerwoman did the best she could. You *must* believe that."

A taut silence reigned until my cuckoo clock sounded its wacky tone three times. Rola and I jumped, startled by the sudden racket. Then, with the tension broken, we both laughed at the ironic intrusion.

"I believe you, Pug, I do," Rola announced, her voice breaking. "It makes sense now."

Once the reasons for the deception were made clear, Fawn's mother understood that Badgerwoman had held no malice. I brewed another pot of raspberry tea. While I poured the warm liquid into Rola's mug, she smiled and said, "I was at Badgerwoman's funeral, hidden from sight. I prayed for her help and understandin'. It looks like she heard me."

"Perhaps she did," I answered, beaming with self-satisfaction.

The witch's eyes glazed over as she thought aloud. Her voice was low, awestruck. "The old woman planned this. She knew you and I were friends. She meant for us to come together. To help each other. She was a fox, that one."

"A silver fox," I said. Awash with emotion, I could barely speak.

"There's something you should know," Rola said, her tone mysterious. "It might be hard to hear, but you need to listen. It's about Badgerwoman bein' branded."

I nodded; the memory made me shiver.

"There was strong purpose at work that day," Rola continued. "Cherokee medicine. Badgerwoman shifted the men's anger away from you by turnin' it on herself. She protected you by absorbin' their hatred into her own flesh." My eyes glistened, and Rola took notice; she placed her hand atop mine and said, "If you search your heart, you'll know it's true."

I hugged myself with awed wonder and gratitude. *Cherokee medicine.* I'd been blessed with a double dose.

"Thank you for givin' me back my life," Rola whispered.

"Thanks for showin' me mine," I answered.

Before she returned to her cabin, Rola asked me to speak to Fawn as soon as possible. At dawn, I found Rola's daughter sitting under an oak tree, nursing one of Olive Kate's pups with a baby bottle. I sat beside her to nurse Piper, small talk hiding my nervousness. I babbled incessantly about the long Indian summer, my winter garden, and a tooth that'd been bothering me.

"What's going on? You're as fidgety as this puppy dog," came Fawn's blunt response.

I said, "Listen, you might find what I'm about to tell you hard to believe, at first." I paused. Fawn playfully punched me. I gathered more courage and continued, "Your granny told me a story before she died. I'm gonna repeat it for you now, as best I can remember." I thought for a moment, then launched into the truth. After I'd finished all but the naming of her mother, Fawn stared at me with her eyebrows scrunched together; it was a look that penetrated my soul.

"What are you tellin' me?" Fawn's question was delivered as a command. She absently dropped the baby bottle, and the puppy wriggled out of her lap.

My face flushed and reddened. "Your mother isn't dead. Circumstances kept you from knowin' her, but she's alive. Your granny brought you to Village Springs to be near her, just like your daddy planned before he died."

The look on Fawn's face reflected a lifetime of loss. No longer sure of the task at hand, I pressed on anyway. "Fawn, I survived my snakebite because you moved here. We're part of an unyieldin', invisible web, you and me, one that's connected and tangled our lives. We're linked to other people, too. Your granny understood that. She did everything she could to keep the web whole."

Comprehension dawned in Fawn's eyes. "Pug, do you know who my mother is?"

I stalled a little longer. I knew the blunt answer would be a blow. "Well, your mama is someone who's lived her life in two parts. She's wise and good-willed. She's also misunderstood. That's because she doesn't hide behind pretense."

Annoyed with my answer, Fawn angrily yelled, "Damn it! I deserve to know. What's her name?"

"Rola Moon."

"The witch? The witch is my mother?"

"First of all," I replied, "Even if she calls herself that, as far as I know, she's never done harm. I've told you about my visits. She's kind-hearted and quite lonely.

"Recently, she's recalled some things. It's a big step. The past is still a blur in her mind, but she now knows you are her child."

"I have a…Oh my God, *I have a mother*." Fawn chanted these words, over and over again. Blessed with such knowledge, Fawn fully emerged from her shadow play into the light of the passing day. She wanted to go, immediately, to Rola's house.

I packed Piper into her Cherokee-styled papoose and saddled two horses. Rola was standing on her porch when Fawn and I rode into the yard.

"Mama?" Fawn cried, hastily jumping from her horse. She almost tripped as she bounded to her mother's open arms, but Rola caught her before she could fall.

"Yes, baby, I'm here," came Rola's choked sob.

The reunion unfolded from the inside out, like a delicate seed, opening fully to a season of faith. Rola and Fawn wept as though they shared one breath, pausing to reflect on the unseen gifts they already possessed. I nestled my own child as I watched the gentle sway of their tight embrace. As one life story had closed, another had been born anew.

TWENTY

They say when calling a dog, you shouldn't hold a stick in your hand. Daddy was armed for bear when he left Village Springs aboard the L&N, bound for Washington. Sadly, the trip was a waste of time. Change within the corrupt, convoluted federal bureaucracy was as likely as a sudden shift in the cycles of the sun and moon.

Alabama's representative, Senator Doolittle, was aptly named; he even refused to support an anti-lynching law. A Southern Democrat willing to use any means necessary to end Republican control of his state, he saw the Klan as his ally. After returning to The Hill, T.H. renamed all Sheridan canines "Doolittle."

As a rule, *nobody* in Washington showed an interest in Klan atrocities. Political attention was focused across the Atlantic Ocean, where our entry into the European war seemed imminent. That fact hit home when Arious received a draft notice, ordering him to appear at Camp McClellan by mid-November to train medics for the war effort. Afterwards, as he was young and battle-worthy, he'd serve in Europe on the front lines.

Arious and Fawn had planned to marry during the spring of the following year. Instead, they decided to wed before he left for war. Family and friends helped execute the hurried arrangements, setting the wedding for November 1st, All Saints' Day. Fawn believed the auspicious date would bring good luck.

Egypt made the bridal gown from a pattern she designed herself; God had given her a genius's talent for working with fine fabric. She sewed the white velvet dress by hand, guided by a pattern cut from sheets of newspaper, some containing articles describing the Great War's bloody battles. She spent late hours attaching the delicate pearls that enhanced the fitted bodice of Fawn's gown; tireless, loving patience attended every stitch. When finished, Egypt presented her friend with a dress fit for royalty. I was in Fawn's cabin when Egypt delivered her completed work.

"Do you like it, Calaeno?" Egypt's question coyly used Fawn's secret name for emphasis, fishing for a well-deserved compliment.

"There are no words big enough to thank you," Fawn replied with a wide smile. "Will you accept this gift as a token? The Cherokee call such a swap a 'giveaway.'" With deliberate formality, she presented Egypt with an exquisite quilt; its intricate Indian design was called "Return of the Swallows." It was the last one Badgerwoman had sewn, and everybody knew how precious it was to Fawn.

After the future bride excitedly slipped the smooth, elegant dress over her head, the three of us shared a precious moment as she proudly pranced around the room. Fawn glowed with an undefinable radiance; she looked like an empress, majestic and grand.

Ruby came home for the wedding. I'd prepared myself, but it was a jolt when she stepped off the train wearing her nun's habit. She looked like a different person, and that fact rapidly became a barrier for everyone who knew her. I noticed that no one cussed in front of Ruby anymore, not even T.H., not even me. Ruby was used to deferential treatment, but not from her childhood friends.

When Seven Sisters met to plan Fawn's pre-nuptial party, Ruby grew exasperated by our stiff behavior. "Relax, for Heaven's sake. It's still *me* you're talkin' to!"

"Can't help it!" Fanny exclaimed. "Every time I look at you, it feels like I'm starin' at the Virgin herself. Like she's right here with us, takin' notes whenever we do something wrong."

"You said it yourself; you're God's handmaiden now, Ruby," Egypt explained. "I think He pays closer attention, watchin' over you, I mean."

"I think it's that outfit you've got on," said Newt. "Such a fancy garment is hard to get past."

"Well, y'all have to get beyond it," Ruby sighed. "Besides, I'm not a real nun yet. Since I haven't taken my final vows, I'm called a novice."

"You mean a baby nun," I joked.

Ruby laughed. "Something like that. Would it help if, just for tonight, I changed into regular clothes?" This question was answered with a chorus of nods, so I loaned Ruby a long-sleeved, navy blue dress. "One night only," Ruby reminded us as she reluctantly changed. "I'm a Catholic Sister, that's true, but I'm also a Seven Sisters lifetime member. Nothin' is *ever* gonna change that." Our friend's noble gesture helped us realize how silly we'd been. It was time to stop living in the past; Ruby had every right to honor God in her own way.

Halloween arrived, the eve of Fawn's wedding, and the perfect time for our "hen party" at Sheridan House. Seven Sisters were joined by Mama, Mamau Maude, Sara, and Rola Moon. Although Rola had risked tentative contact with my family since reuniting with her daughter, these were short visits, little snippets of trust. Her eccentricities continued to be marked, but my relatives accepted her without condition. Rola returned the sentiment, albeit hesitantly. She'd made considerable progress; joining our party was another milestone.

Fawn's bridal shower blossomed into a night of song and sport, its rituals worthy of heathens, an evening that embodied the female soul. We played apple games, contests handed down from medieval times. Rola told us that the old tradition of bobbing for apples symbolized the practice of drowning convicted witches; the game's participants, therefore, were cheating death.

I was concerned that Mama or Mamau Maude would be vexed by some of Rola's notions. On the contrary, they remained highly entertained by her stories; they also understood how well-meaning, yet vulnerable, Rola was.

The night of magic charms quickened when Rola read each woman's future in nutshell ashes. She told Ruby that her true path would someday find her teaching school in Village Springs. The witch predicted that Mama and Sara would take a wonderful trip together, accompanied by two men. In good fun, we teased the older women, accusing them of a covert rendezvous with undisclosed lovers.

Fanny was assured a secret admirer. Newt's future promised a long and healthy life. Our sorceress told Egypt that her life's gift was her beautiful voice. "The angels love to hear you sing," Rola affirmed. "You should do it more often."

When Mamau Maude's turn came, she declined any exploration into the time to come. Instead, she sweetly offered to read tea leaves for Rola, who was delighted by this kind gesture. My grandmother spooned exotic Darjeeling into a china cup filled with warm water, then waited for the tea to settle to the bottom. "I see May Boughs on your door and Easter Eggplant blossoms sprinkled across the threshold," Maude began, her voice a soft echo of conviction. "They are signs that your new life blooms into its flowerin' time. There are still secret parts to survey. But God's blessin's will find you." Mamau Maude spoke to Rola in her own language, words of reassurance that could be readily heard. The witch nodded appreciatively.

Rola's soothsaying session with Fawn followed. She assured her daughter that she'd give birth to three children, all boys. In her own way, she was telling Fawn that Arious would survive the war. That uncertainty had caused a cloudy veil of tension to hang over the party; the open, positive acknowledgment helped brighten the mood.

When the divining tools were packed away, Ruby said, "Miss Moon, Pug didn't get a readin'. Maybe you could see into her future as a writer."

"I'm sorry, Pug," responded Rola. "I guess I'm a little tired. I didn't mean to slight you."

"That's all right," I answered, but in truth, I *did* feel snubbed. In an attempt to soothe my hurt feelings, Rola dramatically stirred new ashes. After studying them for several moments, the look on her face became one of concern. "What's wrong? What do you see?" I asked impatiently.

Rola abruptly pushed aside the soothsaying bowl and mumbled, "I'm more worn-out than I thought. I don't see anything. It's time for me to go." My witch-friend wouldn't look at me, even as she stood to leave. She laid her hand upon her daughter's shoulder with the words, "I'll see you tomorrow," then walked outside, visibly upset.

I followed Rola to the porch. "You're holdin' back. It was something bad, wasn't it?" I told myself there was no harm in asking, but knew better.

Rola leaned on her walking stick, gazing at the twinkling sky. When at last she looked at me, her stare bored into my skull. Strangely, the witch's words were both vague and specific. "You'll twice see his shadow before you see him as he is. Ugly, angry features. He thinks he's been cheated. He hates your pure spirit, something he can't share." Rola made her way down the narrow steps, then suddenly turned to me again. "To take revenge is to sacrifice oneself. As the wind blows, that's all that can be told now." She hesitated before whispering, "Hold on to that rabbit's foot I gave you. And keep your door locked."

My body slowly sank, landing upon a porch swing. A gusty current of air picked up some dead leaves, forming a miniature whirlpool that whisked past me. For a chilling moment, evil rode the brisk breeze, the night wind's prophecy of fate.

Early the next morning, Rola lingered outside my cottage, aiming her bow and arrow at a rudimentary target tacked to a nearby oak. Amazed, I watched as she fired three arrows, each one a bull's eye. Commanding my attention, she barked her orders. "I'll teach you how to do this. I dip the arrow tips in Serpentina, to ease the pain of my prey. The right amount would down a horse." Rola gave me a knowing look. "It'd also stop a human animal, dead in his tracks."

"I'm interested," I said.

"Well, let's get started," Rola answered, before thrusting the bow into my clumsy hands. Our friendship was never boring; each new day was a clean slate.

Fawn and Arious were married that same afternoon. Reverend Tidbow performed the ceremony in the Sheridan House library. Among the well-wishers was Doc Self's son, Calvin, handsome in his Army corporal uniform. Calvin's presence brought the future into clear focus, but didn't detract from a sweet service. The minister sealed the marriage with a fitting quote from Corinthians. "There are three things that last: faith, hope, and love. And the greatest of these is love."

For me, the occasion was bittersweet, a time to remember my own wedding—destiny's promise sealed with a kiss. During the informal reception in the grand hall, I waited until the newlyweds opened all their gifts. "This is from Alton," I said, handing them a single sweetheart rose. Understanding its significance, tears streamed down their cheeks. After I read them the wedding poem I'd composed, the music started; the jovial party gathered steam when Rola led a lively Greek circle dance.

A few hours later, just as Fawn and Arious prepared to leave for their honeymoon, all Hell broke loose. Two of Daddy's deputies raced up the road to The Hill, pressing their horses hard. They took T.H. aside, conveying their urgent message with agitated hand gestures.

When my father returned to the party, everyone gathered to receive the news. "It's started again," T.H. said. "The Tennessee boys are back, settin' more fires. Includin' your barn, Arious. These deputized men will ride with you to see to your place. I suggest the rest of you folks go home and stay on guard."

Fawn turned to her husband. "I'm comin' with you."

"I'll change and get our horses," I added.

"No, you're safer here," my brother-in-law answered, admonishing his bride with a kiss. "Wait for me. Watch over Aunt Caroline until I get back."

Organized chaos followed. The party-goers left with expressions of apprehension—especially our colored friends, those with the most to lose. The smell of fear hung in the air, an odor akin to overripe apricots, sickeningly sweet. Emmer Faulk spirited his children home, including Storm and Sheridan, but Newt insisted on staying.

Daddy discharged a deputy to patrol The Hill, then rode off to round up a posse. Before T.H. left, I heard him caution Finas, "You and Azberry should help Deputy Grayson keep a close watch while I'm gone. With all the weddin' fuss, and the number of folks on The Hill today, I doubt there'll be any problems. But the Klan's got a grudge against me. They've upped the ante. Settin' fire to the Strawbridge place was a clear message."

After Daddy left, Rola decided to check on her own cabin before returning to sit with Fawn. She couldn't be talked into waiting, and she refused an escort. "I've got my bow. That's all the company I need," the witch declared as she headed for the woods.

Fawn fretted and paced like a caged cougar as Seven Sisters comforted her. Mama and Sara calmed us with mounds of fudge wedding cake; time passed quickly, but not fast enough.

Azberry and Finas realized it'd been too long since Deputy Grayson was due to check in. Together, they left to look for him. Piper sensed the anxiety around her, fussing more than usual; I carried her to my cabin, where she could suckle and fall asleep. "I'll come with you," offered Fawn. The remaining Seven Sisters agreed to stay with Arious's Aunt Caroline, and to let us know if there was any word from T.H., Rola, or Strawbridge Mansion.

We crossed the well-worn path in silence. Once home, I settled myself and my babe into a rocking chair in the bedroom. Fawn rested, eyes closed, on a nearby sofa. After an Irish lullaby, Piper fell asleep, and I placed her into her cradle. As I turned to get a blanket from the armoire, I thought I saw a shadow pass the window. When I looked out, no one was there. I smiled at my own unease, then walked to the front room where Fawn and I remained lost in our own unspoken thoughts.

The new bride tapped her foot in sync with the loud ticking of my Swiss-made clock; its hands appeared frozen in time against the ornately numbered dial. Suddenly, the front door flew open and we both jumped—startled. It was Azberry. He was trying to act grown-up, but was obviously upset. "Pug, I can't find Deputy Grayson. And now, I can't find Finas. What should I do?"

"Calm down," I answered. "I just saw somebody walk past the window. I'm sure it was one or the other. Deputy Grayson forgot to check in, and Finas has probably wandered off. You know how scatter-brained he can be. Let's go talk to Mama. We'll round up more people and scour the area."

Piper was still sleeping, so I glanced at Fawn. "I'll stay with the baby," she volunteered.

"Nobody would dare try anything on The Hill. Not even the Klan," I said. "But, just in case, your granny's grubbin' knife is on the shelf above the sink."

I walked with Azberry to the main house, then explained the situation to those gathered there. When she heard Finas was missing, Sara had a swooning spell; Essie and Mamau Maude stayed with her and Caroline, treating their nervous exhaustion with steaming pots of warm milk. The rest of us divided into small groups, armed with Daddy's pistols. If one of our search parties found Finas or the deputy, we'd fire two rounds as a signal to the others.

I teamed with Fanny and Mama; for fifteen minutes, we searched the far side of the lake, but saw no one. Then, we heard two shots fired from Posie's Peach Orchard. When we arrived, the shock of our find took a few moments to sink in.

Newt and Egypt had found Finas and Deputy Grayson in Essie's fruit cellar; both men were unconscious. The deputy had a fist-sized bump on his head. Finas was bleeding; he'd been cut on the arm, and his collar bone was broken. Each man had been attacked, then unceremoniously dumped into the dark storeroom. Ruby ran to Sheridan House for help; we heard Sara's shrill shriek when she was told about Finas.

"Whoever did this without gettin' caught knows the layout of The Hill," I said as we struggled to drag the men up the narrow steps.

"Why would anybody set upon our home this way?" Mama tearfully asked. "It makes no sense. Not considerin' who your father is." Many tense moments passed before Mama murmured, "Unless that's the point." My mother turned to look at me, then added, "You'd better sit down, hon, you look pale."

"Mama," I yelled as I ran toward my cabin, "you've gotta find Daddy right away. Arious, too! Oh my God. I left them alone! I'm so stupid!" My family and friends were torn; they didn't know whether to follow me or help carry the wounded men. I heard footsteps behind me and turned to see Egypt and Fanny close on my heels.

The front door to my cabin was standing open, the interior in disarray. Furniture, lanterns, and knick-knacks either lay broken or were knocked over, signs of a ferocious struggle. I stood in the doorway for a moment, weak-kneed, staring at the trail of blood leading to my bedroom. I called Fawn's name, but there was no answer. I swallowed hard, then followed the blood.

Piper was gone, but her cradle wasn't empty; a small, dead fawn, its throat slashed, lay in her place. The scream that'd been gathering in my solar plexus burst out of me. I fell to my knees, overtaken with despair and disbelief, a feeling of impotence bordering on paralysis.

"Piper!" I pounded the floor until my fists swelled with bruising. I beat my own body with a viciousness I didn't know I possessed. Egypt and Fanny tried to stop my self-inflicted battering, but each time they touched me, I struck out at them like a wild animal. Before it was over, Fanny had a black eye, and Egypt's nose was bleeding.

My sanity was restored when somebody poured a pitcher of ice-cold water over me. I looked up to see my mother's horrified face.

Shaking with disbelief, she lowered herself to the floor, then took me in her arms. Summoning dignity amidst the tumult, Mama said, "Get a hold on your senses, Pug, and tell me what's happened."

When at last I could speak, all Seven Sisters were there, minus Fawn. "Y'all don't know this, but before Piper was born, I made a hateful enemy. He's done this for revenge. If Toad hurts Fawn or my baby…" The pain of the thought caught in my chest, and for a moment, all I could see were shades of gray. I turned to face my mother. "Please, don't ask me what I did to Toad or why. But we have to find this man. He's a leader in this Klan thing. Now, he's usin' the Ku-Klux to get to me."

"Are you talkin' about Wilburn Crowe?" Mama needed clarification.

I nodded, ashamed. "How's Finas? And Deputy Grayson?" My voice was a low whisper; the air had been knocked out of me.

"Maude and Essie are seein' to 'em now, but a doctor's needed. Since Doc Self is ailin', Azberry's gone for Arious."

That's when Ruby called out, "There's a note attached to this poor, dead creature."

Everyone encircled Piper's cradle. Ruby was right, and it was a grotesque revelation. A small, wooden stake secured a flimsy piece of paper onto the animal that took its eternal rest where my child had been sleeping minutes before. The note hadn't been previously noticed because it was covered with blood. Ruby quickly wiped it with the edge of her skirt, then passed the grisly message to me. The ink was smeared, but I carefully deciphered the wording:

Pug, Here's a riddle. I wait for you where it all began. When the cries of one babe, long dead, was drowned by running waters. If you dare cross it, the real Devil will be after you this time—Toad

I felt a glimmer of hope. I knew where they were. My determination to take immediate action was written all over my face. My mother saw this and said, "Arious's deputy escort will come back with him. They'll be here within the hour."

"No, Mama," I pleaded. "We can't wait that long." I gestured to my friends and continued, "We'll ride ahead. When Arious comes, have his deputies get word to Daddy about where to meet us."

Mama could see there was no talking me out of my plan when all Seven Sisters strapped on holstered guns, even Ruby. We saddled the best of Daddy's thoroughbreds, then hurriedly galloped past Warnock's Peak toward Crybaby Bridge.

TWENTY-ONE

As the old structure came into view, it appeared ominous and brooding, darkened by the lowering shadows of the setting sun. We slowed our horses to a trot when we reached the two unmarked graves that rested several hundred yards from the lower end of Crybaby Bridge, burial places made manifest by oblong depressions of collapsed ground. The site was an unnerving, familiar signpost.

The spookily nebulous quietude was shattered when Seven Sisters heard an unexpected sound, a mother's lullaby sifting through the treetops. The music came from no particular direction as a faint and distant melody, one that defied place and time.

"It's the dead baby's mama. Callin' for her child." Egypt's words were breathless.

We stopped our horses and listened intently to the lilting, ghostly song. I'd hoped it might be Fawn, singing to Piper somewhere nearby, but I was sure it wasn't. The sound slowly faded as it merged with the river's rushing waters.

Newt's mare reared back, resisting forward motion, and the other horses responded in kind. Only with patient effort, and much coaxing, were we able to persuade the skittish animals to move ahead.

When we arrived at the lower end of the covered bridge, I glimpsed a moving shadow on the other side. It was Toad. He was holding Piper, clutching her under his arm the way one would grasp a sack of potatoes. I was amazed to see that my child was still sleeping. Toad was standing tall, with calm deliberation, but his black eyes revealed cruel intent.

Fawn stood stiffly next to Toad. She looked like she wanted to speak, but the pressure of a gun barrel at her back kept her silent. "Evenin' ladies. Nice night for a stroll on the river, ain't it?" Toad's harsh voice echoed through the tunnel-like structure.

I got off my horse, and my friends did the same. "I'm the one your fight's with, Toad," I pleaded. "Please, don't hurt my baby. Let me trade places with her and Fawn. You can do what you like with me. Just let them go."

Toad viciously kicked Fawn behind the knees, forcing her to kneel on the ground. Then he walked forward, with Piper still in his arms, toward a small opening at the side of the bridge. I saw his intention—and screamed, "No!"

Toad grasped my child under each shoulder, holding her over the fast-moving water. Piper awoke and began to wail. The evil distraction worked; we were ambushed from behind by Toad's friends, Rattler and Jabbo. They emerged ten feet from us, their revolvers pointed our way.

After forcing us to drop our guns, Jabbo and Rattler lassoed Egypt, Ruby, Newt, and Fanny like heifers, then tied them tightly together. Leaving me unbound, Rattler pressed a gun to my ribs, and all five of us were marched across the bridge. I breathed a cautious sigh of relief when Toad pulled Fawn to a sitting position and placed Piper in her lap.

Rattler leaned close to me and asked, "How's that Injun granny of yours?" I ignored him, keeping my gaze focused on my daughter as I walked. Within the warmth of Fawn's embrace, Piper eventually stopped crying.

When we reached the end of the bridge, Toad grabbed me roughly by my hair, forcing me to the ground next to Fawn. Jabbo secured the rope that held the other Seven Sisters, binding them to the trunk of a nearby tree; then he and Rattler stood guard nearby.

Toad towered above me, his tone condescending, fraught with feigned frustration. "Pug. Pug. Pug. You've pissed off a lot of 'brothers' who run things around here. This is a message to you from them." Terrified, I shook my head in disbelief as Toad slowly unzipped his pants, encouraged by the taunting, sadistic gibes of his amused friends.

I was horribly certain that Toad was about to make me watch as he raped Fawn for a second time. Instead—he urinated on us both.

Fawn was able to shield Piper, but Toad delighted in scoring us, the way an animal would mark its territorial domain. Indeed, it occurred to me that Toad was governed, body and soul, by the basest of animal instincts; he'd become a slave to brutish male barbarity.

From within her dress, Fawn produced her feather bundle and angrily shook it at her enemy. She passionately delivered a Cherokee chant that got everyone's attention, then deliberately translated her curse into English so that all could understand its meaning. "True time is approachin'. Downstream you must go!"

I feared that Toad would retaliate with all the savagery he was capable of, but instead he only laughed. Mocking Fawn, he addressed his friends, "Whoa, boys! We'd better make a run for it. I never guessed they'd have secret weapons. I think they plan to tickle us to death!" All three men doubled over with laughter, but while she was being heckled, Fawn's expression reflected a unique combination of anger and self-satisfaction.

I tried to hide my own rage as I wiped the urine from my face with the driest part of my skirt. It was hard to maintain my dignity, and Toad enjoyed the moment.

Ruby prayed aloud, "Sweet Jesus, in the name of all that's Holy, shine Your precious light on these wicked men. You know their names, Lord. Show them their sinful ways. With Your grace, they can be reborn. Amen."

Jabbo abruptly stopped laughing when he finally took notice of Ruby's attire. "I'll be damned," he said. "We've done shanghaied ourselves a candle lightin', Bible thumpin', card carryin' nun. A bride of Jesus." Jabbo continued to joke as he fingered the crucifix that hung around Ruby's neck, humor serving to hide the uneasiness that showed through his mockery.

A piece of KKK doctrine, part of a flyer, buzzed in my head. As written, it was meant in reversed context. But I bet on Jabbo's noticeable uncertainty. "It's better to commit ten sins against God than to commit *one* against a servant of God."

"Shut up!" Toad yelled as he kicked me.

"We're not gonna hurt the Sister, are we fellas? About that, she's right." Jabbo's voice was shaky; he'd gotten my message.

"Never mind her 'holiness,'" Rattler growled. "Or the rest of 'em for that matter. Just keep those women quiet while Toad conducts his business." As he spoke, Rattler lit two torches, then tossed one to Jabbo.

Toad turned to face me and hissed, "The tables have turned. How does it feel?"

"Rot in hell," I spat, still rubbing my thigh where he'd kicked me.

"Now, that's the puzzle between you and me," Toad answered, his tone sarcastic. "You're a woman who doesn't know her place. With all your fine raisin', how come you don't know how to treat a man with respect? I'm forced to teach you what you refuse to learn. There's just one problem—how to make the end result look like an accident."

I was scared. My voice betrayed me, squeaking like a broken accordion. "If you kill me, T.H. won't stop 'til you're hunted and trapped like the animal you are. One way or another, you're gonna pay."

Toad pretended surprised disgust. "I ain't plannin' on killin' you, woman. I just want to settle the score." He pulled the shiny blade of a long knife out of a leather waist holder. The six-inch slice of metal twinkled in the light of nearby torch flames. "You see, I think we'd be even," he said, pausing to test the blade, "if your face looked like mine."

Piper began to fuss, her protests gradually becoming screams. Fawn tried to soothe my babe to no avail; my child wanted her mother.

Taking up the noble cause of Piper's tiny mutiny, Ruby led Seven Sisters in the Lord's Prayer. The familiar verse echoed past the bridge, "As we forgive those who trespass against us…"

"Shut them up!" Rattler ordered Jabbo. When his subordinate didn't move, Rattler slithered nearer to the roped women, focusing his anger on Egypt. "Keep your place, Nigger, or here's a taste of what you'll get." Rattler struck, biting Egypt hard enough to break skin; then he repeatedly hit her until she begged him to stop.

Losing interest in Egypt, he threatened the others with a closed fist; my friends continued their prayer in silence. Unsatisfied, Rattler turned his rage toward Fawn. "Make that kid be quiet, or I will!"

Thinking quickly, Fawn did the most loving thing she could possibly do. She offered Piper her breast to suckle. It was dry, of course, but my babe wasn't hungry for milk; she was starved for reassurance— that's what Fawn offered, and Piper gratefully accepted. Instinctively, my own body responded to Fawn's maternal gesture. Milk poured forth, like a fountain stream, from my own full breasts.

"I guess all sows have their milkin' time," snarled Toad.

I reached for my daughter, but he blocked me with the point of his knife. "Un-uh. You and I ain't done yet. You're out of time, Pug." Toad looked at my baby and sighed, "She's a pretty little thing. Too bad for her. Her mama's gotta pay the piper!" Toad and company thought his perverse joke clever. However, his smile disappeared when he looked back at me. Somehow, his voice sounded even darker. "That's life in the mean world."

Desperate, I tried to appease the man I faced with lies, forcing sincerity into my words. "I took the easy road when I shot you, Toad. I was wrong. I'm sorry."

My groveling tack surprised him. A flicker of doubt flashed in his eyes, but the coldness quickly reappeared. "Too little, too late. Besides, I'm already a marked man. I've got nothin' to lose." Toad raised his knife to cut me. I closed my eyes, but opened them again when I heard Toad screech in pain.

Fawn had concealed more than her feather bundle inside her dress. Badgerwoman's grubbing knife was firmly planted in Toad's right leg. As Toad reached down to pull the blade out of his calf, his own knife fell to the ground.

In rapid succession, two arrows whistled out of the darkness. One found Rattler's shoulder; the other speared Jabbo's left side. Within moments, Jabbo grew noticeably drowsy, a result of the arrow's Serpentina-dipped tip. He dropped his torch; it rolled toward Fanny, setting the hem of her dress on fire. The flames spread rapidly, igniting the skirts of all four women; their distressed cries were answered by the caw of a nearby crow.

Rola Moon stepped out of hiding and rushed to help them. As she fervently stomped the flames, Rola commanded the women to "turn in little circles" against the tree's huge trunk. The rope that bound my friends allowed just enough sag for these tiny movements, and the flames were snuffed out against the bark.

Simultaneously, I raced toward Jabbo, grabbing his gun just as he dropped to the ground, drugged and unconscious. Toad, quickly tearing his shirt in half, tied it tightly around his wounded leg; he slowly stood upright, keeping his back to me.

I pointed Jabbo's gun at my sworn enemy; his head tilted alertly when I cocked the hammer. "Turn around, Toad," I hissed. "Unholster your pistol and drop it on the ground." Indignant and wracked with pain, Toad ignored me and hobbled away—headed for the river bank.

"Stop where you are, damn you. If you don't turn around, I'll have to shoot, and we've already played that song once before." My determined tone proved that I meant every word.

Finally, Toad turned to face me, his expression shaded with anger. Another emotion also showed in his eyes, a surprising one, something resembling sadness.

"Your gun, Toad, *I said drop it.*"

Again, he ignored the order. Instead, Toad calmly addressed me, his manner contrite, even brotherly. I was lured into a relaxed stance by his earnestness. Guessing he was about to give up the fight, I let him have his say. "It's not over, Pug. But it will be soon." Toad touched his scarred cheek. "You took more from me than you know. You took away my pride. To be shot by a baby-carryin', breast-milkin' *female!* How's a man to get over that?

"Every time I look in a mirror, I remember. I'm tired of thinkin' about it. And about you. I need to find some peace." Toad hesitated before adding, "Don't forget, Pug, the Devil never knocks." With lightning speed, Toad drew his gun and shot in my direction.

The bullet ripped the skin along my temple. A bright flash of light preceded the searing pain, like a hot coal pressed against my head. I shrieked like a bobcat, lost my balance, then fired as I fell.

The bullet hit Toad's chest. It was a gushing wound. His expression of surprise quickly gave way to blankness. I could see the white underside of his eyeballs before Toad crumpled onto his side, and rolled into the river.

I crawled to the river's edge, numbly watching as the cold current carried Toad's body downstream; he floated in the water at a strangely misshapen angle, like he'd been broken in half. I sat, frozen in place, while comprehension of the night's events washed over me. Piper was wailing, frightened by the gunfire—but the sound of her cry faded as I fought the sinking blackness that enveloped me.

Rola tore a strip from her slip, wrapping the makeshift bandage around my forehead. "It's deep, but I can handle it," she assured me. "Right on the hairline. Try to keep still while I look for some red beth root to stop the…"

Before Rola could search for the herbs, I clasped her by the arm. "It hurts like hell," I confessed.

Somehow, Rola understood my meaning, my shame. At the moment of Toad's death, I'd felt corrupt satisfaction with my deed. I could argue self-defense in any court of law. *But did you have to kill him?* demanded my conscience. Rola's Halloween prediction echoed in my mind: "To take revenge is to sacrifice oneself."

"Where's the other one?" I heard them call. Seven Sisters were roaming the perimeter of our camp, armed and scared.

Still holding Piper, Fawn came to sit beside me. "Rattler's gone," she announced, her voice strained.

Rola returned with her herbs. "With that much Serpentina pumpin' through his veins, he won't get far," Rola answered, matter-of-factly, when she saw our concern.

"Are you all right?" Fawn asked. "You're bleedin' pretty bad."

"I'll live," I answered. "How about you?"

"I *hated* seein' Toad again." Fawn sounded tired. "Havin' him so close brought it all back. But, Piper needed me to stay strong."

As Fawn lovingly laid my baby in my arms, Ruby purposefully walked to the river's edge before making the sign of the cross and praying in Latin. Fanny held a gun on the sleeping Jabbo while Newt and Egypt tended his wound. He still hadn't moved when T.H. arrived an hour later.

My father turned tomato red as the story gushed forth from all seven excited women; the veins in his neck popped out like overcooked spaghetti as he tried to keep up with the necessary details. Admirably, T.H. regained enough of his professional composure to discharge his deputies, ordering them to take Jabbo into custody and search for Rattler and Toad.

"Did one of you girls pick up Wilburn's gun?" asked Daddy, searching along the bank.

"It must've gone into the water when he fell in," I answered; the echo of my words sounded lame and ineffectual.

Once satisfied that the immediate area was secure, T.H. rushed to my side. My father kept one arm around me while he used the other to wipe his sweaty face with a handkerchief. Every few minutes, he would touch Piper's cheek, reassuring himself that she was unharmed.

Daddy delivered news from home. The Strawbridge barn had been burned to the ground, but the mansion was unscathed. Arious had returned to The Hill to care for Uncle Finas and Deputy Grayson. My father turned to Fawn. "Your husband will be sufferin' the worst of miseries 'til you're home safe and sound, hon. I'm beholden to him for stayin' behind. I know it wasn't easy."

Deputies Coal and Janson emerged from the other side of the levee. "No sign of either culprit, sir," deputy Coal informed my father. "We've eight more men lookin' though. And a couple of dogs. We'll check farther down the river for a body. As for the other, if he's on foot, we'll find him."

When we arrived at The Hill, the yard was filled with worried, waiting loved ones. Word had traveled fast. Emmer Faulk was happy to see Newt's safe return. Even Grady Holt was there, waiting for Fanny. Essie ran to get ice for Egypt's swollen face, crying, "Dear Lord, what have they done to my baby?"

Fawn and Arious embraced in a frenzy of emotion. She began to sob as pent-up feelings were released. "Toad's gone downstream," she said. "He can't hurt us anymore."

That's when I fainted. Mama, standing beside me, grabbed Piper before I could drop her. Daddy caught me as I fell and carried me to Sheridan House. Safe in the bed of my youth, I succumbed to the feeling of comfort and safety, vaguely aware of subsequent ministrations.

"This will calm you down, help the pain," Mamau Maude promised as she guided French brandy to my sore mouth.

Arious sewed closed the gash in my head. "The excitement increased the swellin'," he told my mother. "It's gonna take at least twelve stitches."

Family and friends took turns sitting with the ailing and tending to Piper. Fawn and Arious spent their wedding night in the main guest room of Sheridan House for safety's sake and in case the doctor's services were required.

I slumbered in a heavy cloud of forgetfulness. Facts, images, and conversations entered the slippery places of my mind like water softening clay. Nothing stuck for long. Then, it was all kneaded together with what was left of my wits.

At dawn on the third day, I came to myself, waking when Daddy placed a spoon filled with warm oatmeal to my lips. "Mornin', lassie," he smiled, pleased to see my return to the land of the living.

I took a quick look around. We were alone. "Where's Piper?"

"She's fine, darlin'. Your mama's givin' her a bath about now."

"Finas?" I asked, feeling worried.

"He's a tough old bird, that one. It'll be weeks before his shoulder will support crutches, and that's made him grumpy. Given time, Finas will pull through fine." Daddy cocked his head thoughtfully. "I've been waitin' for *you* to feel up to answerin' an important question. Are you strong enough?"

I nodded.

Daddy's query was blunt, straight to the point. "Is there any reason why Toad would single you and Fawn out for harm?"

I stalled. "Have you asked Fawn what she thinks?"

"She believes the man was a lunatic." T.H.'s words were a slow, deliberate drawl.

I couldn't tell my father about the rape; my lie would be one of omission, in good conscience. I squirmed between the rumpled sheets and said, "Fawn's right. Toad was crazy. He had some screwy notions about how the law should work. Personally, I think the name Sheridan was enough to set him off."

T.H. nodded, his expression more serious. "It looks like Toad was helpin' the Klan get even with me. For all I've done to stop 'em. Kidnappin' my grandchild would accomplish that."

Daddy's voice softened. "Yesterday, they found Toad's body on the riverbank, near Mardis Falls. There was a bullet in his chest, near his heart. A grievous injury, just as you described. And his leg was badly mangled. With that said, Arious believes neither of those wounds would've killed him in the short term."

My heart began to race. "What are you tellin' me, Daddy?"

"Well…there's no easy way to put this. He was also shot in the head at close range. I believe it was self-inflicted. His family identified his clothes and other effects. Otherwise, he was unrecognizable as Toad. Are you *sure* you fired only once?"

I managed another wordless nod, then pushed the oatmeal away.

Daddy patted my hand. "I'm rulin' the final cause of death a suicide. That'll deflect some of the blame where you're concerned." T.H.

tried to lighten the moment by pinning a deputy's badge onto my night-gown. "I wish I could sit with you longer, but I've got to go," he said. "Deputy Grayson's wife has come to take him home. I'm gonna drive the wagon, keep it a smooth ride."

As if to downplay the point, Daddy casually added, "Don't worry about that scoundrel Rattler gettin' away. Probably well into Tennessee by now. He wouldn't dare come this way again. Too many witnesses to identify him. Put all this behind you as best you can." Before walking away, my father kissed my cheek and whispered, "An old legend claims that it takes a woman to outwit an evil mind. Justice was served when you shot that man. Undue regret brings no interest to the lender."

Later, I awoke from a nap to the shrill cry of a butcherbird as it flew past my window. I thought about what a strange creature it was, surviving as a predator by impaling its prey on thorns. Its victims final-ized their own death by enlarging the fatal gash as they tried to wriggle free. Butcherbirds were small, but they were warriors, not afraid to act on their own behalf, kindred spirits to my own willful nature. I'd pierced Toad, and he'd finished himself off. His final act had been to destroy that which he despised most, his face.

Though we were children, I'd impaled Toad upon the thorny brier of disgrace the first time I'd called him "Whomperjaw." Over the years, the prickly stems of bitterness and rage had caused his fatal undoing. *He pulled the trigger, but I'm the predator, the murderer,* I decided.

I jumped when something crashed into my window. Easing my way out of bed, I steadied myself, then slowly made my way across the room. Peering past the glass, I saw a small sparrow lying on the ground. It flinched twice before taking its last breath.

✶ ✶ ✶

Days later, I moved back to my cabin; immediately, I knew some-thing had changed there. I noticed little things—strange sounds, including bumps and scraping noises I couldn't account for. Olive Kate's pups crouched and growled at empty spaces. Piper cried more than usual. I felt I was being watched by an unseen presence, a troubling awareness that continued day and night.

Fanny insisted that my house was colder than it should have been, considering I constantly kept the wood stove hot. Egypt noticed that the curtains would move for no apparent reason, as if blown by an eerie, slight breeze. We checked the door and windows, but could find no draft. It was a mystery I couldn't solve.

As my anxiety heightened, I developed a curious need to wash my hands habitually, finding myself at the basin up to twenty times a day. As a result, my palms were blood red, sore and raw with dry, peeling skin.

One day, I arrived home to find my *Collected Works of Scottish Poems* fallen from the bookshelf; the book was lying on the floor as if someone had just finished reading it. The last ballad on the opened page read, "Listen carefully, especially on starless nights, for the ticking of the deathwatch spider."

I shivered and slammed the book closed. Turning in a tight circle, I yelled, "You may be back, Toad. But you're not drivin' me out! Do you hear? Dead is dead, damn it. I won, and I'm not leavin'. You are!" I gasped when a small black spider fell upon my arm; I quickly shook it off, then smashed it with my shoe.

The next evening, I invited Rola Moon to dinner. We were well into dessert before I mustered the courage to ask, "Rola, is my house haunted?"

Rola put down her fork, stood, then walked in a slow zigzag while pointing her stone-encrusted walking stick toward each corner of the room. Finally, she aimed the bewitching cane at me. Her reply was succinct. "It's not your house that's bein' haunted. It's *you*. I've suspected it for a while, a year in fact. There's no doubt. He's still here."

I was confused, thinking I'd misunderstood her meaning. I said, "Toad hasn't been dead for a year. How could he be a haunt for that long if he was still alive?"

It was Rola's turn to be baffled. "Pug, what are you talkin' about?"

Not knowing what else to say, I babbled about bumps in the night, the opened book, unexplained cold spots, and the spooky feeling that someone was always behind me.

"You say it was a spider that jumped on you when you talked to the spirit? A *black* spider?"

I nodded, then rattled on about indoor wind.

Rola put her finger to her lips, motioning for me to stay quiet. She closed her eyes for a full minute, then said, "The spider is many things, includin' the spinner of fate. She's also the cutter of life's threads, especially love and death. If it'd been a grasshopper or a locust—the destroyers—that would represent your enemy."

"Most of me is glad Toad is dead," I confessed, my voice a whisper.

Rola nodded and said, "But another part's not so sure. I can see it's a problem. You shot Toad, and now you feel his blood on your skin. After shinin' a light on your enemy's black heart, he surrendered to his own ignorance." Rola took my chapped hands in hers and examined them. "You damn yourself with shame, though the blame is two-sided. Since you willed him to die, you can't deny your role. However, you *can* make peace with your dark side, then call the ocean's crystal spirals to cleanse you."

I looked down at my oozing palms, my cracked and swollen fingers; they felt separate from the rest of me. I registered little pain from their withered and parched condition. "I feel like I've had blood on my hands for a long time. Ever since Brother Watkins died. I was there when he was murdered, you know. With snakes. It was horrible."

Rola's response was straightforward. "Your history with death is long for one so young. The Ancients would say that Toad was your *khaibut*, your shadow. He was the noonday devil fated to be your enemy in this life. That's why his death has addled your mind; a part of you died that night, too—necessary though it was."

"So, what do I do now?" I pleaded. I thought my head might explode from fatigue, lack of sleep, and countless simultaneous thoughts. Absently, I stroked the wound I'd received from Toad's bullet.

Rola sighed deeply as she stared at Piper's sleeping form. Her subsequent words came as a soft whisper. "You have what's called a lotus light. It's shinin' can only be seen by those departed from this world. They're drawn to it. To you. Your light gives them comfort. The more they love you, the harder it is to stay away—to go on, move forward, and remain there.

"Sometimes you'll see the spirits, other times you can hear 'em. Mostly, you'll just sense their presence. You will bear the lotus light to your death. Most carriers consider it both a blessin' and a curse. With your khaibut's end, his shadow gone, your gift has been heightened."

"Who's hauntin' me, Rola?" I pressed the question.

"The deathwatch spider was your clue: the cutter of bonds between souls. Between love and death. Your husband is still with you. Some unfinished worry keeps drawin' him away from the place of dawnin'. Before he passes through the crack between worlds, your lover seeks that which only you can give."

My reaction was one of panic. Quiet desperation took over my mind. "What is it, Rola?" I begged. "What does Alton need from me?" I felt weak. I walked to my bed and lay down.

Rola followed, then sat beside me. "Only *you* can answer that question," she murmured, patiently holding my hand while I cried myself to sleep.

I dreamed of rolling, misty bluebonnet fields as I searched for understanding. When I awoke a few hours later, I had it. "Alton wants my forgiveness," I said aloud. "For dyin' and leavin' me to grieve. He's been as lost as I have."

Rola had spent the night in my rocking chair. As sleepiness left me, I saw that Piper was cooing happily in her arms. The witch seemed pleased. "Are you ready to free him from the foggy meadow of souls?"

It was then that I realized she'd known the answer all along. However, Rola could help me only if I came to the truth on my own, by pushing past selfish longings. "Yes! Of course. Please, Rola," I begged. "Help Alton."

My witch-friend placed Piper on my bed before shuffling out the door, on her way to make the necessary preparations for what she called "circle magic."

That night, I arranged for Mama to care for Piper at Sheridan House. As the ritual began, Seven Sisters joined Rola as we sat inside a ring of burning white candles in the middle of my cabin's front room.

After a silent, meditative period, Rola spoke. "Let this night in visions see this lovin' spirit, by the name of Alton, find his way to the Holy Mountain, the place of rest. May each invocation, as it is given, guide him forward."

Rola nudged her daughter, letting Fawn know that her turn had come. Fawn pounded her chest with both fists, like a drumbeat. "Hear me, Alton. My brother. I send you a lovin' prayer. Be untied this night from the knot that binds you. Find the maker of the trees. Go home."

Newt spoke next. "Be released through your own gentleness. And your faith. Float like a feather back to Heaven."

Fanny's words followed, strong and clear, "Dear Reverend, reveal your light. Though you must leave us, you'll be remembered in the sweetest corner of our minds."

A sudden, loud popping sound made all of us jump. It came from right outside our circle, just behind me. "Something brushed past my cheek," I announced, fighting the tears that came anyway. "It felt soft, like a kiss."

Rola squeezed my hand to reassure me, then nodded to Egypt, whose invocation was an old Irish charm, one I'd taught her when she was five years old. Egypt's tears flowed unhindered as she spoke. "I will kindle my fire this evenin', without malice, jealousy, or fear—a flame of love for my neighbor. I will kindle my fire this evenin'…"

Ruby fingered her rosary beads before praying. "In the name of the Father, Son, and Holy Mary, may the shadow of Christ fall on you, Brother Alton. And His garment cover you. May His breath set you free!"

Everyone gasped when a swishing noise, accompanied by downy puffs of air, made its way around our circle.

"Alton," I whispered. "I lost my way for a while, vexed by a fairy wort at high tide. But I'm all right now, husband. Your love is proof that the sun encircles everything. I forgive your death. I see that I can stand alone. Go with my blessin'."

My heart skipped a beat when the front door blew open and a gusty draft put out the candles. It was followed by more whooshing noises within the cabin, like a funnel cloud finding its way to the exit. A sweetened breeze, bearing the soft scent of roses, hung over me for a few precious moments. Then, it found its way outside, joining the crisp, evening wind blowing past the house. Alton's spirit was gone. Afterwards, all was silent.

Like a consoling, protective shield, Seven Sisters surrounded me. Along with Rola, they stayed close as the long night passed. Near dawn, we walked to the river. There, Fawn led us in the sacred Cherokee ritual of greeting the sun. As fleecy snowflakes fell upon us, we faithfully followed her graceful movements.

Our final invocation was one that Badgerwoman had repeated hundreds of times. "The mornin' star reminds us that all will someday fly back to the heavens. There, within the sparklin' brilliance of the Seven Dancers, we'll find our real home."

* * *

When Arious left for Camp McClellan, many townspeople gathered to see him off. They brought loving, farewell wishes for Ruby, too. The train platform was overrun with warm bodies. It was a vantage point that overlooked our village's expansive landscape. The lower valley shimmered with the reddish-orange haze of late-blooming cannas.

The spirited music of banjoes filled the air, a gift from Azberry and some of his friends. They chose the old tune "Wildwood Flower" for their send-off. The melody was bittersweet, setting the mood while Ruby and I exchanged promises of weekly letters.

I turned to my brother-in-law, then gave him a farewell kiss, squeezing him hard. He lifted Piper from my arms and held her close before handing her back to me. The train's whistle blew, but no "good-bye" was spoken.

Fawn thrust her precious feather bundle into her husband's hands. She pressed his fingers around it with the tearful words, "Granny said there's more power in an eagle feather than in both our fists. Keep it close. It'll protect you."

Arious responded by giving his bride a prolonged, passionate kiss. With resigned determination, he jumped onto the passenger car, fighting naked emotion without success.

Everyone cheered, waving as the smoky locomotive moved along the track. Braving the crowd, Rola came to stand between me and her daughter. She put her arms around our waists and held firm, like an anchor. Rola's ensuing chant was for our ears only, hinting at secrets yet to be learned while reminding us of enduring courage and the oldest of lessons.

Like phantoms in the wind, hope's bounty wafted upon Rola's whispered words: "She cut and peeled a hazel wand, then sent his name upon feathered wing. He answered her call when the seasons changed, and the ancient rite traced the path to Spring."

THE END

AUTHOR'S NOTE

Some works mentioned in *Pug Sheridan* are real, and appeared during the time period about which Pug writes. Thomas Dixon's novel, *The Clansmen*, and the D. W. Griffith film, *Birth of a Nation*, affected popular culture and impacted history. Today, our country is still recovering from such extremist, prejudicial depictions of black Americans.

Birth of a Nation premiered in 1915, yet unbelievably, the film is still used as a recruitment tool for the Ku Klux Klan. In the early part of this century, the KKK used Sir Walter Scott's *Letters on Demonology and Witchcraft* as a reference guide for intimidation and scare tactics.

Nevertheless, the twin flames of hope and justice were reflected in the passionate work of brave women. Sojourner Truth was a former slave who became a dynamic, traveling preacher, described as "a strange compound of wit and wisdom, with wild enthusiasm and flint-like common sense." Her memoirs were published in 1850 as *The Narrative of Sojourner Truth: A Northern Slave*.

Poetess Bessie Stanley won first prize in a contest sponsored by the magazine, *Modern Women*. Written in 1905, Bessie titled her piece "Success," and it is reprinted here in its entirety.

Success

He has achieved success who has lived well,
laughed often and loved much,
who has enjoyed the trust of pure women,
the respect of intelligent men,
and the love of little children,
who has filled his niche and accomplished his task,
who has left the world better than he found it,
whether by an improved poppy, a perfect poem,
or a rescued soul,
who has never lacked appreciation of earth's beauty,
or failed to express it,
who has always looked for the best in others,
and given them the best he had,
whose life was an inspiration,
whose memory a benediction.

ACKNOWLEDGMENTS

Thank you to the supportive friends who read early drafts of this work and gave helpful feedback and encouragement, including: Trudy Burling, Denise Jiminez, Susan Heinz, Anne Denton, Joetta Scott, Yvonne Wise, Joan Smithline, Claudia Sattler, Shelby Chant, Kerri Howland, Gayle Davis, and my sister, Barbara Stonich.

To my wonderful children, Michelle and Chris Cline: Your insight was more helpful than you know; your belief in me kept me going. I am so grateful for God's gift, to have you in my life. I will always be with you as you trace the path to Spring.

My appreciation also goes to the numerous "old-timers" in Alabama who generously shared personal highlights of "the good ole days" during the research phase of this book.

I am grateful to Mimi Von Litolff, not only for her friendship, but for her brilliant cover illustration work.

My gratitude also goes to Allan Burns, editor extraordinaire. His keen eye and kind professionalism were invaluable assets to the overall creative process.

And finally, to those special few who shaped the story of "Pug Sheridan" with wise advice, suggestions, sidebars, and tender coaxing. These four people molded me as a writer with caring attention, open-hearted honesty, and creative brute force: Cynthia Lazaroff, Jeff Bricmont, Cherie Burns, and most of all, my husband, Ron.

To those dear ones mentioned here, as well as the many others in my life who brighten my spirit by your very existence, I Love You. Namaste.

S.C.
June, 2004

ABOUT THE AUTHOR

Pug Sheridan is the first novel written by Alabama native Sandra Cline. This debut work marks a career departure for the author, who previously worked in broadcasting as the producer and host of a successful radio talk show. Cline is an avid supporter of Pro-Literacy and an ardent environmentalist. She resides in the high desert of the Southwest with her husband and editor, Ron.